THE BLACK PHARAOH

The temples of northern Egypt lie deserted, the gods forgotten. All people care about is lining their own pockets. Injustice and corruption reign. Five centuries after Ramses, its former splendours long past, the empire seems to be hurtling towards irretrievable ruin. One man, a Nubian, rejects this dark destiny. Piankhy, the 'living one', the Black Pharaoh, governs his kingdom from the South with wisdom and kindness. In his heart, he has only one desire: that the gods should once again dwell in a united Egypt, nurtured by justice and love. But the price to pay is a heavy one for this man of peace: it means confronting the Libyan Tefnakt, an authoritarian, ambitious Northern prince, who is determined to restore order and reign in splendour—by forcing the country to submit to his yoke. War between the Black Pharaoh and the Libyan prince is inevitable. And the survival of a thousand-year-old empire hangs on the victory of one of these two inflexible wills . . . Despite his own courage and his wife's magic, is the Black Pharaoh really capable of achieving the impossible?

THE BLACK PHARAOH

Translated by Sue Dyson

Christian Jacq

CHIVERS PRESS
BATH

First published 1999
by
Simon & Schuster
This Large Print edition published by
Chivers Press
by arrangement with
Simon & Schuster UK Ltd
2000

ISBN 0 7540 1510 6

British Library Cataloguing in Publication Data available

C404055861

Printed and bound in Great Britain by
REDWOOD BOOKS, Trowbridge, Wiltshire

*And the sun rose over the earth, as a
new day dawned.*

Stele of Piankhy

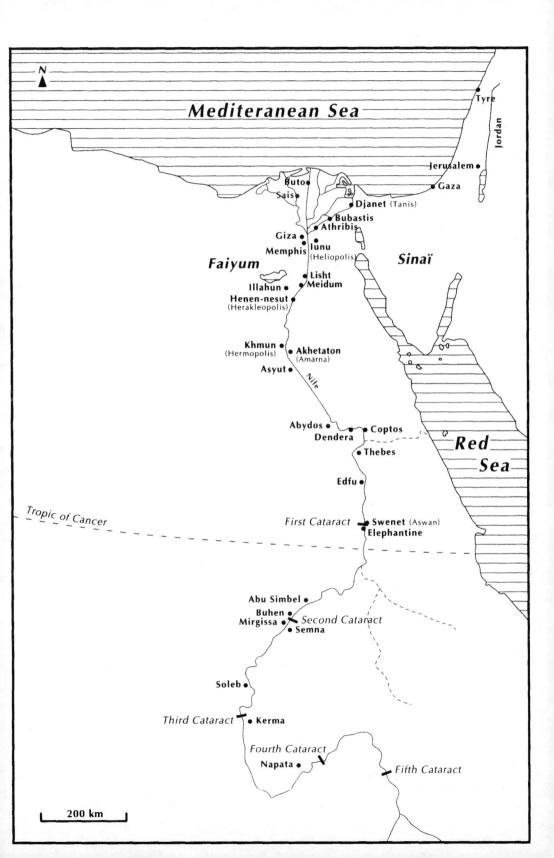

N

Mediteranean Sea

Tyre

Jordan

Jerusalem

Gaza

Buto

Sais

Djanet (Tanis)

Bubastis

Athribis

Giza

Memphis

Iunu
(Heliopolis)

Faiyum

Sinaï

Lisht

Illahun

Meidum

Henen-nesut
(Herakleopolis)

Khmun
(Hermopolis)

Akhetaton
(Amarna)

Asyut

Nile

Abydos

Coptos

Dendera

Thebes

*Red
Sea*

Edfu

Tropic of Cancer

First Cataract

Swenet (Aswan)

Elephantine

Abu Simbel

Buhen

Mirgissa

Second Cataract

Semna

Soleb

Third Cataract

Kerma

Fourth Cataract

Napata

Fifth Cataract

200 km

CHAPTER ONE

When she saw her husband returning from the temple, the village headman's wife tried to make herself believe that he was carrying a sack of wheat on his shoulders. The night before, the couple had celebrated their daughter's birthday. The little girl was delighted with her present, a rag doll her father had made. And now she was playing with other little girls in the middle of the road which ran through Hill-of-the-Fledglings, a village in the Middle-Egyptian province of Henen-nesut.

The headman threw his sack on the ground. It was empty. 'There's nothing left,' he said. 'Even the priests themselves are at risk of starvation, and it won't be long before the gods return to heaven, since no one gives a thought to respecting the laws of our ancestors. Lies, corruption, selfishness: these are our new masters.'

'Go and tell that to the grand vizier, and then tell it to Pharaoh, if that's what it takes,' said his wife.

'There isn't a pharaoh any more, only chieftains who fight among themselves, each claiming to exercise supreme power. The north of the country is under the yoke of the Libyan princes, who revel in anarchy and internal squabbles.' [Events take place around 730 BC.]

'What about the Black Pharaoh?'

'What indeed?' said the headman. 'He has left an army in Thebes to protect the holy city of the god Amon, where his sister rules as Divine Wife of Amon, while he locks himself away in his capital,

1

Napata, on the far side of Nubia. He's been so far from Egypt for so long that he's forgotten all about us.'

'He'll help us, I'm sure he will.'

'Don't deceive yourself. He couldn't if he wanted to. It's all very well him claiming to be King of Upper and Lower Egypt, but all he controls is his own remote province and the south of the Nile valley. He's abandoned the rest of the country to chaos and confusion.'

'We must tell him what's happening, warn him that we're facing poverty and disaster.'

'We'd be wasting our time,' replied the headman. 'The Black Pharaoh is quite content with his hollow kingship. As far as he's concerned, we don't even exist.'

'I still have some dried fish left,' said his wife, 'but only enough for a few more days.'

'People will blame me for the famine. If I don't find a solution, we shall all die. All we can do now is beg the Prince of Henen-nesut to help us.'

'But he's loyal to the Black Pharaoh.'

'If he shows me the door too, I'll look further north for help.'

His wife clutched at his arm. 'The roads aren't safe. The Libyan militia will arrest you and slit your throat! No, you mustn't go. We're safe here, in Hill-of-the-Fledglings. The Northern armies would never dare venture this far south.'

'Very well then, we shall starve to death.'

'No. We'll stop collecting taxes. We'll ration ourselves and share what we have left with the other villages. That way, we'll hold out until the Nile floods again.'

'And if the flood fails us,' said the headman, 'we

2

shall be condemned to death.'

'Don't lose hope. We'll pray day and night to the goddess of the harvest.'

The headman gazed into the distance. 'What is there left to look forward to? Happy times have gone for ever, and life has become a burden. How can we believe the promises the men of power make to us? The only thing they care about is making themselves rich. Their fine words deceive no one but themselves.'

The little girls went on playing with their dolls, in a wondrous universe to which they alone held the keys. They scolded them over and over again, for the naughty dolls would not stop being disobedient.

The peasant woman smiled. Her husband was wrong. Hope did still exist. It lived on in the laughter of these children and in their instinctive refusal to accept misfortune.

The north wind was getting up, bringing with it a cloud of dust which covered the doorsteps of the houses. Sad-faced, the headman sat down on a stone bench in front of his home.

Just as his wife was picking up a broom, the earth began to tremble. A dull sound was heard in the distance, coming from the direction of the road to Memphis, the largest city in the land and its main trading centre. Memphis knew nothing of the Black Pharaoh's inglorious reign, and each day grew more and more resigned to Libyan occupation.

Forming a circle, the little girls explained to their dolls that they must be very obedient if they were going to wear beautiful clothes when they grew up.

A new cloud of dust rose up to meet the sky, and the dull sound became the sort of deafening uproar that might accompany the charge of a herd of enraged bulls. The peasant woman walked forward and looked towards the north, but she was dazzled. The sun's rays were reflecting off metallic surfaces, transforming them into a blaze of blinding white light.

'Chariots,' said the headman, snapping out of his trance.

Chariots, soldiers with helmets and body-armour, shields, spears . . . The army of the North had left the Delta, and was bearing down upon Hill-of-the-Fledglings. The woman screamed at the top of her voice, but the little girls did not hear her, for her voice was drowned by the thunder of horses' hooves and the grinding of chariot wheels.

Intrigued at last, the children turned their heads to look at the invaders, and did not see the headman and his wife running towards them, shouting at them to run and hide in the palm-grove. The little girls stood and stared, their dolls clasped to their chests, fascinated by this wild, unreal torrent of humanity.

And the torrent swept over them, crushing both children and adults, breaking their bodies beneath chariot wheels and horses' hooves. These were the first victims of Tefnakht, head of the Libyan coalition of the North, whose footsoldiers massacred the remaining inhabitants of Hill-of-the-Fledglings, and burned down the little white houses.

What did a few corpses matter, when you were preparing to become Lord of the Two Lands, Upper and Lower Egypt? For General Tefnakht, the time had come to strike down the Black Pharaoh.

CHAPTER TWO

Tefnakht had been born at Sais, in the Delta. He was a powerfully built man with fiery black eyes set deep in their sockets. His harsh, bony face was the outward expression of an iron will; a deep scar, the souvenir of a fierce hand-to-hand struggle, ran right across his forehead.

Ever since he was a youth, Tefnakht had inspired fear. Accustomed to command, he had no time for the mild-mannered or the fearful; he had used threats to drag the Northern princes into a war to reconquer the South. Now he was acknowledged leader of the Libyans, sovereign ruler of the lands west of the Delta, and administrator of the territories of Lower Egypt. Although he was not good at masking his impatience, he had had to learn to be less brusque with those who claimed to be his allies.

A meeting of those allies had been convened at their camp, and the princes and chiefs had gathered outside their tents. Tefnakht prepared to address them. He unrolled a sheet of top-quality papyrus on which was drawn a map of Middle Egypt.

'Memphis is ours,' he declared. 'We have taken Lisht, and we are advancing towards the town of Henen-nesut. My friends, our advance has been remarkable—I promised you a string of victories, didn't I? But if we wish to go further, we must strengthen our alliance. That is why I am asking you to appoint me leader of the entire country.'

The spokesman for the Libyan tribes who had

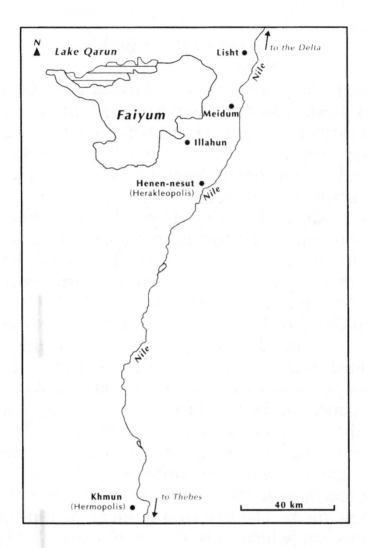

ruled over the Delta provinces since invading them was Akanosh. Like his compatriots, he wore a fine pointed beard, and his shoulder-length hair hung in braids, each decorated with an ostrich feather. There were bracelets on his wrists; and on his arms and chest warlike tattoos depicted bows and daggers. He wore a long red cloak knotted at the left shoulder and decorated with floral patterns,

6

and took great care to look elegant. At the age of sixty, he would have been quite happy with the power he exercised over his domain of Sebennytos, but he had allowed himself to be persuaded to take part in Tefnakht's military adventure.

'We congratulate you on leading us this far,' said Akanosh in a calm, steady voice. 'But Henen-nesut is loyal to our enemy, the Nubian Piankhy, who believes himself to be the rightful sovereign of Egypt. Up till now he has not reacted, for our raid caught him unawares.'

'The Black Pharaoh is vegetating in far-off Sudan, many weeks' march from here,' said Tefnakht scornfully.

'True, but he has troops stationed in Thebes and it won't be long before they take action.'

Tefnakht smiled. 'Do you think I'm feeble-minded, my friend? Certainly they will be ordered to counter-attack, sooner or later. But we are ready to face up to them, are we not?'

'Some of us consider our alliance rather fragile,' said Akanosh with a frown. 'You are a fine war leader, Tefnakht, but several of us enjoy a form of sovereign power which we wish to hold on to. Going any further could lead us all to ruin.

'What will ruin us—and rob us of our power—is doing nothing,' snapped Tefnakht. 'Do I have to spell out the chaos we were in before I took charge of this coalition? There were four false pharaohs in the Delta and at least a dozen claimants to the throne, the most insignificant tribal chief acted like an absolute monarch, and everyone had to endure a state of lawlessness punctuated by bloody fighting.'

'That's very true,' Akanosh agreed, 'and you

have given us back our sense of honour. But we mustn't lose our heads. At present we hold half the country, so wouldn't it make sense to divide up the lands we have acquired, rather than take foolish risks?'

Tefnakht would have liked to strangle this coward, but he managed to contain his anger. He did not yet have sufficient armed forces at his disposal to act alone, and in the short term he must come to an arrangement with this band of barbarians.

'I understand your caution, Akanosh,' he said. 'Up to now, we have been consolidating our positions in the North and abandoning the South to Piankhy, with Middle Egypt acting as a neutral zone. But to achieve happiness and prosperity, Egypt must be united and governed by a true Pharaoh. To think that we can continue living in a state of division would be a fatal mistake—we would lose everything we possess. The only solution is to conquer the South and wipe out the Black Pharaoh's armies.'

'That is your opinion, Tefnakht, and I respect it But you have before you several independent rulers who govern their lands as they see fit.'

'Why are you challenging my authority, when we are on the path to ultimate victory?'

'You have brought us together in an alliance,' conceded Akanosh, 'but we have not granted you supreme power over us. We wished to do something new: move out of the Delta, take possession of Memphis, which has fallen into our hands like a ripe fruit, and conquer a few provinces of Middle Egypt. We have done all we wanted. Shouldn't we be content with that?'

Tefnakht ordered his cup-bearer to serve strong beer to the Libyan princes. Most of them appreciated this diversion, but Akanosh refused to drink.

'So far we have won without fighting,' he reminded Tefnakht. 'The villages we overran were unable to offer the slightest resistance. Henennesut is a fortified city and will be defended by a garrison of experienced soldiers. How many men will we lose—and are we all prepared to face up to that kind of sacrifice?'

'That is the price of victory,' declared Tefnakht. 'To deny it would be a lie, but going back now would be a defeat.'

'We need time to consider.'

Tefnakht hid his disappointment. Whenever the Libyan chiefs met, they invariably became bogged down in interminable wrangling which never led to concrete decisions.

'In that case, give me a clear answer to one question. Do you or do you not give me full powers to undertake the conquest of the whole of Egypt?'

Akanosh stood up and went into his tent, followed by the other Libyan chiefs. For Tefnakht, it meant the beginning of a long wait.

Angrily, he seized a low branch of a tamarisk tree, snapped it and flung the pieces far away from him. Then he walked quickly to his own tent, where his two inseparable advisers were waiting for him.

The two men, Yegeb and Nartreb, made an odd couple. Yegeb was tall, with immensely long arms, an even longer face, and swollen ankles; Nartreb was short and pot-bellied, with fingers and toes as chubby as a baby's, a round face and a thick neck. Yegeb was sly and calculating, and somewhat older than Nartreb. He gave Tefnakht the advice he needed to take action, whereas his accomplice enjoyed an inexhaustible fund of energy and unhesitatingly used any means at all to increase his own wealth. Yegeb, although just as corrupt as Nartreb, was always protesting his spotless honesty; he dressed in old clothes, ate sparingly and claimed to have no interest in material things. A single passion drove him: his taste for manipulation and clandestine power. With Nartreb's support, he was pushing Tefnakht to become the uncontested Lord of the Two Lands, convinced that in return he would reward them well.

'Did it go well?' asked Nartreb, chewing on a papyrus stalk.

'Those imbeciles have decided to have another discussion,' Tefnakht revealed.

'That's the worst thing possible,' Yegeb agreed, scratching his nose. 'There's no doubt what the result of their deliberations will be: the offensive will be called off and we will head back to the North.'

'So what do you suggest?' asked Tefnakht.

'For many years, we have been learning all about these petty Libyan despots and we do not lack the means of action.'

'Then use them,' ordered Tefnakht.

CHAPTER THREE

The young Nubian dived into the Nile, in hot pursuit of the buffalo which were wallowing in the fast-flowing water and in danger of drowning. That,

10

at least, was the convincing tale that Puarma had spun to impress three splendid young women with copper-coloured skin.

They were naked, and had been preparing to laze in a natural bathing-place between two rocks when the buffalo, overcome by the heat, galloped into the river. The errant animals belonged to one of Puarma's cousins, and he was determined to recapture them while the women looked on in admiration. The young man was powerfully built and an excellent swimmer, and he had set his sights on conquering all three women. Since they hadn't run away, he considered that they had given their tacit consent.

However, the desolate terrain around the Nile's Fourth Cataract did not inspire thoughts of love. Flowing, surprisingly, from north-east to south-west, the river used all its formidable power to force a passage between the blocks of granite and basalt and the inhospitable islets that tried to obstruct its course. On the hostile banks, sand and stones left little space for the sparse crops; and for almost the entire year the wadis sunk into the desert remained dry. Sturdy date palms clung to perilous slopes, which here and there suddenly turned into blackish cliffs. To travellers passing through, this region seemed like an antechamber of hell.

But Puarma had spent a marvellous childhood in these solitary wastes, and he knew every nook and cranny of the rocky labyrinth. With elegant skill, he lured the buffalo into a side-channel, where they could drink in perfect safety.

'Come,' he urged the three beauties. 'It's perfectly safe.'

They exchanged looks and a few giggly comments, then sprang nimbly from rock to rock to join the young man. The bravest of the three leapt on to the back of one of the buffalo and stretched out an arm to Puarma. When he tried to take it, she pulled it away and swung backwards. Swimming underwater, her two companions grabbed the boy by his legs and dragged him towards them before resurfacing.

Delighted to become their prisoner, Puarma took the opportunity to caress a magnificent pair of breasts and press kisses on passionate lips. Never had he been so thankful to his cousin's buffalo for taking it into their heads to run away. The young Nubian girl was supple as a liana. Indulging in love-games with her was to enjoy a moment of grace, but to become the plaything of three lusty, inventive mistresses seemed like an impossible paradise . . . In the water, Puarma pretended to struggle to retain some control of the situation, but when they dragged him to the bank he gave up all resistance and abandoned himself to their boldest kisses.

Suddenly, the one who had stretched herself on top of him let out a cry of terror and jumped up. Her two companions did the same, and all three darted away like gazelles.

'What's got into you? Come back!' Bitterly disappointed, Puarma got to his feet and turned round.

Standing on a rock overlooking the love-nest was a giant of a man, over three cubits tall, with ebony skin that shone under the fierce sun. He was dressed in a kilt of immaculate white linen, with a narrow gold collar at his throat. Arms folded, the man gazed before him with exceptional intensity.

Puarma knelt and pressed his forehead against the ground.

'Majesty! I did not know you had returned.'

'Rise, Captain of Archers.'

Puarma was a bold man, who would have fought ten men at once without hesitation. But the Black Pharaoh's gaze was more than he could bear. Like Piankhy's other subjects, he knew that there was a supernatural force within the pharaoh, and that it was that force alone which enabled him to reign.

'Majesty,' he asked, 'is there going to be a war?'

'No, don't worry. The hunting was excellent, and I decided to return earlier than expected.'

Piankhy often came to this chaotic, rocky place to think, to contemplate the remote country he loved so much. Wild, hostile, secret, and at first glance impoverished, darkest Nubia, so far from Egypt, produced strong souls and powerful bodies. Here, each day, the marriage of sun and water was celebrated, here blew a violent wind, sometimes icy, sometimes burning hot, which fashioned the people's will and made them capable of withstanding each day's ordeals.

Although he bore the title of King of Upper and Lower Egypt, Piankhy never left his capital, Napata. Crowned at the age of twenty-five, the Black Pharaoh had reigned for twenty years, and was only too well aware of the political and social divisions which were making Egypt as weak as a child. In the North, the occupying Libyan forces were still fighting among themselves to obtain more power. In the South was the holy city of Thebes, where Nubian troops were garrisoned, their task to protect the domain of the god Amon

13

against any attack. Between the North and the South lay Middle Egypt, with two loyal allies of the Black Pharaoh, the princes of Henen-nesut and Khmun. Their presence alone was enough to dissuade the forces of the North from leaving the region they controlled.

Admittedly, this was not a satisfactory situation. But Piankhy was committed to the well-being of Thebes and the embellishment of his own capital city, where he was building a magnificent temple to the glory of Amon, a faithful copy of his shrine at Karnak. Piankhy's sole ambition was to be a masterbuilder, following the example of the great monarchs of the past. The gods had presented him with a magical land where the voice of Ma'at, the goddess of justice and truth, continued to make itself heard. And that was one treasure he would fight to the limits of his strength to preserve.

'Have you been continuing your men's training?' asked the king.

'Of course, Majesty. My archers are ready to go into battle at any moment. Otherwise, they would grow unfit. Just give the order, and we will fight.'

Piankhy had a high opinion of Puarma's bravery. And the captain of archers was convinced that this meeting owed nothing to chance.

'Majesty, should we prepare ourselves for war?'

'No—at least, not in the form you envisage. The enemy does not always attack where you expect. In my own capital, some people are hoping that I will spend less time thinking about the gods and more about their privileges. Be like your men, Puarma: be prepared for anything.'

The captain of archers bowed his head before the king and ran off towards Napata, while Piankhy

14

continued to gaze at the tortured landscape around the cataract. From the fury of the waters and the implacable eternity of the rocks, the Black Pharaoh drew vital resources of energy to carry out his task.

Happiness . . . Yes, Piankhy had the inestimable good fortune to know happiness. A happy family, a people who ate their fill and were nourished spiritually by peaceful days, measured out to the rhythm of festivals and religious rites. He, the Black Pharaoh, had a duty to preserve that tranquillity.

The air was so clear that the slightest sound was audible. Piankhy knew this sound well: the hooves of a donkey striking the pathway, a donkey carrying Cool-Head, a senior scribe and Piankhy's adviser. The donkey was lucky enough to have a lightweight master, for Cool-Head was a dwarf with a stern face and an admirably proportioned torso.

Ordinarily, the scribe rarely moved from his office, the administrative centre of the capital. If he had undertaken this journey, it must be for a serious reason.

'At last I've found you, Majesty,' said Cool-Head.

'What has happened?'

'An accident at the construction site, Majesty. A very grave one.'

CHAPTER FOUR

Gebel Barkal, the 'Pure Mountain', towered over Napata. It stood at the point where all creation had originated, and housed the invisible power of Amon, 'the Hidden One'.

15

Napata was a day's march upstream from the Fourth Cataract and was surrounded by desert, yet it stood at the heart of a fertile plain where several caravan routes met. Consequently Piankhy's subjects did not lack for the essentials of life—or even the luxuries, for that matter.

But the caravan traders were not allowed to settle in Napata, unless they changed their profession. They were allowed into the city only for a brief stay, sufficient time to sell their wares and rest awhile from their labours. Every one of them knew that Piankhy possessed immense wealth, but that he lavished it only on decorating the kingdom's temples and upon the wellbeing of its citizens. Corruption was rare and was severely punished, in the worst cases by execution. The Black Pharaoh would not tolerate any serious deviation from the Rule of Ma'at, and there were few people foolish enough to risk the force of his anger.

Gebel Barkal stood in splendid isolation, rising up out of the desert wastes. The mountain had fascinated Piankhy ever since he was a boy. He had spent many an hour wandering along the base of the steep cliffs that loomed over the right bank of the Nile. And as the years passed an insane plan had formed in his heart: he would make the Pure Mountain speak, carving and shaping into the symbol of pharaonic rule the isolated peak that jutted from one of its corners.

It was a dangerous enterprise, but for the past two years Piankhy had devoted himself to its achievement, with the help of a band of volunteer workmen. As the peak was separated from the main body of the mountain by a ravine twenty-five cubits wide and a hundred and twenty deep, it had been necessary to put up an immense array of scaffolding. This had been done by gouging out hollows in the rock to anchor beams and girders, and by using rudimentary but effective lifting-gear.

The sculptors sat on narrow platforms and, under the pharaoh's strict supervision, carved away the peak of Gebel Barkal. From the east, it would look like an enormous uraeus, the female cobra, head erect and wearing the White Crown; from the west, the peak would resemble the Red Crown and sun-disc. At the summit an inscription to the honour of Amon had been engraved in hieroglyphics. A goldsmith had also erected a panel covered in gold leaf to reflect the dawn light; each morning, in a dazzling display, it would demonstrate the triumph of light over darkness. Beneath the panel, a niche had been hollowed out to house a golden uraeus.

The work was at last nearing its end, and the final baskets of stones and mortar had been hauled up to put the finishing touches to the mountain's new face.

'Tell me what happened,' Piankhy ordered Cool-Head.

'One of the sculptors wanted to take a close look at his work and didn't follow the safety rules. Halfway up, he lost his footing on one of the beams.'

'Are you saying . . .?'

'He is dead, Majesty,' said Cool-Head. 'And his apprentice has fared scarcely better. Stupidly, he ran to help his master, was overcome by vertigo and is trapped up there, unable to move a muscle.'

Piankhy looked up and saw a young man

17

flattened against the rock face, his hands desperately clutching at an overhang, his feet balanced on an outcrop of crumbling stone. In order to get up there more quickly, the boy had not taken the approved route of ladders and ropes, but had thought he could scale the rock face with his bare hands. When he saw the sculptor fall, he had panicked. Powerless, their arms dangling uselessly at their sides, his friends stood and gazed up at him, waiting for his inevitable fall.

'How old is this lad?' Piankhy demanded.

'Seventeen.'

'And how heavy is he?'

'I don't know exactly,' Cool-Head confessed, 'but he's only a slip of a boy.'

'Choose two men to accompany me.'

'Majesty, surely you are not going to—'

'Above him,' interrupted Piankhy, 'the rock faces are closer together. If I can get a secure foothold and take his hand, he has a chance of survival.'

Cool-Head trembled. 'Majesty, in the name of the kingdom, I beg you not to take such a risk!'

'I consider myself responsible for that boy's life. Come, we must not waste another second.'

Two broad-shouldered, sure-footed stone-cutters set off in front of Piankhy, climbing the narrow ladder up to the first platform, which was constructed of solid beams of acacia wood.

'Hold on!' shouted Piankhy to the apprentice, his voice echoing around the sacred mountain. 'We're coming!'

The boy's left foot slipped and, for a moment, dangled in empty air. Then, with an effort he would not have believed himself capable of, he recovered his balance and managed to flatten himself against

18

the rock once more.

'I'll have to climb higher,' the king announced.

'You should use this knotted rope, Majesty,' said one of the stone-cutters.

Piankhy climbed it without difficulty and came to rest on a ledge above the unfortunate boy, whose fingers were turning blue with the effort of clinging on to the rock. The king stretched out his right arm, but he was a good two cubits too far away to reach the boy he wanted to save from a horrible death.

'Bring me a ladder,' he ordered.

The two stone-cutters lifted one up; it was so heavy that all their muscles knotted with the effort. What Piankhy had in mind would demand a superhuman effort: laying the ladder down horizontally and wedging it between the two rock faces.

Slowly, tightly gripping the middle rung, the king swung the ladder round. It took an immense effort of concentration. When one end of the ladder touched the rock it loosened a few fragments, and the boy let out a stifled cry as they rained down, just missing his head.

'Hold on tight, youngster.'

The ladder was jammed in position. As Piankhy began to move across the improvised bridge, the wood creaked beneath him. One of the rungs let out a sinister crack, but it did not give way beneath the king's weight. In a single smooth, athletic movement, he stretched out along the ladder.

'I'm here, boy, right next to you. Now, I'm going to reach out my arm. You're to grab hold of my wrist, and I'll haul you up on to this ladder.'

'I . . . I can't . . . I'm done for. . .'

19

'You must turn round, so you can see my arm.'

'It's impossible—impossible!'

'Breathe naturally. I want you to concentrate on your breathing, nothing but your breathing. Now, turn round so that you're facing me.'

'I'm going to fall, I'll be crushed, I'm going to die!' wailed the boy.

'Just don't look down, do you hear? Look up, look up at my arm, reaching out to you. It's just above your head.'

The ladder let out another groan of protest.

'Turn round. Turn to face me!' Piankhy ordered, his voice filled with stern authority.

Breathlessly, the apprentice obeyed. Although clumsy and uncertain because of his paralysing fear, his feet moved. The moment he found himself face to face with dizzy emptiness, he lost his footing. Eyes wide with terror, he toppled into the abyss.

Stretching so hard he wrenched his shoulder half out of its socket, Piankhy just managed to grab hold of the boy's left wrist. The shock was violent, but the king succeeded in hauling him on to the ladder.

'Majesty!' the boy blurted out. Then he burst into tears.

'If you were any heavier, my lad, we would both be dead. Your punishment for breaking the safety rules is to work in the laundry for a month.'

At the foot of the mountain peak, the survivor's friends congratulated him, after praising the king's bravery. Cool-Head, though, still seemed worried.

'The lad is alive,' said Piankhy. 'Isn't that what matters?'

'Majesty, I did not tell you everything.'

'What else is there to tell?'

'What I feared has come to pass: certain members of your court—and not unimportant ones either—are questioning your right to the throne.'

CHAPTER FIVE

The Black Pharaoh raised his eyes to the peak of Gebel Barkal. 'Look at it, Cool-Head,' he said. 'This achievement will outlive me. Only that which is carved in living stone can survive down the ages.'

Cool-Head's name was well deserved. He was a tireless, single-minded man, and his enquiries had been far from superficial. Convinced that the king had not understood the gravity of his words, the scribe felt he must press the point.

'This is not simply the usual discontent, Majesty, it is a real rebellion against your personal authority. To be perfectly frank, I believe that even one of your junior wives is involved.'

'Must we bother ourselves with such paltry things?'

'The matter is serious, Majesty.'

'If I did lose my throne, would that be so catastrophic?'

'Indeed it would—for your people and for your country. The man who seeks to supplant you does not share your priorities or those of your father before you. All he cares about is getting his hands on Nubia's gold and using her wealth for his personal enjoyment.'

The argument was not lost on Piankhy. Giving up his throne mattered little to him, but it would be unbearable to see the work of several generations destroyed.

'I am going to the temple,' he said. 'My father Amon will guide me.'

Cool-Head would have preferred the king to call an immediate meeting of the court and rule on the matter with his usual authority. But he knew Piankhy would not go back on his decision.

The Temple of Amon stood at the foot of the Pure Mountain, and was the Black Pharaoh's pride and joy. Here, many miles from Thebes, he had recreated the dwelling of the lord of the gods. It boasted an avenue of rams, the incarnation of Amon, leading to a first gateway whose twin sloping towers symbolized the West and the East. This led in turn to the first great pillared courtyard, where important dignitaries were admitted on feast days, then a second gateway and the second pillared courtyard. This was followed by the roofed temple with shrines opening off it, and finally the innermost shrine, which contained the statue of Amon, the material expression of the god's spiritual power, and which only Pharaoh was permitted to enter. Every day at first light, Piankhy opened the doors of this shrine. Once inside, he paid homage to the statue, anointed it with perfume, dressed it in new robes, and renewed its strength with an offering of food, before replacing it within the primordial stone, at the heart of the creation mystery.

During the afternoons, silence fell over the temple. The ritualists were busy washing the sacred objects in their private workshops, and the faces of the gods and goddesses, engraved on the walls, conversed silently with each other.

A priest from Karnak would have felt perfectly at home had he entered the sacred domain patiently built by Piankhy. For the pharaoh continually added to its beauty, to honour the memory of the illustrious pharaohs who had toiled here, at Napata, so that the message of Amon might shine out into the world.

Inside the temple were kept the stelae of Tuthmosis III, upon whom the Black Pharaoh modelled himself, and those of two other kings of Egypt whom he revered, Seti I and Ramses II. For him, these three monarchs embodied the greatness of the Two Lands, in harmony with divine will, for they had carried out their supreme duty with incomparable meticulousness and love. Tutankhamon's little shrine had been piously preserved, too, as had the statues of the gods whose presence guaranteed the transference of the soul.

The further you went into the temple, the smaller and darker its rooms became, until you reached the innermost shrine, whose secret light was visible only to the eyes of the heart. The mystery of life would never be explained, but it could be experienced and shared.

Piankhy stood very still before a limestone statue of a lion, its every detail carved with extraordinary skill. In Nubia, Amon liked to take on the form of this wild beast, for the name of the lion in hieroglyphics was 'mai', meaning 'He Who Sees': not even by hiding in the furthermost recesses of a darkened room could anyone escape the eye of the Creator. On the plinth of the statue an inscription read, 'The god who recognizes those who are faithful to Him, He whose coming is sweet and who answers those who have called upon Him'.

Beyond the stone beast, a carved panel depicted a bow being offered to Amon. The lord of heaven had revealed the path Piankhy must take: he must continue to fight.

*   *   *

The late evening was profoundly warm and gentle. This was the moment when shepherds played the flute, when the scribe laid down his writing-brush, and the mistress of the house finally allowed herself a moment's rest as she watched the setting sun. Toil faded to a distant memory, and the weariness of the day was forgotten in these magical moments, which wise old men considered the expression of blissful completeness.

When Piankhy entered the darkened bedchamber of his principal wife, he thought at first that she was not there. Then he saw her standing on the terrace observing the last rays of the Star of Life, utterly absorbed in its unique, constantly renewed display.

At thirty-five years old, Abilah was at the very height of her dazzling beauty. With her tall, elegant frame, her exquisite oval face—reminiscent of Nefertiti—and her copper-coloured skin, she had a truly royal bearing. Piankhy had turned down all the official candidates in order to marry this daughter of a penniless priest, a man who had a deep knowledge of Egyptian rituals and had passed on all he knew to Piankhy. Time had left no mark upon her. On the contrary, maturity had only increased and refined her beauty, and even the prettiest seductresses in Napata had given up trying to rival her.

Abilah wore nothing but a long chemise made from diaphanous linen. She had unpinned her perfumed hair and her semi-nakedness, worthy of any goddess, was lit by the last dancing glimmers of the sunset.

When darkness fell over Piankhy's kingdom, she turned to cover herself with another robe. It was then that she saw him.

'Have you been there long?' she asked.

'I didn't want to interrupt your meditation.'

He took her passionately in his arms, as though they had been apart for many long months. Even if she had been furious with him, Abilah could not have resisted his magic. The knowledge that she was loved and protected by this king, so strong and yet so sensitive, filled her with such joy that she had no words to describe it.

'Did you have good hunting?' she asked.

'The court won't go short of meat—though that won't stop them grumbling.'

'Are you afraid of them?'

'Anyone who ignores a plot against him is unworthy to reign.'

Abilah laid her cheek on Piankhy's shoulder. 'A plot? Is it as serious as that?'

'Don't tell me that the Queen of Egypt doesn't already know about it.'

'I thought all those rumours were groundless.'

'That's not what Cool-Head thinks.'

'Cool-Head . . . Do you always listen to that scribe's advice?'

'Do you blame me if I do?'

Abilah took a step back and looked up at Piankhy. 'You are right, my love. Cool-Head will

25

not betray you. One of your junior wives, a few envious priests, a handful of stupid courtiers and an over-ambitious minister—how can you take them seriously, when you have reigned for twenty years and the humblest of your subjects would gladly die for you!'

'There is no antidote to the poison of vanity, Abilah. It leads to the worst death of all, the death of a man's conscience.'

'What are you going to do?'

'I called upon Amon to show me the path I must take, and he has answered my prayer.'

CHAPTER SIX

The night was warm and sweet, and Tranan, the king's finance minister, was revelling in his good fortune. Sitting under the tallest palm tree in his garden, he savoured his approaching triumph. At the age of fifty-four, he held one of the most prestigious posts in Piankhy's government and lived in the centre of Napata, in a magnificent house which would not have disgraced a rich Theban nobleman. He was a fortunate husband, father of five children, had spent his entire career in government service in the city, and should have been well satisfied with his comfortable life.

But Tranan was one of the few officials who knew the true resources of Piankhy's kingdom, whose apparent poverty was in fact an illusion. Modest farms along the Nile banks, the products of fishing and hunting, date crops . . . It took only a moment to enumerate the kingdom's natural

26

wealth, and the casual observer might conclude that Napata was the capital of a poverty-stricken province.

But that was to overlook the true marvel which the Nubian land had to offer its ruler: gold. High-quality gold too, in abundance. If former kings of Egypt had bothered to colonize Nubia, they had done so in order to gain control of this precious metal. At present it was the Black Pharaoh who exercised control over mining rights and every aspect of gold production: this was how rivalries and greed were prevented. But how did Piankhy make use of this colossal fortune? He donated it to the Temple of Amon and used it to improve his subjects' lives.

The minister could not stomach this policy. Any ruler who omitted to look to his own wealth was a weak ruler who deserved, sooner or later, to be eliminated. In Piankhy's place, Tranan would have given the populace the bare minimum, and enjoyed a luxurious life with his close friends. As his wife was aging, he would have treated himself to young courtesans and spent his time travelling, so that foreign princes could marvel at the splendour of his sumptuous banquets.

With Piankhy, the future was a dead end. The Black Pharaoh was so obsessively attached to his Pure Mountain, his Temple of Amon and his capital city that he had no spirit of enterprise or business sense. The time had come to make radical policy changes.

Tranan's steward brought him a goblet of cooled wine and a platter of honey-cakes. 'Master, your wife awaits you for dinner.'

'Tell her to eat with the children and to stop

bothering me. As soon as my visitor arrives, show him into the massage room. And make sure no one disturbs us.'

Tranan could not act alone. True, he had the support of a few court officials, but they would throw themselves at Piankhy's feet the moment Pharaoh raised his voice. On the other hand, one of the junior wives, who had been neglected by her royal spouse, dreamt of vengeance and hated him enough to long to destroy him. Most important of all, Tranan would be able to count on the support of someone even more valuable to him: the fat man who was just about to enter his massage room.

Otoku weighed as much as an ox—probably more—because of his habitual orgies of slabs of beef, rich sauces and cream-filled pastries. He was covered in solid-gold necklets and rings; even his robe was embroidered with gold thread, and it was forbidden to touch him, on pain of a deadly blow from his solid-gold club. Otoku was chief of the most distant of the Nubian tribes, most of whose members were involved in extracting the finest-quality gold from a gigantic mine. For many years he had sworn allegiance to the Black Pharaoh, but as time went on his oath had lost its force.

Bearing in mind Otoku's notorious touchiness, Tranan had approached him little by little and with the utmost care, with the aim of gaining his confidence gradually. Fortunately, the fat man loved receiving presents, particularly ebony caskets and woollen scarves which he wound around his thick neck when the nights grew chilly.

But Otoku's real weakness was massage. For several hours every day, he delivered his plump body into skilled hands which made it quiver with pleasure. When Tranan told him that he had just taken on a massage-girl with remarkable talents, the fat man could hardly wait to meet her.

The custom of his tribe forbade Otoku to step on the ground in the presence of an inferior. Since his only superior was the Black Pharaoh, the fat man entered Tranan's house on a gilded wooden chair which four strapping fellows barely managed to carry.

'Your visit confers the highest honour upon me, Lord Otoku,' declared Tranan, who knew how important the correct forms of address were to his guest.

'Quite, quite. I have a backache. See to it immediately.'

Three steps had to be climbed and it took every last bit of the chair-bearers' strength to carry their master up them. With all the grace of a kneeling elephant, Otoku managed to lay himself down on his belly as a servant slid a golden cushion underneath his belly.

'Where is this massage-girl you promised me?'

'She is here, my lord.'

A fragile-looking Syrian girl, with short, dark-blonde hair, climbed up on to the fat man's back, flexed her supple hands and poured warm, perfumed oil on to the mass of wobbling flesh.

'What is this delightful stuff?' asked Otoku, agreeably surprised.

'An oil used at festivals in the city of Thebes, my lord. It is said to have eased the discomforts of Ramses the Great himself.'

The fat man growled with contentment as one by one, the girl's agile, accurate hands eased the knots of tension from his muscles.

Tranan was careful not to interrupt the treatment—after all, Otoku was going to be thoroughly indebted to him.

'Perfect, little one, perfect,' Otoku told the girl when the massage was over. 'You shall have a bag of powdered gold.' She disappeared, and he sat down again on his chair. 'So, Tranan, my friend, why have you brought me to Napata?'

'That little girl . . .'

'Your Syrian is very talented, but let's talk of serious matters. You know how much I hate travelling and leaving my village.'

Tranan paced up and down nervously. 'The matter is extremely serious, my lord. You are the principal producer of gold in the kingdom and I am the finance minister. With Piankhy, we are the only people who know the extent of Nubia's wealth. I must be honest with you: in my opinion, Piankhy is using it badly.'

'Are you accusing Pharaoh of dishonesty?'

'No, simply of a lack of imagination—many officials think as I do. Our capital is slumbering in its wealth because Piankhy is obsessed with respecting antiquated traditions. He has been on the throne for twenty years, and he forgets the demands of the future. Unless you and I intervene, Napata is destined for ruin.'

Otoku's eyes narrowed to slits. 'And how exactly are we to intervene?'

'A section of the court has decided to challenge Piankhy's right to the throne. The very people who elected him are thinking of naming a successor.'

'A successor whose name would be. . . Tranan?'

'Only if Lord Otoku would agree to become the new finance minister and be honoured as he

30

deserves.'

'And am I to receive a larger share of the gold my tribe extracts from the bowels of the earth?'

'Of course.'

The fat man purred, a sign that he was profoundly satisfied. Tranan knew he would succeed: working on a man's greed always produced results. From now on, Piankhy's days were numbered.

Otoku sprang to his feet like a cat and seized Tranan by the scruff of his neck. 'For a long time I've thought you a petty crook, unworthy of the high office Pharaoh has bestowed on you. You have forgotten one detail, Tranan. Piankhy and I have been friends for more than twenty years, and true friends never betray each other.'

CHAPTER SEVEN

Tranan would never return from the gold mine, where he would work until the end of his days. Nevertheless, Otoku was not fully reassured; he had merely crushed a single wasp whose appetite was bigger than its sting, while a serious threat still hung over Piankhy's head.

The Great Council was made up of the friends and supporters of the king, the elders and the ritualists. It had elected Piankhy unanimously twenty years earlier, yet it now seemed determined to express grave reservations about the Black Pharaoh's behaviour. The reservations were based on false reports submitted by Tranan, tittle-tattle hawked around by one of Piankhy's junior wives, and malicious words by priests who wrongly accused the Black Pharaoh of lacking piety towards Amon. If Otoku had realized the danger in time, he would willingly have strangled all these liars with his bare hands; but the Great Council, as unbending as ever, had set in motion a procedure which no one could now halt.

True, Piankhy would have no difficulty in refuting these shameful accusations, but his reputation would be damaged and, even worse, he was quite capable of renouncing the throne and withdrawing into the Temple of Amon. Otoku knew his friend well, and was quite sure that he would not hang on to power if circumstances gave him an opportunity to rid himself of it. But he also knew that there was no one fit to replace Piankhy and that his abdication would be a catastrophe for Napata, for Nubia and for Egypt.

Instead of preparing to defend himself, the king had galloped off into the desert on Valiant, his favourite horse, determined to give the superb animal a chance to enjoy the wide-open spaces he loved. The man and his mount might not even be back before the meeting of the Great Council was convened.

*   *   *

The youngest of Piankhy's junior wives was seventeen years old, and furious. It was true that her father, when he brought her to the court at Napata, had explained that she would never see the pharaoh and that this diplomatic marriage was essential because she was the heiress of her tribe, from south of the Fourth Cataract, and it would seal their alliance with the monarch. But the girl had not thought it would be like this. After all, she was the most beautiful woman in the palace. She deserved to share the king's bed and drive all her rivals from it.

She had mounted a strenuous campaign to force open the doors that would lead her to Piankhy, but her disorganized attempts had led only to repeated failure. The king's entourage, and in particular the accursed dwarf who worked as his scribe, prevented any inconvenience from disturbing his serenity. She, a chieftain's daughter, a junior wife of the king, considered an inconvenience! Enraged by the slight, she had decided to take revenge on this despot who was incapable of appreciating her beauty, by revealing to the Great Council that Piankhy was corrupt and was stealing much of the kingdom's wealth for his own use. When a new pharaoh was appointed, he would be sure to notice her and give her her proper station at court.

She was currently sitting in her bedchamber, trying on a collar of blue pearls, red jasper and cornelian, separated by thin gold discs. 'Fasten it,' she commanded her maid.

'That necklace is worthy of a queen—and you are not a queen.'

Stung by this reproach, the girl looked round and found herself face to face with Abilah, Piankhy's principal wife.

'This palace welcomed you, little one, and you have betrayed its trust. Worse still, you have told lies about Pharaoh and tried to stir up a plot against him.'

Terrified, the girl stood up, unable to do more than stammer a feeble protest.

'Such a crime,' Abilah went on, 'is punishable by a long term of imprisonment, but you are no more than a child, though your heart is already filled with bitterness. Give up all idea of sullying Piankhy's name, or I shall forget my lenience towards you and become fiercer than a tigress.'

'What . . . what are you going to do with me?'

'You will return to your tribe, where respectable women will teach you how to work and keep house. Consider yourself fortunate.'

*   *   *

Kapa, the most senior member of the Great Council, was ninety-seven years old but still clear of eye and speech. He was very thin, for all his life he had eaten only one frugal meal a day; he did not drink date-wine and always took a daily walk. Those around him were wary of his grouchiness, which had grown more pronounced with age. The contrast between him and Otoku, the bon viveur, was striking.

The fat man had no idea how to deal with this grumpy old man, who would not even accept a cup of cooled beer. 'Think of your health . . .' he said.

'You're not interested in my health, Otoku, any more than I'm interested in yours. Where is your friend the king hiding himself?

'He has gone for a long ride.'

'The members of the Great Council have submitted their conclusions to me, and I have examined them carefully.'

'In that case you will have realized that the accusations are absurd.'

'How dare you criticize the work of these men!'

34

snapped Kapa. 'They must be treated with respect.'

'The information they received was a tissue of lies,' said Otoku hotly. 'All the evidence points to a few jealous people who wanted to harm Piankhy, and the correct course of action is to punish them as they deserve.'

'From what I've heard, you yourself punished Tranan, the former finance minister.'

'I put him to work. Piankhy is sometimes too forgiving. It is up to his friends to rid him of vicious parasites.'

'I am the leader of the Great Council and I will not allow myself to be improperly swayed. Whether the king likes it or not, he must appear before us at the earliest possible opportunity.'

* * *

Valiant was five years old, and in his prime. He was the finest horse Piankhy had ever had an opportunity to break in, and he could cover immense distances without ever tiring. Friendship had sprung up between man and beast the first time they set eyes on each other, and though the warhorse was proud, even fierce, the king scarcely had to make any effort for Valiant to understand what was required of him; for the horse wished only to please this man, who had won his complete trust.

Valiant was a bay with a tawny mane as shiny as silk. He stood tall and regal, and seemed almost to be laughing as he gazed straight ahead of him, unblinking. The horsemen in Piankhy's army regarded him with admiration and envy, though they dared not approach him too closely. Everyone knew that Valiant obeyed no one but Piankhy, and that he would revert instantly to a wild beast if anyone else tried to mount him.

The king had introduced him to many of the trails around Napata, and the horse had learnt them astonishingly quickly, without the slightest hesitation. Whenever it was time to return to his personal stable, where Pharaoh himself groomed him, Valiant always chose the shortest route. As well as strength and endurance, the horse demonstrated a keen intelligence.

From the top of a high sand-dune, the Black Pharaoh contemplated the desert wastes that stretched out beneath him. 'You see, Valiant, no emperor would want a land like this. But it's the land we love, you and I, because it never lies, because it forces us to be ruthless with ourselves and to worship the limitless power of the Light. Desert wastes and cultivated earth are strangers to each other; they cannot become one. And yet, each makes you understand the need for the other.'

Crowned cranes flew over the heads of the horseman and his mount. In the distance, at the summit of another dune, a long-horned oryx was standing stock-still, watching them. If Piankhy needed a watering-place, he had only to follow it.

'They're waiting for me in the capital, Valiant, and the people who want to see me are hostile. Still, if I lose everything, there are two beings who will follow me to the bottom of the abyss: my wife and you. Am I not the happiest of men?'

The horse pointed its muzzle towards Napata and set off at a flying gallop. Neither he nor his master feared the trial that awaited them.

CHAPTER EIGHT

Tefnakht knew that war was the only way he would ever acquire supreme power, but he took no pleasure in battle or in bearing arms—let others devote themselves to intensive training in archery and spear-throwing. All the Libyan chiefs were proud of their physical strength, but such things were of no interest to the leader of the alliance.

To overcome his anxieties, Tefnakht had a hundred times reviewed his plans for reconquering and reunifying the Two Lands. Prostitutes had been brought to him but he had sent them away, and he refused to touch a drop of wine or beer. These soothing pleasures would distract him from his one and only goal: to be recognized as the supreme head of the Libyan coalition, to annihilate Piankhy's troops, to reduce the Nubian to powerlessness and be crowned as Pharaoh—first at Thebes, in the South, then in the Northern city of Memphis.

Victory was within his grasp, but he must act quickly, before the Black Pharaoh realized how determined and ambitious Tefnakht truly was. Up to now, Piankhy had regarded him only as one Libyan prince among many, more powerful than his peers, admittedly, but just as mediocre and venal. Piankhy was wrong.

Tefnakht had a Libyan father, but an Egyptian mother. He had studied Egypt's glorious past and had reached an unshakeable conclusion: the country would only rediscover its former greatness when the Two Lands of Upper and Lower Egypt were once again reunited. It was a spectacular project, which Piankhy could never bring to fruition, and which the Libyan princelings poured scorn upon. But Tefnakht believed himself capable of pursuing this difficult path right to its end, and re-igniting the torch that the successors of Ramses the Great had allowed to go out.

Unfortunately, success depended on the goodwill of a collection of petty tyrants who lacked vision and were interested only in hanging on to their own petty privileges. When he obtained supreme power, Tefnakht would end the anarchy which was exhausting the country. All the provinces, whether they belonged to the North or the South, would be brought back under the sole authority of Pharaoh.

Tefnakht was motivated not by any lust for personal glory but by the desire to give back to Egypt her former splendour and, better still, to make the country the centre of the new Mediterranean world which was beginning to take shape under the influence of Greece and Asia Minor.

No one could understand this vision, and the weight of solitude was hard to carry. What's more, he had to resort to the services of Yegeb and Nartreb, two creatures who feared neither the gods nor man, to attain his goals. But, if Tefnakht succeeded, these times of doubt and suffering would quickly be forgotten.

He unrolled a papyrus inscribed with accounting details from an ancient dynasty, that of Ramses the Great. It was a reminder of Memphis's immense wealth in those days: fertile fields, waterways teeming with fish, warehouses bursting with goods, incessant visits from hordes of ambassadors . . . Today, the great city was slumbering, waiting for a true king who would give it back the strength it needed to take on its role as the 'Balance of the Two Lands': a fulcrum between the North, which looked to countries beyond Egypt, and the traditionalist South.

'May I speak with you, my lord?' asked Nartreb from the entrance to Tefnakht's tent. There was a note of exaltation in his voice.

'Is it good news?'

'Excellent. But my throat is parched . . .' The counsellor reached out his pudgy hands, and helped himself to a cup of white wine, which was kept cool in a jar of a type which only the potters of Middle Egypt knew the secret of making.

'Have the provincial chieftains finally voted in my favour?' asked Tefnakht.

'The situation is a little more complicated than that, my lord. To be honest, over the last few days opinion was moving rather against you, and the only people you could rely on were those who opposed you. If Yegeb and I had not intervened, the vote would have gone against you and you would have had to return to your princedom of Sais.'

'So how did you persuade them to change their minds?'

'It wasn't easy. But we knew how to find the right arguments.'

'I want to know what they were, Nartreb,' said Tefnakht sternly.

'Is that really necessary, my lord? You pay us to do a job and we do it. The details are not important.'

39

'That is not how I see it.'

Nartreb could feel Tefnakht's anger rising. He bowed his head, and said, 'For several years, Yegeb and I have been gathering all sorts of information about the chieftains of the Northern provinces, thanks to the cooperation of local officials who are happy to sell us their secrets as long as their names aren't mentioned. Today, we are reaping the benefits of this groundwork. Since the princelings are all more or less corrupt and have all betrayed their own allies in varying degrees, naturally they wish to have these shortcomings well and truly forgotten, so we had little difficulty in negotiating their approval. There's just one small problem . . .'

'Akanosh?'

'Oh no, not him—he's too timid. He came round to the majority opinion. No, I'm talking about the old chieftain who rules the Delta marshes and controls the fishing grounds. He's an imbecile, and a stubborn one at that. He refuses to enter into any conflict with the Black Pharaoh. Unfortunately, his word still carries a lot of weight and it's preventing us from concluding the talks. In fact, his opposition could even threaten our ultimate success.'

Nartreb's stomach rumbled. He gulped down a handful of dates.

'How do you intend to solve this problem?' demanded Tefnakht.

'Yegeb is taking care of it. Ah, here he is now.'

Yegeb's long, thin face bore an expression of profound satisfaction. 'May I sit down, my lord? My legs are aching.'

'Did you succeed?' asked Tefnakht.

'Destiny smiles upon you. The old marshland chieftain has just died.'

40

Tefnakht paled. 'You mean you . . .?'

'Your implacable adversary died during his afternoon nap. It was a perfectly natural death, which just goes to prove your good fortune.'

'I want to know the truth, Yegeb!'

'The truth is that he will be mourned with all due solemnity, and then the Libyan chieftains will vote to give you supreme power over them.'

*　　*　　*

Akanosh's wife was in her fifties and still beautiful. After thirty years of marriage, she could divine her husband's feelings without him saying a word, and when he returned to his tent she saw immediately that things had not gone well.

'Is it war?' she asked.

'They all changed their minds, and our most senior member is no longer there to convince them that in choosing Tefnakht as their commander-in-chief they are making a fatal mistake. Yes, it is war. We are preparing to attack Henen-nesut.'

'You're afraid for me, aren't you?'

Akanosh clasped his wife's hands between his own. 'We are the last people alive who know that you are from Nubia. In any case, no one would dare attack my wife.'

Although she had the fair, sun-bronzed skin of a Northern Egyptian, Akanosh's wife had a Nubian father. For a long time, the Libyan prince had dreamed of an alliance with Piankhy, which would have turned him into a natural negotiator with his fellow Delta chieftains.

'It's Tefnakht who worries me,' Akanosh admitted. 'He is intelligent, cunning and ruthless.

He'll put Egypt to fire and the sword if it will turn his dream into reality.'

'But you must obey him, just as the other chieftains do, and order your soldiers to follow you.'

'It's true that I have no choice. And yet . . . my conscience tells me that I must warn Piankhy.'

'Take care, my darling. If you're accused of treason—'

'Tefnakht will kill me with his bare hands, I know. But don't worry. I know how to do this without anyone ever suspecting.'

CHAPTER NINE

The Great Council had convened before the first gateway of the Temple of Amon at Napata, in the place where 'Ma'at was spoken', the law of truth and justice. Kapa, head of the Council, presided over the meeting. Seated around him were the friends and supporters of the king, the elders and the ritualists. Their faces were uniformly stern.

The Black Pharaoh galloped into view and dismounted a few yards from Kapa, who remained impassive. Piankhy was wearing the crown commonly worn by Nubian kings, a sort of bonnet moulded to the shape of the skull, enclosed within a golden diadem from which darted two spitting-cobras, their heads erect and ready to strike. On his wrists and upper arms, he wore gold bracelets inscribed with his own name. On his golden apron glittered a tiny panther's head, radiating rays of light.

42

At the sight of the monarch, whose powerful physical presence made grown men tremble, most of the members of the Great Council would dearly have loved to run away. But instead they bowed respectfully, following the example of old Kapa, who immediately began to speak, so as to avert a mass flight.

'Majesty, twenty years ago the Great Council elected you Pharaoh of Upper and Lower Egypt. None of the council members has had any cause to complain of your actions, but distressing events have recently disturbed the peace of the court. We have examined the complaints which have come to us by various indirect routes, and—'

'Why,' interrupted Piankhy, 'do my accusers not dare show their faces?'

'Majesty, we approve of the punishment meted out to the Tranan, and also of the banishment of the junior wife who was trying to foment a plot against you. For my part, I would go so far as to say that those measures were too lenient.'

'In that case, what else am I accused of?'

The majority of the Great Council's members hoped Kapa would be satisfied with this brief confrontation, but the old Nubian had an acute sense of the magic of beings, places and moments. For him the form of government was more important than any choice of ministers or policies. A man who was not in tune with the secret harmony of the world had no chance of ruling a country properly.

'For twenty years,' Kapa reminded the king, 'your power has remained intact. If unworthy individuals have tried to sully your good name, it is for a serious reason, namely the fact that your

43

capacity to reign has grown weaker.'

Several members of the Great Council felt that old Kapa was going too far and feared Piankhy's anger. But the Black Pharaoh did not lose his composure.

'The Divine Light has placed the king upon this earth of living mortals to judge human beings and satisfy the will of the gods,' he said solemnly, reciting the coronation text. 'For the king must replace disorder, lies and injustice with the harmony of Ma'at, protect the weak from the strong, make offerings to the Invisible and venerate the souls of the dead. That is the task for which Amon chose me. "Accept the crown," he commanded me, for it is truly Amon who decided my destiny. God makes the king, the people proclaim him. And I adopted the coronation titles of my glorious ancestor Tuthmosis III: "Peacemaker of the Two Nations", "Unifier of the Two Lands", "All-Powerful is the Harmony of the Divine Light". Like him, the son of Thoth, I seek wisdom and knowledge. It is written in the *Book of Going Forth by Day* that knowledge is that which banishes evil and darkness, sees the future and brings order to the land. But perhaps you are right, Kapa. Perhaps my ability to reign is indeed weakening. Perhaps the time has come for me to renounce the throne and withdraw from public life. It is for Amon, not me, to reply; and he will give a sign of his will.'

*   *   *

Piankhy stood on the terrace of his palace, surrounded by palm trees, hibiscus and oleander,

44

gazing down on his city and the far-distant desert. How peaceful it seemed, in the warm, sweet darkness, and yet the night swarmed with prowling demons, ready to devour the unwary traveller. Many times the Black Pharaoh had confronted the dangers of the desert, its shimmering mirages, its illusory paths that led nowhere, its tempting sand-dunes which the eye never tired of looking at.

Abilah stood beside him, her body against his, her fingers caressing his cheek. How he loved this woman, who alone embodied all the beauty and nobility of Nubia. Her dress of fine gauze, diaphanous as a fisherman's net, revealed more of her body than it concealed, and at her throat she wore a golden collar, ornamented with turquoise beads. She was the very essence of seductiveness. She had given Piankhy a son and a daughter, and with the birth of each child she had grown still more dazzlingly feminine.

'Are these our last few nights in this palace?' she asked. Her voice was clear, with no trace of anxiety.

'Yes, if Lord Amon withdraws his trust from me.'

Abilah embraced her husband. 'If I heeded only my love for you, I would beg Amon to remain silent. We could take ourselves away to some palm-grove, and live there peacefully with our children. But I shall not offer up that prayer, for you are the only guarantee of your people's happiness. Sacrificing their happiness for our own would be an unforgivable act of treason.'

'Don't you think you're over-estimating my importance?' asked Piankhy, smiling.

'It is for you to doubt your own power, and for me to proclaim it as it is. Isn't that the first duty of a Queen of Egypt?'

45

'Amon sent me the sign of the bow.'

'And Nubia,' said Abilah swiftly, 'is the "land of the bow". By that sign, he is showing you that you must continue to reign.'

'The bow is also the symbol of war . . . But there is no war on the horizon.'

'Aren't you worried about the unrest being stirred up by the Northern princes?'

'They're too busy fighting among themselves. No Libyan prince is capable of imposing his will on all the others.'

*   *   *

For a very long time, Kapa had slept no more than two or three hours a night. Life had passed too quickly for his liking and, before returning to join the Goddess of the Beautiful West, who brings death with an enchanting smile, he wished to savour every moment.

He had never left the country of his birth, this burning-hot, rugged land whose attractions he knew better than anyone. Nubia gave herself only to those who loved her passionately, with an inexhaustible desire: that was why Piankhy made an excellent ruler. But the old man had acted according to his conscience and had no regrets. Stripped of his magic, even a giant might become easy prey for the forces of darkness.

If the gods disowned Piankhy, Nubia and southern Egypt would be plunged into a crisis whose outcome was uncertain. Only second-rate men dreamt of succeeding the pharaoh, and they would turn a difficult situation into a disaster.

At the heart of the night, in a lapis-lazuli sky, the

46

stars unleashed their splendour. They were doors which opened, letting out the light which was born every second at the ends of the universe. They taught mankind that in order to create you must look up, not down.

Suddenly, a star left its sisters and crossed the sky, as fast as a greyhound in full flight. As though irresistibly attracted by the earth, it rushed towards it, trailing fire.

No, Kapa wasn't seeing things! The star was plunging towards Nubia, towards the Napata, towards the royal palace, which vanished in a sudden blaze of light.

CHAPTER TEN

Insomniacs had seen a ball of flame plunging towards the terrace of the royal palace, and every one of them believed that the wrath of the heavens had destroyed the Black Pharaoh. Amon's answer had been terrifying.

Kapa rushed towards the scene of the drama as fast as his old legs would carry him. The entire population of the capital was already beginning to flock there, awakened by those who had witnessed the catastrophe.

Puarma, captain of archers, had ordered the king's personal guard to prevent anyone entering his apartments. Not even Cool-Head had been allowed in.

'Shouldn't we try to help His Majesty?' asked Kapa anxiously.

'I don't know,' the officer confessed. He was so

overwhelmed that he was incapable of making a decision.

'Well I'm going in,' declared Cool-Head, who was still puffy-eyed from sleep.

'I'm coming with you,' decided Kapa.

At a sign from Puarma, the archers let the dwarf and the old man pass. The two climbed up a staircase decorated with painted flowers and ventured into Piankhy's private apartments.

'Majesty, it is I, Cool-Head. Can you speak?'

No answer.

The bedchamber, the vast bathroom, the massage room, the office, the rooms where the pharaoh received distinguished guests, the library—all were empty.

'There's still the terrace,' said Kapa.

Cool-Head was almost in tears. Inside his apartments, Piankhy might have escaped the devastating effects of the star that had fallen from the sky. But out on the terrace . . .

'My old legs won't carry me any further,' groaned Kapa.

'Stay here and rest. I'll go on alone.'

His chest tight with fear, the dwarf climbed slowly up the flight of steps that led to the terrace. And there, in the moonlight, he saw them. Piankhy and his wife lay side by side, Abilah's head resting on her husband's chest. Lying there, they had died at the same moment, united in their love.

'What are you doing here, Cool-Head?'

The dwarf jumped half out of his skin, shaking from head to foot. It was the solemn voice of Amon, the voice of the heavens come to punish his audacity!

'Has something serious happened in my capital?'

demanded Piankhy, sitting up.

Cool-Head gaped, convinced he was looking at a ghost. 'Is that you, Majesty? Is it really you?'

'Have I changed so much?'

'B-but a star fell out of the sky . . . there was a ball of fire . . .'

'Do you see any traces of fire here?'

The queen awoke. 'I dreamt of heavenly fire. It surrounded us, protecting us like a halo. We were in the heart of a sun, shining in the darkness.'

'It's a miracle!' roared Cool-Head, rushing down the stairs. 'It's a miracle! Lord Amon has turned the royal couple into rays of light!'

*   *   *

The judgement of the Great Council, the advice of the priests and the opinion of the population were unanimous: Amon had indeed chosen to appear in the form of celestial fire—the same Amon who dwelt in the Pure Mountain and recognized Piankhy as his son and the rightful pharaoh.

As the sun rose over Gebel Barkal's crown-shaped peak, the friends and supporters of the king, the ritualists and the elders confirmed Piankhy as king, through their spokesman, Kapa.

'We are your servants,' declared the old man. 'Order, and we shall obey you, since it is the Creator's thoughts which guide your own.'

A broad smile lit up Otoku's face. The fat man was already thinking of the sumptuous banquet he had organized to celebrate the Black Pharaoh's second coronation. With its abundance of exotic dishes, it would take its place in the history of Nubian feasts.

'Nothing is more pressing than the need to honour our ancestors,' Piankhy decreed. 'Without them, we would not exist. They lie not behind us but ahead of us, for they know both life and death.'

Piankhy climbed into the royal ship, whose prow was decorated with the head of a ram, the sacred beast of Amon. He sat down on his throne, Queen Abilah took her place beside him, and he gave the signal to set sail for Kurru, downstream from Napata. The ship was followed by an impressive flotilla containing every single dignitary in the land.

Kurru was the burial place of the Nubian kings, including Piankhy's father. Modest burial mounds, each provided with a recessed alcove for offerings, skirted funerary wells and tombs similar to the Houses of Eternity of the Old Empire. These tombs had walls of smooth limestone, which shone in the sunshine, and chapels which were open on their eastern side, allowing the living to communicate with the dead by means of offerings.

Piankhy, whose name meant 'The Living One', saw that his own tomb was almost finished. He had chosen to build a pyramid, inside which a sloping passage led down to a burial chamber with a vaulted roof. Close by stood the final resting-place of his wife, who would continue to be his companion in the afterlife.

Piankhy's pyramid already contained two faithful friends: his two first horses, which had been mummified and placed, standing upright, in deep pits. They had first been blessed with the ceremonies of opening the mouth, eyes and ears, and their mortal hearts had been replaced with imperishable replicas.

Piankhy offered his ancestors flowers, perfumes,

fresh bread, wine, milk, beer, festival oil, fabrics and golden necklaces. 'Your names are engraved in stone,' he intoned, 'and they shall never be forgotten. I give life back to them, and so in turn shall my son's son. In truth, he who perpetuates the memory of his ancestors, and furnishes their tables with offerings, is a man worthy of the name.'

Abilah was radiant. She shared her husband's belief that every day the Egyptians of the Two Lands were forgetting a little more of their traditions, and turning further and further from the law of Ma'at. Soon, even the holy city of Thebes would start to neglect its sacred duties, and allow itself to be bewitched by mirages of profit and personal ambition. But here at Napata, in this wild, far-off land, the Black Pharaoh kept the true rites alive, reading the ancient texts, sustaining the wisdom of the age of the pyramids and the work of Tuthmosis III, Seti I and Ramses II.

One of the people taking part in the ceremony was filled with great pride. Cool-Head, the stern scribe, extolled the earliest style of hieroglyphic writing, and demanded the use of classical language, free from all the barbarisms and foreign words that were invading the degraded dialects of the Northern tribes. Witnessing the building of the pyramid, a ray of light embodied in stone, reminded him of the golden age of the pharaohs.

Piankhy planted a tamarisk tree in the garden of his father's funerary shrine. At that moment of communion with the world of the Invisible, a vision haunted him: the bow to which Amon had directed his gaze. What dangers and threats did it presage?

CHAPTER ELEVEN

Tefnakht had deployed his entire army against Henen-nesut, the 'City of the Royal Child', a very ancient settlement which was loyal to the Black Pharaoh. The new commander-in-chief of the Northern armies had been surprised by the chiefs' obedience; they had carried out his plan without protest.

The Libyans had attacked in four places simultaneously, causing surprise and panic among the defenders. The Egyptian commander, Prince Peftau, a sixty-year-old scribe, wealthy landowner and son of an eminent local family, had not known how to react in the face of the onslaught. Although well trained, his soldiers were unused to fighting on such a large scale.

Within half an hour, the Northern forces had captured a postern-gate, forced open a fortified gate and poured into the city. Up above on the ramparts, Peftau's bowmen tried to slow down the torrent of destruction, but the Libyan slingshots soon wiped them out.

A few brave civilians threw themselves into the battle, but they were cut to pieces by the Northern soldiers, who were driven into a frenzy of excitement by their impending triumph.

Afraid that carrying on the struggle would lead to the massacre of his people, Peftau came out of the palace, surrounded by his personal bodyguard, and told his men to throw down their swords and shields.

Tefnakht advanced towards the defeated prince.

'Do you agree to surrender unconditionally?'

'We are your prisoners, but spare the inhabitants of the city.'

'Agreed, if all weapons, without exception, are brought to the city square.'

'You have my word.'

Little by little, the madness died down. Henen-nesut obeyed its prince. Women and children huddled together, terrified by their conquerors' cruel expressions. One soldier, who tried to escape, was captured by four infantrymen, who trampled him underfoot before plunging a spear into his back. It was a scene of unprecedented brutality, and it extinguished all lingering thoughts of resistance among the defenders of Henen-nesut. In every part of the city, weapons were laid down.

'Are you not the prince of Sais?' asked Peftau, stunned.

'Today I am the leader of the Northern alliance,' replied Tefnakht. 'And tomorrow I shall reunify the Two Lands.'

'You must know that the only rightful pharaoh is Piankhy, and that this town belongs to him.'

'It's your choice, Peftau. Either you become my vassal, or you die.'

The Prince of Henen-nesut understood that Tefnakht was not joking. The look in his eyes was the look of a pitiless conqueror. Peftau bowed his head and said, 'I recognize you as my sovereign.'

'Do you renounce all allegiance to Piankhy?'

'I do. But what are your plans?'

'Henen-nesut was only a staging-post.'

'A staging-post? Surely you aren't thinking of continuing further south?'

Tefnakht looked around. 'A third of your

53

soldiers have been killed or wounded, which means that two-thirds of your experienced fighters are still alive. They will join with my troops to attack and capture another town controlled by Piankhy.'

'Henen-nesut is a magnificent conquest,' said Peftau, 'and your new-found fame will be enough to terrify the Nubians. Why ask for more?'

'You are a second-rate man, Peftau; you don't see beyond the ramparts of your city. Confine yourself to obeying me unquestioningly, and you will retain your privileges.'

Tefnakht left the defeated prince and summoned the Libyan chiefs to the audience chamber of the palace. Some of them were already drunk, others covered in the blood of their victims, and all were shouting the name of their general. For he had led them to a swift, brilliant victory, when most of them had feared a ruthless show of resistance from the people and soldiers of Henen-nesut. Tefnakht had just demonstrated his ability as a warlord and had opened up the way to an undreamt-of future. He had awakened their desire to fight and wipe out the Egyptians, the hereditary enemies who had humiliated the Libyans for centuries.

Tefnakht had intended to discuss the lessons learnt from this first military operation, but the state of his subordinates persuaded him to abandon the idea. Sickened by so much mediocrity, he abandoned them to their drunkenness.

As he was leaving the palace he bumped into Akanosh, who was wearing a long red robe of pleated fabric.

'Why didn't you take part in the attack?' demanded Tefnakht.

'I am the spokesman for the tribes, not a footsoldier. My job is not to fight my way through enemy lines.'

'You disapprove of my action?'

'You have won a brilliant victory, Tefnakht, and there can be no more challenges to your authority. I shall therefore pass on your orders exactly as you give them to me.'

'Very well, Akanosh, here is one: have the fortifications of Henen-nesut reinforced and organize guard patrols.'

Tefnakht went off to took for Nartreb and Yegeb. He found the latter with a mob of looters sacking the house which had belonged to the city's captain of archers, who had been killed in the attack. Despite his painful ankles and his difficulty in moving about, the counsellor was the most energetic of all, and was busy filling a large sack with golden goblets.

He gave a start when he saw Tefnakht. 'My lord! I, er, I am supervising these people, have no fear! They will take only their due.'

'I have every faith in you,' said Tefnakht drily. 'Where is Nartreb?'

'Upstairs,' replied Yegeb with an odd smile. 'But I think he's rather busy at the moment.'

Tefnakht set off up the stairs. From above he could hear the screams of a woman who was being beaten and raped by Nartreb.

'That's enough, Nartreb!'

The brute continued. 'She's only the daughter of Peftau's captain of archers, and I'm damn sure she's never known a man like me!'

Tefnakht kicked him in the side.

'That hurt, my lord!' protested Nartreb.

'Go and find Yegeb. And check up on Peftau, the Prince of Henen-nesut.'

Nartreb fastened his loin-cloth, paying no heed to the young woman, who was glaring at him with hatred in her eyes.

'Do you doubt his loyalty, my lord?'

'I want to know everything about him—and quickly.'

Before going downstairs, the rapist turned back to his victim and said, 'We shall meet again, my little one.'

The Egyptian girl hid her naked breasts and belly with the tattered remnants of her dress.

'What is your name?' asked Tefnakht.

'Daybreak. Are you the Libyan general?'

'I am the new master of this town.'

'You killed my father. And I am going to kill you.'

CHAPTER TWELVE

The Black Pharaoh's palace stood near the Temple of Amon, and was built on a plinth four cubits high and surrounded by an outer wall. The huge double gates which led into it had been opened to admit the great and good of Napata, who had all been invited to a banquet in honour of Piankhy. As the master of ceremonies was none other than the great food-lover Otoku, everyone expected the evening to be something out of the ordinary.

For Puarma, the captain of archers, the most difficult thing had been choosing a companion for the evening from the dozen or so fine-looking girls who had begged him to take them. All he could do to extricate himself from this awkward situation was to choose a girl at random and placate the rest with long, involved explanations and gifts which plunged him deeper in debt.

As luck would have it, it was the least talkative of the girls who hung on his arm, her eyes wide with wonder at the sights that greeted them. Torches had been planted in the earth all around the gardens, their flames illuminating the palm trees, tamarisks and sycamores and the ornamental lakes where blue and white lotus blossoms opened their petals, shimmering in the dancing light. Servants offered perfumed towels and goblets of cooled white wine to the guests as they marvelled at the palace's columns, which were cleverly designed to resemble papyrus stalks.

Puarma and his companion climbed the staircase of honour, its steps carved from pink granite and its sides decorated with images of prostrate, defeated enemies. Hordes of courtiers had already packed into the huge, pillared audience chamber. The design of the room was enchanting: yellow, green, blue and violet enamelled earthenware tiles, cornices shaped from gilded stucco, carved panels depicting wild bulls, panthers and elephants.

At the far end of the chamber stood a canopy, flanked by two lions carved from limestone. Beneath the canopy were two gilded wooden thrones, on which Piankhy and Abilah sat during official audiences. Puarma's companion was so dazed by all the marvels around her that he was careful not to tell her that beneath the centre point of the palace a huge block of native gold had been buried, as a symbol of light hidden within the

57

darkness.

Somebody bumped into Puarma.

'Who the . . .? Oh it's you, Cool-Head. Why aren't you all dressed up for the party?'

'I have too much on my mind to think about all that,' retorted the scribe, clearly at the end of his tether.

'Why? What's happening?'

'It's the drainage system again. In spite of the strict instructions I gave them, the workmen have done everything their own sweet way. And yet it's all so simple. Line the stone basins with copper strips, hollow out a sufficiently large opening and block it with a metal stopper. Then work out the right diameter for the pipes, which you make from sheets of beaten copper rolled into cylinders. I don't know why I bothered showing them the plans and giving them all the right measurements. The system which drains off waste water from the left wing of the palace is blocked up again—which means no party for me. Instead, I have to go and wake up a mob of useless idiots!'

As the dwarf went off, still grumbling, the musicians entered the great hall. Two girl harpists plucked a delightful tune from their instruments, and were soon accompanied by a flautist, two oboe-players and a clarinettist.

At the end of the concert, a butler asked the guests to proceed to the banqueting room. Puarma's companion almost fainted when she saw the magnificent low ebony tables, the floor strewn with cornflowers and mandragora, the oil-lamps placed on top of high columns of gilded wood, but most of all when she set eyes on the dinner service: serving-dishes, goblets, plates, bowls, basins for

58

washing the hands—everything was made of gold!

Servants wafted fans, some made from reeds shaped into lotus flowers, others made from ostrich feathers, spreading an agreeable coolness around the guests, who were seated comfortably in the vast, subtly perfumed room.

Beautiful ladies dazzled the eye with their elegant six-stringed necklaces, made from gold and semi-precious stones. Puarma's girlfriend had never seen such wild excesses of cornelian, jasper, turquoise and lapis-lazuli. And what could you say about the golden earrings, shaped by goldsmiths into so many inventive shapes?

'Am I wearing enough jewellery?' she asked anxiously.

'You look perfect,' replied Puarma hastily. He could not afford to heap jewels on a girl who was his companion for only one evening.

When Piankhy and Abilah appeared, they provoked gasps of admiration. With their perfect blend of power and beauty, the royal couple easily outshone all those who had hoped to rival them. The contrast between the glittering gold collars and bracelets, Piankhy's black skin and Abilah's coppery complexion, created an almost supernatural harmony. The jewels the king and queen had chosen were so perfect that they could have been offered to the gods. Everyone watching was struck, as though for the first time, by the colossal strength radiating from Piankhy and by his wife's innate nobility. She, too, must be immensely strong, to maintain her station at the side of such an impressive ruler.

Piankhy held up an enormous pearl. All eyes turned to focus on it.

'Look at this masterpiece of nature,' he said. 'It is the visible symbol of the sphere of creation, the symbol of the celestial mother's transparent belly, within which a new sun is born each morning. Worship this light which is given to you in such abundance, worship this generous life which sometimes takes on the appearance of death, the better to wake us to eternity.'

The king picked up a golden goblet, rounded in form and engraved with a lotus with pointed petals. This design was to illustrate the process of resurrection, the rebirth of the soul inscribed in the lotus rising up from the primordial ocean. And the wine within the goblet represented an act of homage to Hathor, the goddess of the stars and of creative love, she who made the constellations dance with joy when divine intoxication filled the human heart.

Piankhy drank a mouthful of wine. The queen followed suit. The celebrations could begin.

*   *   *

Having to stand guard on such a night was rather a disappointment. But the officer and his men, who had been ordered to ensure the safety of the capital, had not been forgotten by the pharaoh: they were to receive double pay and rations and, the next day, a pitcher of the finest red wine.

Although the soldiers regularly complained about not getting promotion and about working long hours, their life in Napata was not too demanding. The city was rich and well governed, its inhabitants were happy and peace-loving, there were never any internal struggles, and there was no sign of war on the horizon. In earlier times, when Nubians had joined Pharaoh's army to fight Libyans and Syrians on dangerous military expeditions, a soldier had needed to carry several protective amulets, and to make sure he was ready to fight at a moment's notice.

If it had been up to him, the officer would have allowed himself to drift off into a nice, restorative sleep, under the protection of the sky's starry vault, where the souls of those pharaohs judged to have spoken with a 'just voice' shone for all eternity. But he would be sure to be noticed by one of the sentries, who would report him to a superior officer.

The officer moistened his lips and forehead with tepid water and continued his watch, eyes glued to the northern road which ended at the city's first fortified guard-post. All travellers wishing to enter the city underwent stringent checks there.

Thanks to a cousin who was a cook in the palace kitchens, tomorrow the officer would enjoy some of the dishes which had not been entirely polished off by Piankhy's guests. It was rumoured that among the delicacies was a sauce called 'Ramses' Delight', the recipe for which had been passed down through the centuries.

Something gleamed in the desert.

At first, the officer thought it was a star shimmering, but he quickly realized the truth: one of the watchmen was signalling the alarm. The signal was repeated several times, stressing that danger was near.

CHAPTER THIRTEEN

The officer hesitated. Should he wake the king, or wait until morning? Rudely awakening Piankhy from his slumbers might anger him, but the consequences of failing to warn him immediately might be even worse. Unable to make up his mind, the officer decided to consult Cool-Head.

The scribe, who had only just got off to sleep after overseeing repairs to the drainage system, let out a long series of grunts and groans before finally sitting up in bed.

'What do you want?'

'There's been a serious incident,' said the officer. 'Perhaps we ought to inform His Majesty.

'Come, come. Surely no one's trying to invade Napata!'

'Well . . .'

By this time, Cool-Head was wide awake. 'Is the situation under control?'

'Yes. The man has been arrested.'

The dwarf frowned. 'The man . . . Are you telling me that Napata has been attacked by one man?'

'Anyone who travels by night is necessarily suspect. But our security has proved very effective, and I hope that my own role in the matter—'

'I will mention it to the king.'

*   *   *

Piankhy was not asleep. For hours he had endured the flattery of courtiers who tried to outdo each other in fulsome expressions of praise. Everyone

62

had remarked upon the excellent quality of the food and wine, and, in recognition of his organizing genius, Otoku had been given his own weight in jars of strong beer.

The Black Pharaoh had not enjoyed the pageantry of the evening for one moment. An obsessive worry gnawed away at him, preventing him from savouring the pleasures of a banquet which the court would be talking about for months. Abilah had noticed her husband's distress, but had decided not to intrude on his thoughts.

Piankhy stood on the palace terrace, gazing up at the sky. The stars alone possessed the ultimate wisdom, for they were the source of true power, the power from which life originated.

A light footstep sounded on the terrace.

'You again, Cool-Head?'

'Forgive me for disturbing you, Majesty, but since you are awake. . .'

'At this time of night you're usually fast asleep.'

'A man attempted to enter the city, but the archers arrested him. The officer responsible would like to see his worth recognized and receive promotion.'

'He shall be given responsibility for night security next month. After that, we shall see. And did this intruder give his name?' asked Piankhy.

'According to the officer, he says nothing that makes any sense. He claims to be a servant of Amon and to have a confidential message for the rightful pharaoh.'

'Have you questioned him?'

'No, Majesty. I thought you would wish to meet this strange traveller as soon as possible.'

'Bring him to the audience chamber.'

It was the first day of the first month of the season of the Nile flood, in the twenty-first year of Piankhy's reign; and the dawn had created a palette of exceptionally intense colours. The light sprang forth from the Eastern mountain, in the form of the sun's disc, the living image of the Creator whose representative on Earth was Pharaoh.

The audience chamber at the palace of Napata was bathed in the gentle rays of the rising sun when the traveller appeared before Piankhy, his wrists held fast in wooden manacles and a soldier on either side.

'Release him and leave us alone,' ordered the king.

For a long moment, the sight of the giant with the black, shining skin left the visitor speechless. Then he said nervously, 'Majesty . . .'

'Who are you?'

'A priest of Amon.'

'What is your rank in the priesthood?'

'I am a ritualist, in charge of purifying the sacred vessels for the evening rites.'

'Which temple do you come from?'

'From Karnak,' said the priest, 'from the temple of Amon-Ra, king of the gods.'

'And how did you get here?'

'I had a map, and I changed boats several times, before finishing my journey on foot.'

'Walking at night is dangerous. You could have been bitten by a snake.'

'I had to take that risk, in order to avoid the bite of a reptile who is more dangerous than all the

64

cobras in Nubia. This reptile is coiling himself round all Egypt, giving her people no room to breathe. Soon he will deprive them of the breath of life.'

'Don't talk in riddles,' said Piankhy.

'Does the name Akanosh mean anything to you?'

'He is a Libyan prince, from the Delta.'

'At great risk to his life, Akanosh sent a message to Karnak. I was chosen to deliver it to you.'

'Give me the papyrus at once.'

'The message is a spoken one, Majesty.'

'Then speak.'

'The chiefs of all the Libyan tribes have formed an alliance, and have named Tefnakht, Prince of Sais, their commander-in-chief. First, he conquered the west of the Delta, then the Delta in its entirety. Thanks to a large army, his has taken control of Memphis and his forces are now heading south. The local princes, mayors and governors are like dogs at his heels—no one questions his orders any more. Every town as far as Henen-nesut has opened its gates to him, and he has become master of them all.'

'But Prince Peftau, my faithful subject, resisted him and prevented him from progressing any further. That braggart Tefnakht has turned tail, and his alliance has fallen apart.'

'I am sorry to disappoint you, Majesty,' said the priest. 'Tefnakht launched an attack on the city of Henen-nesut, and Peftau could not hold out against him.'

'Was Peftau killed?' asked Piankhy.

'No, he surrendered.'

'And what happened to the people of the city?'

65

'They were spared. But Peftau's soldiers are now under Tefnakht's command.'

'And they haven't tried to rise against him?'

'If they don't obey him, they'll be massacred. From now on, they are your enemies.'

'So,' said Piankhy thoughtfully, 'Tefnakht now governs Henen-nesut.'

'Yes, Majesty, and you must understand that he now leads a true army, which speeds from one victory to the next.'

'Have you any information about the strategy he intends to pursue?'

'He is ready to fight each day, and push further towards the South.'

'As far as Thebes?'

'Certainly, Majesty.'

The Black Pharaoh remained silent for a few seconds, as though struck dumb by the priest's revelations. Then he burst out laughing.

CHAPTER FOURTEEN

The priest was completely taken aback by Piankhy's reaction. 'Majesty,' he said, 'don't you believe me?'

'You are a man of prayer and meditation. You understand nothing of war.'

'But Akanosh . . .'

'How can he have an objective view of the situation? Akanosh is a Libyan warlord, under the thumb of that braggart Tefnakht. These events don't seem at all serious to me.'

'But Majesty, the whole of Middle Egypt will soon be under Tefnakht's control!'

'Khmun, city of the god Thoth, will remain loyal to me. Tefnakht will not dare to attack it.'

The priest was dismayed. 'You will not react in any way?'

'Don't be afraid. I shall convene my council of war. As for you, you will be well housed and fed. The Temple of Amon is open to you: you may carry out your sacred duties there.'

'I have a request to make, Majesty.'

'I am listening.'

'Will you grant me permission to live here, in Napata? I have heard that the ancient traditions are still followed here.'

'If that is your wish, it shall be granted.'

*   *   *

The Black Pharaoh's council of war consisted of Abilah, Cool-Head, Puarma and Otoku. Piankhy trusted them completely, for he knew that they would neither lie to him nor try to deceive him. All that ministers and courtiers were good for was talking endlessly, as though their only concern was to safeguard their own interests. Consequently it was preferable to take key decisions in private, and then announce them to the court later.

Piankhy had summoned his confidants to the shadiest part of the palace garden. At its centre was a pool, where the king often swam. The late-July heat might be exhausting, even for Nubians, but Piankhy rejoiced in it. For it liberated the strength of the Earth, putting every organism to a stern test. Overcoming it was part of man's earthly task.

Otoku did not share this view. He was sitting with his feet in a bowl of cool water and had a damp towel, perfumed with myrrh, laid across his brow. As for Cool-Head, he fought off the dog-day heat by drinking pint after pint of sweet beer. The heat did not trouble Queen Abilah, who sat in the shade of a parasol, clad in a simple gauzy robe which scarcely veiled her admirable body. Puarma was naked, in no hurry to don his training armour.

'Relieve me of one doubt, Majesty, said Otoku, rubbing his skin with a sweet-smelling ointment made from frankincense and galingale. 'This meeting is purely social, isn't it?'

'Don't deceive yourself. As you have already guessed, this is actually a council of war.'

The fat man mopped his brow. 'Has one of the tribes rebelled against you?'

'It seems more serious than that. Apparently Tefnakht, a Libyan prince, has succeeded in persuading his allies to form a unified army.'

'That's ridiculous!' exclaimed Puarma. 'A Libyan's worst enemy is another Libyan—they'll never agree on a single leader.'

'But Tefnakht has managed to make them listen to reason, and the Northern provinces have appointed him commander-in-chief. From now on, they will recognize his sole authority.'

'It had to happen,' said Cool-Head gloomily. 'The economic situation in the North is shocking. Thousands of people are out of work, food prices are forever going up, no one worships the gods any more, and the only unopposed rulers are injustice and corruption. There was only one possible outcome: the arrival of a tyrant clever enough to rely on a well-equipped army.'

'Well-equipped? That's impossible!' protested Puarma. 'These days the North is too impoverished to train battle-ready troops.'

'Tefnakht has taken control of Memphis,' Piankhy revealed. 'And he has captured Henen-nesut.'

The Black Pharaoh's words hit his listeners like a thunderbolt.

'Where did you get this information from, Majesty?' asked Otoku.

'From a priest of Amon, who travelled for many days to warn us.'

'But you didn't take him seriously,' put in Abilah.

'That's true,' agreed Piankhy. 'To my mind, this man Tefnakht wanted to score a brilliant victory to consolidate his power over the Northern chieftains. Seizing Henen-nesut is a real coup, but he won't dare go any further—he hasn't got the resources. A bandit chief doesn't turn into a brilliant general overnight.'

The captain of archers nodded his agreement.

'Nevertheless, we must prepare to strike back,' urged Otoku. 'Allowing this troublemaker to act with impunity will only encourage him.'

'I take a more pessimistic view,' confessed Cool-Head.

The dwarf's interjection sent cold shivers round the little group. Everyone respected his remarkable intelligence and took his opinions seriously.

'What is it that you fear?' inquired Otoku worriedly.

'A radical change of attitude among the Northern allies. Up to now, their rivalries have made them powerless—we Nubians lived through a similar state of lawlessness, so we know what it means. But the moment they accepted the sovereignty and strategy of a single leader, it was no longer their shortcomings that were highlighted, but their good qualities. It is in testing times that a leader of men reveals himself. For all its importance, Memphis has long lacked a leader capable of thinking for himself, and it had no hope of resisting any conqueror, even a second-rate one. With hindsight, Henen-nesut was an obstacle to overcome, a stronghold with an experienced garrison commanded by Peftau, a nobleman loyal to Piankhy. Capturing the city took only a little effort, and Tefnakht can congratulate himself on a notable success which reinforces his prestige.'

'Are you trying to worry us or make us angry?' demanded Piankhy.

'Neither, Majesty. I am simply telling you what I think.'

'I simply cannot believe that this man Tefnakht dares to challenge us!' growled Puarma. 'This victory—if it really has happened—won't lead to anything. How dare a mere chieftain provoke the anger of Piankhy, the pharaoh?'

'When I heard about his exploits I burst out laughing,' admitted the king, 'but Cool-Head's conclusions make me think that perhaps I was wrong.'

'An adventurer who knows how to take advantage of the common people's wretchedness is capable of leading them into all kinds of madness,' declared the queen. 'If Tefnakht is drunk with success, he will lose all self-restraint and won't care one jot for the corpses he leaves strewn in his wake. Like Cool-Head, I think this attempt to invade the South should not be passed off lightly.'

'But it's impossible to mount an attack on

Khmun,' objected Puarma. 'Nemrod, its prince, has sworn allegiance to Piankhy, and he has enough troops to fight off any attack.'

'That's what we thought about Henen-nesut,' the dwarf reminded him. 'If Tefnakht becomes lord of all Middle Egypt, the road to Thebes will lie open before him. And after that, who knows?'

'That's hardly likely,' retorted Otoku. 'Our regiments based in Thebes will be more than enough to deter him.'

'Let's hope so,' said Cool-Head.

Head bowed, Puarma asked Piankhy, 'What is your decision, Majesty?'

'I need time to think.'

CHAPTER FIFTEEN

Prince Akanosh's wife was so upset that she had not even put on her make-up. 'Come,' she told her husband. 'You must come *now*.'

'But I haven't finished my breakfast,' objected the prince. 'I haven't shaved, I—'

'Come!'

Akanosh stuck a warrior's feather plume into his plaited hair and hurriedly tied the knot of his long cloak on his left shoulder. Whatever the emergency, he could not step out into the streets of Henen-nesut without the symbols of his power.

'Where are you taking me?' he asked.

'To the hospital, the one where they're tending the civilians who were wounded in the attack.'

'It's not my place to go visiting hospitals—and neither is it yours.'

71

'Are you a member of Tefnakht's alliance?' demanded his wife. 'Yes or no?'

'Yes, but—'

'Then go into that hospital.'

The rough brick building was guarded by two soldiers, who blocked the doorway with their spears and forbade Akanosh and his wife to enter.

'I am Prince Akanosh. Let us pass.'

'Yegeb has not authorized any visits,' said one of the soldiers.

'How dare you oppose me, soldier? Your Yegeb is a mere insect. If you don't let us through, I'll have you both transferred to the Delta marshlands!'

The guards lowered their spears.

The moment Akanosh set foot inside the building, a terrible stench assaulted his nostrils. Blood, gangrene, death . . . Dozens of men and women were laid out in a row on the floor. Those closest to the door were moaning piteously. Those at the far end of the row were all dead.

Two soldiers seized a corpse by its feet and began dragging it out.

'Where are you taking that body?' snapped Akanosh.

'Yegeb ordered us to dig a ditch. We're going to throw it in there—that'll make one more space. When we've taken out all the dead bodies, we'll bring in more wounded. And we'll keep doing that until there aren't any left.'

'What treatment are these poor people receiving?'

'None. The best they can hope for is to die quickly.'

Prince Peftau had given Tefnakht the first floor of his palace. There the conqueror was meeting his allies one by one, to convince them of the justness of his strategy and the effort which must be put into the offensive.

Just outside the audience chamber was Yegeb's office, where all visitors were screened.

'I demand to see Tefnakht immediately,' announced Akanosh.

Yegeb consulted an old scrap of papyrus, on which he had written the date and a list of names.

'You have not been summoned. Request an audience and wait for the general's reply.'

Akanosh's anger erupted. He seized Yegeb by the throat and—although smaller than the counsellor—lifted him right off the ground. 'Don't stand in my way, you vermin! You are a criminal and a butcher. It is my duty to tell your master exactly what you have been up to, and I shall personally mete out whatever punishment he decrees.'

Akanosh let go of Yegeb, who fought to get his breath back as the prince marched into Tefnakht's audience chamber.

On a scribe's tablet, the general was composing the official account of his first great victory over the Black Pharaoh. It would be copied out many times, distributed to senior officers, and read out to their soldiers. The news would spread throughout Middle Egypt, then as far as Thebes. It would sow the seeds of terror among Piankhy's supporters and encourage them to surrender.

Tefnakht's dark eyes fastened on the intruder. 'I

73

don't recall summoning you.'

'I must tell you what is going on in this town.'

'Everything is calm, our army is in control of the situation, and Prince Peftau has become my vassal. What is there to complain about?'

'Are you aware that the hospital reserved for civilians is a charnel-house, and that the patients receive no medical treatment whatsoever? The embalmers simply wait until they die and then throw the corpses into a mass grave, without any funeral rites. And these horrors are being committed on the orders of your devoted slave Yegeb. I demand that those unfortunate people receive better treatment, and that the torturer be punished.'

Tefnakht threw the tablet against the wall. 'You are in no position to demand anything, Akanosh. You seem to have forgotten that you owe me total obedience.'

'But the civilians—'

'It is hardly fitting for a Libyan prince to be as soft-hearted as a grieving widow,' said Tefnakht sarcastically. 'The North is impoverished, you know that, and our army is short of medicines and ointments. Everything we have found in Henen-nesut must be reserved for our troops' use. Those are my orders, and anyone who flouts them will be considered a traitor.'

'So we're just going to let the wounded die, are we?'

'We are at war, Akanosh, and there are certain choices we have to make. Kind thoughts won't defeat Piankhy's warriors.'

'You gave me your word that the population of this town would be spared!'

74

'Do you disagree with my methods?' asked Tefnakht menacingly.

Akanosh would have liked to go on protesting, but the words died in his throat.

'Keep a clear head, my friend, and forget these unimportant details. Do what the rest of us do, concentrate your mind on a single goal: reconquering Egypt. Our victory will bring happiness to the people, you can be certain of that.'

'What about Yegeb?'

'He is devoted to me and he never questions my orders. Do as he does, Akanosh, and you will live to enjoy a happy old age.'

Tefnakht left the room, passing Yegeb without a glance.

*   *   *

'When are the doctors going to treat the sick and injured?' asked Akanosh's wife.

The prince flopped down on to a pile of cushions. 'They aren't.'

'But you . . . Didn't you speak to Tefnakht?'

'Oh yes, I spoke to him.'

'And he refused?'

'You must understand, my darling, that this is war. You, I, Tefnakht—none of us can do anything about that.'

'Tefnakht is the commander of our army, and if he says he is sparing the common people he's a liar?'

'You're right but . . .'

The lovely Nubian looked at her husband sadly. 'You're afraid to stand up to him, aren't you, Akanosh?'

'I feel too old and weak to resist Tefnakht. If I oppose him, he'll just have me killed, and the storm will carry you away with it too. I'm like all the other chiefs, no better than a puppet in his hands—but I'm the only one who realizes it. Tefnakht is prepared to do absolutely anything in order to conquer Egypt, and he's a real warrior. Unless Piankhy reacts very quickly Tefnakht will win, and he'll impose a dictatorship from which the country will never recover.'

CHAPTER SIXTEEN

Barefoot and with his head shaven, the priest from Karnak walked slowly down the staircase which led to the sacred lake, close to the great temple. His fine white linen robe flared about him as he stooped to fill a gold vase with holy water.

This water came from the *Nun*, the ocean of primordial energy where creation originated and which still surrounded it. The Earth was merely an island which had emerged since the 'first time', that moment when divine thought had taken form and manifested itself; and when Pharaoh no longer performed the rites necessary to resurrect that first time, the Earth's island would sink beneath the primeval tides. As it was written, the destiny of mankind would be fulfilled: humanity was born in God's tears and in the end it would disappear beneath the weight of its own depravity.

The role of the gods' servants was to put off the inevitable day by providing them with a dwelling-place and revering their presence so that it might

76

illuminate the hearts of those who tried to walk in the ways of Ma'at, choosing truth above lies, justice above injustice.

The priest found Napata astonishing. He was rediscovering a zeal which he had thought lost for ever, and a strictness in celebrating the sacred rites which was no longer in fashion in some of the shrines at Karnak. Here, close to the Fourth Cataract, Amon was honoured as he should be.

Carrying the precious vase of pure water, the priest continued towards the Hall of Offerings.

Suddenly a gigantic man blocked his way. 'Are you enjoying your stay among us?'

'Majesty!' said the priest. 'My days here are magical.'

'You surprise me. Don't you miss Karnak?'

'If only I could explain to you how much I admire—'

'Finish your devotions, then come and join me in the temple library.'

*   *   *

Pyramid texts, Books of the Dead, rituals for opening the mouth, ceremonial rites for the New Year, lists of auspicious and ill-omened days—all the writings that had been composed and passed down since the age of the pyramids. The priest was thunderstruck by the riches contained in Napata's library. The Black Pharaoh had every element of sacred science at his disposal.

'When I realized that the North was distancing itself more and more from our traditions,' explained Piankhy, 'I decided to form a collection here, bringing together the writings that enabled our civilization to flower.'

The priest went from one shelf to another, his hands wonderingly caressing the carefully arranged boxes of papyruses.

'Tell me,' said the king, 'is Amon no longer fittingly honoured in Karnak?'

'The permanent priests doze a little, the temporary ones sometimes have too frivolous a view of their duties. And the Divine Wife of Amon, whom you appointed to oversee the temples at Thebes and ensure that they are properly run, is worn out and ill. Factions have sprung up, and some priests are more interested in increasing their own wealth than in celebrating the sacred rites.'

'Is that a true picture of the situation?'

The priest felt as though the Black Pharaoh's eyes were boring into his soul. There was only one way to convince him, and that was by swearing a solemn oath.

'Upon Pharaoh's life,' he said earnestly, 'I swear that I am speaking the truth. If I lie, may my soul be destroyed and may the gates of eternal life be closed against me.'

Thebes, the sacred city. Thebes, the city of Amon. Thebes, with its hundred gates, its magnificent temples and shrines and, above all, the great precinct of Karnak. Thebes, where the secret of creation had been revealed . . . A profound sadness gripped the Black Pharaoh's heart. He had come here to the temple in Napata to meditate and to ask Amon to guide his actions; and now he had discovered that the city on which he had modelled his capital was falling into decay.

*   *   *

Cool-Head glared at his twenty pupils. 'Who composed this tablet?' he asked furiously.

The trainee scribes were seated before him in the correct manner, one leg bent, the other raised. A brush tucked behind the ear, they wore short kilts and sat with their heads bowed, terrified by their master's anger.

Once a week, the dwarf taught an advanced class to those who, tomorrow, would occupy key posts in the government. Among the fortunate few to benefit from these teachings were four young women.

'I repeat: who drafted this text?' Cool-Head brandished the tablet.

The students stared down at their knees.

'Well, there are no informers among you. So much the better. If one of you had denounced a friend, he or she would have been immediately expelled from the course. And I don't need any help to identify this script.'

The dwarf walked down the central aisle and stopped by one of the boys, who closed his eyes. He snatched up the boy's brush and snapped it in two. 'Stand up, you young rogue!'

The pupil was the son of a minister who owned several houses and two palm groves in the capital, but that carried no weight with Cool-Head.

'I admitted you to this school because you seemed to have the necessary talent to pursue a career as a scribe, but I can see now that I was sorely mistaken.'

'But, Master, I was very careful to—'

'Be quiet, you conceited little idiot! Oh yes, your hieroglyphs are perfectly drawn, there are no

79

grammatical errors, and every term has been rigorously chosen. But you drew up a land-tax without thinking for a moment of visiting the farm concerned or meeting the owner to ask if he was experiencing any family or working difficulties. If you go on like that, my boy, you'll become the worst type of administrator: an inhuman machine, concerned with nothing but the application of rules, and with no contact with the people whose lives you regulate. One more mistake like this, and I shall certainly expel you from my class. The day scribes spend all their time in their offices and shirk their responsibilities, this country will be ungovernable!'

Suddenly the atmosphere changed. No one had seen Piankhy enter the classroom, but his mere presence had made itself felt. Cool-Head looked up and saw the king standing there, arms folded, and his anger dissipated.

'That is all for today,' he said. 'For next time, prepare the type of letter to be sent to a mayor. Don't waste papyrus. Use limestone fragments and old ink.'

The pupils filed out in silence.

'Are you satisfied with your pupils, Cool-Head?'

'They won't make worse ministers than the ones you already have in your government.'

The scribe washed his brushes and scraped his tablet to produce a fresh surface, smooth enough to write on. Cool-Head was fanatical about waste. He had been entrusted with state property, and he must take the greatest care of it.

'Have you had any recent news from Thebes?' asked Piankhy.

'Some reports drafted by the administrative

scribe.'

'What did they say?'

'Nothing new, Majesty. Thebes is a peaceful town, which lives according to the rhythm of the rites.'

'No incidents?'

'Not according to these reports, no.'

'And is this scribe trustworthy?'

Cool-Head rubbed his chin. 'There is something that bothers me—there's constant repetition of the same banalities, the same words and phrases. In fact, I'd decided to talk to you about it if the next report is no more than a copy of the previous ones.'

'Someone's trying to reassure us and lull us into a false sense of security, aren't they?'

'It's possible, Majesty.'

CHAPTER SEVENTEEN

Nartreb had remembered one basic lesson from his time keeping the accounts on a farm in the Delta: someone who's clever with figures can make them say whatever he wants. Certainly the clumsily made-up accounts of a beginner or a money-maker in too much of a hurry to get rich would deceive few people, but Nartreb didn't make that kind of mistake.

A swift tour had shown him that Henen-nesut was rich and, in particular, housed the families of several landowners who had accumulated nice little fortunes. As the city was now coming under the rule of Tefnakht, the laws laid down by Piankhy must be modified. So Nartreb, who was in charge

81

of carrying out this delicate mission, had issued a lunch invitation to the town's treasurer, a seventy-year-old nobleman, a widower with a well-established reputation for scrupulous honesty.

'Grilled lamb,' said Nartreb, 'puréed figs, haricot beans in cream sauce and red wine from Imau: how does the menu suit you, dear colleague?'

'Colleague?' The Egyptian, who had taken an instant dislike to the moon-faced counsellor, was astonished.

'Tefnakht has put me in charge of financing his campaign. I and my friend Yegeb, a top specialist in accounting procedures, shall relieve him of all material concerns so that he can concentrate on reconquering Egypt.'

'What are your plans for my town?

'I should like to know the taxation system laid down by Piankhy—may his name be cursed.'

'It is in accordance with tradition. For example, farmers pay half their harvest to the city; one part of it is consumed during the year, and the rest is stored in barns in case the Nile flood should fail. In exchange, the government provides them with everything they need to irrigate and cultivate their land. Moreover, if a farmer exceeds the expected yield, he is allowed to purchase land and extend his farm.'

Nartreb pulled a face. 'How very archaic! The state is forgoing a lot of benefits.'

The treasurer said mutinously, 'The farmers are happy with it, and—'

'In a war economy, we must control every stage of food production. Our soldiers must be well fed and enjoy the best possible living conditions if they are to win more victories. I am requisitioning all the farms.'

'That is unjust and unacceptable!'

'Moderate your language, my dear colleague! That is Tefnakht's decision.'

'What will the peasants have left?'

'We shall set food rations adequate for this inferior class, and they will come and fetch them from the central barracks.'

'Most of them will refuse to work for you,' said the treasurer.

'In that case, they will be executed immediately for high treason. When a few of them have been publicly burnt alive, the remaining rebels will quickly return to the fold. As for the tradesmen, they are to work for the army so that our soldiers will be correctly equipped. You have no objection, dear colleague?'

'What good would it do if I had?'

A broad smile spread across Nartreb's face as he rubbed his pudgy hands together: the old nobleman was beginning to give way under the pressure.

'Now,' he went on, 'let us consider the question of Henen-nesut's great riches. The city's notables— of whom you are one—enjoy a wealth of lavish possessions, which should be made use of in the best possible way. Tefnakht must be rich—and so must I.'

'You're nothing but a thief!'

'Come, come, dear colleague, there's no need to get so angry. I have a tempting proposition for you. As you are well acquainted with all the leading citizens of this town, I shall make you responsible for negotiating with them. You will relay my orders to them and arrange for their possessions to be stored centrally, and in return you will receive . . .

let's say, ten per cent. Serving Tefnakht will make you a very rich man.'

Nartreb was gorging himself, but the old man pushed away his meal, untouched.

'What do you take me for? Do your own dirty work! I will not rob my fellow countrymen and I will not help you in any way whatsoever. On the contrary, I shall tell everyone what a bandit you are.'

Nartreb got to his feet. 'There seems to be a misunderstanding between us. I am concerned only for your wellbeing, while at the same time carrying out the tasks assigned to me. A man of your experience should understand how difficult my work is.'

'You cannot speak a single word without lying,' said the treasurer contemptuously.

'Wouldn't you like time to think about this?'

'I shall be your implacable enemy, no matter what it costs me.'

'Please excuse me for a moment.'

Nartreb walked round behind the treasurer and made as if to head towards the kitchen. But he swung round, fastened his hate-filled hands round the old man's neck, and snapped it.

'This has cost you your life, imbecile, and I shall manage perfectly well without you,' he sneered.

*   *   *

'Every obstacle has been removed, my lord,' said Nartreb, bowing obsequiously before Tefnakht.

'So the city worthies have accepted your new taxation system?'

Nartreb had sent out soldiers to fetch them and

had forced them to file past the corpse of the treasurer, who had been accused of disobedience and collaboration with the enemy. No long discussions had been needed, and he considered that his favourite method, brutality seasoned with extortion, was producing excellent results.

'What about you, Yegeb?' asked Tefnakht.

'The town has been cleansed, my lord. Not one useless mouth or undesirable element remains.'

'And is Henen-nesut as wealthy as you thought?'

'Certainly it is well provisioned, but there are fewer weapons than I had expected.'

Tefnakht scowled. 'Fetch me the captain of archers' daughter.'

Yegeb looked uncomfortable. 'I don't know if she's still alive.'

'Fetch her!'

*   *   *

Despite her filthy hair and her bruised and dirty flesh, Daybreak was magnificent and had not lost a shred of her pride.

'Have my soldiers been ill-treating you?' asked Tefnakht.

'What else could I expect?'

'Whatever I want, I get. And what I want is to know where your father hid the weapons.'

'Why ask me?'

'I am a good judge of people. You are spirited and brave, and I believe he confided in you.'

'You believe wrong.'

'I need those weapons, Daybreak. Either you tell me where they are, or every hour I shall have a child beheaded.'

85

CHAPTER EIGHTEEN

She was young, beautiful and passionate. At eighteen years old, she made love like an experienced woman, yet with touching flashes of innocence.

Lemersekny watched her sleeping. She was twenty years younger than he and had tried so hard to seduce him that in the end he had given in. With his beard, shaven head and body covered in scars, Lemersekny did not go looking for women, but they sought him out, and he simply could not resist them.

He ran his left hand gently down to the small of her back. 'By all the gods of heaven and earth,' he thought, 'what a woman!'

His calloused hand slid a little lower, became indiscreet and awoke the young beauty.

'What do you want, my love?' she murmured sleepily.

'We can't leave it at that. I'm sure you haven't shown me everything.'

She curled herself round him like a jungle creeper and lavished passionate kisses on him, then pressed her lips against her lover's right arm, a jointed wooden arm which fascinated her.

'How did you lose your arm?'

'It was an axe-blow. I couldn't get out of the way, because I hesitated for a moment instead of slitting my foe's throat straight away. Since then, I have never hesitated.'

'It's made of acacia wood, isn't it?'

'A very old piece of the finest acacia, which will never warp or decay. It cost me a great deal of money, but the carpenter produced a work of art, you understand. The joints are perfect—and at least I'll never get rheumatism in that arm.'

Suddenly, the young woman sat up and covered her breasts with her hands. 'Someone's watching us—a giant!'

Lemersekny seized his short sword and leapt to his feet.

'Oh. It's you,' he said. His sword-arm dropped to his side. 'Get dressed, little one, and leave us.'

'But the giant . . .'

'The Pharaoh of Egypt doesn't mean you any harm. Now go. Leave us.'

The young woman ran off in terror, not even pausing to pick up her clothes.

'A new conquest,' observed Piankhy. 'She's splendid.'

'A new defeat, more like,' lamented Lemersekny, helping himself to a cupful of beer. 'I've tried desperately to resist that kind of temptress, but I can't manage it. I just hope she's not married. Are you thirsty, Majesty?'

'I need some advice.'

'You, Majesty? That's a bad joke! You always make your decisions alone, and I don't see how I can help you to govern.'

'You're an expert in warfare, aren't you?'

The infantry captain's pale-blue eyes darkened. 'Warfare? Are you talking about a real battle, with real soldiers, real fighting, hordes of dead and injured?'

'I don't know yet.'

'Ah, I thought as much. So it's nothing serious,

then. The kingdom is as quiet as ever, and there's been some trivial squabble between two tribes. I'm going back to sleep.'

Piankhy pushed open the wooden shutters, letting in the light.

'Majesty,' protested Lemersekny, 'you know I prefer the dark.'

'I know that while you're shutting yourself up in this hovel, making love to the most beautiful girls in Napata, you're also keeping up to date with everything—and you're still the only military expert I can really trust.'

'Very true, and you should have promoted me to general a long time ago.'

'The powers that be don't appreciate your excessive fondness for strong drink, nor your passion for women, nor even the way you command your troops. A senior officer is expected to conduct himself properly.'

'The only good conduct in a warrior is victory.'

All the evidence suggested that Captain Lemersekny had no liking for housework. His clothes lay all over the place, in a chaotic mess which defied any attempt at tidying up.

'Do you think the Northern provinces might form an alliance?' asked Piankhy.

'It's inevitable.'

'How can you be so certain?'

'Even in a hornets' nest, one will end up imposing its will on the others.'

'And who, in your opinion, will play that role?

'I can't see it being anyone but Tefnakht, Prince of Sais. He has the biggest princedom and the best army. One of these days he will take possession of the whole Delta, and Memphis will immediately throw in its lot with him.'

'And after that?'

'After that, easy success will go to Tefnakht's head and he'll believe he's a master strategist who can go further and fight a real battle. So he'll consolidate his authority, eliminate all his rivals and venture into Middle Egypt.'

'You have second sight, Captain Lemersekny,' said Piankhy.

'You're not telling me all this has already happened?'

'Unfortunately, yes. And in your opinion, just how far will Tefnakht go?'

Lemersekny scratched his wooden arm doubtfully. 'If he wants to progress further, there are several obstacles he must overcome. First, he'll attack Henen-nesut.'

'Why there?'

'Because Prince Peftau is sixty years old and not as vigorous as he used to be. Because he won't be able to resist a massive, devastating attack.'

'But Henen-nesut has stout defensive walls.'

'They only *look* that way. The defenders are no longer fully alert, and they think that the mere name of Piankhy is enough to ensure their protection. With respect, Majesty, you are a long way from the fighting, and a crazy war won't be stopped by attitudes like that.'

'So you think Tefnakht is capable of capturing Henen-nesut?'

'If he succeeds, his dreams of victory will begin to become reality. Tefnakht the conqueror, that's what he hopes to become, and he'll use any means, even the most barbaric, to achieve his goal.'

'Henen-nesut has fallen to Tefnakht,' admitted

Piankhy.

Lemersekny put down his cup of beer on a low table. 'You're joking, Majesty!'

'No, Tefnakht has succeeded, just as you thought he would.'

'Has he continued further?'

'It seems he has consolidated his position. But I have doubts about the information I am receiving.'

'Yes, consolidation makes sense. He'll use a good rear base to launch other assaults. The first step will be to take Khmun.'

'Prince Nemrod will drive him back.'

'It's true that Nemrod has the resources to do it. But the battle promises to be a tough one. And if Tefnakht is unleashed, if he achieves a fresh victory, the road to Thebes will lie open before him.

'What do you recommend?' asked Piankhy.

'We must alert the troops we have stationed at Thebes, and—depending on how the situation develops—send reinforcements.'

'You are to leave for Thebes with Puarma, my captain of archers, and take command of the troops there. Your objective: to stop Tefnakht.'

'Majesty, I can't stand that fellow Puarma and, besides, I'm only a captain—the senior officers in Thebes will never accept my authority.'

'You will have a warrant from me, detailing your mission, Lemersekny. What's the matter. Are you afraid of fighting?'

The wooden arm slammed down violently on to the low table, which broke in half.

'I shall leave first thing tomorrow, Majesty.'

CHAPTER NINETEEN

Nartreb tore the little boy from his mother's arms. The child burst into tears and tried to resist, but the counsellor slapped him and punched the woman out of the way. Two men who tried to intervene were severely beaten by members of the militia set up by Yegeb.

Nartreb forced the child to lay his head on the execution block, then slid his sword out of its scabbard.

'If you refuse to tell me where the weapons are hidden,' Tefnakht told Daybreak, 'I shall have this child's head cut off. And others will follow.'

'You are a monster!'

'You are wrong. My concern is for Egypt's happiness. In order to obtain it, I must defeat Piankhy, and to do that I need weapons. Speak, Daybreak, or this child will die—and it will be your fault.'

The young woman looked at Tefnakht strangely. 'And what if you are lying?'

'What do you mean?'

'Whatever I tell you, you will kill this child and then kill me too.'

Tefnakht smiled. 'You don't understand me, Daybreak. Besides, you have no choice: you must gamble on the future.'

'What sort of future do you want to build?'

'This country is divided, powerless, more and more impoverished because of this Black Pharaoh, who claims to govern it yet shuts himself away at the back end of Nubia. How can you and your fellow citizens put up with his tyranny? I have already conquered the Delta and the great city of Memphis. Tomorrow, I shall take possession of the South. When that happens, the Two Lands will be reunited and the people will recognize me as Pharaoh.'

Doubt replaced anger in the young woman's green eyes. 'Do you really mean that?'

'You now know my sole ambition.'

'Come with me. Alone.'

Yegeb intervened. 'Don't listen to that girl, my lord. She'll lead you into a trap.'

'I am quite capable of defending myself.'

Daybreak led Tefnakht to her father's house, walked through the kitchens and down a stone staircase which ended in a cellar. There, she knelt down and scrabbled around the floor with her fingers until she uncovered a stone slab marked with a seal.

'The weapons are underneath here,' she said.

Tefnakht slipped the blade of his dagger under the stone and lifted it up. Another staircase led downwards, disappearing in the darkness. The general lit a torch and stepped down into an underground chamber filled with bows, arrows and spears. The entire collection was brand-new and of excellent quality. Thanks to these arms, his ability to launch an attack would be considerably strengthened.

A knife-blade sank into his side.

'You killed my father,' Daybreak reminded him in a voice of ice-cold hatred, 'and I am going to kill you.'

'Your father died a soldier's death. He believed he could save his town, and he considered me his enemy. He was wrong, but I salute his bravery and I shall have a stele engraved in his memory. It's a pity. If he had been more clear-headed, he could have joined me in my campaign, and I would have given him an important post in the new Egypt I am building. I didn't kill your father, Daybreak, it was this war—this necessary war, which we must continue to its end.'

The point of the blade slid in deeper, and a little blood gushed out.

Tefnakht ignored it. 'If you kill me,' he went on, 'you will regret it all your life, because you will be the cause of your people's misery. In your heart, you know that I am the only one who can save this country from ruin and give meaning to your father's death.'

'How dare you!' she spat.

'It is the truth. Have the courage to admit it.'

The blade hesitated; then, very gradually, it slid gently out.

Tefnakht looked into the young woman's eyes. 'Will you help me?'

'Me? Help you? But. . .'

'You know this region and its leading citizens. With your help, we may be able to avoid some bloody battles. Instead of rotting in a prison cell, wouldn't you like to make yourself useful by saving many lives?'

'Help you?' she repeated.

'Whatever you decide, I shall attack Khmun. If you manage to persuade Prince Nemrod to renounce his allegiance to Piankhy and become my ally, the townsfolk will be spared much suffering.'

Daybreak bit her lip. Tefnakht's arguments had all hit home. She hated him, but he had

93

reawakened hope in her heart. And she could not go on any longer, in this state. She could wash, remove the traces of beatings and defilements, take up the struggle again, avoid a massacre . . .

Tefnakht could not admit to the girl how much she disturbed him. The Prince of Sais was surrounded by an army of courtesans always eager to satisfy him, but, haunted by his plans to reconquer Egypt, he paid them no heed. Daybreak was not like them. She was wild and untamed, capable of meeting challenges far beyond the ordinary. Up to now, Tefnakht had not burdened himself with a wife; but once he was crowned pharaoh, he would have to bring a Great Royal Wife to the throne. Only Daybreak was worthy of that office.

*   *   *

The Libyan chiefs were still celebrating. Not in their wildest dreams had they ever imagined that they would spend nights feasting in the palace of the Prince of Henen-nesut, the vassal of the Black Pharaoh. Forced to accept his fate, Peftau joined in the general rejoicing. He had ordered his officers and soldiers to obey Tefnakht without question. Since the supreme authority had changed, it was useless to oppose it.

Yegeb observed each of the revellers in turn. If one of them was preparing to betray Tefnakht, he would know. As for Nartreb, he was gorging himself with food and gulping down goblets of white oasis wine without bothering to dilute it with water.

'What do you think of Peftau, Yegeb?' asked

Nartreb.

'At his age, his main concern is to avoid unpleasantness and live a comfortable life. Since Tefnakht is the strongest man, he will follow him blindly.'

'The general shouldn't have become so infatuated with that girl Daybreak. Women sap a warrior's strength. And that one will never stop hating him.'

'I'm not so sure,' said Yegeb. 'Tefnakht fascinates her. And after all, he is her only future.'

'All the same, we must watch her closely.'

'Someone else worries me more.'

'Who?'

'Prince Akanosh. He has the face of a worried, disappointed man, and he shows no enthusiasm for our war of conquest.'

'Akanosh will never challenge Tefnakht's authority,' said Nartreb.

'It's more subtle than that. We must watch him closely, too.'

Tefnakht entered the banqueting hall, still dressed in his breastplate. It took only a few seconds for complete silence to fall, and even the most drunken reveller heard his announcement.

'Our weaponry has been strengthened and our troops have had time to rest. The time has come to return to combat. Before heading further south, we must control the whole of Middle Egypt and seize the city of Khmun, its weapons and its wealth. We shall try to persuade Prince Nemrod to surrender. If he refuses, we shall lay siege to Khmun.'

CHAPTER TWENTY

Captain Lemersekny was fuming. Organizing the expedition to Thebes seemed utterly impossible. The store-suppliers refused to show any initiative, and every scribe referred him to a superior, who in turn claimed not to have the necessary authority. The captain's only remaining option was to force his way into Cool-Head's office and obtain some proper explanations. Did the king, or did he not, wish to send an armed force against Tefnakht?

Lemersekny was disagreeably surprised to find Puarma in the scribe's office. The archer flexed his muscles, as if to prove to his rival that strength was on his side.

'Sorry to see you again, Puarma,' said Lemersekny.

'Why have you left your lair? Don't tell me you've managed to sober up for once.'

'I'd rather be a drunk than a stupid braggart.'

'Let's go outside and settle this with our fists.'

'That's enough!' cut in Cool-Head. 'You'll soon be fighting the enemy—and you'll be doing it together.'

'I'm more than ready to do so,' declared Lemersekny haughtily. 'Why is this incompetent fool trying to put a spoke in my wheel?'

Puarma stared at him in disbelief. 'What are you talking about? I have received an order: I am to leave for Thebes.'

Lemersekny's lips twisted into a sneer. 'We are to work together, I know.'

'I refuse!'

'An officer does not have the right to refuse His Majesty's orders,' snapped Cool-Head, outraged by Puarma's behaviour. 'One more insubordinate remark like that, and you will defend yourself before the Council of War.'

Lemersekny was delighted by Puarma's discomfited expression. He decided to press his advantage, and asked, 'Which of us will be the senior officer?'

'You will have the same rank,' said Cool-Head, 'you in the infantry, Puarma in the corps of archers. During the journey, you will have to get on together. At Thebes, you will hand over your written orders to the commander of our troops.'

'Why aren't we leaving immediately?'

'Because of some new information that has just reached us,' said Cool-Head. 'It seems that Tefnakht is less ambitious than we thought. He has left Henen-nesut and is heading back towards the North.'

Lemersekny was cruelly disappointed. 'I might have known it! The war is over before it's even started. This man Tefnakht is less than nothing.'

'All the same,' said the scribe, 'we remain on the alert. In what state has the enemy left Henen-nesut? If Prince Peftau does not succeed in re-establishing order and proclaiming that his town is once again Piankhy's vassal, we shall intervene. The Pharaoh will not leave Middle Egypt to sink into lawlessness.'

'In other words, we must be patient,' complained Lemersekny.

'My archers will start training again,' declared Puarma.

'They certainly need it,' said his rival. 'Now, my

footsoldiers, they're already battle-ready.'

*   *   *

Shepena, [Her full name, Shep-en-Opet, means 'Gift of the goddess Opet' (spiritual fecundity)] the Black Pharaoh's daughter, was a magnificent young woman of twenty, tall and supremely elegant, with her mother's copper complexion. As a very young girl, she had been initiated into the mysteries of the goddess Mut, wife of Amon. Unlike other girls of her age, she did not spend most of her time swimming, dancing, making music and being courted by boys. In the workshops of the temple, where she had first served as assistant to a ritualist, she had discovered a passion: the manufacturing of perfumes.

She had had to undergo a formidable examination, conducted by an old perfumer priest who had criticized her sternly before acknowledging her gifts. Since he wished to retire to a little official residence in the shadow of Gebel Barkal, he had consented to reveal the secrets of his trade to her. In this way, she gained the benefits of years of research and experimentation.

Shepena had thanked the specialist and the gods for granting her such a favour, and she felt a debt towards them. Henceforth, she would devote her existence to the continual improvement of perfumes destined for shrines and holy statues. When a worshipper entered the temple, wondrous scents would enchant his soul and make it light as a bird.

As Napata was rich and Piankhy demanded that the gods must be served to perfection, Shepena had at her disposal the rarest and most costly materials,

98

such as myrrh from Yemen, known as 'tears of Horus', incense from the land of Punt, or *moringa* oil, which was sweet and colourless and never grew rancid. She had just received a large quantity of styrax, imported from Syria, which was indispensable for fixing fragrances. And her stocks contained abundant supplies of linen and balanite oils, beef-fat, resinous gums, balm, Persian galbanum, essences of rose and lily, and salt for drying her preparations.

For the next festival of Amon, Shepena had decided to fill some phials with the most wondrous of perfumes, *kyphi*, which was extremely difficult to make successfully. Only master perfumers set out on this adventure which, only too often, ended in failure. According to the ancient recipes, ten or twelve ingredients made up this perfume, and some specialists went as far as sixteen. Shepena had chosen juniper berries, sweet-smelling galingale, dried myrrh, lentisk (mastic-tree), aromatic tree-bark, resin, Phoenician reeds, styrax, dyer's bugloss, fenugreek and pistachio. After scrupulously measuring out the precise proportions, she spent a long time grinding all the ingredients finely in a mortar, then sieved the concoction to produce three-fifths of its initial volume. She checked that the powder was sufficiently fine, and mixed it with wine of exceptional quality, before heating up some honey, resin and serpentine, which she added to the scented powder.

'Have you succeeded?' asked Piankhy.

'Majesty, your visit is an honour.'

'People say such good things about your workshops that I wanted to see them for myself.'

Shepena uncorked a phial. Instantly, the king

99

felt himself transported into an unreal world where neither trials nor sufferings existed. The power of the *kyphi* his daughter had made exceeded any he had encountered before.

'You're a magician, Shepena!'

'No work could be more inspiring than striving to satisfy the gods.'

Piankhy tried to forget the perfume's attraction. 'You might be able to serve them more publicly and more effectively.'

The young woman frowned. 'Would I have to give up my work as a perfumer?'

'Of course not. But you would have to take on other, equally demanding, duties.'

'Father, I don't understand.'

'Your aunt, the Wife of Amon in Thebes, is elderly and very sick. She can no longer ensure that Karnak's many temples are run as they should be. The time has come to choose a successor, so that your aunt can adopt her and pass on the secrets and duties of her high office.'

Shepena turned pale. 'Father, the Wife of Amon is a queen who rules a temple-city and issues decrees to thousands of people. But I love solitude, and the only thing I rule is my workshop, far from the cares of daily life.'

Piankhy took Shepena in his powerful arms. 'My beloved daughter, you are the one I have chosen.'

CHAPTER TWENTY-ONE

At almost fifty years old, Prince Nemrod was proud of himself and his successes. His life had been one good thing after another, from his happy childhood in a marvellous palace where he had been pampered by devoted servants, to the day when he had inherited from his father the rich, much-envied city of Khmun.

Besides graduating top of his class of scribes, Nemrod was an excellent bowman, a practised horseman and blessed with an iron constitution, and he had always effortlessly seduced the prettiest of women. He never put up with a mistress for more than six months; moreover, she must hold her tongue and not bother him. So as not to offend conventional morality, Nemrod had married an aristocratic woman who remained confined to her apartments and made do with a life of idle luxury.

To tell the truth, the prince was bored. It was Memphis he would have liked to rule. There, life was lively, the influence of the North was growing from day to day, and it was easy to get involved in the sort of dubious deals in which the old law of Ma'at no longer had any place. Here, at Khmun, the sacred city of Thoth, the god who had revealed the secret of hieroglyphics and the sacred sciences to mankind, everything was suffocated by tradition.

The great Temple of Thoth, which was almost as vast as the temple of Amon-Ra at Karnak, was a haven for scholars of noble descent: ritualists who took their inspiration from the ancient texts, astronomers and astrologers, physicians and surgeons, magicians, perfumers and architects—each day they gained deeper knowledge through further study. But it all left Nemrod unmoved.

When, from time to time, he was obliged to receive representations from these learned men, he pretended to listen attentively to their boring speeches, while dreaming of the magnificent woman he would take to his bed that very evening, after a succulent meal. The next day, he would take a chariot ride into the fifteenth province of Upper Egypt, which had been placed under his jurisdiction, or perhaps sail idly along the Nile, drinking sweet beer.

Each day, Nemrod put himself in the hands of a masseur, barber, hairdresser, manicurist and pedicurist. He selected his own wigs, clothes and perfumes, and was constantly on the lookout for the slightest sign of aging. Thanks to balms which a serving-girl smoothed delicately into his skin, the prince was not afflicted by a single wrinkle.

The administrative skills of the scribes employed in Nemrod's government relieved him of any worries about day-to-day management; his province was fertile, checks on harvests were rigorous, and taxes were gathered without difficulty. So the prince was content to cast a brief glance over the figures which were handed to him and which never contained any mistakes. His only real concern was the upkeep of the regiment Piankhy had placed under his command. It was made up of elite archers and experienced footsoldiers, capable of repelling any attack. Engineers maintained the fortifications, which Nemrod had reinforced at regular intervals.

It was a peaceful existence—too peaceful. Egypt was deadlocked. To the north of Khmun lay the Libyan princes and anarchy; to the south the holy city of Thebes, just as much a prisoner of its traditions as Khmun. And in the lonely wastes of Nubia, far from civilization, was Piankhy, whose reputation alone was enough to terrify his foes.

When Nemrod first learnt of the attack on Henen-nesut, he had not believed it. Yet another of these empty boasts the Libyans were so fond of! And then the news was confirmed. Peftau had been unable to hold out against Tefnakht.

Tefnakht . . . Nemrod would never have imagined the fiery Prince of Sais as a brilliant strategist, leading an alliance. And that judgement was correct, since he had not dared to attack Khmun. After a period of rest and carousing in Henen-nesut, the Libyan army had not marched on towards the Theban region where Piankhy's troops would have cut them to pieces; it had turned back towards the Delta. In short, it was a minor episode.

Henen-nesut would come back under the control of Peftau, who would once again proclaim himself the Black Pharaoh's subject; and changelessness would take on the force of law. Nemrod would still have to endure peasants and artisans moaning on endlessly about tax increases and working conditions, which were becoming more and more difficult. He would respond by toughening up the legislation and, at the first sign of rebellion, would send in his police to re-establish order. In other words, boredom.

Nemrod was choosing a wine for dinner when his head minister requested an audience. The man was usually unflappable; he would not depart from protocol without good reason.

'Prince Nemrod,' said the minister, 'we're surrounded.'

'That's impossible! It's Piankhy's army—it must be Piankhy's army coming to protect us.'

'These soldiers aren't Nubian.'

'Then who . . .?'

'It's Tefnakht. I have put the troops on high alert.'

'Will we really be able to defend ourselves?' asked the prince.

'The attacking forces are substantial, but we can hold out. The water-tanks are full, and we have ample food reserves. As they will lose a great many men, perhaps they will give up.'

'Every man to his post.'

*   *   *

The young woman was dressed in a long green robe with shoulder straps, and a very plain black wig. When she walked forward, alone, through the great fortified gate of Khmun, the archers stood amazed, waiting for orders.

Daybreak was led under armed escort to Nemrod's palace.

'Who are you?' he asked.

'The daughter of a Henen-nesut officer, who was killed by Tefnakht.'

'And yet he freed you?'

'I am his envoy.'

The prince was astonished. 'Are you making fun of me?'

'The soldiers of Henen-nesut are now under Tefnakht's command. He has decided to take possession of your town.'

'Isn't he being rather over-ambitious?'

'You may believe that, Prince Nemrod, but the aim of my mission is to change your mind. I know that Tefnakht seeks to save Egypt from decadence, and give her back her former greatness. If you continue to serve Piankhy, your city will be

104

destroyed and you will die with it.'

'What other options does Tefnakht offer?'

'Open the gates of Khmun and become his ally,' said Daybreak. 'Your soldiers will be placed under his command, and the war of reconquest will be directed south, towards Thebes.'

'That's an amusing attempt to frighten me, young lady, but Khmun will resist the attack.'

'Tefnakht is implacable. He won't stop until he has achieved his goal, no matter what his losses. Khmun must fall—and Khmun *will* fall.'

'If I surrender my town to him, he'll have me killed.'

'Prince Peftau is still alive, and still governing Henen-nesut. Why continue to suffer the yoke of this man Piankhy, who never leaves his precious Nubia and laughs at the future of Egypt, while reducing her to the status of a slave? It is because of him that prosperity has disappeared and stagnation deepens. Under Tefnakht, the Two Lands will rediscover their lost unity, and those who have helped him to victory will be rewarded.'

Nemrod thought for a moment. It was true that the Black Pharaoh was nothing but a distant tyrant to whom, in the final analysis, he owed nothing. Of course, he had sworn an oath to remain loyal to Piankhy in all circumstances, but that promise had been lightly given and the current emergency freed him from it. Tefnakht was at the gates of Khmun. He had a grand plan and he would allow Nemrod to escape from his boredom to another, far more exciting, way of life.

'You're a very persuasive envoy,' he told Daybreak. 'There'll be no bloodshed. I shall open the gates of Khmun to Tefnakht's army and place

105

myself under his command.'

CHAPTER TWENTY-TWO

Tefnakht entered Khmun at the head of his troops, to the cheers of the townsfolk. Nemrod had addressed them an hour beforehand, and had announced that he had averted a bloody struggle and that they could now look forward to the brightest of futures. Day-to-day problems, tax increases, inflation, failure of the Nile flood, children's illnesses—all these misfortunes were the doing of a single man, Piankhy, the Black Pharaoh. For several years, Nemrod had tried in vain to escape from his tyranny. Now, thanks to Tefnakht, the future Pharaoh of Egypt, the people would come to know a new era of prosperity.

'Why are these poor people so gullible?' wondered Akanosh. His horse trotted beside those of the other Libyan princes, who were delighted at this easy success, universally attributing it to Tefnakht's military genius. Nobody thought of challenging his authority any more. In taking Khmun, he had made himself master of Middle Egypt, ensured the cooperation of noteworthy scribes, and considerably increased the power of his army.

This time, people could not talk of a simple raid or an achievement that would lead nowhere. Tefnakht really was gaining the stature of a conqueror. But Akanosh was haunted by another question: 'Why didn't Piankhy react?' Either the message had not reached the king, or he had underestimated the seriousness of the danger. And now the road to Thebes lay wide open.

*   *   *

Nemrod had welcomed his new master in a manner befitting a king: a pavilion with elegant gilded wooden columns to protect him from the sun, a throne with feet shaped like lions' paws and decorated with palm fronds, a little footstool carved in the shape of a prostrate, vanquished Nubian. The message was clear: the Prince of Khmun did indeed consider his conqueror to be the new Pharaoh of Egypt, lacking only the official coronation rites.

Perfumed with essence of roses, Nemrod wore a wig, elegant sandals, a fine linen robe and a wide necklet of turquoises. He bowed low before Tefnakht, and said, 'Henceforth this town is yours, my lord. Command and I will obey, if you will grant me the immense privilege of continuing to govern it.'

'You are a reasonable man, Nemrod. In time of war, that is a rare and precious virtue. Who knows this ancient and glorious city better than you?'

Nemrod knelt and kissed the greaves that armoured Tefnakht's legs; he also wore a breastplate and helmet.

'Thank you, my lord. You may count upon my absolute fidelity.'

'Rise, vassal.'

The Prince of Khmun cast a glance at Daybreak, who stood one pace behind Tefnakht.

'The intelligence and beauty of your envoy—'

'She is much more than that,' said Tefnakht.

'Daybreak is the future Queen of Egypt.'

A smile of astonishment and delight lit up the young woman's face. The wound inflicted by her father's death still gaped wide, but she was falling under the spell of this conqueror, who was so certain that his cause was just. He had awakened the same fire in her. Although hatred had not disappeared from her heart, it battled with an admiration that was close to love, and she wanted to help him. Tefnakht had not deceived her: thanks to her intervention, thousands of lives had been spared. Tomorrow, at Thebes, she would try to repeat that success. Perhaps the Wife of Amon would understand that the Black Pharaoh was a bad master and that opposing Tefnakht was tantamount to betraying Egypt.

Becoming queen . . . the thought slid over Daybreak like a soothing balm. Suddenly this girl, who had only lived for the moment, without ever thinking about the future, lost all the light-heartedness of childhood. She felt true terror, certainly, but she had a passionate desire to live, to be useful, to prove that she shared Tefnakht's determination.

At the first banquet organized to celebrate the liberation of Khmun, Daybreak was seated at Tefnakht's left hand. Before the whole world, the conqueror was stressing the rank he had given her. Although very attracted to her, Nemrod was careful not to flirt with her.

'I'm sorry to broach serious and tiresome matters so soon,' Nemrod whispered in Tefnakht's ear, 'but what about the taxation system laid down by Piankhy? Do you wish to change it?'

'For now, the war economy takes precedence

108

over everything else. My counsellors Yegeb and Nartreb will explain their requirements to you, and they will take care of the details.'

'And about my personal deductions . . .'

'Since you have done well, increase them,' said Tefnakht. 'Now, what state is your weaponry in?'

'It's been carefully maintained.'

'And are your soldiers battle-ready?'

'They're expert archers and long-serving footsoldiers, all first-rate professionals, and they'll inflict heavy losses on the Nubians.'

'Enjoy your good fortune, Nemrod, and don't bother about anything else.'

* * *

Akanosh's wife was weeping. 'Yegeb and Nartreb are using the same methods here as they did in Henen-nesut. The old and the sick are being systematically killed, and so is anyone who dares express the slightest doubt about Tefnakht's plans. But why doesn't Piankhy respond? He should send his army from Thebes to crush these monsters!'

Akanosh was close to collapse. 'Perhaps the Theban priest who was meant to brief him did not arrive in Napata. I shall have to carry out this mission myself.'

She caught him in her arms. 'No, Akanosh! They'll never let you leave this town. You'd be arrested for treason, and tortured.'

He bowed his head. 'You're right, it would be madness. But there is one possibility left: the priests of Thoth must be opposed to what is happening.'

'Do you know one?'

'No, but we shall have to take that risk. Go to the temple workshops and ask for help. Tell them that the house we have been given is infested with fleas and we need special oil of wild mint to get rid of them. In view of my status and the substance we're asking for, they will send us a specialist.'

*   *   *

The specialist was a middle-aged priest who carried his phial of oil of wild mint with the greatest care. Moving about slowly, he inspected the reception rooms in Akanosh's house.

'My lord Prince, I don't know what to say. This house seems in perfect order, and I cannot see any traces at all of fleas.'

Akanosh took the plunge. 'Are you still loyal to Piankhy?'

'To answer you might cost me my life,' said the priest nervously.

'Don't be afraid. It's true that I am a Libyan prince and that I obey Tefnakht—if necessary, I will fight at his side. But I cannot tolerate his agents acting like torturers and making the people suffer like this. It's vital to warn Piankhy. Perhaps a devastating war will break out, or perhaps—as I hope—the situation will stabilize again. At least the civilians will be spared and Tefnakht's tyranny will extend no further.'

'Doesn't saying this make you guilty of high treason?'

'I am heeding the voice of my conscience. Can the Temple of Thoth send a messenger to Piankhy to warn him that Khmun has fallen into Tefnakht's hands?'

'Take this phial of wild-mint oil, Prince Akanosh, and spread the contents around your home. After all, you did ask for my help to combat harmful vermin.'

CHAPTER TWENTY-THREE

The flask Piankhy's daughter had given him was made of glass, one of the most precious of all materials. He opened it. Her *kyphi* was truly exceptional. The gods themselves breathed in this perfume in the otherworld paradise where the thorn did not prick and the crocodile did not bite.

Abilah took the flask from him gently and anointed Piankhy's powerful torso with perfume. 'This scent is magical,' she said.

The queen entwined her naked body round her husband's. She was all flowers and all essences, the spell of the Nile banks, the magic of a fertile, enchanting, sunlit land.

'I have only ever loved one woman,' he said, 'and I shall never love another.'

'I believe you, for I know that your word is truth.'

With her long, slender, goddess's fingers, Abilah unfastened her husband's kilt. The Black Pharaoh tasted the matchless perfume of her loving body, with the same surge of emotion as if it were their very first time together.

*   *   *

Cool-Head did not know what to do. The guards

111

had not forbidden him to enter the monarch's private apartments, but the king and queen were lying together, their naked bodies curled together. Should he wake them to tell them the bad news? The dwarf was a scribe in the service of the state, and he must take account of rank or privilege. So he touched the king's forehead lightly.

'Majesty, wake up.'

Piankhy opened one eye. 'Oh it's you, Cool-Head. What are you doing here?'

'I'm sorry, but it's very urgent.'

The pharaoh looked down at his wife's exquisite body. He wished he had the right, like any other man, to be with the woman he loved and forget the world's heavy burdens for a while. Then Abilah, too, awoke and stood up. Sublime in her nakedness, she walked with a light, supremely noble step towards the bathroom.

'Cool-Head,' said Piankhy, 'if you've disturbed me for nothing, it'll be the end of our friendship!'

'Matchless though it is, Majesty, I would sacrifice it for the sake of peace if peace can still be saved.'

'Have you had news from Middle Egypt?'

'Unfortunately, yes.'

*   *   *

The messenger sent to Pharaoh by the Temple of Thoth was a young man with a steady gaze and strong, well-muscled legs.

'Where have you come from?' asked Piankhy.

'From Khmun, Majesty.'

'Who sent you?'

'The High Priest of the Temple of Thoth.'

112

'What is the name of the valley where the temple stands?'

'The Valley of the Tamarisks.'

'What is made in the workshop near the temple entrance?'

'Scribes' palettes,' said the messenger.

'What is Khmun's sacred name?'

'The city of the Ogdoad, the eight gods who created the world and today lie at rest in Thebes.'

Piankhy was reassured: the messenger was not an impostor.

'Why did you speak to Cool-Head of a "catastrophe"?'

'Because Prince Nemrod has betrayed you and opened the gates of Khmun to Tefnakht.'

'That's hard to believe. Nemrod swore allegiance to me and he had the armed strength to resist.'

'All the same, it is the truth, Majesty. Nemrod has pulled down the city walls, and he has broken his oath and become Tefnakht's vassal. He did not hesitate to offer him the treasures of Khmun and put his soldiers under the Libyan's command. Forgive my impertinence, Majesty, but how much longer will you stay silent while Tefnakht extends his conquests unopposed? Majesty, it is your reputation that creates your power; and it is that alone that will dissuade your foes from laying waste to Egypt.'

*   *   *

The horse with the tawny mane carried Piankhy far out into the desert. The Black Pharaoh devoured the open spaces, drew nourishment from the crystal-clear air and communed with the

113

uncompromising blue of the sky. Seeing that his master was troubled, Valiant changed rhythm and direction before he had even been told to. Man and horse were one, absorbed in their strenuous exertions, which were accompanied by flights of white ibis and crested cranes.

Eventually, Piankhy stopped at a well. He gave Valiant a drink before slaking his own thirst, then gazed admiringly at the desert. Nothing tainted this immense vista, which lay wide open to the sun and the wind. No wicked being could disturb this harmony created by the Hidden One, whose presence asserted itself beyond all human knowing.

For long hours, Piankhy meditated. His lips murmured the ancient prayer that his predecessors had addressed to Amon:

Perfect god, you give life to every being. Hail to you, Unique One, Master of Ma'at, you who cross the distant sky in peace. You give life to the Light, your word is the Word. O you who remain one though you create the many, my heart's desire is to welcome you. How sweet it is to speak your name, for it has the taste of life. You are the herdsman leading the bulls to pasture, the bronze gate that protects its town, the pilot who knows every bend in the river. You are Amon, Master of Silence, you who reveal yourself to the humble. You who give breath to those in need, save me, for I am sorely afflicted with pain and uncertainty.

When the sun went down, the Black Pharaoh turned and rode back towards Napata.

* * *

On Piankhy's orders, the priest of Thoth gave the

114

court a detailed account of all that he had told the king.

Faces grew long, all except Captain Lemersekny's—he was glimpsing joyous tomorrows, in which he could quite lawfully massacre Libyans. His presence shocked many members of the court; they were unpleasantly surprised by the favour granted to this warrior, who feared neither the gods nor man.

'What do you intend to do, Majesty?' asked Otoku, suddenly losing his appetite.

'We must consider the evidence: the fall of Henen-nesut was not one isolated blow, and Nemrod is a traitor of the worst order. By surrendering his town to Tefnakht, he has turned him into a formidable enemy, who must be fought with every last bit of our energy.'

The fat man had dreaded hearing these words. 'Majesty, I hope you aren't thinking of leaving Napata at the head of an army? Your presence here is vital, and you have no right to risk your life.'

'I agree with Otoku,' declared Queen Abilah. 'The disturbances in Middle Egypt have taken on a worrying dimension because of Nemrod's treason, but swift intervention by our troops based in Thebes should be sufficient to re-establish order.'

'I shall strengthen them with an army commanded by Puarma and Lemersekny,' decreed Piankhy. 'Their mission is to liberate the towns of Henen-nesut and Khmun, to break up the enemy alliance and beat back the remnants of their army to the North.'

Otoku was relieved. By adopting this course of action, the king would remain in his capital city and leave it to his best troops to take care of ending a futile rebellion.

CHAPTER TWENTY-FOUR

Nemrod was delighted. Not only had he retained all his princely prerogatives but he had also been freed from all administrative cares. Nartreb and Yegeb were dealing marvellously with the affairs of the city, which they were carving up with real zest. No area of public life escaped them, and their methods were even more brutal than those they had used in Henen-nesut.

On Tefnakht's instructions, these two damned souls had transformed Khmun into a giant barracks where all the inhabitants, from children to old men, worked in one way or another for the army. Those who had fought in the army of liberation had to be pampered, and their smallest need satisfied. It did not worry Yegeb or Nartreb that mothers had to prostitute themselves or that ten-year-old children had to carry heavy baskets of food. The demands of the war economy were not open to discussion. Now that all the useless mouths had been dispensed with, the whole of Khmun was available for use in battle.

Tefnakht held a meeting of his council of war in the palace dining-hall. Present were Nemrod, Yegeb, Nartreb, the Libyan chiefs, Prince Peftau and Daybreak—her presence was resented by most of the participants, but one did not criticize the general's decisions.

'Have we any news from Thebes?' asked Tefnakht.

'Yes, my lord,' said Yegeb eagerly. 'We have more and more supporters there. Our seizure of Khmun showed them that your reconquest has really begun, and that the hope of reunifying the Two Lands is not an impossible dream.'

'Have you infiltrated spies into the city?'

'We have one or two informants we can trust. They have to act with extreme caution, for Thebes is still trumpeting its allegiance to Piankhy.'

'What have they told you?'

'The Black Pharaoh has just reacted by sending an army to Thebes.'

Everyone's face fell. Up to now, the Libyans' victories had been swift and easy. The prospect of finding themselves up against formidable Nubian warriors, with their legendary cruelty, did not exactly fill them with delight.

'What if we negotiated?' ventured Prince Peftau, in a quavering voice.

'What are you suggesting?' asked Tefnakht.

'My lord, you have conquered two great cities and you are now the master of Middle Egypt. If Piankhy recognizes that, why go further? An exchange of envoys will ratify this new situation.'

'You don't understand why I'm fighting, Peftau. I'm not interested in adding to my own lands. What I want is for Egypt to be united as she used to be, a nation which will once again become the most important empire in the world. Piankhy will negotiate with me when his troops have been wiped out and he believes himself condemned to solitude and misery, in a Nubia which Egypt will once again control and whose wealth she will exploit. Not that I shall make the mistake of allowing the usurper to live. A Nubian rebel deserves no lenience.'

Prince Peftau did not dwell on the matter.

Much to everybody's surprise, Daybreak began to speak. 'If Piankhy has sent an army,' she observed, 'it is not to negotiate or to make peace. He will certainly have chosen his best men to lead his Theban troops into battle.'

'Surely we aren't going to take lessons in strategy from a female,' protested one of the chiefs.

'Why not? This lesson seems excellent,' replied Tefnakht.

'Well then, let's push on to Thebes and attack it,' said the chief.

'Idiot!' cut in Daybreak. 'We'd come up against Piankhy's troops, and we can't be sure what the outcome of the battle would be. On the contrary, let's wait for them to come to us. They will have to divide their forces. Only part of their army will try to retake Khmun, so as not to strip Thebes of protection and leave it defenceless. It is up to us to prepare by deploying our troops in a way which will guarantee us victory. Then, and only then, will we head for Thebes, whose ability to resist will have been considerably weakened.'

The chiefs grumbled, and some shrugged their shoulders, but many had to admit that the young woman's analysis was perceptive.

'My lord, why did you have the walls of Khmun destroyed?' asked Akanosh.

'To make the enemy believe that the town has been laid waste and that they can enter it easily. Once inside, Piankhy's soldiers will be caught in a trap.' The general unrolled a papyrus scroll on which was drawn a detailed map of the region. 'The rest of his Theban troops will be caught in a pincer movement on the plain, and we will lay several

118

ambushes along the hills so as to cut off any chance of retreat. Piankhy knows nothing of the art of war—he believes that any battle can be won by sheer brute force. The time has come to teach him a sound lesson.'

'Isn't there a risk that the people will rise up against us?' asked Akanosh.

'Why on earth are you worried about that?' asked Tefnakht, astonished.

'Because we treat them so harshly.'

'This is war, Prince Akanosh. Any sign of weakness would incite the civilians to disobedience. My two advisers are doing excellent work.'

A faint smile played about Yegeb's lips. 'Thanks to us,' he said, 'the common people feel governed and protected. After all, what do we ask of them? Only that they obey Tefnakht and give him their trust—that's all. And they know we are working for their own good, even if at first they don't understand the sacrifices we demand.'

Akanosh challenged the hypocrite with a hard stare, but did not dare utter the criticisms that gnawed at his heart.

'Can anyone suggest a different plan?' asked Tefnakht.

The only reply was silence.

'Then we shall begin intensive training. The different divisions of the army will be trained at the locations where they will fight, according to the plans I shall show you. On the day of the battle, I shall tolerate no hesitation. Now, let's get to work.'

*　　　*　　　*

Nartreb was chewing a papyrus stalk, Yegeb was

119

doing his accounts.

'We're starting to get rich, my friend,' said Yegeb. 'Thanks to the powers Tefnakht has granted us, we are legally and discreetly making ourselves a charming little fortune. Houses, land, consignments of clothing, sandals and crockery—when we attack the country areas, I'm hoping to get my hands on entire flocks. This war is a lovely war!'

'As long as it continues,' commented Nartreb, 'and as long as the fortunes of war smile upon us.'

'I've paid the officers at Henen-nesut and Khmun handsomely to obey Tefnakht blindly. As long as he is victorious, they'll ask no questions. All a soldier expects are clear orders and good pay. If he has those, he'll kill without a moment's thought.'

'I can't help wondering whether all our allies genuinely want this victory.'

'You're thinking of Prince Akanosh, aren't you?' said Yegeb.

'I have the feeling that he'd be glad to see the war end, and that he doesn't approve of our way of running a town.'

'You're right, Nartreb. That man Akanosh could become a hindrance.'

'Do you want me to take action—in my own way?'

'No, a violent death would make the other chiefs suspicious of Tefnakht, and a split would appear in the alliance. I have a better idea: we'll set a trap for him.'

Nartreb rubbed his pudgy feet with an unguent made from acacia leaves, zizyphus leaves, Nubian earth, chrysocolla and the interior of a freshwater shell. The counsellor detested walking, which inflamed his big toes.

'Daybreak is getting above herself,' he complained. 'If we let her go on like this, Tefnakht will relegate us to the second rank and will end up forgetting us—perhaps even getting rid of us altogether.'

'I hate women,' said Yegeb sourly. 'All they ever do when they leave their bedrooms and kitchens is cause chaos. When Tefnakht is king, we should advise him to pass a law forcing them to be veiled from head to foot, give up working and stay mewed up in their houses.'

'An exellent idea, Yegeb! While we're waiting, we must prevent this ambitious woman from becoming queen—without setting Tefnakht against us.'

'It won't be easy, my friend, but we'll succeed.'

CHAPTER TWENTY-FIVE

Good weather, a powerful current, swift boats and excellent pilots: all the conditions had combined to favour an easy journey. In just twenty days, the army commanded by Lemersekny and Puarma reached its first destination, Thebes, 'the Powerful One', city of Amon.

To avoid having to talk to each other, the two officers had not travelled in the same boat. Yet the Black Pharaoh had ordered them to take joint command and to implement very precise plans which would end Tefnakht's offensive. Lemersekny had objected that conditions on the ground might make it necessary to modify the plans, but Puarma

121

had promised the king to be his sword-arm and to refrain from taking any personal initiative.

If there had not been many fine battles to look forward to, Lemersekny would happily have knocked Puarma senseless with his acacia-wood arm. But he had managed to control himself, and between Napata and Thebes he had calmed down somewhat, thanks to the passionate embraces of two young Nubian girls he had secretly stowed away on board, contrary to regulations. The beauties were so happy at the prospect of becoming dancers in an ale-house in the great Southern city that they lent themselves enthusiastically to all the hero's fantasies.

As they approached the town, army boats barred the river. The Nubian flotilla hove to. For a moment, Lemersekny thought that Tefnakht had taken Thebes and that he was going to have to stage a fight, one against thousands. But the presence of a Nubian officer in the prow of the flagship reassured him.

Puarma did not want to leave the privilege of this first contact to his rival, and joined him by jumping from one boat to another.

'A rather strange welcome, don't you think?' he said to Lemersekny.

'Are your archers in position?'

'We are at Thebes, and—'

'Tell them to be ready, *idiot*! We're at war, remember, and anything could happen at any moment.'

Puarma was annoyed, but gave the order anyway.

The Nubian officer looked the new arrivals up and down. 'Identify yourselves.'

'Lemersekny, captain of infantry, and this is my colleague Puarma, captain of archers.'

'I have orders to take you to the temple at Karnak.'

'What on earth for?' protested Lemersekny. 'We're soldiers, not priests. We wish to see the garrison commander immediately.'

'The Wife of Amon commands here. She has given me an order, and I am carrying it out.'

Lemersekny was ready to draw his sword, but Puarma laid a hand on his wrist, and said, 'Very well, we will follow you.'

The two captains were taken aboard a heavy warship which carried a hundred sailors.

'Don't ever do that again,' Lemersekny told Puarma, 'or I'll break your arm.'

'It was for your own good, idiot. You're supposed to fight our enemies, remember, not our friends.'

The sight of Karnak quelled their bickering. They were astounded by their first glimpse of the immense sacred dwelling-place of Amon-Ra, King of the Gods, which was enclosed within a high wall behind which could be seen the tips of obelisks covered in gold. The temple at Napata was certainly imposing, but this one exceeded anything the imagination could conjure up. For centuries, the pharaohs had enlarged and embellished it; it bore the name 'That which Fixes the Sites of All Temples'. Life had appeared for the first time in the form of a little island emerging from the primordial ocean and, since then, the breath of Amon had never ceased to make its presence felt by swelling the sails of boats.

'Well I'll be damned! What a fine fortress it

would make!' exclaimed Lemersekny.

Puarma's eyes were fixed on the twin towers of the main gateway, which symbolized at once the mountains of West and East, and the goddesses Isis and Nephthys. Between them, and thanks to them, the sun was reborn each morning. 'It was the gods who built Karnak,' he murmured, 'not men.'

A shaven-headed priest led Piankhy's emissaries to a side door in the curtain wall, where a stern-faced ritualist took their names and asked them, 'Have you been with a woman in the last three days?'

'Of course not,' lied Lemersekny. 'We've come from Napata by boat. All we had on board were soldiers.'

'In that case, you may cross this threshold.'

'We were sent by the pharaoh to fight the Libyans, and there is no time to lose.'

'Follow me.'

Lemersekny let out an exasperated sigh: they were in Karnak, and would have to put up with the priests' whims. Very slowly, which irritated Lemersekny still more, the priest led his visitors towards the sacred lake. Puarma was fascinated by the splendour of the coloured temples, which seemed to fit inside each other like boxes, while Lemersekny allowed himself to be enchanted by the sweet perfumes, which reminded him of exquisite mistresses. The size of the lake stunned the two officers. Hundreds of swallows were flying over the blue-tinged water, on which the priests floated miniature boats on festival days.

'Take off your clothes,' ordered the priest.

'You're allowing us to swim?' asked Lemersekny.

'You must purify yourselves.'

'We've no intention of becoming priests.'

'The rule demands that anyone admitted to the temple, even for a short time, must be purified. Undress, walk slowly into the lake down the stone staircase, enter the water, remain there without moving for a few seconds and collect your thoughts, while directing your spirit towards the Light.'

'I'm keeping my sword,' Lemersekny announced.

'Out of the question: all weapons must be left at the gateway to the temple.'

'Come on,' urged Puarma.

When Lemersekny took off his rough shirt, the priest could not hide his astonishment.

'A funny kind of arm, eh?' said the captain. 'Before we left Napata, I had the wooden frame reinforced with metal, and the master chariot-maker coated the whole thing in resin for me.'

Naked, the two soldiers purified themselves in the sacred lake. Then they were robed in dazzlingly white linen kilts, shaved and perfumed with incense.

'Before God,' the priest urged them, 'do not boast that you possess power. Without him, the arm is deprived of strength. It is God who makes a weak man strong; it is he who enables a single man to vanquish a thousand.'

Now that they had become 'pure priests', members of the lowest rank of the priesthood, Lemersekny and Puarma were invited to pour a little holy water on to the foodstuffs deposited on the altars, and to recite a ritual text addressed to Amon: 'Show us the path; permit us to fight in the shadow of your power.'

'Now,' said the priest, 'you may enter the great

125

Hall of Pillars.'

It took their breath away. The Hall had been built by Seti I and Ramses II. The pillars resembled gigantic stone papyrus stalks, on which coloured scenes were painted, showing the pharaoh making offerings to the gods. Tiny openings allowed rays of light to pass through the enormous stone slabs which formed the ceiling.

In the centre of one of these shafts of light, Lemersekny saw an apparition: a young woman dressed in a long white robe with shoulder straps, her breasts covered with a pale yellow shawl.

'A goddess,' he stammered. 'It's a goddess!'

CHAPTER TWENTY-SIX

'Are you Captain Lemersekny and Captain Puarma?' asked the apparition.

'Lemersekny, that's me! I have always respected the gods, especially the goddesses. But Puarma, he's an infidel. He's not worthy to listen to you.'

The apparition smiled. Her features were so delicate that Lemersekny felt intimidated.

'Are you the Wife of Amon?' Puarma asked.

'No, only her assistant. Her Majesty is gravely ill and no longer leaves her bedchamber. So she asked me to welcome you and to question you before you meet your colleagues.'

'Question us? What about?'

'Please, come with me.'

The beautiful priestess guided the two officers to the Wife of Amon's temporal dwelling, which comprised a shrine, private apartments and scribes'

126

offices. It was into one of these last that she showed her guests.

Bewitched, Lemersekny could not take his eyes off her. 'What is your name?'

'Marjoram.'

'Are you married?'

'Neither the Wife of Amon nor the priestesses who serve her may marry. Are you interested in religious matters, Captain Lemersekny?'

'Passionately.'

'I have sad news for you: the commander of the military base at Thebes died four days ago.'

'That's tough for him. Who's his replacement?'

'That is what the Wife of Amon wants to know as quickly as possible, for she is greatly concerned about the security of Thebes. Since your arrival was announced, the whole town has been waiting to know which of you is to take command of the troops.'

Lemersekny and Puarma looked at each other, lost for words.

'We have the same rank,' said Puarma.

'The infantry is the oldest and most traditional of the armed services,' argued Lemersekny. 'So—'

'The corps of archers contains only handpicked soldiers,' Puarma objected. 'So—'

'The Wife of Amon,' said Marjoram, annoyed by their wrangling, 'wants to know what orders Pharaoh gave you.'

'We were to work together and place ourselves under the orders of the Theban commander,' said Puarma.

*   *   *

127

Lemersekny and Puarma debated for over an hour, throwing endless specious arguments in each other's faces.

'Why don't we simply carry out Piankhy's orders?' suggested the latter. 'He decrees that we should share command—fair enough, let's do that.'

'Impossible.'

'We have no choice.'

Lemersekny had had enough of talking—he preferred action. 'Well, all right, but we will talk to the men together, on a strictly equal footing, and you are not to try to establish your authority at the expense of mine, on the grounds that you're an archer.'

'Let's make up for the temporary lack of a commander and fulfil our mission. Pharaoh will be grateful to us for doing so. If we don't, his anger will be terrifying.'

'At last you've come up with a persuasive argument. Basically you're right, Puarma. Let's make a joint effort to succeed. But leave the tactics to me—you aren't up to it.'

*   *   *

The soldiers billeted in Thebes were not easy to convince. First of all, they were grieved by their commander's death and demanded that they should wear mourning for several more days, with a bonus into the bargain; next, they knew Puarma and Lemersekny only by reputation and were suspicious of these new leaders; finally, they had become accustomed to a rather peaceful, comfortable life and hadn't the slightest desire to fight, particularly since Tefnakht was not threatening Thebes. The best solution, they concluded, was to wait for new orders from Napata. The spokesman for the troops, a junior officer, even presented a list of grievances relating to the quality of the food, uniforms and the number of days' leave.

Puarma was afraid Lemersekny might smash the spokesman's skull with his wooden arm, but the captain remained impassive.

*   *   *

Tefnakht caressed Daybreak's naked breasts very slowly. 'You're a sorceress. What did you do to enchant me like this?'

'It is you who have cast a spell on me, since I share your hopes. What task could be more exciting than to reconquer this country and make it as powerful as it used to be?'

Tefnakht had fallen in love with the young woman's body, stirringly curvaceous, naively passionate; he never tired of exploring it. Daybreak responded to his caresses, but she never stopped talking to him about his great project, which she had made her own with an all-consuming passion.

'Have you any children?' she asked him.

'At Sais, I had several women at my disposal, though I did not love any of them, and they gave me children. The women have remained in the North, but two of my sons who are old enough to fight are officers in my army. None of them is capable of succeeding me. After me, it is our son who will mount the throne.'

Daybreak took his face in her hands. 'I love you, Tefnakht. I love you because your heart is fired by a grand vision. But I do not want a child until you are Pharaoh and the Two Lands bow their heads before you.'

Her resolution impressed Tefnakht. She was not made of the same stuff as the other women he had known, and from time to time she almost frightened him.

'As you wish,' he said.

To thank him for his consent, she covered him in kisses, as fiercely as a lioness bent on devouring her prey. Tefnakht had little taste for playing the victim; he rolled her on to her back and regained the mastery.

Someone knocked at the bedchamber door.

'Who dares disturb me?' thundered Tefnakht.

'It's Yegeb, my lord. I have important news, very important.'

'Can't it wait?'

'I don't think it can.'

The general opened the door.

Yegeb bowed low. 'Our spy network has just informed us that the garrison commander at Thebes has died. Piankhy's army has arrived, but it is mired in confusion. The officers are at each other's throats, nobody can give clear orders and there will be no movement of troops before new instructions have been drawn up by Napata. Isn't this a wonderful opportunity?'

Tefnakht's eyes flashed. 'We'll attack Thebes from the Nile and inflict heavy losses on the garrison. Yes, the time has come!'

'We did agree another plan,' Daybreak reminded him. She was indifferent to the presence of Yegeb, who stared at the young woman's body with a mixture of interest and disgust.

130

'We must learn to adapt to circumstances,' said Tefnakht. 'We can take a decisive advantage! The first wave of attackers, commanded by one of the chiefs, shall set sail immediately.'

CHAPTER TWENTY-SEVEN

The garrison was slumbering soundly. Since the commanding officer's death, training had been suspended, and the soldiers were sleeping late.

But one soldier, Ricin, had suffered from insomnia ever since he had witnessed his best friend's death in a bloody fight against the 'sand-travellers', the Bedouin plunderers of the desert; and he did not appreciate this extended sleep as much as his comrades did. He preferred exercise. Tiring himself out physically chased away his bad memories. Ricin lay with his eyes wide open, staring up at the wooden ceiling of the barrack block.

Suddenly, as though it had been sawn in half, a roof timber gave way and fell into the dormitory. Two palm-tree trunks suffered the same fate, jolting the soldiers into wakefulness and spreading panic.

'Listen to me!' roared Lemersekny, who was perched on the roof with Puarma and twenty archers. 'Get out of your pits this minute, and put on your armour. Roll-call on the parade ground. Anyone who disobeys will be executed for insubordination.'

The same scene was repeated in every barrack block, and by the end of the morning the Theban garrison was on a war footing.

'You see,' Lemersekny told Puarma, 'you just have to know how to talk to them. Those little lads needed to be woken up, that's all. Now it's up to you to take them in hand. I'm off up north with a well-equipped little fleet of ships.'

'That's very risky.'

'It's the only way to uncover any traps laid by the advance guard of Tefnakht's army.'

*   *   *

Puarma was worried sick. He bitterly regretted accepting Lemersekny's proposition; he should never have allowed him to leave in sole command of several hundred sailors. An infantry captain commanding a naval force! It was bound to end in disaster.

And yet they had to do something. Piankhy had ordered the two captains to advance in battle formation, to engage Tefnakht in combat, to surround him and to capture him. They were to begin by destroying his boats, while at the same time guaranteeing the safety of Thebes.

Under Puarma's protection, Amon's sacred city was in no danger. As for the rest, everything depended on Lemersekny's luck.

The officer in charge of mail appeared before Puarma. 'I await your orders, Captain.'

'Has the messenger left for Napata?'

'First thing this morning, with a squad of archers. You can be certain that he will reach his destination safely.'

Puarma had drawn up a long report, omitting not one single detail. It was for Piankhy to take decisions based on the way the situation had evolved, and to send him his orders as quickly as possible.

'Make sure that another messenger is ready to leave. From today, there will be a constant traffic between Thebes and Napata.'

'Understood, Captain.'

The Wife of Amon was on the point of death. Puarma was the lone master of Thebes, and this unexpected responsibility terrified him. But he would defend the city to the last drop of his blood.

*　　*　　*

'Faster!' raged the Libyan chieftain, urging on the oarsmen. 'You're going to sleep, you good-for-nothing oafs! Soon we shall be in Thebes, and you will have the most beautiful girls in Egypt and all the wine you can drink.'

These alluring prospects had no effect at all. The civilians from Henen-nesut and Khmun, who had been forced into service, were in no hurry to face Piankhy's troops and die in a battle they had no wish to fight in.

Consequently, Tefnakht's attacking fleet had progressed much more slowly than expected. Killing the Egyptian oarsmen was no answer, for no Libyan soldier would agree to replace them.

When the north wind rose, they could at last hoist the sails and travel more quickly. The chieftain, an old sand-traveller won over by the good living and softness of the Egyptian land, was rediscovering his killer instincts. He could already imagine himself setting fire to the Temple of Amon, raping the Wife of Amon and her priestesses, and emptying the sacred city of its treasures.

Tefnakht was a good general. By ordering this surprise attack, which would disrupt the enemy's defences, and in ensuring victory by deploying the greater part of his troops, he would win the war in a few weeks.

*   *   *

Lemersekny was enjoying his new position. Settled in a comfortable cabin, stretched out on a first-class bed, he ate grapes by the bunch and sipped sweet beer, cool and slightly sparkling, just the way he liked it.

The navy had its good points, and war was truly the best thing life could offer a man. While poor old Puarma was worrying himself senseless, trying to organize the Theban defences, he—the warrior with the wooden arm—was sailing along the Nile.

When they approached Khmun, it would be time to think about Tefnakht. That cowardly Libyan would never dare venture beyond Middle Egypt.

Ricin, whom Lemersekny had chosen as his assistant, entered the cabin. 'Captain,' he said, 'it seems there are boats ahead.'

'Merchant vessels?'

'No, warships. And they're heading straight for us.'

'You must be mistaken, Ricin.'

'The lookout says there are at least twenty.'

Intrigued, Lemersekny left his cabin and walked up to the bow of the ship. Ricin was not mistaken. These were neither ferry-boats nor barges; they were indeed Libyan vessels, heading up the Nile in the direction of Thebes.

'Hmm,' he said, 'Tefnakht is more dangerous than I thought.'

'Are we to beat a retreat, sir?'

Lemersekny cast Ricin an indulgent look. 'How long is it since you fought, soldier?'

'A few years. At Thebes, things were pretty quiet.'

'Do you know Piankhy's reputation?'

'They say just speaking his name is enough to put the enemy to flight.'

'That's right. And you also know that Piankhy has ordered me to drive Tefnakht and his rebels northwards.'

'Yes, sir, but these rebel forces are big, much bigger than ours.'

'We shall fight as one against ten, but in the name of Piankhy. The Libyans have absolutely no chance.'

'Do you really think so?'

'Lemersekny never lies, soldier. Clear the decks for action: send the order to all our boats.'

'What tactics will we use?'

'The simplest: we're going to charge straight at them.'

*   *   *

The Libyan chieftain could not believe his eyes. Spread out across the Nile, the Egyptian boats were heading straight for him. Lemersekny had set up veritable walls of shields across the bows, so the Libyan archers' volleys were futile. On the other hand, many of the archers died in the rain of stones, some round, some pointed, hurled by the

135

enemy slingshots.

These missiles also spread panic among the cattle and horses Tefnakht had had loaded on to the ships, the bullocks to provide food, the horses to pull the chariots, which would be assembled from prefabricated sections as soon as they landed. The terrified animals snapped their tethers, trampled on many of the soldiers and even made one of the boats capsize.

The Libyan chieftain did not know what to do. Some of his junior officers urged him to attack, others urged retreat. The oarsmen escaped from their benches and dived into the river.

Even before the prow of his ship had stove in the front of the Libyan vessel, Lemersekny, sword in hand, leapt on to the enemy craft with a yell and slit the throats of all those who got in his way. Inspired by his example, the footsoldiers of his force followed the path opened up by their captain.

CHAPTER TWENTY-EIGHT

'That's our first objective achieved,' declared Lemersekny proudly. 'All the Libyan boats heading for Thebes have been destroyed. There were no survivors, and my losses were negligible. The Northern princes have just suffered their first defeat.'

'You're quite a fellow,' acknowledged Puarma, who had just rejoined him, 'but that was only a minor skirmish. Any booty?'

'Weapons, provisions, wine jars.'

'We must send everything to Thebes.'

'What about our share?'

'Piankhy has forbidden it.'

The two officers had met again in the south of the Province of the Hare, some distance from its capital, Khmun. As soon as he received Lemersekny's message, Puarma had set off with the rest of the army to continue carrying out the Black Pharaoh's orders.

'Tell you what, colleague,' said Lemersekny in dulcet tones that did not suit him at all, 'I have a new plan.'

'What is it?'

'Attack Khmun and capture it. A surprise attack by all our troops would destroy the town's defences.'

'We'll forget about your eccentric behaviour on the Nile. But where Khmun is concerned, there's no question of improvising. We must follow the pharaoh's plan and we must keep to it.'

Lemersekny realized he was getting nowhere. How irritating these tactical wars always were!

*   *   *

In the audience chamber at the palace of Khmun, the members of Tefnakht's council of war could not hide their dismay.

'Is this information reliable?' asked Prince Akanosh.

'Our boats were sunk,' Tefnakht confirmed, 'and not one of the sailors in our assault force survived.'

'No one could have foreseen that we would come up against an enemy fleet,' protested Yegeb.

'I warned you this strategy was dangerous,' Daybreak reminded him.

137

Yegeb and Nartreb glared with loathing at her.

'We mustn't dwell on the past,' declared Tefnakht. 'This was merely a skirmish which proves—if proof were needed—that our enemies are determined.'

'There may still be time to negotiate,' suggested Prince Peftau.

'I shall never negotiate!' snapped Tefnakht. 'Are we going to lose heart at the first setback? We knew very well that capturing Thebes would be difficult and would take several battles. Piankhy will believe we are weaker than we really are, and will make mistakes he can't undo. The first will be when he falls into our trap at Khmun.'

'There's one important requirement,' opined Daybreak. 'This council of war must move its base further north, to Henen-nesut. When the Nubian troops pour into Khmun, believing the town is at their mercy, the fighting will be extremely fierce. We must not continue our march towards the South until the Nubian force has been wiped out.'

Nemrod paled. 'As Prince of Khmun, must I remain in my city?'

'That won't be necessary,' decided Tefnakht, 'since you are a member of my council. You will return there after our victory is won.'

Relieved, Nemrod gave his approval to the general's plan.

'In future,' Daybreak told Yegeb, 'don't give military advice. Confine yourself to running our cities.'

The young woman had expressed herself with the authority of a queen. Yegeb stared back at her, open-mouthed with astonishment.

Although it was a little low, the Nile flood could be considered satisfactory. The waters were already draining away from the high ground, and the old peasant, who managed a farm with twenty workers, had just ordered his men to prepare the swing-ploughs to till the earth before using bulls to trample in the seed.

His grandson, an eight-year-old urchin, grabbed his arm. 'Grandfather, who are those people on the path leading to the hillock? The ones with the spears?'

'Go back to the house, little one.'

The soldiers approached the farm. Their leader was a bearded, shaven-headed man with a fearsome face. The farmhands trembled as they formed a huddle behind their master.

'What do you want?' asked the farmer.

'I am Captain Lemersekny, and I order you to stop work immediately.'

'But we're just about to start the ploughing!'

'There will be no ploughing, sowing or harvest in the Province of the Hare for as long as it is occupied by the Northern army. Those are the orders of Piankhy, the pharaoh.'

'Are you planning to starve out the Northern forces?'

'They will surrender, and that will mean fewer deaths.'

'But what about us?' asked the farmer. 'How will we feed ourselves?'

'Pharaoh has made arrangements: you will be fed from the reserves held at Thebes. But don't try any tricks, whatever you do. Anyone who flouts the orders will be imprisoned immediately.'

'Is this war going to last long? Since the Libyans took over Khmun, they have been holding us to ransom! In the next village, they even burned two farms and forced their owners to become oarsmen. If the Black Pharaoh is a just man, let him bring peace again.'

'We're taking care of that, grandpa.'

*   *   *

It was dawn when the Libyan soldiers from Khmun entered the village. They had marched by night, at the head of a convoy of donkeys and porters carrying baskets. In the city of the god Thoth, food reserves were running low, and the leading citizens had complained about the mediocre quality of their recent banquets.

So the commanding officer of the garrison, on Nemrod's orders, had sent out several convoys like this one to replenish stocks of fruit and fresh vegetables. The peasants protested, but beating up the most vociferous was enough to silence the others. The Province of the Hare must recognize the need for a war effort in favour of its capital city.

Nemrod's soldiers marched past the enormous jars which held water for the village's use, and past the bread oven, and stopped opposite the headman's house, a whitewashed building decorated with delicately painted garlands of cornflowers.

A footsoldier banged on the door. 'Open up immediately!'

A grey cat hid itself in the thick grasses that bordered the roadway. The soldier thumped the door again, and a few moments later it creaked open.

'I was fast asleep. What's going on?'

'Wake up the peasants. We're requisitioning all foodstuffs.'

'Er . . . that's impossible.'

'Obey my order!'

'I give the orders here,' replied Lemersekny, smashing his wooden forearm down on the soldier's head.

Archers came out of the other houses; Nemrod's troops realized it was useless to fight. None of the traitor prince's food convoys returned to Khmun.

CHAPTER TWENTY-NINE

'There they are!' shouted a watchman.

The commander of the stronghold of Khmun immediately deployed his troops as Tefnakht had stipulated. The civilians were sent to their homes, where they closed their doors and windows, while footsoldiers and archers hid in every nook and cranny of the city, whose encircling walls had been partly demolished.

The Nubian army would be irresistibly attracted by the abandoned town. The commander's men must have patience and wait for the greater part of the attacking force to be caught in the trap, so that they could be wiped out. After such a defeat, the Black Pharaoh would give up trying to reconquer the Province of the Hare, which would become Tefnakht's forward base.

'Are they coming closer?' asked the commander.

'Yes,' said the watchman. 'Ah . . . wait. The leading rider is stopping.'

* * *

Puarma gazed at Khmun. At first glance, the city seemed to have suffered. Not a single archer stood on the ramparts. No doubt Nemrod's soldiers had fled north.

Lemersekny, who preferred walking to riding on the back of a quadruped with unpredictable reactions, was in a bad mood. To respect Piankhy's orders, they must neither attack by night nor throw all their available men into the battle, and yet they must wipe out Tefnakht's army and capture the rebel general. It was like trying to walk on ripe fruit without crushing it. In these conditions, how could you wage a serious war? And then there was Puarma, an obedient, zealous officer who was preventing him from acting as he wished.

Lemersekny walked over to join his colleague. 'A fine prize, don't you think?'

'Knowing you,' said Puarma, 'I'm sure there's only one thing you want: to attack Khmun and capture it.'

'You don't know me very well, bow-handler! My nose tells me it's a superb trap. You don't abandon a town as important as this. Tefnakht has ordered several hundred veterans to hide there and ambush us. But they've overdone it: there isn't even a single archer on the ramparts.'

'Whether you're right or wrong, it doesn't matter. The pharaoh ordered us to give it a wide berth and attack Henen-nesut.'

'All the better for us.'

Ignoring Khmun, the army continued northwards. Lemersekny could feel tiny pin-pricks all over his back. He didn't doubt that hundreds of pairs of eyes were watching their victims disappear into the distance.

*   *   *

Villages laid waste, houses burnt down, dead dogs, cats and little monkeys lying in the alleyways, lost children crying out for their mothers, old men dead from hunger, their bodies propped up against the wrecked wall of a farmstead . . . Lemersekny was used to the cruelties of war, but never had he witnessed such terrible sights. Puarma couldn't bear it and had to go off on his own, to weep in private. Even experienced soldiers were overwhelmed.

Lemersekny tapped Puarma on the shoulder. 'Come, we can't stay here. We must gather up the survivors and send them south.'

'Forgive me, but. . .'

'No need to apologize. A good soldier has no taste for this kind of slaughter.'

Puarma clenched his fists. 'If Tefnakht and his allies really are in Henen-nesut, we shall kill them! And the pharaoh will be proud of us.'

It was the same scene of desolation on the road leading to the city. Close to the river bank they saw burning ferry-boats, which Tefnakht's men had set alight. A passer-by explained to the two captains that the Northern armies were burning all the crops and destroying every single farm, in order to prevent the Nubian army feeding itself and moving about easily.

'It's not going to be easy,' commented Lemersekny. 'If the enemy forces have all gathered at Henen-nesut, they'll outnumber us.'

'Piankhy has given us a mission, and we are going to accomplish it.' Puarma's warlike rage was a pleasure to hear.

'Agreed, bowman! But let me do the planning. I've no wish to die.'

                    *   *   *

When he emerged from the room where the council of war had just met, Akanosh was in pensive mood. He had hoped that the reverse suffered by Tefnakht would be enough to persuade him to give up his plan of conquest, but he had been sorely mistaken.

Tefnakht had been scarcely weakened by the loss of his first wave of assault troops, and he had reinforced his army by bringing up reserve troops from the Delta. In falling back to Henen-nesut, the general was adopting an ingenious tactic, which consisted of luring his adversary towards him in order to annihilate him if, by some miracle, he had escaped from the trap of Khmun.

Tefnakht was right: Egypt must be reunified. But not this way! A population conquered by force would never love the tyrant who had made them suffer, and sooner or later they would rise up against him. Unfortunately, the general listened only to his two advisers, Yegeb and Nartreb, because by using corruption they had allowed him to form a coalition and become its leader.

As Akanosh walked into his private apartments, an old man with sunburnt skin and frizzy hair

144

dropped an empty pitcher on the floor. It fell near to him, shattering into a thousand pieces.

'Forgive me, my lord, I could have hurt you.' Suddenly, the man lowered his voice to a whisper. 'I must speak with you, my lord. Order me to bring you fresh water.'

Intrigued, Akanosh did so.

When the man came back, carrying a beautiful pitcher decorated with lilies, the prince and his wife received him.

'My lord, I must speak with you alone.'

'I have no secrets from my wife. Explain yourself, or leave.'

'Can anyone hear us?'

Akanosh's wife checked that no indiscreet ear could overhear the conversation.

'I'm working as a water-carrier,' revealed the man, 'but I was sent by Piankhy. I have taken these risks to meet you, because we must act, and quickly. With your help, Prince Akanosh, my mission is to burn down the warehouses where Tefnakht's chariots are kept. Without them, he will feel so vulnerable that he will give up the fight and return to Sais.'

'I am neither a traitor nor an ally of Piankhy.'

'I know that, Prince. But, like Pharaoh, you wish to stop the massacre of the population. Tonight I shall station myself near the warehouses with a dozen men. If you have the guards relieved by soldiers from your own tribe, we can make this fire look like an accident, and peace will return to the region. Act now, I beg of you.'

'You belong to the Baksim tribe, don't you?' asked Akanosh's wife. 'The tribe closest to Piankhy?'

'That is true. We enjoy his trust and we try to show that we are worthy of it. I must go. Until tonight, Prince.'

Akanosh looked at the bows and daggers tattooed on his arms. 'I can't remain idle,' he decided.

'Tonight,' his wife objected, 'you will sleep in my arms.'

'No, I—'

'It's a trap, my darling. This man is a spy, and he's trying to find out if you intend to betray Tefnakht.'

'How can you be sure?'

'Because the Baksim tribe doesn't exist.'

CHAPTER THIRTY

'Disappointing,' commented Yegeb, massaging his swollen ankles with a salve made from wheat flour, fatty meat, aromatic galingale and honey. 'Are you sure our man carried out the scheme properly?'

'I'm sure,' replied Nartreb irritably. 'He sensed that Akanosh was ready to betray Tefnakht. But the prince didn't go to the warehouses that night.'

'Because he knows we set a trap for him, he is now utterly powerless. He knows he'll be watched day and night, so he won't be able to communicate in any way with the enemy. In the end, the result isn't too bad.'

A servant dashed into the advisers' room. 'It's the enemy—the enemy is at the gates of Henen-nesut!'

Lemersekny ate his fifth raw onion as he stared fixedly at the fortress. 'A fine beast. But,' he concluded, 'too big for us.'

'Piankhy ordered us to take it,' said Puarma emphatically.

'He didn't know the place. To the left our opponents hold the canal; to the right the river is blocked by their boats; and in the centre we have this stronghold, with hundreds of Libyan archers on its ramparts. How many more soldiers are there inside? If Tefnakht is there, his troops will feel they are invincible.'

Henen-nesut was three days' march south of Memphis, and ruled a prosperous region. A gap in the hills which ran along the edge of the desert had allowed a canal to be constructed, linking the Nile to the rich province of Faiyum. Its principal shrine, protected by a ram god, held a pool containing the primordial water from which life had first appeared.

The softness of the countryside and the little breeze which made the Nile waters sparkle did not inspire thoughts of battle.

'What's the matter, Lemersekny?' asked Puarma. 'Has that legendary courage deserted you?'

'I like being a living legend,' retorted Lemersekny. 'And when my wooden arm itches as if it were still made of flesh, I know I'm on the wrong track.'

'Surely we aren't going to turn back?'

'There's more than one way of attacking, Puarma.'

147

'What do you mean?'

'Tefnakht is convinced we're going to launch an assault on the city, so he has stationed his best men there. On the Nile side, we haven't enough boats to break his blockade. On the other hand, we can take the canal.'

'Which is the least important objective.'

'I agree, but even a minor gain should provoke a reaction. And I intend to exploit that reaction.'

*   *   *

Prince Peftau was standing at the top of the central tower in Henen-nesut, behind perforated wooden panels which provided protection against enemy arrows.

A broad smile spread across his face. 'Aren't my town's fortifications impressive, general?'

'You've done well,' Tefnakht acknowledged.

'Piankhy thought they would prevent you taking my city. Today, those precautions are turning against him. The Nubians are helpless. Their miserable army doesn't know what to do next.'

'They're withdrawing,' observed Daybreak. She was dignified, almost austere, in her long, plain red dress.

Peftau's shrill, nervous laugh assaulted the young woman's ears. 'They're afraid—those famous Nubian warriors are scared to death! We must spread the news throughout Egypt. It will destroy Piankhy's reputation for invincibility and his name will no longer frighten anybody.'

'Look,' urged Daybreak. 'They're heading east.'

'That's stupid,' said Peftau. 'Why head for the hills?'

'You're the stupid one,' snarled Tefnakht. 'They're going to attack the canal.'

'Even so, my lord,' the old dignitary stammered, 'its loss wouldn't matter much.'

'Since the Nubians are happy with such small prey,' thought Tefnakht, 'the moment has come to strike a hammer-blow at them.'

'We're going to mount a raid,' he announced.

*   *   *

Puarma's archers were remarkably successful. Over half their arrows struck the enemy in either the head or the chest. A single volley was enough to scatter the Libyan guard, which was made up of inexperienced young recruits who immediately panicked. Puarma took on the job of shooting their officer in the throat as he tried to regroup his soldiers, who were on the verge of flight.

Lemersekny's soldiers wiped out the last of the Libyans with spear-thrusts, their bodies falling into the canal. Meanwhile, Lemersekny himself made no move; he thought it beneath him to get involved in such an insignificant scuffle.

Suddenly, his attention sharpened. 'There you are,' he said. 'They've just opened the great gate of the city and they're sending out a raiding-party to cut us to pieces.'

Puarma looked towards Henen-nesut. 'It looks as if they're not using chariots. Just footsoldiers.'

'Are your archers in position?'

'In the bushes, on either side of the plain.'

'I'll deal with the frontal assault. As soon as I sound the retreat, it's your turn.'

The Libyans wore their hair divided into three sections, with a thick central pony-tail coiled at its base, and a plume of two tall, curled feathers. Tattoos decorated their chests, bellies, arms and wrists, and with their criss-crossed shoulder-belts and phallic sheaths they were fit to terrify any foe—except Lemersekny and his Nubian warriors.

Wielding a short, light, double-bladed axe, the captain sliced necks and forearms with such speed that almost single-handedly he slowed down the advance of the Libyans as they came out of Henennesut. With its hollow back, fashioned with three jutting tenons sunk into the heft and solidly bound in place, Lemersekny's axe caused havoc, while his acacia-wood arm shattered skulls.

Once the effect of surprise was gone, the Libyans, who were commanded by a chieftain who had got drunk on palm alcohol before leading the offensive, resumed their march forward.

'Retreat!' yelled Lemersekny.

The captain protected his men for a few moments as they ran towards the right-hand side of the plain, then followed suit. The Libyans pursued with shouts of triumph. They were easy prey for Puarma's bowmen, and the remainder of the army struck at the Libyans' left flank, breaking it in two, while Lemersekny and his best men, racing back along the enemy column at top speed, cut off all attempts at retreat. The Libyans' raid ended in crushing defeat.

But Lemersekny did not want to leave it at that, and he pressed his advantage. 'To the Nile,' he ordered.

Archers and footsoldiers hurled themselves into an assault on the Northern boats, which were simultaneously attacked by the Nubian flotilla. Piankhy's men outnumbered the enemy; and, excited by their success, they easily won the day and burned Tefnakht's boats.

'Now for Henen-nesut,' declared Puarma.

'No,' objected Lemersekny. 'Look.'

The city walls were intact and bristling with archers, and the neighing of horses could be heard, ready to pull the chariots massed to the north of the town. The major part of Tefnakht's army was intact.

'All we've done is scratch them,' said Lemersekny.

CHAPTER THIRTY-ONE

Piankhy and Abilah sat in the shade of a canopy supported on little columns of gilded wood, close to an ornamental lake where they bathed whenever the heat became unbearable. They were playing the game of dogs and jackals. Thirty holes had been bored into the smooth surface of a small sycamore table; in these, the opponents placed little pointed sticks, each tipped with the head of a dog or a jackal.

The king and queen were both naked, but their skin was coated with moringa oil and perfumed with *kyph*i, their daughter's wonderful creation. They had made love in the delicious waters of the pool, and were now locked in serious competition.

After a brilliant manoeuvre, Piankhy was

151

convinced that his jackals were going to beat his wife's dogs. But, distracted by Abilah's wild beauty, he was finding it harder and harder to concentrate. Feeling his gaze slide over her like a caressing hand, the magnificent Nubian woman began to move her body, almost imperceptibly, in a way calculated to distract her opponent even more.

She stretched out her hand very slowly to the sycamore table, moved a dog with a narrow, aggressive head, and took five jackals.

'You win,' conceded Piankhy. 'But you cheated.'

'Cheated? Me?'

'You cast a spell on me.'

'Do the rules of the game forbid that?'

The Black Pharaoh embraced his wife as though confessing his love to her for the first time. 'Like every Queen of Egypt, you are a great enchantress. Your eyes know the secret of worlds that I cannot reach.'

'You are too modest, Majesty,' said Abilah. 'After all, it's you who hold the power.'

'May it serve me to protect Nubia from all danger.'

'What have we to fear?'

Piankhy's eyes darkened. 'This generous sun hides dark shadows.'

A little monkey scuttled to the top of a palm tree, and a plump ginger and white cat slunk under a clump of hibiscus. Someone was coming.

'It is I, Majesty,' announced Cool-Head. He was carrying a heavy box filled with papyrus scrolls. 'I have Puarma's reports.'

* * *

152

On the orders of Pharaoh and his Great Royal Wife, and in their presence, Cool-Head revealed the reports' contents to the members of the Grand Council.

'Captains Puarma and Lemersekny met very strong opposition in Middle Egypt. In accordance with His Majesty's orders, they have saved and protected Thebes, but have not attacked Thoth's sacred city, Khmun, whose prince, Nemrod, betrayed Pharaoh's trust. However, they have tried to retake the town of Henen-nesut, which also fell into enemy hands because of Peftau's defeat. The city has been transformed into a fortress, and our experts believe that it is currently impregnable.'

'Then the army's mission is a failure,' said Kapa, head of the council, stunned.

'The situation is more serious than we had supposed,' admitted the scribe. 'Tefnakht is a true war leader, and he has massed a large number of soldiers to the north of Henen-nesut, whose city walls are defended by skilled archers. So Lemersekny and Puarma must be content with harassing the enemy and barring his way to the South.'

'Can Tefnakht still attack Thebes?' asked Kapa.

'No, Thebes isn't at risk. Our troops have closed off the Southern border and the Province of the Hare, and the garrison in the city of Amon is on permanent alert. In reality, Tefnakht cannot go any further.'

'And we can't go any further North,' Kapa pointed out bitterly. 'Pharaoh's prestige is sullied— he no longer rules his own country.'

'Puarma and Lemersekny are not relaxing their efforts, but they need to handle their men carefully

153

and not cut themselves off from their bases by undertaking too risky a venture. According to Lemersekny, whose bravery and experience are beyond doubt, it is impossible to wipe out Tefnakht's forces.'

A heavy silence followed this declaration.

Then Queen Abilah said, 'How are the people of Middle Egypt being treated?'

The scribe looked uncomfortable. 'Majesty, I don't . . .'

'Tell me the truth, Cool-Head.'

'The armies of the North are at war. They pay no heed to the well-being of those they regard as their subjects. Our troops are trying to come to the aid of the most vulnerable, but many villages have been destroyed and hundreds of innocent people have died.'

'Egypt is sinking into chaos,' declared Kapa. 'There is no justice, no safety, no respect for others, only hideous violence and misfortune, creeping like a snake.'

'We should stop endangering our soldiers unnecessarily,' recommended fat Otoku, 'and build a chain of forts to the north of Thebes. Let's accept that Middle Egypt is lost, and learn lessons from our defeat.'

'Piankhy is Pharaoh of Upper and Lower Egypt,' protested old Kapa. 'He must not abandon more than half his lands to a vicious rebel who is suffocating their people under the yoke of pitiless tyranny.'

'That is a very noble vision, but it is out of date, and I am the first to lament that fact,' said Otoku gravely. 'The golden age is over and no one will ever bring it back. Let's stop dreaming and face the facts. Piankhy rules a kingdom comprising Nubia and Upper Egypt. Tefnakht has seized the rest of the country and he won't let go of it. Let us have only one goal: to preserve our sacred values, our joy in life and our peace. Consequently, let us negotiate and recognize the new border which has been established by these battles.'

Piankhy rose to his feet. Abilah knew from his posture and the look in his eyes that he was as furious as an enraged panther.

The king's voice filled the audience chamber. 'I utterly reject the injustice and barbaric demands of him who considers himself to be the strongest man in Egypt. Tefnakht has violated the law of Ma'at, and he will continue to violate it unless I take action. When I sent the two captains to wipe out the Northern army, I hoped that they would swiftly bring an end to this insurrection. But what have our soldiers done? They have left the enemy almost unscathed, and reinforced his determination to harm us. As true as I live and am loved by Ra, as true as my father Amon guides me, I shall go into Egypt myself and put an end to Tefnakht's pernicious plotting. I shall make him renounce warfare for ever, and the Northern princes shall feel my iron fist!'

No one dared utter a word after the king had spoken. He swept out of the audience chamber on to the palace terrace, followed by Abilah.

'I know you don't agree with me,' he told her, 'but I no longer have the right to enjoy a selfish happiness while Egypt is in the grip of suffering. I truly hoped that Lemersekny and Puarma would spare me the need to leave Napata and take part in this battle myself. But I underestimated my

155

adversary, and I was sorely mistaken. Now, my heart is filled with anger against myself, my lack of foresight, my failure to think clearly. It was because of my weaknesses that Tefnakht thought he could conquer the Two Lands. It is up to me to relieve Egypt of the burden which weighs upon her—a burden for which I feel I am responsible.'

'You're wrong about Tefnakht,' said Abilah. 'The desire to conquer and destroy, to slake his thirst for power, is his only reason for living: nothing and no one could have made him turn back.'

'He will turn back. I swear it!'

'Piankhy—'

'No, Abilah. I must go, so that the law of Ma'at may live. If the pharaoh does not fulfil his first duty, happiness will disappear from this earth.'

'I'm not asking you to stay. I want to go with you.'

CHAPTER THIRTY-TWO

When the two armies clashed, the violence of the impact had been terrible and huge numbers of young men had been killed. That appalling vision haunted Prince Nemrod's dreams. The explosion of violence had shown him a world whose existence he had never suspected, a world where uncontrollable instincts were unleashed, instincts for which his noble upbringing had not prepared him.

A strange feeling crept over him: he missed his own town. He had dreamt of leaving it for Memphis, but now he longed to see its monuments,

156

its narrow streets, its houses. Locked away in Henen-nesut, he had left his people in the hands of a soldiery who thought of nothing but spilling blood and who, tomorrow, might destroy the ancient city of Thoth.

Nemrod went to Tefnakht's headquarters, but Yegeb barred his way.

'I'm sorry, Prince, but the general is very busy and—'

'Stand aside.'

'I assure you that—'

With unaccustomed firmness, Nemrod pushed the counsellor aside and opened the door to the office. The general had laid out a map of the region on which he had underlined in red the places under his control, and in black those which still obeyed Piankhy.

'I must talk to you,' said Nemrod urgently.

'Come in, Prince, and close the door behind you. This map is my most precious military secret.'

'Why am I not allowed to study it?'

A glimmer of surprise appeared in Tefnakht's dark eyes. 'Are you developing an interest in the art of war?'

'I wish to defend my town in person against Piankhy. Who but myself knows Khmun so perfectly? Since our trap did not work, I shall rebuild the section of the ramparts which we destroyed and have the walls reinforced.'

Tefnakht was sceptical. 'Your attitude is unexpected, Nemrod.'

'You brought me into this war, General, and the blood of its victims has tainted my sight. In my torment, a truth appeared to me: my city is my dearest possession.'

157

'If Piankhy counter-attacks, you will be in the front line.'

'I know the Black Pharaoh well: he'll never leave Napata. His men will continue to make no headway, and in the end they will establish a kind of frontier in the south of my province.'

'I shall break through it,' promised Tefnakht.

'You may count on my city and on my help, General.'

'Very well, Nemrod, go back to Khmun and turn it into an impregnable stronghold.'

*   *   *

Lemersekny was asleep under the stars. On either side of him lay a sandy-coloured dog which would alert him to the slightest danger. As he slept, as lightly as a wild creature, he dreamt of Nubia and his long, solitary treks in the grasslands. He had left to wage a joyous, open war but now he was becoming bogged down in a cruel, unending conflict.

Denied reinforcements from Thebes, which must maintain its defences at full strength, the Nubian army's only option was to safeguard its resources by restricting attacks to skirmishes that left the major part of Tefnakht's troops intact. The Nubians would retake a village they had liberated a fortnight earlier, but then have to withdraw, leaving it exposed to a Northern counter-attack. These comings and goings translated into an immobility which ate away at Lemersekny's morale. They were sinking ever deeper into a cesspool, into a situation that was neither war nor peace, without hope or future, and the poorest people were becoming even poorer.

What was the point of fighting if that was the only result you could expect? Lemersekny felt like resigning his commission and handing his sword back to the Black Pharaoh. Let younger, more committed soldiers take over and believe that the same sun would rise tomorrow.

The two dogs growled in unison. Lemersekny leapt up immediately, sword in hand.

'It's me, Puarma.'

'Why have you woken me up in the middle of the night?'

'Tefnakht's men are trying to force their way through and cross the border into the Province of the Hare.'

'Oh, is that all?' yawned Lemersekny.

'If they succeed, they'll strike at Thebes.'

'Next time, let me sleep. The detachment of men I've deployed will give them no chance of getting through.'

'What if you're wrong?'

'Sleep tight, Puarma.'

*   *   *

Nartreb was red-faced with anger. 'Useless cowards! You must punish them, my lord!'

Tefnakht's unattractive, bony face showed no sign of annoyance. 'How? All the members of the raiding-party—and you picked them yourself—are dead. They will have neither tomb nor funeral rites. What further punishment can I inflict upon them? You wanted to check the effectiveness of the enemy defences, and we've done precisely that. The border with the Province of the Hare cannot

159

be crossed.'

A rictus sneer of anger distorted Nartreb's moon-shaped face. 'At least we know . . . Piankhy has realized that attacking you was useless. He has taken up a defensive position.'

'If he still sees himself as Pharaoh of Upper and Lower Egypt, he will not long tolerate a situation which denies his sovereignty so blatantly.'

A questioning look came into the counsellor's small eyes. 'Do you think he'll intervene in person?'

'No,' said Tefnakht scornfully. 'The Black Pharaoh is too conceited to leave his Nubian capital, where he leads a happy life, worshipped by courtiers who heap flatteries upon him.'

'So what are you thinking about?'

'The expression of his anger: in other words, an attack on Khmun.'

Nartreb rubbed his pudgy fingers together. 'Yegeb has no faith in Prince Nemrod's loyalty—and neither have I.'

'Do you take me for an idiot? Loyalty is a notion invented by moralists who know nothing of the constraints of war. Like anyone else, Nemrod is ready to commit treason to safeguard his own interests, but his actions are influenced by love, his love for his city. He knows that Piankhy will never forgive his defection, so there remains only one solution open to him: he must turn Khmun into a fortress capable of resisting all attacks, and then defend it with every last bit of his strength. Nemrod the indecisive has become one of the pillars of my strategy.'

'My lord, do you wish me to order another raiding-party to cross the border into the Province

160

of the Hare?'

'These crude plans lead nowhere. Daybreak is right: you and Yegeb should confine yourselves to the management of the lands we control.'

The counsellor withdrew, quivering with rage.

Barefoot, the general's mistress silently approached her lover and laid her scented hands on his chest.

She said, 'Get rid of that man and his accomplice, Yegeb. They don't care a snap of their fingers for your destiny. All that interests them is increasing their own wealth.'

Tefnakht kissed her exceptionally slender fingers. 'Do you think I don't know that? Every king needs vermin like them to hunt down waverers and root out the stubborn. To keep their position and their privileges, Yegeb and Nartreb won't hesitate to use corruption or murder. That's why they are my most valuable helpers.'

CHAPTER THIRTY-THREE

The priest wore a panther-skin robe. 'Majesty,' he told Piankhy firmly, 'it is impossible.'

'Nevertheless, I must go.'

'And it will remain impossible, for as long as the stars do not favour you. If you pay no heed to them, your undertaking will be doomed to failure. We are the sons of the stars, and we must respect their message.'

'How long must I wait?'

'A few days, Majesty,' said the priest, 'until the new moon. When the moon, Horus's left eye, is in

161

harmony with your journey, Set the destroyer will not be able to break it into pieces, and the cosmic struggle between the two brothers will subside. Their strength and energy will become yours, and your power will grow with the waxing moon. Remember, Majesty, when the moon is restored and full, it is the image of a happy Egypt, complete with all its provinces.'

*   *   *

Piankhy himself checked his soldiers' equipment. He examined their kilts, sandals, belts, swords, scabbards, shields, bows and arrows, and rejected anything of poor quality. Then he turned his attentions to the Nubians' favourite food, fish which had been dried and stored in jars shaped like enormous sausages. In view of the length of the journey and the number of warriors he was leading into Egypt, fish-sellers and the makers of preserved foods were working day and night. Abilah, too, was far from idle. With her husband's agreement, she took charge of important matters concerning health and cleanliness, particularly the stocks of soap, which was made from the bark and flesh of the balanite, a tree rich in saponin. The whole of Napata was involved in preparations for Piankhy's departure.

As the day approached, Otoku lost his appetite. He badly wanted to talk to Piankhy, so he went out to look for him. He found him just about to enter a wheelwright's workshop, and, summoning up his resolution, the fat man accosted him.

'Majesty, I've been thinking.'

Piankhy feigned astonishment. 'What terrible

162

thing is troubling you, my friend?'

'Leaving here is madness. Napata needs you.'

'This city is rich and peaceful. What does it have to fear?'

'Either Tefnakht will kill you and invade Nubia, or you will stay in Thebes to govern Egypt and Nubia, so as to stave off another rebellion from the North. Either way, Napata will be abandoned.'

'What you say makes sense,' said the king, 'but my destiny does not belong to me. Amon chose me to be Pharaoh and he has given me much happiness. Today, when my country is suffering and in danger of disintegrating, what right have I to display ingratitude?'

'You could simply send another army.'

'Pharaoh's reputation has been tainted. Neither you nor the humblest of my subjects should tolerate that outrage.'

'But how will Napata survive without you?' asked the fat man despairingly.

'I am entrusting my capital to an official who loves it and will know how to safeguard it against any attack: to you, Otoku.'

'But Majesty—'

'You will make an excellent governor, as long as you consult old Kapa from time to time and take account of his opinions. There will be a constant stream of messengers travelling from Thebes to Napata and from Napata to Thebes, so I shall be able to guide your decisions. Does that reassure you?

'No, Majesty.'

'So much the better. You'll stay on your toes.'

Piankhy turned away and went into the workshop, where the wheelwright was hard at

163

work; he was a highly skilled expert craftsman, who specialized in making chariot wheels. The king knew that the outcome of the war might turn on a single detail: the solid construction of these wheels, which would be severely tested in battle.

The craftsman had perfected his own methods, and guarded the secret jealously. The positioning of the spokes, in particular, was astonishingly precise, and the choice of size of wheel was absolutely perfect. Piankhy had tried out several chariots on difficult terrain, and they had proved remarkably resilient.

'Are you nearly finished?' asked the king.

'Another two or three days, Majesty, and I shall deliver all the wheels you ordered.'

'Can you guarantee their quality?'

'On my life, Majesty! Pebbles, sand, soft ground, slopes—you will have victory on any type of ground. The Northern forces' wheels will break long before ours do, I promise you.'

Full of emotion, the craftsman gazed at the work he had just completed. 'What a beautiful thing a wheel is. It seems fixed, immobile, and yet it contains the secret of movement. All ways originate within it, and when it stops it remembers the roads it has travelled. But it is better that it should never travel at all, since it is used only in time of war.'

'Unless I fight the Northern armies, they will flood on towards Napata, and they will destroy what we have built. Thanks to you, I will prevent that disaster.'

Shepena was in her workshop, putting the finishing touches to a perfume as fresh as a spring dawn, when her father came in.

'Are you ready, daughter?' he asked.

164

'I wanted to forget that one day I would have to leave the land of my birth, my town and this place where I have known so many joys. Father, tell me you have abandoned your plan.'

'You know I have not.'

'Must I live at Thebes until the end of my days?'

'That is the rule, and the Wife of Amon must obey.'

Shepena was on the verge of tears. 'You are breaking my heart!'

Piankhy took her tenderly in his arms. 'I know, Shepena, but it is your own genius which led me to name you as the future sovereign of Thebes. You shall reign over Karnak, the temple of temples, and safeguard the sacred heart of our civilization.'

'This mission is terrifying!'

'No, daughter, it is exciting. As soon as you don the ritual robes of the Wife of Amon, the wisdom of those who have gone before you will become your most precious help. Have no fear, Shepena: you are the guardian of a force whose true nature you do not yet know. It will be revealed to you once you hold the office for which you were born.'

'I shall meditate in the temple until it is time to leave.' Shepena kissed her father's hands.

*　　　*　　　*

Piankhy left the town to gaze at the distant Pure Mountain and its peak, lit by the setting sun.

The sculptors had finished their work. Gebel Barkal would ensure that the seal of pharaonic rule was imprinted for ever in the heart of Nubia. Piankhy felt his throat tighten with emotion. Would he see it again one day, this mountain in whose

165

shadow the Temple of Amon had been built, as a far-off echo of the temple at Karnak? He had hoped never to leave it, and to grow old peacefully under its protection.

But destiny had suddenly taken on a new face and was making demands the Black Pharaoh could not escape. His happiness, the peaceful, regular succession of days, the spendour of his palace—none of this mattered any more in the face of the tragedy which was plunging the people of Egypt into despair.

Less than a pace from Piankhy's feet, the bushes moved. Out darted a black cobra, aggressive and ready to strike. The pharaoh had no time to react, for a mongoose, [The ichneumon species was nicknamed 'Pharaoh's rat'.] swifter than the reptile, sprang at it and sank its teeth into the serpent's neck.

The mongoose was one of the manifestations of Atum, the Creator. It sometimes allowed itself to be tamed, and would keep its owner's house free of lizards, rats and mice. By way of thanks, when it died the mongoose was mummified and its eternal body placed in a tiny sarcophagus.

Its fur bristling with anger, the little carnivore with the triangular snout and the long, flexible tail knew all the right fighting moves to avoid being bitten. The struggle was brief and fierce. Panting, the mongoose stared down at the cobra's dead body.

Piankhy picked it up, and it did not try to get free.

'You have shown me what to do,' he said. 'I shall take you with me.'

CHAPTER THIRTY-FOUR

It had been a satisfactory week. The Nubian army had lost control of two villages and had not attacked any Libyan patrols. Tefnakht received regular and abundant supplies from the North, and was continually reinforcing the defences at Henen-nesut.

He sat on a low chair with feet shaped like lions' paws, watching Daybreak smooth down her hair before covering it with a luxurious wig.

'This situation has lasted long enough,' he said. 'We must find a way of provoking the Nubians into attacking, then wipe them out and ensure that some of the troops stationed in Thebes are sent to help them. After that, nothing will stand in our way.'

'There could be no better plan, my darling.'

'Then let's put it into practice. We must try to convince the enemy that Henen-nesut is easy to take.'

'Why not let it be known that you have left the town, and that Peftau has once again become Piankhy's vassal? The Nubians won't be suspicious of their ally, and the trap will close on them.'

Tefnakht planted a kiss on Daybreak's neck. 'You could do the work of a council of war all by yourself.'

'I want victory for your sake—for Egypt.'

A junior officer on Tefnakht's staff announced that Yegeb wished to see the general.

'Later!'

'He says it's urgent, my lord.'

'Oh, very well, send him in.'

There was fear in Yegeb's eyes. 'My lord, terrible news!'

'Where from?'

'From our network of informants in Thebes. Piankhy has just sent a message: he is leaving Napata and will be travelling to the city of Amon.'

'I would never have believed it,' said Tefnakht slowly.

Daybreak covered her perfect body with a white shawl. 'This changes everything,' she said. 'Soon, we shall be fighting the leader of the Nubians. Tefnakht and Piankhy face to face . . . As soon as the Black Pharaoh is dead, his supporters will throw down their weapons.'

'Precisely,' hissed Yegeb. 'And it would be best if Piankhy never reached Middle Egypt.'

'An excellent idea,' nodded Tefnakht, 'but how would we organize an ambush? The South belongs to him.'

'His journey will be long and difficult. Let's try to sneak a few determined men through, by way of the Eastern desert. If they fail, Piankhy will arrive in Thebes—and find that the city of Amon will be his tomb.'

*   *   *

Thanks to a bold young peasant girl who was eager to hone her skill at games of love, Lemersekny had spent an entertaining night. For several hours, he had managed to forget the failures of recent weeks. Not a single Libyan patrol in his nets, no battle worthy of the name, and every day the situation becoming more and more bogged down.

168

Lemersekny had more than once tried to persuade Puarma to call in the troops stationed at Thebes. The idea was not to attack the enormous obstacle of Henen-nesut, but to take back several parts of the Province of the Hare once and for all, and make the area more secure. But Puarma refused to weaken Thebes's defences.

This time, Lemersekny's mind was made up. He was going to hand Puarma his resignation and turn over the command to him. What he'd do with himself, he didn't yet know; all he knew was how to be a soldier—any other kind of life seemed completely incongruous.

It pained Lemersekny to give ground to an archer who would never learn how to lead a proper offensive, but the prospect of staying bogged down in this war of position was even more unbearable. Deprived of the invigorating air of adventure, he was slowly withering away.

When he saw Puarma coming towards him smiling broadly, Lemersekny knew the archer had guessed his intentions and was already revelling in his new freedom of action—a career soldier willing to make any compromise, that's what he was.

'A message has come from Thebes,' Puarma said.
'New orders?'
'Better than that, Lemersekny, much better.'
The captain frowned. 'I don't understand.'
'Piankhy is on his way.'

*   *   *

Since his return to Khmun, Prince Nemrod had taken on a new lease of life. He had rediscovered his old routines, his courtiers, his palace, his

169

favourite cook, and spent most of his time walking the streets of the city he had almost lost.

Women and feasting were secondary amusements; his one and only mistress was Khmun, and he would increase its beauty season after season, until he had made it into the most attractive city in the land. When his butler reminded him tactfully that the war was still raging, Nemrod simply replied that this situation would no doubt last for decades and it was better to forget about it. Yes, forget all about it, just as he had forgotten his own treachery.

The prince drank cool white wine as he sat in the shade of a pavilion with clematis-covered walls, listening to a harpist singing in the Valley of the Tamarisks, not far from the great Temple of Thoth. The commander of his troops dared to interrupt this cultured moment.

'Not another administrative problem?' groaned Nemrod.

'No, Prince. A messager has just brought a papyrus scroll bearing Tefnakht's seal.'

Nemrod broke the seal and unrolled the papyrus. He read and re-read the few lines, written by the general himself, and tried to convince himself that this was a bad dream. No, the Black Pharaoh could not have left Napata for Thebes. No, there was no way he was going to attack Khmun.

*　　　*　　　*

Despite his appointment as governor of Napata, Otoku still refused to set foot on the ground in the presence of an inferior, and his sweating servants

170

had to carry his great bulk in a litter from place to place around the city.

The fat man was in such a state of anxiety that he sometimes cut short one of his five daily meals. He had delegated his tribal responsibilities to a cousin, who would be beheaded if he dared steal the tiniest particle of gold for himself. Meanwhile he, Otoku, had devoted himself to mastering the arcane arts of government.

When the fat man took on an obligation, he did not do so lightly. Even if it cost him his health, he would safeguard Napata's prosperity. But he still had to make the scribes respect him, and show them that he was no man of straw.

The only way to achieve this was by obtaining Cool-Head's unconditional support. That was why Otoku was being swiftly carried in the direction of the scribe's pretty fifteen-roomed house, which nestled in the heart of a luxuriant garden filled with palm-trees. When Otoku reached the entrance, the gate-keeper bowed low, and the litter-bearers set off up the sandy pathway which led to the main doors.

Otoku found the dwarf's wife standing on the threshold, weeping. She was a full-breasted Nubian beauty, who had produced a son and a daughter, now aged fourteen and twelve—they were destined to become scribes, and paid great attention to their father's teachings.

'Lady Cool-Head, I don't wish to disturb you, but I must speak with your husband at the earliest opportunity.'

'Unfortunately, that is impossible.'

A shiver ran over Otoku's massive frame. 'Surely you don't mean . . .?'

171

'No, no, my lord, Cool-Head is alive—but Piankhy has taken him with him.'

It was a heavy blow. Well, Otoku would manage on his own somehow, and the Black Pharaoh would be proud of him.

CHAPTER THIRTY-FIVE

The mists of morning had lifted and the air was crystal-clear, throwing into sharp relief the yellowish undulations of the desert sands. Piankhy's fleet travelled on through countryside which drew gasps of wonderment from his troops. There were tawny plains, sandstone with its orangy hue, countless palm trees, a wide strip of well-irrigated earth, and shimmering stretches of wheat and barley: the overall effect was far gentler than that of the Fourth Cataract. Surging vigorously northwards, the Nile seemed to issue a challenge to the more conciliatory desert. It flowed through little villages of white-painted houses whose inhabitants, crowded on to the river banks, cheered the king and queen, who could be seen sitting in the bows of the royal ship.

Piankhy gripped Abilah's hand tightly. His eyes drank in the luminous beauty of the Nubian land, whose fire nourished his soul. Monkeys laughed in the tops of palm trees; swallows danced in the blue sky, swooping and curving around flocks of white ibis as they flew steadily and majestically on.

Cool-Head brought goblets of fresh carob juice. 'Majesty, may I point out that your position is far too exposed. Here, in the bow of the ship, you are an easy target for any experienced archer.'

'Don't be such a pessimist. We haven't yet reached the territory occupied by Tefnakht.'

'But what if he knows you have left Napata, and has sent killers to stop you reaching Thebes?'

'Impossible.'

'I hope so, Majesty,' said the scribe, 'but shouldn't we be ready for the worst from an enemy like Tefnakht?'

'What would the Nubians think if I shut myself up in my cabin? They would say Pharaoh was a coward and would no longer trust him. Don't you agree, Abilah?'

'Cool-Head is right, but so are you,' she said.

The king and queen remained sitting in the bow of the ship, gazing towards the North, where violence and death awaited them.

*   *   *

'Majesty,' said the captain, 'we are approaching the Isle of Argo. The way through looks simple, but I don't like this place. The island is immensely long, and where the river divides to go round it we must choose one branch or the other. If we choose the wrong one, we might encounter an unfavourable current.'

'Would that endanger the fleet?'

'The supply boats, certainly.'

The barges were forty cubits long, and were laden with grain, jars of oil, wine and beer, poultry, cattle, vegetables, salt, cheese, preserved meat and fish, and all the weapons the army needed, not to mention the horses, which were treated with the utmost care.

173

'How will you make your decision?'

'I'll trust to luck, Majesty.'

'Show me a chart.'

Piankhy examined it not with his eyes but with his hands. Touch was a far more subtle sense than most men believed. The hand could see, and even discern invisible things, if you knew how to educate it wisely. Piankhy had chosen his horse by laying his hand on its neck, and that was how he would choose the safe channel.

'We shall sail to the right of the island.'

The captain would probably have chosen to go the other side, but he could offer the king no firm reason why.

When the long convoy entered the right-hand channel, it was attacked by such huge clouds of flies that they prevented the pilots from correctly sounding the depth of the river with their long poles. In trying to wave them away, one pilot toppled into the water. Two sailors immediately raced to help him, and threw him a rope; he grabbed hold of it and clambered back on board.

'Issue oriole fat to all the crews,' ordered Piankhy.

They all covered themselves with the precious grease, and the flies stopped biting.

But the king saw another danger: although the wind was light, ripples were forming in the river. It was an unmistakable sign that there were submerged sandbanks, just below the surface of the water.

'Stop!' yelled a pilot.

The warning came too late for the leading boat and the flagship, which struck a sandbank and ran aground. The rest of the fleet managed to avoid the

174

obstacle.

There was only one solution: they would have to haul the boats off. Piankhy leapt on to the sandbank and took personal command of the manoeuvre, heaving on the rope with the strength of ten of his sailors.

Soon, the Isle of Argo channel was no more than a bad memory.

*　　　*　　　*

The Nubian fleet passed through the Third Cataract without difficulty, slipping between banks of granite and porphyry, and emerged into a strange land where the sand was grey and the rocks blackish. A few antelopes fled in fright, leaping the sparse bushes of an empty savannah in a series of graceful bounds.

Then it was back to dunes of ochre-coloured sand, the tender green of the palm trees, and banks covered in reddish silt which held the secret of fertility. Piankhy felt an intense surge of emotion when his journey took him past the sites of the temples of Soleb and Sedeinga. They celebrated the love Amenhotep III had felt for his wife Tiyi, and the sacred nature of the royal couple.

The king embraced Abilah. 'Amenhotep III also built the temple at Luxor,' he told her, 'one of the jewels of Thebes, in a time when the Two Lands were united, rich and joyful'.

'If we succeed in defeating Tefnakht, perhaps that happy age will return.'

'We have never fought a war as serious as this before, Abilah. Will the Nubians' bravery be equal to it?'

'It isn't like you to harbour doubts.'

'I don't, since I have no choice. But how many dead will there be before we can lay down our arms? Tefnakht has made a serious error in disturbing the fragile harmony of the North, but he has drawn me out of my lethargy. You were wrong to think that the Libyan princes would be satisfied with their own lands and would restrain their crazy ambitions. But I was wrong too. One must never give one's trust to men who crave power. And cowards like Peftau and Nemrod are no less dangerous, for they will betray you at the first opportunity. I was mistaken in thinking that fear would be enough to keep them in line. Perhaps you should return to Napata, my love.'

'I want to go through this ordeal with you,' said Abilah. 'And if we have to die to defend our cause, I shall be by your side.'

The mongoose climbed on to Piankhy's shoulder, as if to prove that it, too, was ready to fight.

Suddenly Cool-Head raced up, galloping along the slippery deck so fast that he was in danger of breaking his neck. This could not mean anything good.

'Majesty,' he wailed, 'there's been a catastrophe! And it's all my fault!'

'What have you done?'

'I didn't check all the boxes of amulets, and one of them contains nothing but pots. Some of the sailors will be without magical protection—they'll refuse to go on.'

'Calm down,' said Abilah firmly. 'I shall share out my serving-women's amulets. They have plenty.'

There were amulets made from faience, from quartzite, cornelian, red jasper and serpentine. Some were carved in the shape of a hand, others resembled a pillar, a sphinx, a falcon's eye, or a hippopotamus's head. Cool-Head was reassured. Since every member of the army would be sheltered from hostile forces, it would assuredly reach its destination safely.

CHAPTER THIRTY-SIX

Many horses had died of exhaustion, but Tefnakht's message had reached a tribe in the extreme south of Libya. In exchange for a dozen bars of silver, high-quality ointments and a hundred donkeys, fifty young huntsmen had agreed to slip secretly across the Egyptian border and attack Piankhy when he reached the Second Cataract, a particularly suitable place for an ambush. Too sure of himself, the Black Pharaoh would not expect this kind of attack on territory under his control.

Despite the generous sums of money offered, not many volunteers had come forward. Piankhy had a reputation as an invincible warrior, and experienced men were in no hurry to confront him. Only young lads in rude health had been willing to attempt this mad adventure, in the hope of bringing back the Black Pharaoh's severed head to their village. Kafy, the younger son of the tribal chief, had taken on the role of ringleader. Knowing he had little chance of winning power because of his elder brother's hatred, Kafy saw this as a chance to demonstrate his true worth.

The raid promised to be a dangerous one. By day, they could travel only on those stretches of the Nile which were not under surveillance by Piankhy's soldiers; by night, they risked hitting a rock and sinking. But they must not think about failure; they must move as quickly as possible, so that they could surprise Piankhy in the allotted place.

*   *   *

The king gazed admiringly at the rectangular linen sail, which began at the top of the double mast and draped down to the deck. His sailors relied mainly on the strong current to move the ships forward, but they also used delicate manoeuvres so as not to waste the power of the wind. Whenever the wind fell, they furled the sail round the yard, lowered the mast and laid it down on two fork-ended posts.

On the flagship, next to the royal couple's cabin, a large open-air enclosure had been set aside for Piankhy's horse. Valiant had been provided with two stalls, and the king ordered regular stops to allow him to gallop. Like the soldiers, Valiant behaved impeccably; he, too, understood the importance of their mission.

Piankhy often talked to his horse, who answered him with looks and whinnies, showing his approval or displeasure. The king took account of these opinions to improve the horse's daily life and keep him in excellent health. Moreover, Valiant possessed a rare quality: he could foresee danger, and displayed his fears through noisy outbursts of anger.

178

An anger which exploded into life as they approached the Second Cataract. None of the sailors dared intervene, for fear of being kicked; and Valiant would allow no one but Piankhy to go near him.

The king stood by the enclosure and watched the animal buck and kick. 'Hush, my friend. Calm down,' he urged in his steady, serious voice. But Valiant did not calm down.

When Cool-Head saw the king enter the enclosure, he was afraid. The horse was so enraged that even the sight of his master did not calm him. But Piankhy looked Valiant straight in the eye and walked towards him without hesitation. The horse's anger faded.

*   *   *

'Valiant is warning us of danger,' Piankhy told his wife.

Abilah was stretched out on a bed whose head was inlaid with ivory and whose feet were shaped like a bull's hooves. There was a rare anxiety in her eyes. 'I had a nightmare,' she said. 'Gigantic crocodiles came out of the Nile, then giant hippopotamuses rose up out of the soft earth of the river banks. At first they challenged each other, and I thought they were going to tear each other apart. But they held each other in respect and in the end they even formed a kind of alliance against a monster who had come out of the desert, a monster I couldn't identify. The battle began, and I woke up.'

'A dream? Or a vision?'

'I don't know which it was. But we shouldn't

179

ignore these warnings.'

Piankhy sat down on the edge of the bed, and his wife nestled against him.

'In other words,' he said, 'return to Napata, and forget Tefnakht and the war.'

'Why hide it from you? I am afraid.'

'Only a man without courage would deny his fear. But we have no right to turn our backs on danger. I shall warn the sailors and soldiers that we shall probably have to fight sooner than we expected.'

The information caused consternation. What risks could a Nubian army possibly face on its own territory, so far from the enemy? Nevertheless, the fleet's captains put their crews on high alert, and archers watched the riverbanks day and night.

*   *   *

Kafy and his men had succeeded. Taking difficult paths, which fortunately led past watering-holes, they had at last overcome all obstacles to reach the area around the Second Cataract.

The terrain was daunting: rocky ridges that rose up out of the Nile, whirlpools expressing its anger, rapids attacking islets of granite, cliffs that seemed to guard the way, only to bar it. Some of the Libyans trembled with fear, convinced that evil spirits lurked in these places. One of them even tried to run away, but Kafy calmly drew his bow and felled the man with an arrow in the back.

'That is the only fate cowards deserve,' he said.

Kafy was more terrifying than the evil spirits, and the young Libyans kept their fears to themselves.

180

'This is where we shall kill Piankhy. When he is dead, his body bristling with our arrows, his soldiers will scatter like terrified animals. We shall seize the corpse and take his head to Tefnakht. Then we shall demand double what he promised us. Soon, you will be rich men.'

The prospect gave them renewed heart for the task in hand.

'These cliffs are our allies,' declared Kafy. 'If we position ourselves at the top, we'll be out of range of the Nubian archers, but we'll be able to hit our own targets easily.'

The only task left to the little band was to cross the Nile by jumping from islet to islet, then climb up the cliff face, so that they would not be facing into the sun and the wind.

Kafy took the lead. Just as he reached halfway, a yell made him turn round. One of the rocks had just risen up, throwing a Libyan into the river. It wasn't a block of granite; it was a gigantic hippopotamus, disturbed during its sleep. A dozen of its fellows, just as monstrous as the first, opened wide their jaws and let out a horrible chorus of bellowing.

In panic, the Libyan made the mistake of sinking his dagger into the river-horse's fragile skin. Maddened by rage and pain, the hippopotamus speared the swimmer on his two razor-sharp canines, which were well over a cubit long. The others followed suit, piercing the flesh of the Libyans, who tried in vain to escape.

Kafy saw something move on the bank. At first he thought they were tree trunks, lying in the mud. A long head appeared, then scales, a reptilian tail and legs that were short but swift, oh so swift . . .

181

Although it was heavier than four big sacks of grain, the Nile crocodile was amazingly agile.

'Crocodiles!' he shouted. 'We're saved—they're going to attack the hippos!' He knew that a merciless war had existed between the two species since the dawn of time.

In panic, one of the Libyans struck the water with his spear, hoping to produce intolerable vibrations that would drive the crocodile away. In fact, he produced the opposite of the desired result and attracted it towards him. And since the prey was sizeable, the reptile let out a kind of whistle to call for its fellows' help.

Kafy was stunned. Not one of the crocodiles was taking any notice of the hippos, and the hippos were ignoring the crocodiles. Both were killing the members of the raiding-party.

A crocodile rushed towards him. Kafy didn't have time to shoot an arrow into its open mouth, for a female closed her jaws on his right leg and bit down so hard that tears poured from her lachrymal glands. Indeed, all the crocodiles shed tears of joy on the occasion of this exceptionally fine feast.

*   *   *

The mongoose was sitting bolt upright on Piankhy's shoulder, its muzzle sniffing the wind, its eyes fixed on the horizon. The king and queen, too, were gazing into the distance. Deep in the Second Cataract, which they had begun to cross slowly and very carefully, they made out turbulent water and hoarse cries.

'It must be a fight between crocodiles and hippopotamuses,' ventured Piankhy. 'Yes, I can see

182

them now. The reptiles seem to be going away.'

'The water is tinted red,' commented Abilah.

'You're right. But . . .'

'My dream was right. Monsters were lying in wait for us, but they weren't hippopotamuses or crocodiles.'

The fleet sailed on. The crocodiles had not left a single morsel of flesh and, thanks to the strong current, the blood of their victims was quickly diluted in the dark-blue water.

For the first time since they had left Napata, Shepena left her cabin and came and stood by her father's side.

'I prayed to Amon,' she said. 'I invoked his Invisible Presence so that his gaze would become the pilot of your boat. Terrible trials await us, and I shall continue to pray for his help.'

The mongoose fell asleep on Piankhy's shoulder, and the fleet crossed the stone belly of the Second Cataract without further incident.

CHAPTER THIRTY-SEVEN

The trained maid had just finished working on Daybreak's slender, delicate feet; she was followed by a massage-girl who rubbed Daybreak's pearly body with a salve made from incense and perfumed reeds which would keep her skin supple and sweet-smelling all day long.

Her preparations were almost complete. All that remained was for the hairdresser to come, and to choose a wig. Daybreak was still dreaming of the passionate night she had spent with Tefnakht. The

183

general might be a cold, austere, abrupt man in his public life, but when he was with her he was transformed into an ardent lover, full of surprises. And yet, even at the height of pleasure, she felt he was haunted by his great plan. If he loved her, it was not because of her beauty or her youth, it was because she was driven by the same ambition.

When the hairdresser arrived, she was in tears.

'What's the matter?' asked Daybreak.

'Mistress, it's that monster Nartreb.'

'Has he raped you?'

'No, he wouldn't dare touch me, because I'm in your service. But my younger sister is eighteen years old and as pretty as a lily, and he raped her.'

Robed in transparent linen, with her feet bare and her hair flowing free, Daybreak hurried out of her bedchamber, past the guards who stood at every corner of every palace corridor, and almost knocked over the head steward, who bowed to her respectfully. Flying into the council chamber, she found Tefnakht listening to Yegeb's report on the economic situation in the region.

'Your adviser Nartreb is a brute and a criminal!' she told Tefnakh furiously.

'Why are you so upset, Daybreak?'

'Because he has raped my hairdresser's sister.'

'That's impossible,' protested Yegeb. 'I can vouch for his good conduct.'

'Make him come and give an account of himself,' ordered the young woman.

Yegeb's expression darkened. 'Shouldn't it be the general who gives the orders?'

'Go and find your friend,' Tefnakht told him.

The counsellor bowed and left.

'Get rid of them,' advised Daybreak. 'In the end

184

they'll make the people hate you. And under our laws rape is punishable by death.'

'My advisers' efficiency is undeniable,' objected Tefnakht. 'Even if their methods sometimes seem brutal, they get excellent results because I allow them to grow rich. Thanks to them, the people are afraid of me and know that they must obey me.'

'So you would exonerate a rapist?'

'First, let us hear his version of events.'

When Nartreb appeared before Tefnakht, Daybreak repeated her accusations forcefully.

'This is just a simple misunderstanding,' said Nartreb. 'The truth is that I went to the aid of this poor girl, who had just been manhandled by a peasant. I saw immediately that she had been the victim of horrible sexual abuse, and I ordered that she must receive the best of care, at my expense.'

'It is you she accuses, not some peasant.'

'She was almost unconscious—the shock must have made her delirious. It's perfectly understandable, and I forgive her for it.'

'Before a court,' insisted Daybreak, 'it will be her word against yours.'

'Not at all, for I have three witnesses. Three soldiers were escorting me and saw the peasant run away. Their testimony will be decisive.'

Yegeb smiled. 'As you see, General, Nartreb is a man above suspicion.'

'The matter is closed,' declared Tefnakht.

*   *   *

Prince Akanosh's wife accompanied herself on the lyre as she sang him a song of the Great South, at once sun-soaked and full of melancholy. It evoked the cool water that the woman and her lover drank together on the banks of the river, in the sweet, shared dawn of their love. It spoke of youth, which fled with the river current and was lost in the yellowish sands that slid down towards the Nile.

Moved to tears, their steward waited until the song ended before speaking to his master. He was the only servant allowed access to the couple's apartments; swift investigations by Akanosh's wife had revealed that the others were in Yegeb's pay and seeking to compromise her husband.

'Tefnakht is furious,' said the steward.

'With me?' asked Akanosh.

'No, Prince, you may set your mind at rest on that score. He has just learnt that the Libyans who were paid to kill Piankhy during his journey have failed. The Black Pharaoh has crossed the Second Cataract and it won't be long before he reaches the isle of Elephantine.'

'Piankhy in Egypt . . . Is that mad dream really going to come true?'

*　　　*　　　*

The mongoose spent most of its time asleep, Valiant was perfectly calm, it was pleasant sailing along the river, and Piankhy and Abilah were enjoying wonderful times together. At Napata, their respective duties often made it impossible for them to enjoy the intimacy they longed for; here, in this spacious, airy cabin, they savoured each moment of happiness with ever-greater intensity, as sombre reality crept inexorably closer.

Abilah had the mysterious charm of deep waters and the magical charisma of a cat. Even in wild

186

outbursts of desire, her bearing was never less than noble. She was an adventure, begun anew each day, and she fascinated Piankhy. Without her, he would have stood no chance of victory.

The mongoose awoke and stood up on its hind legs, front paws pressed against the wooden door of the cabin. A few moments later, Cool-Head knocked.

'Enter,' said Piankhy.

The dwarf opened the door a fraction. 'Majesty, the captain is worried. The wind has started blowing from the south. It's already whipping up waves on the river and it's gathering strength abnormally quickly. If it continues like this, it will become frighteningly strong. We should stop and moor the boats at the first possible opportunity, otherwise we'll capsize.'

'We are approaching the First Cataract, are we not?'

'Yes, Majesty.'

'We must go to the library at once.'

There were a certain number of papyrus scrolls which Cool-Head had refused to leave behind. Among the most important were the ordinary and extraordinary rituals, the calendar of festivals, the list of temples and a hundred other essential subjects, without a knowledge of which it would be impossible to govern. Piankhy unrolled a dozen or so before he found the one he was looking for.

Immediately he summoned the officers in charge of supplies, and headed for the bows of the ship, where the things he had requested were brought to him without delay. Wearing the Blue Crown, the pharaoh offered the spirit of the Nile a kilt of royal linen, a blank sheet of the finest papyrus, festival

187

oil, a jar of wine dating from the first year of his reign, a honey-cake and a gold ingot. Queen Abilah, clad in a long red dress, shook two sacred golden rattles to drive away harmful forces and re-establish harmony between humans and the river.

Little by little the south wind abated, the whirlpools disappeared and the river resumed its peaceful course.

'Make offerings,' murmured Piankhy. 'That is what the old writings teach us to do. That is the only way to ward off evil and open the way. Let us never again forget, Abilah, that the whole of Egypt is an offering to the Creator. On that truth, I shall base my strategy.'

CHAPTER THIRTY-EIGHT

The Nubians were appalled by the granite chaos of the First Cataract. Many wondered how on earth they were going to pass through this rocky barrier, for the river raged between the rocks in terrible bursts of anger.

With the aid of detailed charts, Piankhy had no difficulty in finding the channel created by Pharaoh Senusret III a thousand years before. Even during periods of danger, it was free of reefs and remained navigable. In order to facilitate trade with Nubia, the rulers of a later dynasty had widened the passage to turn it into a real canal which even cargo boats could pass through.

And this was the entrance to the land beloved of the gods, to the first province of Upper Egypt, the head of the Twin Nation, symbolized by an elephant whose name also meant 'Cessation', since the border marked the end of Egypt proper.

The fortress of Elephantine had formerly posed an insurmountable obstacle for the Nubians, but from now on its great walls were destined to halt the Northern invader. The entire garrison lined the ramparts and hailed the Black Pharaoh. They all expected him to disembark at the fortress to establish the first link between the two sections of his army, but Piankhy had more pressing business.

The king had the royal ship brought to a halt beside the temple of the god Khnum, the ram god who created beings on his potter's wheel and who lifted his sandalled foot from the waters to let loose the annual Nile flood. He stepped down on to the jetty alone, watched by the sailors of his fleet and the soldiers of the garrison, who were awe-struck by the Black Pharaoh's formidable appearance.

Piankhy passed through the first gateway of the splendid temple, and was welcomed by the High Priest of Khnum. The temple was built from sandstone, with doorways and gates of granite. Its interior was filled with the scent of incense.

'Majesty, this temple belongs to you,' said the High Priest.

'Take me to my father's shrine.'

It was a small room, whose walls were decorated with sculpted scenes showing Kashta, Piankhy's father, founder of the Nubian dynasty, presenting offerings to Khnum. At the foot of the statue of Kashta, a stele recorded the fact that he had visited Elephantine and had richly endowed its principal shrine.

Piankhy read the columns of hieroglyphics which conjured up the perpetual resurrection of his

189

father's soul, in the eternity of the Light, in the company of the just. Kashta spoke to him, through signs which could endure through the ages without losing any of their power of expression. Nourished by the permanence of stone, the hieroglyphs preserved the words the gods had uttered at the dawn of life. And his father asked Piankhy to continue his work, as Ramses had continued Seti's work, as every pharaoh must continue the work of his predecessor, for the happiness of the Two Lands.

Piankhy could have explained to him that the situation had changed, that Tefnakht's invasion should have prompted him to remain in Napata, the better to protect Nubia, that it was no longer possible to reunite Upper and Lower Egypt. But, out of respect, a son did not question the instructions of a father who had become eternal.

*   *   *

There were three of them, two tall and one short. The short one was in charge. He gave terse, precise orders, for he knew the terrain perfectly. Before Tefnakht's invasion, he had lived in the southernmost village of the Province of the Hare, on the frontier fixed by Piankhy's Nubian army.

At regular, frequent intervals along the border, encampments of soldiers formed an impenetrable line of defence. Impenetrable, that is, except by three men who had been trained to crawl on their bellies like snakes. But they still had to find a way through, which would enable them to slip through the net and reach Thebes. There, they would make contact with the Libyan spies and prepare for

190

Piankhy's murder.

Four times already the short man had been thwarted, because the patrolling guards were more diligent than he had expected. His comrades suggested they turn back, but the short man had one last idea, the abandoned cemetery on the border between the fields and the desert. The Egyptians were superstitious: there'd be no soldiers on watch there, where ghosts might be roaming. If they slipped between the tombs, the trio would escape the enemy's vigilance.

As soon as he set foot in the cemetery, the short man knew he had found the enemy's weak point. Nevertheless, he did not let his guard drop, and insisted that the other two were equally careful. As soon as they were out of Province of the Hare, they would swim across the canal, steal a fishing-boat and sail to the outskirts of Thebes, where the leader of the Libyan spy network was waiting for them.

Organizing Piankhy's assassination would not be easy, but there would undoubtedly be opportunities. The Black Pharaoh's arrival was such an extraordinary event that his safety could not be constantly guaranteed throughout the long round of festivities and official receptions.

The trio crept past a ruined tomb, the last in the cemetery. One of the taller men was in the lead. He had just turned round to announce delightedly that they were through when Lemersekny's wooden arm smashed down on the back of his head. The other tall man brandished his short sword, but the captain's axe sliced through his neck. As for the short man, he tried to flee through the cemetery, but a soldier felled him with his spear.

'I knew they'd try something stupid like that,' said Lemersekny to his men. 'That's why I left just one way open. These imbeciles probably thought I was afraid of ghosts! Any survivors?'

'No, Captain.'

'That's a pity, we could have interrogated them—mind you, they'd certainly have told a pack of lies.'

When they returned to camp, Lemersekny slaked his thirst with strong beer, then went into Puarma's tent.

'I stopped three Libyans who were trying to get out of the Province of the Hare,' he said. 'You know what that means, don't you?'

'Deserters?'

'Heading south? Of course not. They were on their way to Thebes.'

'Can you prove it?'

'My instinct is all the proof I need. And if they were on their way to Thebes, that's because they were sure of a warm welcome there.'

'That's nonsense, Lemersekny. Thebes is loyal to Piankhy.'

'Do you really think Tefnakht has no supporters there? Even if there aren't many of them, a few Thebans are bound to have gambled on a Northern victory.'

'What do you make of it?' asked Puarma worriedly.

'These three crafty devils were taking instructions to their Theban allies to prepare a strike against the Black Pharaoh.'

'You mean an assassination attempt?'

'If Piankhy is killed, we'll return to Nubia to protect Napata, and Tefnakht will have free rein.'

'You're right—worse luck.'

A horse galloped towards them out of the darkness. An army courier jumped down and saluted the two captains. He handed Puarma two thin wooden tablets, one from Thebes, the other from Cliff-of-Great-Victories, a village in the Province of the Hare.

Puarma's face lit up. 'Piankhy has just set foot on Egyptian soil! He went to the Temple of Khnum at Elephantine to honour his father's memory, then set sail again for Thebes.'

'Piankhy in Egypt,' murmured Lemersekny, astounded. 'It's incredible.'

Puarma's jubilation faded. 'The other news isn't so good. Under the command of one of Tefnakht's sons, the Northern princes mounted a surprise attack on the fortified village of Cliff-of-Great-Victories and recaptured it, cutting off our route to Khmun.'

'That's quite enough of that!' roared Lemersekny, making Puarma jump out of his skin. 'We're going to retake that village, and prove to the Black Pharaoh that we aren't incompetent fools.'

CHAPTER THIRTY-NINE

Within Tefnakht's council of war, conflict reigned. Some of the members wanted to return to the North, others wanted to strengthen the defences of Henen-nesut and Khmun, and there were some who recommended fighting Piankhy head-on.

Prince Akanosh rose to his feet. 'Like you,' he said, 'I am a tribal chief and a warrior, and I have

193

many times proved my valour and my courage. Today, we must weigh up our military gains and losses, and we must show that we can do so with clear heads. Neither we nor Piankhy can achieve outright victory, for our forces are too evenly balanced. We have promised obedience to Tefnakht, and thanks to his vigorous leadership, we have conquered a prosperous region, extending from the furthermost edge of the Delta to the south of the Province of the Hare. Let us be content with that and proclaim Tefnakht pharaoh of this vast territory.'

'You are forgetting Thebes,' protested Daybreak. 'Without the city of Amon, the god of victories, Egypt is nothing but a sick, maimed body. If we weigh up our achievements as you suggest, it gives us good cause to hope. Our positions are firmly established, and we have succeeded in drawing Piankhy into Egypt. And what does his unexpected journey mean? It means that the Black Pharaoh's Nubian army has failed, and that he is so afraid of Tefnakht that he has to fight him himself. This is the usurper's first admission of weakness, and none of our soldiers need fear him.'

Daybreak's eloquence took the wild Libyan chieftains by surprise, and even Akanosh dared not argue.

'Now that he is on Egyptian soil,' pointed out Tefnakht, 'Piankhy is no longer safe. Thebes may still be under the enemy yoke, but we have supporters there who will they do all they can to ensure our victory.'

Peftau was intrigued. 'General, are you saying that Piankhy might be . . . disposed of?'

'We must have victory, and any means are

194

justified in order to achieve it. The Black Pharaoh is wrong to believe in his own sanctity, and to think that he is invincible because he is in the holy city of Amon. What he does not realize is that he is the past, whereas I am the future.'

* * *

The head of the Libyan spies in Thebes was vexed to hear that the three soldiers sent by Tefnakht had failed to cross the frontier from the Province of the Hare, and had been killed. With them, the job would have been much easier. But the important thing was to overcome setbacks and take whatever risks were necesssary in order to kill Piankhy. For months, the spy had been sending Tefnakht regular information on the situation in Thebes and the progress of the Nubian army. His last message had consisted of only five words: 'Tomorrow, Piankhy arrives at Karnak.'

It was the Black Pharaoh, and he alone, who could prevent Tefnakht conquering Egypt and imposing his law upon it. No one else among the Nubians was capable of succeeding him. When Piankhy was dead, his troops would withdraw and head back to Napata. The fortress of Elephantine would block their way for ever.

But, the spy reminded himself, you should not sell the skin before you had killed the panther. And Piankhy was a formidable creature, with an unerring instinct. He would have to be taken by surprise in a moment of weakness, when he had no reason to be suspicious. The spy felt well able to carry out this assignment.

'I should have strangled that damned Daybreak long ago,' cursed Nartreb as he rubbed his aching toes. 'She's dangerous. She's gaining more and more influence over those stupid chiefs—they can't take their eyes off her and hang on her every word.'

Yegeb, who was writing rows of figures on an old wooden tablet, fully agreed. 'We could easily poison her, but the shock of her death would unman Tefnakht for weeks, or even months, and we need him at his most warriorlike just now, with Piankhy bearing down on us.'

'So what do you suggest we do?'

'We must thoroughly discredit her, prove to Tefnakht that she's nothing but a schemer he should get rid of—certainly not the future Queen of Egypt.'

'Anything new on Akanosh?'

'Not yet,' replied Yegeb, 'but I'm having him watched closely. He'll betray us, I'm sure of it, unless he gets too scared and continues to shut himself away in his apartments with his wife. In any case, he won't give us any trouble.'

'Do you think the Theban plot against Piankhy will succeed?'

'If it was only a plot, no, but it's something much more subtle than that, and the snake's bite will be as swift as it is unexpected. Piankhy is finished.'

'Good!' said Nartreb. 'So what shall we do about Daybreak?'

*　　*　　*

'They call it the orb of the whole world,' went the

sacred song, 'for the stones at its corners correspond to the four pillars of heaven. Thebes is the queen of cities, the Divine One, the eye of the Great Creator; all the cities glorify her name. At the dawn of time, a mound of sand formed and emerged from the water. On this mound the world was born, on it was built Thebes, the eye of the Light.'

Piankhy and Abilah wept with joy when they saw the city, with its hundred gates and countless temples. It was unsullied by the grievous degradation of pharaonic power, and preserved the ancient traditions that the North, subjugated by the Libyan invaders, had forgotten. Thebes, the shrine of Amon, the Hidden One, who had neither father nor mother; Thebes, the great work which God had used his magic to create, by heating it with the flame of his eye; Thebes, where the Invisible One revealed his message to light up the Two Lands in the midst of darkness; Thebes, which held both ends of eternity.

Piankhy's eyes opened wide, as though he had been reborn to a world he had dreamt in every tiny detail, but whose sublime reality he was only now discovering. And Thebes spoke to him, uttering the words it had uttered since its beginnings: *It is here, and here alone, that a pharaoh is crowned, because this celestial city, established on earth, gives the king a country and the chance to endow human lives with the harmony of the gods.*

'Come to Pharaoh, O Amon,' chanted the queen, 'you who are brave as a ship's captain, and permit him to reach the shore of victory. Come to him, O Amon, saviour of the shipwrecked, and permit him to reach the land of happiness. Come

197

to him, O Amon, the ferryman, and permit him to reach the Western land of peace.'

The royal couple left the ship and stepped down into a small boat, which moved slowly along the canal joining the Nile to the temple at Karnak. Shaven-headed 'pure priests' rowed in strict time, beneath a scorching sun filtered through willow-trees.

The pharaoh and his wife hoped to be welcomed by the Wife of Amon despite her failing health. But it was an elderly priest who bowed before them.

'May Amon grant you his protection, Your Majesties. In the name of the priests and priestesses of Thebes, permit me to welcome you.'

'Why is my sister not here?'

'Alas, Majesty, the Wife of Amon is dying.'

Piankhy wanted to rush to his sister's bedside, but ritual demanded that he must fulfil a first duty at the moment he entered the sacred domain of Amon: he must make offerings to the god. So he ordered his sailors to bring the offerings to the temple: solid gold vases, each weighing as much as a ram; silver ewers; sheets of gold which would be applied to the bases of columns; offertory tables in granite and diorite, so massive that it took six men to carry each one; and huge quantities of gold, which Karnak's goldsmiths would use to make ritual objects and cover the holy statues.

Piankhy put aside the grief tearing at his heart, and turned his mind to the gift of these riches, the visible sign of his trust in Amon. Without the support of the Invisible One, all his actions would come to nothing.

CHAPTER FORTY

Marjoram, assistant to the Wife of Amon, placed a moist, scented towel on the ruler of Thebes' forehead.

'Hold my hand,' the old woman begged her.

Marjoram tried to hide her anguish. 'You don't seem quite so weak.'

'Don't lie—I know I am dying. Is Piankhy here yet?'

'The watchmen have sighted his fleet.'

'May Amon give me the strength to wait for him. I would so love to see him again.'

'You will live, I am sure,' said Marjoram. 'Oh, my lady, if only I could give you a little of my youth!'

'No, you must guard it carefully, Marjoram. The span of my life is almost done, and I thank Amon for giving me so many happy hours in this temple, far from human depravities. Please . . . a drink . . .'

Marjoram hid her face and wept.

Just as she was pouring cool water into a cup, a giant with skin as black as ebony entered the Wife of Amon's rooms. He was dressed in a gold-edged kilt and accompanied by a young Nubian woman with delicate features.

Marjoram was overcome by awe. 'You . . . you are. . .' she stammered.

'Is my sister still alive?'

Marjoram bowed low. 'Yes, Majesty, and she has been longing to see you.'

When the old priestess saw Piankhy, she managed to overcome her exhaustion and sit up for a few moments. Brother and sister joined in a long

199

embrace; they had no need of words.

Then the Wife of Amon's eyes fell on Shepena. 'Your daughter,' she said. 'How beautiful she is, and there is such depth in her eyes. She is the one, isn't she? The one you have chosen to succeed me? You have chosen wisely. Come here, child. My last words are for you. I shall tell you the secrets of your office so that you may unfailingly fulfil your duties as Wife of Amon.'

*   *   *

That evening, an hour after her predecessor's death, Shepena was raised to the high rank of Wife of Amon and sovereign of all the temples of Thebes. After purifying herself in a lake, she was given the sacred robes, and dressed in a long, tight-fitting dress and golden sandals. On her head she wore a vulture's-skin headdress, evoking the cosmic mother, the goddess Mut; on her forehead sat the female cobra, the golden uraeus; round her neck hung a wide golden collar symbolizing spiritual fertility.

Like the Wives of Amon who had gone before her, Shepena vowed never to marry or to have children. Her only husband would be the god, into whose mysteries she was initiated during a 'royal ascent' to the temple.

Then the new Wife of Amon drove a skewer through the wax figurine of an enemy, which she plunged into a brazier to drive evil forces away from Thebes and render them powerless. Lastly, as the earthly representative of the goddess Tefnut, the secret fire of creation, she offered up a figurine of Ma'at, symbol of the eternal harmony of the living.

Before all the religious and lay officials of the city of Amon, Piankhy recognized his daughter as Wife of Amon, placing her at the head of a true government comprising a steward, an overseer of the granaries, scribes and workshop overseers. Shepena would have the right to have a shrine built within the walls of Karnak and there, after her death, she would be worshipped.

*   *   *

Dawn was breaking. At the end of the long night of rituals, Shepena didn't feel at all tired, although within the space of a few hours she had lost both her youth and her native land. Henceforth, she would never leave the walls of Karnak, except to go to the temple at Djamet on the west bank, where she would be buried alongside other Wives of Amon, close to the mound where the primordial gods slumbered.

As Shepena was gazing into the sacred lake, her mother came to her, haloed by the first glimmers of daylight.

Abilah said, 'This is your first day as ruler over this sacred domain, Shepena. When you celebrate the Invisible presence of Amon every day, you will be maintaining the link between Egypt and the world beyond. I am so happy for you—and so sad to know that you will never return to Napata. But forgive me for burdening you with my feelings. You need strength, and I give you my trust.'

The two women fell into each other's arms.

'I shall show that I am worthy of the task my father has given me,' said Shepena, 'even if this destiny is greater than I am.'

'I, you and your father no longer belong to each other. Since Tefnakht invaded, the soul of Egypt is dictating what we must do, and we must serve it with all our hearts, so that future generations may know the happiness we have known.'

'Would the Queen of Egypt agree to assist the Wife of Amon in celebrating the dawn rites?'

With measured tread, mother and daughter walked towards the Temple of Amon.

*   *   *

Thebes was in turmoil. The Black Pharaoh's presence had enlivened the ancient city and given it back a hope it had thought lost. Suddenly it began to dream of a reunified Egypt, ruled by a monarch who would walk in the footsteps of his ancestors and would re-establish the law of Ma'at, even in the North.

Everyone knew that this improbable future could come to pass only after a ruthless war against Tefnakht, a lengthy, bloody conflict which would lead to the deaths of thousands of men. Still, until Piankhy launched his great offensive, there would be time to organize banquets and enjoy oneself, as though tomorrow was bound to be another happy day. Every eminent citizen in Thebes invited the pharaoh to dine at his table, in the hope of spending an unforgettable evening, but the king declined all invitations. Eventually, the dignitaries realized he had no intention of leaving the barracks, where he was inspecting the troops who had been stationed at Thebes since the beginning of his reign. The town sank gradually into sadness, waiting for the Black Pharaoh to signal that it was time to leave.

This time, to crush Tefnakht, he would not send only his Nubian army to Middle Egypt. This time, all his troops would be involved.

When Piankhy called a meeting of important Thebans in the great open-air courtyard of the temple at Karnak, no one doubted that he was going to announce the start of the campaign. For several days, the Nubians had been undergoing intensive training and all leave had been cancelled.

Those who did not know the pharaoh were astonished by his power and his magnetism. Faced with a warrior of this stature, the Northern army would have only once choice: flight or defeat. The Thebans' dream of victory reappeared with renewed force. What if this Nubian, from the depths of the Great South, really did have the courage to follow his quest to the very end?

'I have called you here to make an important proclamation,' said Piankhy.

Everyone held their breath. The destiny of the country and its holy city was in the balance.

'Before waging war against Tefnakht and the Northern armies, I wish to endow the festivals of the new year and Opet with the grandeur they once enjoyed. There is no more vital duty than the celebration of these ritual moments which have permitted us to commune with our ancestors since the origin of our civilization.'

His words were greeted with utter amazement. Instead of attacking Tefnakht immediately, Piankhy was planning to revive an ancient festival, one to which the Thebans themselves, because of circumstances, attached less and less importance.

Had the Black Pharaoh lost his mind?

CHAPTER FORTY-ONE

All Henen-nesut was singing Tefnakht's praises. His plans were proceeding without a hitch, and there could be no doubt about the final victory. The prince relished his growing popularity.

Daybreak was becoming more enthusiastic by the day about the idea of at last attacking and defeating the Black Pharaoh. She often went to the barracks to spur on the soldiers, who were delighted to feast their eyes on such a lovely woman—one who, thanks to their determined efforts, would soon be their queen.

Tefnakht was watching the archers training when Yegeb brought him a message from Thebes.

'Why do you look so worried, Yegeb?'

'It's incomprehensible, my lord . . . and yet, this message is genuine. It definitely includes the code used by the leader of our spies.'

'Is he refusing to kill Piankhy?'

'Not at all, but the Black Pharaoh's behaviour is absurd. Instead of preparing his troops for war and giving the signal to leave for Middle Egypt, all he cares about is celebrating the old Festival of Opet. Many people think he's lost his mind and that the gods of Thebes have cast such a spell on him that he's lost touch with reality.'

'Piankhy is no madman,' said Tefnakht. 'This is a ruse, designed to make us drop our guard. He'll delegate control of the rites to the Wife of Amon and launch a surprise attack in the middle of the festival. We must be doubly watchful and intensify our preparations.'

*   *   *

Lemersekny was so stunned that he dropped his cup of strong beer. '*What?* The Festival of Opet?'

'Pharaoh has decided to make it especially splendid this year,' said Puarma calmly.

'Don't play games with me, archer. You're as astonished as I am. How can a pharaoh think about enjoying himself when his country's in the grip of lawlessness and war?'

'This festival isn't just about pleasure—as you know very well. It's an essential act of worship to the gods.'

'Oh, the gods! They're not the ones wielding the swords and the javelins, are they?' said Lemersekny.

'Legend has it that it was Amon who made it possible for Ramses the Great to beat thousands of Hittites single-handed at the battle of Kadesh. And Piankhy, too, is under Amon's protection.'

'I'm too old to believe in legends. Are your archers ready?'

'You always want—'

'I'm going to celebrate this festival *my* way.'

*   *   *

The head of the Libyan spies in Thebes was wondering what plan to adopt. At first, it had seemed that Piankhy's words were just a fable, designed to win the goodwill of the local priests and ensnare Tefnakht. Later, it had become

205

obvious that the Black Pharaoh really was going to celebrate the Festival of Opet with a maximum of pomp, and also restore the ancient traditions which had sunk, little by little, into oblivion. Piankhy believed that communion with the gods and respect for rituals were essential if the country was to have any hope of a bright future.

Rank upon rank of courtiers, jubilant crowds, the population in a state of high excitement . . . these were excellent conditions in which to strike a decisive blow. But what if this was a trap? Getting close to Piankhy would not be easy. His personal guards were always on the lookout for trouble, and then there was the queen, that statuesque Nubian, who was as watchful as a tigress and quite capable of singlehandedly foiling an assassination attempt. It would be necessary to act more subtly.

An idea began to form in the assassin's mind.

*   *   *

The Libyan commander who had seized the fortified village of Cliff-of-Great-Victories had had the unexpected good fortune to stumble on a real treasure-trove: in the mayor's cellar, he had found jars of red oasis wine over ten years old. So every evening there was a banquet with the officers and a few local beauties who weren't put off by military high spirits.

According to information from headquarters at Henen-nesut, the situation was deadlocked and it would be weeks—maybe several months—before it altered. For his part, the officer was convinced that Piankhy would settle in Thebes and give up all thoughts of fighting a war whose outcome was

206

uncertain.

Consequently, he was sleeping peacefully and the sentry's arrival was most unwelcome.

'Quickly, Commander, quickly!'

'What's the matter? It's too early to get up.'

'We're under attack!'

Suddenly he was wide awake. 'Is it Piankhy?'

'I don't know. They're Nubians, but there don't seem to be many of them.'

'So it must be a raiding-party.'

A horrible cracking noise half deafened the commander. Using a battering ram, Lemersekny's soldiers had just broken through the main gate of the village, while Puarma's archers, clinging to the top of a mobile siege-tower, were picking off the defenders on the ramparts, one by one.

The commander was hurriedly buckling on his breastplate when Tefnakht's son, a rangy young man with an unattractive face, burst into his room.

'Nubians—they're Nubians! You said they wouldn't attack us!'

'I'll see that you get away.'

'They . . . they're not going to take this village?'

'If Lemersekny is leading his men, it's only a question of minutes. We've no chance against a devil like him.'

'We must fight! Tefnakht will never forgive cowardice.'

'Hurry up, lad. Your life's in the balance: Lemersekny doesn't take prisoners.'

The commander leant out of the window and saw that the situation was desperate. The attack had been so violent that half the Libyan garrison had been killed in less than an hour. From the top of their mobile tower, the Nubian bowmen, tireless

207

and precise, were causing havoc and making it impossible for the defenders to put up any organized resistance.

Lemersekny's troops followed their leader unquestioningly, and poured into Cliff-of-Great-Victories with a fury that froze their opponents with terror. The captain swung his double-edged axe, slicing the throats of the bravest men, and with his wooden arm, in which two arrows were embedded, he struck down the cowards as they begged for mercy. Puarma's archers captured the ramparts, and felled the few remaining Libyans who were crazy enough to resist.

The commander and Tefnakht's son would have had a chance to escape if the terrible cries of mortally wounded men had not made their horses panic. Whinnying and rearing up, the beasts were uncontrollable.

'Follow me, lad. We'll have to run very fast.'

'No! No, I want to fight!'

Tefnakht's son stared blankly about him, hearing nothing now but the cries of the dying and the sound of arrows whistling through the air. The commander took him by the arm, but Lemersekny's axe sank into his shoulder and forced him to let go.

'Don't . . . don't kill him,' gasped the commander with his last breath. 'He's Tefnakht's son.'

Thinking Lemersekny was in trouble, Puarma unleashed a powerful shot, straight to the target. The arrow passed right through the young man's throat, and he slumped over the commander's corpse, stone dead. Tefnakht's son was the last victim of the brief assault on Cliff-of-Great-Victories.

'The festival has started well,' declared Lemersekny, who was scarcely out of breath.

CHAPTER FORTY-TWO

As he handed Piankhy the report drafted by Puarma, Cool-Head hoped that the pharaoh would be satisfied with his expeditionary force's behaviour. So he was astonished by the king's reaction.

'I ordered them to wipe out Tefnakht's rebel army, and to seize that vile creature. Instead of doing that, they go and recapture a little fortified village—and they think they've won a great victory!'

'Majesty, Tefnakht's son was killed,' said Cool-Head.

'One of Tefnakht's sons,' Piankhy corrected him, 'and his death won't make the Libyan give up the fight. Even if all his children were executed before his very eyes, he'd still pursue his dream of absolute power. He is the one we must strike down, no one else. But my officers don't seem able to do it.'

'What are your orders, Majesty?'

'Tell Puarma and Lemersekny to hold their position and wait. The time has come to observe the holy festivals and to worship the gods.'

*   *   *

The High Lector-Priest, who was in charge of ensuring that festivals ran smoothly, could not believe his eyes. Thanks to the hard work of the new Wife of Amon, efficiently assisted by Marjoram, it had been possible to unearth a very ancient text of the new-year ceremony, which took place at the height of the summer, and enact it. The Black Pharaoh had offered up matchless treasures, such as bronze vases decorated with horses and bundles of papyrus stalks. And there were still more extraordinary works of art, like the bright-blue glass chalices with the conical bases, each decorated with a figure of Osiris and a text inviting the faithful to the banquet in the world beyond: 'Drink and you shall live'.

The pharaoh and the Wife of Amon had driven back the demons, the miasmas, sicknesses and other messengers of death sent by the lion-goddess Sekhmet during the last five days of the dying year, the most worrying period for the country's future. Through magic, they had persuaded her to transform her rage into positive energy, by placing offerings before the two series of three hundred and sixty-five statues of Sekhmet arranged inside the sacred precinct of the goddess Mut.

Once the transformation had been achieved, the dignitaries gathered at Karnak in a great open-air courtyard, beneath the hot sun, and presented the pharaoh with gifts to mark the new year. They included necklaces, linen-chests, armchairs, a carrying-chair, vases with lids shaped like a ram's head, bows, arrows and quivers, and even statues of the gods, which would henceforth be kept in the temple. The sculptors had created a carved panel showing Thoth writing the name of Piankhy on the 'Stem of Millions of Years'.

Queen Abilah felt intense pride. In these happy

hours, she had become more and more aware of Pharaoh's most exalted mission: to turn the Two Lands into the living image of heaven and transform daily life into a spiritual festival.

Through its fertilizing waters, the Nile flood hailed the coming of Piankhy. In each village tables were laid out, groaning with food, thanks to the king's generosity, and his fame was celebrated in banquets washed down with plenty of strong drink.

As the sun reflected off the tides, turning the whole land into light, the monarch and his wife gathered the water of the new year in vases of gold, silver and copper. Standing before the people, Piankhy drank the liquid contained in a gold and silver vase, a mixture of wine, beer and rye-wine. Then he spoke the ancient text: 'O Hidden One, we offer you this meadow of mysteries, endowed with all virtues. In it grows the earth's hair, the wheat and barley which give life even though they are surrounded by rye-grass.'

Abilah felt a moment's anxiety. What if a murderous hand had poisoned the mixture? But at once her mind was set at ease: it was their own daughter, the Wife of Amon, who had herself measured out the brew. At Thebes, Piankhy was in no danger, for he was under Amon's protection.

And now it was time for the secret rites that took place inside the temple, where only those initiated into the mysteries of Amon and Osiris might enter. The initiates formed a procession of sixty priests and priestesses, each carrying one of the items used during the daily acts of worship; the most important were a censer, a purification vase and a sceptre of consecration. Because the energy of these symbols was exhausted, it was the royal couple's task to regenerate them by climbing up to the temple roof and there presenting them to the powerful sun of the new year.

In the full blaze of noon, the Divine Light accomplished its task.

*   *   *

A little before dawn, in the innermost shrine of the temple, Piankhy opened the mouth and eyes of the statue of Amon, dressed it in new robes, anointed it with perfume and presented it with the *ka* of food and drink. Then the king opened the mouth of each statue, each bas-relief and each hall of the temple of Karnak. This action was designed to give back strength and vigour to this immense living being, within which flowed a new energy which would nourish the shrine.

While the harpists and flute-players made their musical offering to Amon, Abilah watched her husband. She saw that he was on the verge of being swallowed up by this sacred universe, to which he had just given back its full intensity. The queen bore the very ancient title of 'She who sees Horus and Set'; she knew there were two irreconcilable aspects to reality, the powers of construction and destruction, and that these powers, which warred ceaselessly in the universe, were miraculously harmonized within the person of Pharaoh.

She knew it was her duty to intervene. She asked Piankhy, 'Have you forgotten the war, Majesty?'

'Thebes is celebrating, Abilah.'

'Nevertheless, you cannot allow your thoughts to wander so freely in these holy places that you forget what tomorrow will bring.'

212

'Why are you so cruel to me, when I love you so dearly?'

'It is my duty as queen. You are the spouse of Egypt, as were all the pharaohs who went before you, and Egypt is suffering—and may even die— while you dream of staying here in Karnak and thinking only of holy things. That's what you're planning, isn't it?'

Piankhy felt a stab of pain. Abilah had read his mind. Yes, he dreamt of withdrawing into Amon's dwelling-place, of doing nothing but celebrating the rites each day and living like a reclusive priest, far from the demands and the depravities of the outside world. If he stayed here, wouldn't that guarantee peace—admittedly only relative peace, but none the less real, and he could consolidate it through the power of hymns and prayers. If he chose that path, the military situation would be deadlocked for years on end.

But Abilah was trying to shatter this dream by forcing Piankhy to accuse himself of selfishness, and to remember the cruel fate of the Egyptians in the North, who were subject to Tefnakht's tyranny.

A land that was unified once more, a land liberated from the evil that gnawed away at its heart, a people at last delivered from war . . . But was the Black Pharaoh capable of winning such an enormous victory? Rather than delude himself and shed blood, was it not better to be content with beautifying Thebes and contemplating God?

Abilah kept silent. She sensed that her husband was in the grip of a conflict that was tearing him apart. The destiny of the whole country and all its people rested upon the Black Pharaoh's decision.

CHAPTER FORTY-THREE

Lemersekny was sitting with his back against a block of limestone, on which he had laid his weapons, eating onions and smearing linseed oil on his acacia-wood arm. At one time, he had debated cutting a notch in it for every enemy he killed, but the numbers had mounted up too quickly.

Puarma sat down beside his colleague.

'Well, are we going to attack another stronghold?' asked Lemersekny.

'Piankhy's furious,' said Puarma gloomily.

'What? That's a good one! We recapture Cliff-of-Great-Victories, we kill one of Tefnakht's whelps, we prove that the enemy can't move an inch, and the king isn't happy?'

'The pharaoh has ordered us to hold our positions.'

'What have we been doing all these months? I hope Piankhy's coming soon—at least then he can show us what to do.'

'I don't know anything about that.'

'What do you mean, you don't know? You've just received new orders.'

'Yes, but they don't say anything about that. Piankhy's going to celebrate the Festival of Opet, and—'

'That damned festival again!' exclaimed Lemersekny, picking up a stone and flinging it away from him. 'But what good are we doing here? I'll wager the king's decided to settle in Thebes and won't be going any further.'

'You mean . . .?'

'Piankhy has no intention of waging total war against Tefnakht: that's the truth. And we shall stay stuck here until the end of our days, guarding this damned border.'

*   *   *

The accuracy of the skilled archers was sometimes astonishing, and Daybreak never missed one of their training sessions. A young officer had just shot three arrows into the centre of a target a hundred paces away, a small shield that many veterans would have missed. The young man had an assured bearing, though his face was that of a boy. His movements seemed instinctive, effortless.

'Remarkable,' commented Daybreak, her green eyes sparkling with excitement.

'In my heart, I dedicated the third arrow to you. Will you forgive my impertinence?'

She smiled. 'I consider it a thoughtful gesture, even if it is an act of war.'

'Not yet, Princess. For the moment, it's only a game. Soon, I hope, there will be a Nubian in place of that target, then another and another . . .'

The intensity in the archer's eyes disturbed Daybreak. 'Do you really want to fight Piankhy?'

'It is my dearest wish, but I know I must be patient. Everyone knows this war will be decisive.'

'What if it never happens?'

'That's impossible—Tefnakht is just waiting for the right moment. And it will be glorious, I'm certain of that.'

The young man's freshness and enthusiasm charmed Daybreak. He was the same age as she was, believed that the whole world could belong to

215

him, and hadn't the slightest doubt about his commitment.

'You are right,' she said. 'His victory will be dazzling.'

As she walked away, his eyes never left her.

*   *   *

The Festival of Opet, which released the secret of spiritual fertility, was the high point of the flood season. It had lasted no fewer than twenty-four days, and soon the Nile waters would recede, after depositing fertile silt on the land. During this period of celebration, the pharaoh's *ka* had been regenerated, allowing him to carry out his duties with the maximum of energy, an energy which he communicated to his people and his land.

Piankhy had escorted the statue of Amon, which had left Karnak for Luxor, where the mystery of divine revelation had taken place. The visible had communed with the Invisible at the moment when the King and Queen of Egypt had been united once again under Amon's protection. The god's great cedarwood boat had appeared before the jubilant crowds. It was covered with gold and decorated with precious stones, but the veil draped over the boat's cabin would never be raised, for it covered the place where the god's effigy dwelt, and his true form would never be made known to ordinary mortals.

All along the river, little wooden shrines had been built, as they had along the sides of the road which led between the temples at Karnak and Luxor. These shrines formed a series of stopping-places for the procession, which was accompanied

216

by male and female singers, musicians and dancing-girls, while the ordinary folk gorged themselves with the food liberally handed out by the priests. For the gods commanded that places of refreshment be prepared both for the boat's bearers and for those who trod more earthly paths.

By celebrating the presence of Amon, the father, his wife Mut, the mother, and their son Khonsu, 'He who Crosses the Sky', Piankhy was asserting the omnipotence of the divine trinity, thanks to whom a new sun was reborn.

Piankhy knew that the secret of governing Egypt rested on the strict observance of the calendar of festivals, as it had been revealed in the beginning. In peace, he experienced the reality of Amon when he carried his statue into the innermost shrine of the temple during the night, which was brightened by a light which human eyes could not see. As he returned the god to his dwelling and positioned him upon his throne, the pharaoh was bestowing honour upon the instigator of creation and returning all things to their rightful place.

*   *   *

Thebes was reluctantly emerging from several weeks of celebration, which had been on a much grander scale than usual, by order of Piankhy: it was his intention to create a dazzling assertion of his domination over Southern Egypt. Leading citizens had convinced themselves that the spectre of war was moving away and that the king would abandon Napata in favour of Thebes, embellishing the city of Amon and covering its temples with gold.

217

Everyone knew that Piankhy had been won over by Thebes, where he celebrated the daily rites fervently. Thanks to him, some of the priests had rediscovered the path of faith, and the sacred songs sung in the Temple of Amon resounded with the same grandeur as in the age of Ramses.

As for the Wife of Amon, she thanked heaven for granting her precious time with her father. Without him, Shepena would have felt abandoned to a life of loneliness and crushing responsibility, for the obligations of her new office were frighteningly numerous and heavy. Running all the temples in Karnak efficiently seemed beyond the scope of a young woman who, up till then, had devoted herself to the art of making perfumes. But the advice she had been given by her predecessor and by the king and the queen, and the help she had received from Marjoram and a devoted steward, had allowed Shepena to shoulder her responsibilities quickly, and forget her fears. Like most members of the Theban priesthood, she hoped that Piankhy would choose Thebes as his permanent residence and that violence would be banished for ever.

*　　*　　*

When Queen Abilah awoke, she turned her head to look at Piankhy, who last night had made love to her with the enthusiasm of a young lover setting out to discover a marvellous, unexplored land. But the king had left their bed.

She went out of the bedchamber on to the palace terrace, which looked over one of the courtyards of the temple at Karnak. She was sure he would be there, gazing down at the sacred dwelling-place of Amon.

She stood beside him and slid her arm round him, in the gesture of magical protection the sculptors represented in stone when they created statues of an eternally happy couple.

'Has Pharaoh taken his decision?' she asked.

'Today, we shall go to the Temple of Mut, to carry out the rites of anathema against visible and invisible enemies. Tomorrow, I shall lead out my army to strike down adversity and re-establish harmony.'

CHAPTER FORTY-FOUR

Crying with rage, Daybreak ripped up a delicate linen shawl Tefnakht had given her. For several minutes, her past had overwhelmed her like the unstoppable tide of the Nile in full flood. Her father's death, her rape by Nartreb, the Northern general's arrogance, the treason of which some would undoubtedly accuse her . . . She should leave Henen-nesut, run away, disappear—wasn't that the best solution?

No, she had must fulfil her destiny. Even if she had to trample her memories underfoot, endure Nartreb's lascivious glances and Yegeb's hypocrisy, and struggle against the cowardice shown by some of the Libyan princes, she would not abandon Tefnakht. She would throw all her energies into helping him achieve the vital reconquest of Egypt.

A man entered her bedchamber carrying a dish of grapes, pomegranates and dates. She recognized him instantly: it was the young officer from the corps of archers.

'Forgive this intrusion, Princess,' he said. 'I thought you might like to taste this delicious fruit.'

'Who let you in?'

'The guards know me. And I wanted to surprise you.'

Daybreak suddenly realized that she was almost naked. A simple veil, reaching down to mid-thigh, did nothing to conceal her lissome form.

'Put down that tray and go,' she ordered.

'Until today, archery was my only passion. Will you grant me your permission to leave the army and become your servant?' The young man's voice was unsteady.

Overcome by emotion, Daybreak turned her back on him. 'Don't even think of such madness. You are an elite archer.'

'What does that matter to me, if I can no longer see you, speak to you, breathe in your perfume, if ... if I can no longer touch you?'

He laid his hand hesitantly on her shoulder. She should have moved away, ordered him to leave, but his caress was so gentle, so sweet ...

'I love you,' he whispered, delicately kissing her cheek.

Daybreak's heart began to pound, and a strange warmth pervaded her body. 'No, not here.'

As if he had not heard, the officer stroked her hair. She knew that, if she allowed him to continue, she would lose all power to resist him.

'If Tefnakht catches us,' she said, 'it will mean death—for you as well as me.'

She turned to face the young man, whose eyes were filled with desire.

'When . . . when shall I see you again?' he asked.

'Tomorrow, in the early afternoon, in the palace storeroom where they keep fabrics. Tefnakht will be at the main barracks to inspect the infantry's weaponry—No, this is madness!'

He kissed her hands. 'I love you, Daybreak. I'm mad with love for you! And I swear that I will keep this secret, for it is the key to our happiness.'

'Go! Go quickly!'

He gave her such a fevered kiss that she wanted to hold him back and give herself to him, but the danger was too great. When he had gone, desire still burned in the young woman's heart. She longed to enjoy that virile body and share its passion.

*   *   *

The young officer emerged from the palace and turned into an alleyway which led to the barracks.

Yegeb was waiting there. 'Well,' he asked, 'did you succeed?'

'No woman can resist me—I told you that. Daybreak is no exception to the rule.'

'Are you sure she's attracted to you?'

'I know women, Yegeb. They can pretend up to a point, but in this instance Daybreak is sincere. What's more, she's a superb filly, and if I'd pushed her a little, we'd have slept together this very evening.'

'That would have been too soon. Tefnakht must catch you together, and have absolutely no doubt about the infidelity of the woman he was going to make Queen of Egypt.'

'She's taking a big risk.'

221

'That's not your concern,' said Yegeb.

'And you can definitely guarantee me immunity?'

'I shall tell Tefnakht the whole truth: I paid you to seduce that slut and prove that he was wrong to trust her. You will be regarded as a loyal follower and promoted to high rank.'

'In the meantime, pay me what you owe me.'

Yegeb handed the officer a small leather purse containing gold nuggets. The young man checked the contents.

'You're a rich man now,' said Yegeb.

'So I should be—I'm taking a lot of risks. And this is only the first half of the fee?'

'You'll have the other half as soon as Tefnakht is rid of that lying, treacherous woman.'

'Why do you hate her so much?'

'Do your job properly, soldier, and don't ask pointless questions.'

Weighing the purse in his hand, the officer walked off towards the barracks.

Of course, Yegeb mused, he'd get his gold back. He'd take it from the corpse of that imbecile, who, together with the adulteress, would be executed for insulting the general. And Tefnakht would never know the truth.

*   *   *

As night fell, Karnak's astrologers climbed slowly up the stairs to the temple roof. Each one took up a specified position to observe the movement of the planets, 'the tireless stars', and the circular course of the thirty-six candles, the groups of stars that burned in the firmament. The specialists

222

constantly refined their knowledge of celestial phenomena and used them to try to read messages from the gods.

Before beginning his work, the head astrologer filled a cup with clear water and placed it on a smooth, flat flagstone. Ordinarily, the liquid surface formed a perfect mirror, the symbol of Hathor, mistress of the stars, and linked the spirit of the observer with the spirit of the goddess.

He thought his eyes were deceiving him. Such a phenomenon, when there was not a breath of wind . . . He looked closer, and had to admit the terrible reality: there were ripples on the surface of the water! Terrified, he rushed down the stone staircase and almost ran to the royal palace, but the two Nubian soldiers guarding the gates barred his way.

'I must speak to the king,' panted the astrologer. 'Tell him!'

When he was shown into Piankhy's apartments, the astrologer could not disguise his alarm. 'Majesty, I have just witnessed something ominous: there are ripples in the water-mirror we use on the temple roof.'

'How do you interpret this sign?' asked the king.

'As the herald of great misfortune, Majesty. Such an inexplicable phenomenon indicates an imminent disaster which will touch at the very heart of the kingdom. That is why I had to warn you without delay.'

'What precautions do you suggest we take?'

'The magicians must spend all night reciting incantations to prevent death from seizing and abducting her prey.'

'Can you be more specific about your fears?'

The astrologer hesitated, then said, 'Majesty, your life is in danger.'

CHAPTER FORTY-FIVE

When Tefnakht, accompanied by Daybreak, entered the audience hall, one look at his expression was enough to tell the members of his council of war that the situation had suddenly changed. Clearly, the general had vital information to impart.

'Piankhy is leaving Thebes,' he revealed.

'Is he going back to Nubia?' asked Akanosh.

'No, he is preparing to attack us.'

Tefnakht omitted to mention that his Theban spies had failed to kill the Black Pharaoh, and that he was not sorry to hear of this failure. Naturally, it would have been easier to defeat the Southern army if it had been deprived of its leader, but the prospect of battle was welcome. If he could personally kill his enemy, it would prove his supremacy once and for all.

'Are we going to wait for him to attack, or shall we act first?' asked Peftau anxiously.

'There is no reason to change our strategy. We'll let Piankhy batter his troops to pieces against the walls of Henen-nesut. When he's lost enough men, we'll launch a series of attacks which will end in the total destruction of the enemy.'

'Will you grant a pardon to any survivors?' went on Peftau.

'No,' replied Tefnakht. 'We must exterminate this Nubian scum without pity. That is the price of this country's future.'

*   *   *

Piankhy had drawn water from the Temple of Mut's sacred lake, which was shaped like a crescent moon. The water would be kept in jars, and would provide magical protection for the Southern army, which was preparing to depart. Freely given by the celestial river, this other-worldly energy would ensure that the strength of those who were determined to reconquer the North would never wane.

Dressed in a long red robe which left her breasts bare, Queen Abilah looked magnificent; but she could not overcome her anxiety. 'The astronomer established that the stars were unfavourable to you, didn't he?'

'There were ripples on the surface of the water-mirror,' Piankhy reminded her. 'That means there will be a death. It may mean my death, but why shouldn't it refer to the end of an era?'

Abilah looked her husband in the eyes. 'First I wanted this war, then it filled me with horror. Then I realized once more that it was vital if happiness was to flower again, and I forced myself not to think about it. But here and now, I am at a loss. All I know is that I am afraid for you. If you gave up everything to remain in this temple, I would understand, whatever other people might say. You are the life I dreamt of, my love, and yet you are very real. I want to keep you beside me.'

Piankhy held her close. 'Perhaps death awaits me at the end of this adventure. But we have a chance of victory. Unless I carry out the duties of

225

my office, unless I try to make the law of Ma'at respected throughout the land, I shall be justly sentenced to a second death and annihilation by the court of the hereafter. We have made our choice, Abilah; now we are free to act.'

Realizing that she would never succeed in changing Piankhy's mind, Abilah went with him to the temple of the fearsome Sekhmet, where the necessary rites of conjuration would take place, in order to reduce their enemies' destructive power. All night long, the magicians of Karnak had chanted incantations to protect the king, in the hope that death the abductor had not devised some new trick to steal away Piankhy's soul.

As agreed, the Wife of Amon was to celebrate the birth of the new sun while the royal couple, assisted by Marjoram and the priestesses of the scorpion-goddess Serket, waged the first great magical battle against Tefnakht and his allies, who were symbolized by figurines crudely carved from alabaster and limestone.

'A few decades ago,' mused Piankhy, 'it was the Nubians who were hated like this. But today they have come from the far-off South to fight and die in order to save the country that embodies the essential values of civilization and spirituality. It is a strange reversal of fortunes: those who were persecuted yesterday have forgotten their legitimate grievances and grudges, and have become today's liberators.'

On the figurines, scribes had written in red ink a short text describing the destructive nature of the enemies of Ma'at, the rebels and their allies, who were shown kneeling or lying on their bellies, with their hands tied behind their backs.

226

Marjoram addressed Piankhy. 'Pharaoh of Upper and Lower Egypt, may the gods protect you from those who speak evil words and perform evil deeds. May your power be stronger than theirs, may they be terrified by your might, may they be trampled under your feet. May those who try to hinder the voyage of the sun be for ever deprived of the Light; may their lips be sealed and their arms cut off.'

A priestess closed the mouths of the figurines with Piankhy's seal and broke their limbs. Then Marjoram threw them into a brazier; moans seemed to rise from it, scaring those taking part in the ceremony—even the mongoose became nervous and took cover behind his master's feet.

Queen Abilah felt that this ancient magic was not an illusion but really was unleashing waves of strength which would attack the enemies of Ma'at at the same time as Pharaoh attacked them. And she understood why, since the earliest times, no King of Egypt had neglected his ritual obligations before leaving for war.

While the fire crackled, Marjoram handed Piankhy a fine alabaster goblet inscribed with his name. 'Majesty, before this vase is placed in the temple treasury to commemorate your fame, please drink this beer created by the god Ra so that your courage may shine out through all the provinces of the kingdom.'

Just as the pharaoh was stretching out his hands to take the goblet, the mongoose darted up on to his shoulder, stood stock still for a brief instant, then leapt on to Marjoram's wrist and bit her so hard that it drew blood.

She let out a cry of pain and dropped the goblet,

227

which fell on to the stone floor. A yellowish liquid ran out, driving the mongoose into a fury. With its fur standing on end and its whiskers bristling, it twisted and turned as though attacking a snake.

'That creature has gone mad. Kill it!' demanded Marjoram.

But Abilah, when she saw how the animal was behaving, immediately realized the truth. 'Marjoram,' she said, 'you tried to poison the king with snake venom given to you by an accomplice, one of the priestesses of Serket. You are in Tefnakht's pay, aren't you?'

Unable to bear the queen's accusing stare, Marjoram backed away, clutching her bloodied wrist with her other hand. She was about to deny everything, when two terrified priestesses of Serket tried to run away. Piankhy's soldiers stopped them roughly.

'Why did you do this,' asked the king, 'you who were the faithful servant of my dead sister, the Wife of Amon?'

His voice was so stern that Marjoram began to shake, but she managed to say defiantly, 'The new Wife of Amon is a Nubian, like the last one. Isn't it enough for you to govern Thebes through her? Tefnakht's cause is just. His victory will give us back our lost unity.'

She threw herself to her knees and licked up the deadly liquid. 'I have failed, but the North will have victory!' Her eyes stared fixedly ahead, her limbs stiffened, she vomited bile and collapsed, clutching at her throat.

With her death and the arrest of her accomplices, Tefnakht had no spies left in Thebes.

CHAPTER FORTY-SIX

In the Libyan ranks, enthusiasm mingled with fear. On one hand, the soldiers were longing to fight; on the other, they were afraid of the Black Pharaoh's savagery. But Tefnakht knew the way to inspire trust and keep a sometimes flickering flame burning brightly. By making his men train all day long, he prevented them falling prey to fear-ridden imaginings.

One thing was certain: Piankhy would not succeed in capturing Henen-nesut. All that remained was to find out how he would react. Would he fight on and lose thousands of men, or would he beat a retreat? It was up to Tefnakht to find the right moment to launch an overwhelming attack which would break the back of the Nubian army.

The general was reassured by his inspection of the armoury and warehouses. There were plenty of weapons, all in good repair, and there was enough food to withstand a long siege, particularly since the Northern provinces were having little difficulty in sending supply convoys.

As he was returning to the palace, Yegeb came up to him, looking worried. 'My lord . . .'

'What is it?'

'I have two pieces of bad news for you. But perhaps I have chosen the wrong moment.'

'Tell me,' ordered Tefnakht.

'Marjoram is dead, and the other priestesses have been imprisoned. We no longer have anyone in Thebes to send us information on Piankhy's decisions.'

'That is not too serious, since we no longer need that kind of information. We know the Black Pharaoh's strength and we shall not alter our plans. What is the other bad news?'

Yegeb looked deeply apologetic. 'It's a delicate matter, my lord, extremely delicate.'

'Speak out, man.'

'It's about Daybreak.'

'Has someone tried to harm her?'

'To tell the truth, my lord, the way she's behaving it's likely that she'll be the one to do harm, serious harm—to you.'

'Be careful what you say, Yegeb,' said Tefnakht menacingly.

'Listen to me, my lord, I beg of you. Our watchers believe they have chanced upon a . . . a liaison between Daybreak and a young officer in the corps of archers.'

Tefnakht's dark eyes grew darker still. 'Can you prove what you are suggesting?'

'Unfortunately, yes. If you will follow me . . .'

* * *

Daybreak was still full of desire for the young man who was going to become her lover. In the room where linens were stored, which was filled with delicious scents and the pleasing smell of clean sheets. And as he walked towards her, he too felt passion rising.

'You came,' he said softly. 'It's a dream, a wonderful dream!'

She smiled. 'No, I'm not a dream.'

He closed his eyes. 'Let me imagine you first,

then look at you as you really are. You are by far my most beautiful conquest.'

'Have there been so many?'

'Now that I've seen you, no other woman even exists.'

Slowly, he slid down the left strap of her dress then, still more slowly, the right strap, baring her magnificent breasts. As he kissed them, she quivered and, bowing her head in utter intoxication, gazed deep into his eyes.

What she saw there horrified her. His eyes were filled with the same contempt, the same arrogance, the same brutality, as she had seen in Nartreb's eyes when he raped her. He did not love her. All he wanted was to possess her in the most bestial way.

Suddenly, she understood. 'Turn round,' she said. 'I'm going to take off my dress.'

'I didn't think you were so modest.'

'Please.'

Amused, he obeyed.

Daybreak seized one of the leather straps used for binding bundles of linen and used this improvised weapon to strangle the archer. He struggled, but her grip was remorseless. And her strength grew even greater when she saw that Tefnakht was standing watching the scene, arms folded.

The officer stopped struggling. His throat crushed, he had suffocated to death.

'He threatened me,' Daybreak said to Tefnakht. 'He brought me here and tried to rape me—by humiliating me, he wanted to soil your name. And the traitor confessed to me that he was in Piankhy's pay.'

She spat on the corpse then collapsed, weeping,

into Tefnakht's arms.

*   *   *

Yegeb's head was wrapped in a damp cloth, his torso covered in a salve designed to relax his tense muscles. He was suffering from an attack of indigestion, which was causing painful bilious spasms. He growled to Nartreb, 'That damned Daybreak made me apologize to her, and the general ordered me to check my information properly before sullying the reputation of the future Queen of Egypt. I was worried I might even be dismissed in disgrace.'

Nartreb shrugged and went on rubbing his painful toes. 'Tefnakht can't do without us—he delegates all his dirty work to us. But how did that girl manage to turn the situation to her advantage?'

'By killing the officer,' said Yegeb uneasily.

'You're not afraid of her, are you?'

'I'm not used to failure. And at the moment, Daybreak hates us.'

'That's nothing new,' said Nartreb. 'But if she thinks Tefnakht really takes any notice of her opinions, she's sorely mistaken. Ambition is the general's only mistress. And we are by his side to satisfy that need. The decisive attack is coming, and we, my friend, are going to make a great deal of money out of it.'

*   *   *

Otoku had noticeably lost weight, and his food no longer tasted as good as it once had. The fat man was conscientious, and ruled Napata with

232

meticulous care. Both local dignitaries and administrators missed Piankhy, who, although stern, had been less demanding than Otoku.

The news from Thebes was not calculated to restore the fat man's appetite, and the news that Kapa wished to see him made him feel no more cheerful. Otoku put down the alabaster serving dish, on which a roasted goose leg awaited his attention, and told the steward to show the old man in.

'If you've come to criticize, Kapa, you've chosen a bad moment. I'm drowning in a Nile flood of work.'

'Why are you so jumpy? Your scribes and I have reason to be proud of you. I only came to offer you my congratulations.'

Otoku couldn't believe his ears. Kapa must be mocking him. And yet, the old man had abandoned his usual irony. No, he wasn't jeering at the new governor of Napata; moreover, he looked just as sad as Otoku.

'You're thinking the same thing, aren't you, Kapa? You think Piankhy's not coming back.'

'Why delude ourselves? Either he will lose the war and be killed, or else he will establish his capital at Thebes and never leave there again.'

'Never . . .?' said Otoku, aghast.

'Yes, never. You're going to have to rule Napata until the end of your days. Piankhy made a good choice when he appointed you.'

'Will this city ever know happiness again? Without the Black Pharaoh, it's nothing but a little town buried in a remote oasis.'

'Do as I have done, Otoku. Grow old. Then you will accept the unacceptable.'

233

CHAPTER FORTY-SEVEN

The royal ship's prow was shaped like a snake with a ram's head, covered in gold, and was as eloquent of kingship as the peak of the Pure Mountain. In the bows sat the Black Pharaoh and his Great Royal Wife, gazing north towards Middle Egypt and the Province of the Hare, which they would reach in ten days' time.

The king was wearing the White Crown, symbol of Upper Egypt, enclosed within the Red Crown, symbol of Lower Egypt; on it were fixed two gold figures of female cobras, whose rage would drive away the king's enemies. His feathered corslet had straps which knotted on the shoulders, and he wore a linen loincloth. Gold bracelets inlaid with glass encircled his wrists; on the clasp of each was a representation of Nut, the sky-goddess. Under his gold collar, which was made up of miniature cobras, hung a blue-green ceramic amulet nearly a hand's-breadth long, shaped like a ram's head crowned by the solar disc. These items evoked the secret of the Divine and his revelation through the Light.

Abilah sat at her husband's side, her right arm proudly threaded through his left. She wore a long red dress, caught at the waist by a white belt which hung down in long bands. She wore gold earrings in the shape of the key of life, a reminder that the hieroglyphic name for the ears was 'the living ones'. A decorative collar of glass, ceramic and cornelian beads hung at her throat, the beads interspersed with little scarabs, embodying the idea of transformation, and pillars, which evoked stability. Her pendant was shaped like a lotus flanked by two falcon's eyes, holding all the dimensions of the universe.

'Amon is coming in the wind,' chanted Piankhy, 'but the eye cannot see him. The night is filled with his presence, the day glorifies him. That which is above reflects that which is below, and it is he who brings it about.'

'O great soul of Egypt,' prayed Queen Abilah, 'give breath to all those who are about to fight for the reunification of the Two Lands.'

Piankhy opened a silver-gilt case and took out a dagger. Where the blade joined the hilt, a lion was devouring a Nubian. But the weapon dated from the glorious days of Tuthmosis III, and it had been piously kept in the temple of Amon at Napata. The sun glinted off the long, thick blade, giving the sign that it was time to set sail.

*   *   *

Golden fields of barley, herons soaring above thickets of papyrus, falcons drifting with the wind, the gentle slopes of the riverbanks . . . the landscape was dreamily beautiful. But none of the Nubian soldiers had the heart for idle reveries. Their thoughts were dominated by the terrible battle they would soon have to fight—all were thinking of the wives, mothers, fathers and children they might never see again.

Before they set sail, Piankhy had spent a long time talking to his horse, whose sparkling, intelligent eyes were tinged with anxiety. He had

235

not concealed the truth, but had warned Valiant that he was about to confront formidable dangers. Valiant grew calm and lifted his head proudly. He, too, was ready to fight.

Waiting on the riverbank, at the southern border of the Province of the Hare, Lemersekny and Puarma were both overwhelmed and anxious. Overwhelmed to see the Black Pharaoh approaching on his horse, which he had harnessed himself; anxious because they knew they must bear the brunt of his criticism.

'Is Tefnakht still a free man?' he demanded, visibly irate.

'Yes, Majesty,' replied Puarma.

'I gave you a mission, and ordered to you put an end to that renegade. I trusted you because I was confident that you would drive these Northerners away. But today the cities of Khmun and Henen-nesut are occupied by the enemy and the name of Pharaoh is scorned because of your incompetence!'

Puarma hung his head, but Lemersekny protested, 'We have spared no effort, Majesty, but Tefnakht is not some petty chieftain leading a band of disorganized rebels. What we are faced with is a real army.'

'Do you think I don't know that?' demanded Piankhy.

'The siege of Henen-nesut will be long and difficult,' observed Lemersekny. 'We shall lose many men, but I hope to find a way to crush the city's rebellion. Once we are the masters, Tefnakht will be forced to surrender.'

'So we are facing the prospect of heavy losses.'

'Alas, Majesty, the walls of Henen-nesut are thick and the Libyan archers are skilful.'

'Send out scouts immediately,' ordered Piankhy. 'Tell them to make a point of showing themselves, so that the watchmen will notice they are there.'

Lemersekny was astonished. 'But Majesty, wouldn't it be better to—'

'Tomorrow morning, instruct a detachment of soldiers to set up camp a good distance from the town. They are to make plenty of noise.'

'A detachment . . .? If we're going to take Henen-nesut, we're going to need all our forces.'

'Have the soldiers pitch plenty of tents to form a vast encampment, as if the whole of my army was preparing to attack.'

'You mean, we aren't going to attack?'

'Of course we are,' said Piankhy. 'But not where the enemy expects.'

*   *   *

Feeling nervous and irritable, Nartreb was pacing up and down the battlements of Henen-nesut. A watchman suddenly noticed two Nubian scouts clumsily trying to hide behind a thicket of thornbushes, and he alerted the counsellor immediately.

'There are two others down there,' he said, 'and another two at the edge of the fields.'

Nartreb ran down from the battlements and hurried to the main barracks, where Tefnakht and Daybreak were addressing the soldiers.

'They're there,' announced Nartreb. 'Many scouts. That means Piankhy's army will be here tomorrow, or in a few days at the latest.'

Daybreak smiled, but Tefnakht controlled his joy.

'This evening,' he declared, 'there shall be meat

237

and wine for all our soldiers, both officers and men. Piankhy has fallen into our trap. His vanity will make him launch an attack against this impregnable fortress. We shall kill thousands of Nubians, and the North will be victorious!'

Tefnakht's men cheered him loudly. Then he went back into his apartments with Daybreak. Both were in a state of high excitement, and the young woman was shivering in spite of the heat.

'Your dream is going to come true,' she said, 'a dream which is now mine too.'

She undressed the general, untied the shoulder-straps of her own dress and made passionate love to the man who was going to defeat Piankhy, and impose his law on a reunified Egypt.

*   *   *

Yegeb was putting the finishing touches to the plan for government requested by Tefnakht. The pharaoh would be crowned at Thebes and at Memphis, all Nubians, including the civilians, would be killed, and Napata would be destroyed. The gold mines would be taken over, the police and army would be enlarged, and a strict system of administration would be set up to ensure that the population could be properly supervised. Individual freedoms and property rights would be abolished, as would the privileges granted to the plethora of temples, most of which would be transformed into barracks. No one would be permitted to leave Egypt except soldiers with direct orders from Tefnakht. Taxes and levies would be increased, to facilitate the creation of a government entirely loyal to the king. Production of defensive and offensive arms would be increased, more fortresses and prisons would be built, and anyone who challenged these measures would be immediately put to death.

As they re-read this list of measures, Yegeb, the future minister of state finance, and Nartreb, the future head of state security, were well pleased with their work.

However, one last detail worried Yegeb: he must bring to heel certain Libyan chieftains who still clung to the notion of their independence and believed, naively, that Tefnakht intended to respect it. Most of these cases would be resolved either by the authority of the new master of Egypt, or by handing out the kind of presents which would persuade the dissenters to keep their mouths shut.

That left only Prince Akanosh, who was neither corrupt nor corruptible, and was sufficiently stubborn to protest openly against the new policy. Before resorting to arranging his sudden death, which would cause disagreeable repercussions at a time when Tefnakht was consolidating his power, it might perhaps be possible to find a weak link in his entourage, and discredit him once and for all.

CHAPTER FORTY-EIGHT

Nemrod, Prince of Khmun, was in an excellent mood. How right he had been to betray Piankhy and back Tefnakht! Just as the latter had predicted, the Black Pharaoh was going to batter his troops against the stronghold of Henen-nesut, and he would not realize until too late that he had so

239

weakened his own army that he had lost all chance of winning.

With his perfumed hair, and carefully tended nails, Nemrod felt more handsome than ever. In fact, he was so pleased with himself that he had sent for his wife, Nezeta, whose existence he had for a long time virtually forgotten—much to the benefit of a string of mistresses, all of them well versed in the games of love.

Nezeta was over fifty but still stylish and charming. However, she could not compete with pretty twenty-year-old schemers who thought, mistakenly, that they could conquer the Lord of Khmun. Soberly dressed, and wearing an old-fashioned wig, Nezeta showed no sign of resentment when she entered.

'Why did you summon me, Nemrod?' she asked.

'Soon Tefnakht will be crowned Pharaoh, and he will offer me my choice of posts in his government. So as not to shock the court, I must be seen with a submissive, discreet wife on my arm. Do you accept this role?'

'What if I refuse?'

'I shall renounce you on some pretext or other—perfectly legally of course—and another woman will take your place. Naturally, you will lose all your privileges and you will have to live far more frugally.'

'What will my duties be?'

'Simply to appear at my side, to pretend to be happy and to talk of nothing but trifles. There are more unpleasant jobs, Nezeta. At least with you beside me, no one will criticize me and there will be no dramas. I need calm in order to fulfil my future responsibilities. Do I have your agreement?'

'Yes.'

'Perfect!'

The whole world was smiling on Nemrod. Thanks to the instinct that had led him into Tefnakht's camp, his city would become one of the richest in Egypt and he would become one of the most visible and important members of the new pharaoh's court.

The prince was already excited as he walked towards the bedchamber of his latest mistress, a Syrian lute-player with wondrously nimble fingers.

Suddenly his chief bodyguard barred the way. 'Prince Nemrod—'

'Later. I'm in a hurry.'

'Prince Nemrod, we're under siege!'

'Under siege? But by whom?'

'Nubians—thousands of Nubians.'

'You're talking nonsense,' said the prince. 'Piankhy's army is marching on Henen-nesut!'

'No, Prince. The Black Pharaoh really is here, with his soldiers.'

At the risk of getting out of breath, Nemrod climbed right to the top of the highest tower in the fortifications.

What he saw appalled him. The men the Northerners called 'braid-wearers' and 'burnt-faces' were unhurriedly bearing down on Khmun, and at their head was the Black Pharaoh, sitting astride a magnificent bay warhorse with a tawny mane. The Southern soldiers had jet-black skin and scarred cheeks, and wore small gold rings in their ears. The front portion of their heads was shaved, their hair was short and curly, and they wore short kilts held up with a red belt. They seemed invincible. The officers were identifiable by their

241

white robes, necklets of multicoloured beads and red wigs.

'There are so many of them, Prince, so many!' moaned the commander of the guard.

Though terrified, Nemrod tried to keep calm. 'Our fortifications are strong.'

'They say the Nubians rip out their victims' entrails and feed them to the crocodiles! They say that, when they attack, blood rains down from the skies! They say—'

'That's enough! Every man must stay at his post and defend this town as if it were his most treasured possession. We shall drive the Southerners back.'

So Piankhy had let his foes believe that he would swoop down like a bird of prey on Henen-nesut, all the better to concentrate his efforts on Khmun, the city of Thoth, whose favour the Black Pharaoh wished to be certain of having. Being so steeped in tradition, Piankhy would never have taken a step forward without the help of Thoth, the Master of Knowledge. Neither Tefnakht nor Nemrod had perceived this aspect of the Nubian's personality. By reducing him to the level of a simple conqueror, they had forgotten the sacred dimension of his office.

But now was not the time for regrets. Nemrod must try to save his city; and save it he would. After all, his fortifications were just as strong a deterrent as those of Henen-nesut.

*   *   *

Lemersekny was more poorly dressed than the soldiers he commanded, and he hadn't even

242

bothered to shave. His only concession to vanity was the strip of coarse linen which concealed his wooden arm.

For several long minutes, he had been staring fixedly at a particular section of the fortifications.

'Do you think we should concentrate our attack there?' asked Piankhy.

'Certainly not, Majesty. That's the section that Nemrod had destroyed, hoping to lure your first army into a trap. I'm convinced that when he realized his ruse had failed, he had that wall strengthened with particular care.'

'Then what do you suggest?'

'If it was up to me, I'd simply attack on all fronts. But this isn't some little stronghold like Cliff-of-Great-Victories. Look how high and thick the walls are. Throwing ourselves full-tilt at Khmun would just lead to disaster. We'd lose a lot of men without being certain of gaining even a foothold on the battlements. Frankly, Majesty, I am ready to fight, but why die in a charge that would be as stupid as it was heroic?'

'And there is no other way?'

Disappointed, Lemersekny shook his head.

Puarma would have liked to steal his rival's thunder and impress the king with his brilliance, but he, too, was short of ideas. In spite of their numbers, it seemed that the Nubians had no chance of taking Khmun. Undoubtedly they would deal it a serious blow, but at what price?

'Pitch the tents,' ordered Piankhy.

Lemersekny himself supervised the work. The men moistened the soil to damp down the dust, marked out paths and put up tents of different sizes, from the vast many-roomed one set aside for

243

the royal couple down to the little shelters used by junior officers. The horses, donkeys and cattle were fed, and the chariots, which had been transported in sections on the cargo boats, were reassembled. The doctors tended the sick, and everyone played dice and talked loud and long, to forget tomorrow's bloody fighting.

Queen Abilah was far from idle. In the royal tent, she arranged ceramic cups, glass phials of perfume, vases with lids shaped like rams' heads, and little lotus-shaped fans, not forgetting the cosmetic boxes containing pots of make-up and salves. A procession of serving-girls brought in the vital linen-chests and gold and silver dishes.

When Piankhy entered, he was dazzled. 'You have recreated our palace in Napata, Abilah!'

'Only a few rooms, and not very well, but this campaign against injustice doesn't mean we should sink into barbarism.' She took Piankhy's head in her gentle hands. 'You look worried. What can I do to help you?'

'Khmun seems impregnable. Even Lemersekny is ready to give up.'

'But not you!'

'All repeated attacks will do is bring us heavy losses. If we want to take Khmun, we shall have to find another solution.'

'When you are faced with an insurmountable obstacle, isn't the right thing to do either to go round it or else to destroy its very nature?'

'You mean . . . if there was something we could do so that the battlements weren't battlements any more? Yes, you're right!'

CHAPTER FORTY-NINE

The Nubian carpenters had worked day and night to assemble giant catapults, while the footsoldiers set up raised platforms mounted on wheels, and the donkey-drivers loaded their beasts with heavy baskets of earth.

Lemersekny sat with his back against a palm tree, chewing on a papyrus stalk and watching all this activity with a sceptical eye.

'Have a little faith,' Puarma advised him. 'These are Piankhy's orders.'

'Capture a fortress with donkeys? Can you really believe that?'

'You're forgetting the catapults.'

'I don't know how to use those things.'

'The army the king brought from Napata contains men who are skilled in the use of these war-machines,' said Puarma.

'They're just meant to impress the enemy, nothing more.'

'You're only sulking because your men aren't in the front line for once.'

Lemersekny growled like a Syrian bear.

*   *   *

Standing with his garrison commander at the top of the watchtower, Nemrod observed the Nubian preparations. He didn't understand them at all.

'Why don't they attack?' he asked.

The commander was equally puzzled. 'It's certainly surprising. And yet the habits of Nubian warriors are well known.'

'What are those strange machines for?'

'I have never seen anything like them, Prince. In my opinion, they don't know how to attack us and are trying to frighten us.'

An enormous stone, flung from a catapult, destroyed several crenellations of unbaked brick, killed two Libyan archers and wounded another ten. The skilled Nubians had judged the distance correctly with their very first shot. Twenty catapults swung into action and caused serious damage to the battlements.

Piankhy signalled to the donkey-drivers to advance, followed by the oxen, which drew chariots laden with tons of earth. To protect the convoy and unloading, Puarma's archers stood on the raised platforms and felled the Libyans, very few of whom were able to make use of their bows. Caught in the heavy, accurate fire from the catapults and bows, many defenders were struck down, while the army labourers built up an embankment which would surround the curtain wall and reach three-quarters of the way up it.

The walls of Khmun were no longer impregnable.

*   *   *

Without losing a single man, Puarma's archers took up position on the battlements. When Piankhy joined them, he noted that the town's defences had not been totally destroyed. The survivors still held the palace, the armoury, the barracks and the granaries. But already a putrid stench was rising from the narrow streets and the nooks and crannies where bodies lay piled high. Soon, no one in

246

Khmun would be able to breathe.

Lemersekny was growing impatient. 'Majesty, leave the job to me now. My men won't take long to flush out these cowards.'

'You're wrong, Captain. They'll defend their lives fiercely. Why should we risk the lives of our own men?'

'So what are your orders?"

'We shall wait for a reaction from Nemrod, our former ally.'

*   *   *

'We're all going to die,' predicted the garrison commander. 'We can hold out for a month, maybe two, but after that. . .'

All the officers shared his opinion. As for the city dignitaries, they were moaning with fear at the prospect of what the Black Pharaoh had in store for them.

'We must resist,' said Nemrod, whose face had visibly aged. 'Even better, we must counter-attack. Piankhy thinks he has already won, but let's prove him wrong!'

'Khmun is surrounded,' objected the commander, 'and we have lost half our men, while Piankhy's army is intact. If we try to counter-attack, we'll be wiped out.'

'Then what do you suggest?'

The commander hung his head. 'We should negotiate, Prince Nemrod.'

'You mean . . . surrender?'

'It's the best solution.'

'Have you gone mad? Piankhy will slaughter us all.'

A prominent citizen cut in. 'You were his ally, Nemrod, and you betrayed him. It is you the pharaoh will blame, not this town. He has no reason to punish its inhabitants if they submit themselves humbly to his will.'

'I am your prince. It is I you must obey!'

'The commander is right,' said the man. 'We must negotiate.'

*   *   *

The wealthiest citizens of Khmun passed through the gate in the city wall which led from Nemrod's palace. Their hair was braided, their beards had been groomed into sleek points, and they wore robes decorated with floral patterns.

Instantly, the Nubians drew their bows.

'Hold your fire,' ordered Puarma. 'They aren't armed.'

Laden with caskets filled with gold, precious stones and expensive fabrics, the envoys crossed a roadway littered with Libyan corpses and headed for the postern gate where Lemersekny was stationed.

The eldest envoy addressed him. 'Will you permit us the honour of placing these gifts at the feet of Pharaoh?'

'I'm going to search you first.'

The worthies submitted to the humiliation without turning a hair. Then Lemersekny led them to the centre of the camp, where Piankhy was seated on a gilded wooden throne, his fan-bearers providing him with a little cool air.

The citizens' spokesman bowed before the Black Pharaoh. 'Majesty, please accept these gifts from

248

the city of Khmun. Here are treasures which we have gathered together to offer you. Our town grovels on its belly to worship your greatness and to implore your mercy.'

'Did Nemrod send you?'

'We took the decision ourselves, but the prince was in agreement with it.'

'Why did he not accompany you?'

'He fears your anger, and—'

'He is right!' snapped Piankhy. 'When is he going to open the gates of this city, which is mine and which he stole from me?'

'Majesty, I beg you to understand Nemrod's fears.'

'Your prince is nothing but a rebel—and, worse than that, he is a traitor! No king would be weak enough to grant him a pardon he does not deserve.'

The spokesman was terrified, but nevertheless he tried to defend the cause of his town. 'Nemrod has committed a grave offence, Majesty, and we deplore it. But must Khmun suffer the consequences of your just anger? The city's walls have been destroyed, and half its garrison killed. Today, our families are afraid, and no one knows what tomorrow has in store for us.'

The Black Pharaoh got to his feet. 'Nemrod and Khmun have violated the law of Ma'at and forgotten the oath of allegiance they swore to me. Such a betrayal demands the severest punishment.'

CHAPTER FIFTY

Nemrod's mistress was rubbing his back with rare and precious oil of moringa, but she was having no success in relaxing him. Tender caresses produced no better result, and the young woman was rather piqued when Nemrod pushed her roughly away.

His lawful wife, Nezeta, was standing in the doorway of the bedchamber.

'What do you want?' he asked.

'If I'm disturbing your love-affair, I'll come back later.'

'Go away,' Nemrod told his mistress.

Annoyed, the girl left.

'We're all going to die,' said the prince to Nezeta. 'Piankhy will have no pity, neither for me nor for the inhabitants of this city. I'm sorry, my dear. You'll never be a great lady at Tefnakht's court.'

'Since there is no longer any hope of escaping the Black Pharaoh's fury, will you allow me a last attempt at negotiation?'

Nemrod was astonished. 'What kind of negotiation?'

'Since I am your wife, I shall lead out a procession of women and children, and I shall beg Piankhy for mercy.'

'You have no chance of succeeding.'

'At least I will have tried.'

*   *   *

Lemersekny stared in disbelief at the strange

procession as it passed. At its head walked a proud, simply dressed woman with a high forehead. The captain dared not search her, but he urged Puarma to be ready to let fly an arrow if she showed any sign of being a threat. Behind Nezeta walked fifty or more women and children, some afraid, others almost amused to see the formidable Nubian warriors at such close quarters. A little girl touched a footsoldier's shield, and he took her in his arms and joined the procession, telling her a story from far-off Nubia as they walked along.

It was Queen Abilah who received this surprising delegation.

Nezeta knelt before her. 'I am Nemrod's wife, and I have come to beg you to spare our lives.'

'Get up.'

'Not until I have permission to speak with the pharaoh.'

'Do you believe he will grant you mercy?'

'A King of Egypt rules according to his heart.'

'Follow me.'

Abilah led Nezeta into Piankhy's tent. He was sitting on a sycamore chair with feet shaped like a bull's hooves, slaking his thirst with a cup of fresh milk. He was struck by his visitor's noble bearing.

'Majesty,' she said, 'my name is Nezeta. It was my ill fortune to marry Nemrod because I loved him—he made me so unhappy that I lost all interest in life. Today, I wish to plead the cause of my city and its people. They have been placed under a traitor's yoke and forced to obey him. Why should they suffer an unjust punishment? It is Nemrod, and he alone, who should answer for his actions.'

Piankhy considered. 'If that is true, let him

251

appear before me.'

*   *   *

Nemrod listened carefully to his wife, not daring to interrupt her. What was she offering him, if not a death sentence?

Appearing before Piankhy was tantamount to suicide. Without the shadow of a smile, Nezeta appealed to the prince's courage, through which he would save thousands of lives, spare his town horrible suffering, and prove his devotion to his subjects.

No woman had ever mocked him like this. No one had ever placed him in such a position of inferiority without even raising their voice. Nezeta went away, leaving Nemrod alone to ponder his responsibilities.

He loved his city, but not as much as he loved himself. That meant there was only one way out for him: he must try and escape and rejoin Tefnakht. The changing of the guard took place just before dawn. For a few minutes, he would have free access to one of the small gates. Dressed as a peasant, Nemrod would slip past the granaries and the parade ground, through the outer wall of the city and across enemy lines. It was a risky enterprise, but he no longer had anything to lose.

Nemrod opened the door of his bedchamber. His wife and several guards were waiting for him.

'The nobles, officers and population are unanimous,' said Nezeta. 'The Prince of Khmun must appear before his king.'

*   *   *

Fear. A hideous fear which stuck his skin to his ceremonial robe and made acrid sweat flood from every pore. Against fear like this, Nemrod's will was powerless. If only he could faint, and be swallowed up in nothingness! But he went on walking forward, like a drunken man who unfortunately was still clear-headed, as he entered the Nubian camp, watched with hatred by thousands of warriors.

If Lemersekny had not received the order to make sure Nemrod reached the pharoah in one piece, he would happily have smashed the traitor's skull with his wooden arm. But he had to admit he understood why Piankhy might want to assuage his anger himself. Perhaps the king would stage a fine display of torture for his troops, to remind Nemrod that a man's word was a sacred thing.

Puarma raised the tent flap to admit the Prince of Khmun; but he hesitated on the threshold.

'Enter!' said Lemersekny, giving the prisoner a shove in the back.

Nemrod closed his eyes, in the hope that this nightmare would disappear. When he opened them again, the Black Pharaoh was before him, his athletic body towering over him.

'As elegant as ever, Nemrod. Your reputation does you justice.'

'Majesty . . . Can you accept that the heart is a rudder which sometimes makes its owner capsize, for it is in the hands of God? It is that which decides our destiny and makes us what we are. My heart led me astray; it led me into wickedness. Thanks to you, I have realized the error of my ways and I have come to beg your forgiveness.'

Piankhy slid his dagger out of its scabbard, and contemplated the blade. 'You are right, Nemrod. The heart forms ideas, it thinks, gives orders to the limbs, commands the tongue and creates the capacity for knowledge. "Follow your desire in the time of your existence," wrote the sage Ptahhotep. "Do nothing to excess, but do not cut short the time of following your heart, for the *ka*, the creative power, hates to be destroyed even for a moment." A man whose heart is powerful and stable, a man who is not the slave of his belly's demands—that man can hope to receive God and hear his voice. Are you that man, Nemrod?'

'No, Majesty.'

'The ancients state that our four enemies are greed, deafness, negligence and obstinacy. One after another, they vanquished you, didn't they?'

'Today, you are the only victor and I wish to become your servant again.'

'Life is like a gaming-board, made up of white and black squares. One colour is favourable to us, the other is not. And then comes death . . . What is important is not death itself, but our state of mind when it catches us by surprise. Are you ready to die, Nemrod?'

The Prince of Khmun knelt down on the ground, his eyes fixed on the dagger-blade. 'No, Majesty, I am not ready! Death terrifies me, and no matter how old I may grow, I will never lose my taste for life.'

'What can a traitor possibly offer me?'

'All the treasures of Khmun belong to you: gold, silver, lapis-lazuli, turquoise, bronze. The taxes will be paid to you regularly, and everyone will obey you without question—especially me!'

254

'I have already chosen your successor,' said Piankhy.

Slowly, the prince got to his feet, hypnotized by the dagger. He wanted at least to die standing up and, despite his terror, he asked the question that burned in him. 'Who . . . who is he, Majesty?'

'You yourself, Nemrod. Who knows better than you how to govern Khmun wisely?'

CHAPTER FIFTY-ONE

Cool-Head was sulking as he drafted his report, which would be filed in the royal archives.

'Why are you so annoyed?' asked Piankhy.

'Don't oblige me to criticize your decisions, Majesty. I have always served you faithfully and I shall continue to do so.'

'Let me guess. You were hoping Nemrod would be tortured in front of the whole army, weren't you?'

'I have no taste for cruelty,' said the scribe. 'But you must understand that confirming a traitor in his office may go against a lot of people's thinking.'

'People don't yet properly understand my real decision. Is the queen ready?'

'She is waiting for you, Majesty.'

*   *   *

Seated on their thrones, Piankhy and Abilah watched Nemrod, Prince of Khmun, and his wife, Nezeta, approaching them. Nezeta held a golden sistrum in her right hand and another, made of

255

lapis-lazuli, in her left. The metal rods of these two musical instruments quivered gently, sending out waves of sound which drove away baleful influences.

Behind a guard of Nubian soldiers crowded the population of Khmun, anxious to hear the Black Pharaoh's words.

'This town has suffered serious wounds because of Nemrod's behaviour,' declared Piankhy. 'So it is up to him to bind those wounds and to make Khmun prosper, thanks to the peace which I have just re-established. Any man who recognizes his mistakes can make amends, on condition that he never again strays from the path of Ma'at. Nemrod, do you swear, once and for all, to fulfil your duties?'

'On the name of Pharaoh and on my life, I swear it.'

'Bearing in mind the serious mistakes you have made, it is not advisable for you to rule alone. Therefore your wife will be my special representative, and will report to me on your every action. If there is any dispute, her opinion will take precedence. She will lead a council of elders, which will manage the city's wealth and watch over the well-being of its inhabitants, who from now on will be your sole concern.'

Not a trace of emotion crossed Nezeta's noble face. Nemrod swayed, as though he had been struck by the pharaoh's sceptre.

'Control yourself,' said his wife in a low whisper. 'Do not forget that the Prince of Khmun must set an example.'

The citizens began a heartfelt song: 'How perfect your deeds are, Piankhy, Son of the Light—

you who offer us peace, protect the Province of the Hare and our town, and permit us to celebrate this day.'

Under Cool-Head's watchful eye, a priest ritually sacrificed a bullock which had been declared pure by the animal-doctor. He cut off its front right leg, the symbol of strength, then dipped his hand in the animal's blood and held it out to a priest of Sekhmet, who sniffed it and pronounced his verdict: the beast's vital energy was healthy, and would give *ka* to all those who ate its flesh.

Reassured, freed and happy, Khmun opened wide its gates to the Black Pharaoh, who headed along the avenue of tamarisks that led to the Temple of Amon. Before the gateway in the surrounding wall stood two immense statues of Ramses the Great.

After worshipping the Hidden God, Piankhy walked to the great Temple of Thoth. At the feet of a stone baboon ten cubits tall, he was welcomed by the High Priest, a smiling old man who at eighteen had been initiated into the mysteries of the god of knowledge. He saw that the shadow of God protected the Black Pharaoh, and that the celestial *ka* guided his actions.

Piankhy was filled with wonder at the sight of the park, where he found the lotus pool, birthplace of the first sun. The park also contained the Island of Illumination and the Lake of the Two Knives, sites of its victorious battle against darkness; and the shrine of the primordial egg, which contained all the elements of creation.

*　　　*　　　*

Nemrod was thinking things over. Although he had been humiliated in front of the people of Khmun, his life had been spared and he had retained certain not-inconsiderable privileges. It was true that he had to obey his wife, but he had retained the title of Prince of Khmun. Perhaps there was still a chance of convincing Piankhy that he, Nemrod, was fit to rule alone as he had done in the past, and that Nezeta would have neither the strength nor the ability to rule such a large city.

But before that could happen, the Black Pharaoh would have to emerge from the Temple of Thoth, where for the last few days he had been studying the old mythological texts and spending hours talking with the priests to sample the depth of their scientific knowledge.

At last the king reappeared and agreed to visit the palace.

'Majesty,' announced Nemrod enthusiastically, 'I am going to show you the most wonderful things. If I manage to impress you, will you allow me to plead my cause again?'

Piankhy's expression was unreadable.

Quivering with excitement, Nemrod led the way into each of the palace's hundred rooms, each one filled with flowers and perfumes. In the audience chamber, the reception rooms and the bedchambers, open chests had been arranged, containing gold, jewels, fabrics and salves. But Piankhy showed no signs of admiration. He walked on, unmoved, as though these splendours did not interest him.

Nemrod was disappointed but not discouraged; perhaps the king was hiding his true feelings. Besides, there still remained one last treasure,

258

which would enchant the most austere of men.

The Prince of Khmun made a great show of pulling aside a curtain. 'Majesty, here is my most precious possession. It is yours.'

Ten beautiful girls, naked and carefully made-up, were lounging on many-coloured cushions. Some were reading poetry, others playing sweet melodies on lutes and little harps.

'Take me to the stables, Nemrod,' was Piankhy's only reaction.

'To the stables? If you want a horse, I'll have one brought to you immediately.'

'I dislike having to repeat an order.'

'Yes, yes, of course.'

Not once had Nemrod ever ventured into that stinking place, the preserve of the grooms. No doubt Piankhy was putting him to the test. So he guided him there, chatting cheerfully all the way.

The pharaoh stopped to inspect the reserves of fodder and grain. He took a handful of grain and let it trickle down on to a flagstone. 'It stays on the ground,' he commented.

'Is that important?'

'If the grain had been completely dry, as it should be, it would have bounced back up. This fodder is of poor quality.'

'I shall deal with it, Majesty.'

Piankhy approached a horse with a swollen eye and with dark patches all over its head and legs. At first fearful, the animal allowed itself to be stroked.

'He has a fever. Why is he not being cared for?' demanded Piankhy.

'He shall be, I promise you.'

The king entered one of the stalls, where he found a horse with a sprained hip and muscle

259

strains.

'Bring me some salve.'

The king himself rubbed it into the beast, whose back was so sore that he should not have been ridden. Piankhy was overwhelmed by the look of gratitude in the sick creature's eyes.

'Injured, starving, neglected horses. As true as I speak and the god Ra loves me, it is more painful to see these animals mistreated than to list all the crimes you have committed! Nemrod, all your treasures shall be brought to the temple at Karnak. And you, unworthy prince, may count yourself fortunate that I have shown you such mercy.'

CHAPTER FIFTY-TWO

The Nubians had feasted long into the night, gorging themselves on their favourite dishes: eggs, curd cheese and kid's flesh. Although moderately drunk, Lemersekny was still sufficiently clear-headed to harangue his drowsy soldiers and promise them a fine battle when they took Henen-nesut. This time, they would prove their valour through deeds which future generations would remember.

Standing on the palace terrace at Khmun, Piankhy looked out at the city's celebrations.

Abilah took his left hand tenderly. 'You have prevented a massacre, Piankhy.'

'And the horses have been cared for. But we were lucky. Nemrod loves himself so much, and has such a taste for compromise, that he didn't dare risk the destruction of this magnificent city. That won't be the case with Tefnakht. He is pursuing a true goal, and he would rather sacrifice all his men than give it up.'

'I've been thinking a lot about Nemrod.'

'Are you going to scold me for not punishing him more severely?'

'Actually, his obvious gift for treason could be used in the cause of peace, don't you think?'

'Whatever do you mean?' asked the king.

As the queen set out her plan, Piankhy thanked the gods for allowing him to marry such an exceptional woman.

*   *   *

Tefnakht was furious.

'Thanks to me,' he told Nartreb and Yegeb, 'you have become rich, influential men, and you continue to swell your own coffers in ways which I would rather not know about. But I demand information on the movements of Piankhy's army.'

Yegeb's voice became syrupy. 'My lord, we are not trying to deceive you. But we are receiving so many contradictory messages that we cannot be certain of anything. According to some sources, the Black Pharaoh has already left to return to Nubia; but according to others, he has been besieging Khmun for several days.'

'I will not tolerate this uncertainty! Do whatever you have to do, but I must know the truth.'

Daybreak entered the general's office; she looked dazzling. She cast a disdainful glance at the two advisers.

'My darling,' she said, 'instead of listening to useless chatter, wouldn't you prefer to know the

261

fate of Khmun?'

Nartreb's lips tightened. 'With respect, my lady, we are dealing here with important business, and—'

'Would you consider Prince Nemrod's request for an audience sufficiently serious?' asked Daybreak sweetly.

*   *   *

The news had spread round Henen-nesut like a jackal in full flight, so Tefnakht deemed it wise to convene his court in the great pillared hall of the palace. Nemrod looked so elegant and relaxed that his appearance reassured the assembled throng.

'What a joy to see you again, General Tefnakht,' he said.

'Your presence fills me with pleasure, Prince Nemrod. Does it mean that Khmun is free and that Piankhy has lifted the siege?'

'The Black Pharaoh made a great show of force. His men launched an assault on my fortifications and they failed miserably. In the face of heavy losses, the Nubian beat a retreat. Now Thebes is the place where we must flush him out.'

Enthusiastic cheering greeted the Prince of Khmun's warlike speech. Tefnakht congratulated him and promised him an unforgettable banquet.

*   *   *

Henen-nesut was celebrating. Young boys and girls crowned with wreaths of flowers were playing catch-and-kiss, watched with amusement by revellers who emptied jar after jar of the beer that had been generously shared out among the people.

While the victorious Tefnakht and Daybreak were turning away one supplicant after another, Nemrod was taking the air under a tall palm tree, in the company of Akanosh and Peftau, Prince of Henen-nesut. Peftau had grown fatter, and there was an expression of intense satisfaction on his ruddy face.

'What a wonderful evening, my friends,' he said. 'And how right we were to follow Tefnakht, who has led us to this glorious victory—it will be followed by many others. I am certain now that we shall soon enter Thebes and that we shall be welcomed there as liberators.'

'I'm getting weary of this campaign,' confessed Akanosh. 'I want to go home, to the Delta, and forget this war.'

'Don't talk like that,' protested Peftau. 'None of us can abandon Tefnakht just when our troops are about to inflict a crushing defeat on the Black Pharaoh.'

'Don't get so carried away,' advised Nemrod.

'I see that my attitude surprises you, but I was so afraid that the walls of Khmun wouldn't be strong enough to withstand Piankhy's soldiers. Now, I am reassured, and—'

'You shouldn't be,' cut in Nemrod.

Peftau reddened. 'I don't understand.'

'Listen to me carefully, Prince of Henen-nesut, and you too, Akanosh. Isn't life your most precious possession?'

'Of course,' said Peftau, 'but why do you ask?'

'Because you will soon lose it if you take the wrong decision.'

'It's Tefnakht who takes the decisions,' Akanosh reminded him, 'not us.'

'In the current circumstances, you're wrong.'

'Are you going to tell us what you're talking about?' asked Akanosh.

'I lied.'

Akanosh and Peftau looked at each other, bewildered.

'You lied?' said Peftau. 'About what?'

'The Black Pharaoh has taken Khmun.'

'You're making fun of us, Nemrod!' said Peftau.

'I tried to resist, but Piankhy has weaponry against which our defences are useless, in particular catapults which hurl enormous stones, destroy the city walls and kill the soldiers stationed on the ramparts. And then there are his artificers and his archers.'

'Does this mean that no stronghold can hold out against Piankhy?' asked Peftau anxiously.

'Not one like Khmun, that's certain. Henennesut's defences will be no more effective than mine were.'

'What . . . what will happen when the Black Pharaoh attacks?' asked Peftau.

'Thousands of Libyans and men from your province will die. The city will suffer grave damage and will fall into Piankhy's hands.'

'We must prevent this disaster!' exclaimed Peftau.

'That's why I've come here,' said Nemrod, 'to reveal a truth which Tefnakht is incapable of admitting. This very night, I am leaving to return to Khmun. There, I shall give an account of my mission to Piankhy, the sole master of Egypt.'

Peftau was distraught. 'But . . . what are we going to do?'

'You said it yourself: prevent a disaster.'

CHAPTER FIFTY-THREE

It had been a long night of love, and Daybreak had played every note in the scale of his desire. Now, in the light of day, Tefnakht had reached a decision: he would attack Thebes with the main body of his troops, augmenting them with the garrisons from Henen-nesut and Khmun. Piankhy was in full retreat and would not be expecting a massive, brutal offensive. Either he would continue to retreat, leaving the field to the Northern armies, or the two forces would clash violently and there would be many dead. But the defeat of the South was inevitable, so long as the offensive was launched from Memphis.

'I'm coming with you,' said Daybreak. 'When we get there, I shall take care of the preparations for the coronation.'

The general caressed her breast. 'Do you really want to be Queen of Egypt?'

'Do what you will with me, but win this war!'

'You're much younger than I am, Daybreak. What if you fall in love with a younger man?'

Her green eyes shone with anger. 'Do you really think this Queen of Egypt would be stupid enough to become the slave of her emotions? All she will dream of is rebuilding this country—and even a long life may not be enough for that.'

Tefnakht leant back and gazed at her. 'I know what I want to do with you, Daybreak, and I also know that you will be worthier of your rank than any other woman could ever be.'

Nartreb and Yegeb had two main enemies, both of them particularly difficult to overcome: women and the heat. The heat made their ankles and toes swell up, and even slowed down their thought processes. The prospect of going back to the North, even for a few days, seemed to them like a precious gift, even though they had not yet succeeded in getting rid of Daybreak, whose influence was still a hindrance to their plans.

The two men were packing pots of refreshing salve into a wooden box when a small, rat-faced man came to give them his report.

'Have you at last found something that will compromise Prince Akanosh?' asked Nartreb irritably.

'Unfortunately not, but—'

'We're leaving in an hour and we haven't time for long discussions. Keep trying, and be more efficient in future.'

The rat-faced man went on, 'Akanosh's life seems blameless, but there is one thing that intrigues me.'

'What's that?' inquired Yegeb.

'It's about his wife. No one can tell me what she did before she married him.'

'That's of no interest,' remarked Nartreb.

'It might be,' put in Yegeb. 'Just suppose she has something to hide . . . Continue your investigations,' he ordered the rat-faced man. 'When we return from the North, try to come up with something worthwhile, if you want to be well paid.'

At break of day Tefnakht and his court,

266

including Akanosh, left Henen-nesut with an escort composed of charioteers and archers. In a very short time, the powerful Libyan army would leave its rearward base to cross Middle Egypt and conquer the South.

*   *   *

Piankhy had left only a hundred or so footsoldiers in Khmun, under the command of Nezeta, who from the moment she took up her duties had shown great authority and diligence. In her hands, her husband would weigh hardly heavier than a scribe's writing-brush, even if he did remain the arbiter of all things elegant.

On his return from Henen-nesut, Nemrod had been doubtful. Yes, he had fulfilled his mission by lying to Tefnakht and telling the truth to Akanosh and Peftau, but how would Peftau react? He was fascinated by Tefnakht and believed that the North would ultimately be victorious. Nemrod believed that the general would pretend to leave the town, the better to prepare an ambush.

Although the Prince of Khmun filled him with contempt, Lemersekny shared his opinion. Peftau, another traitor, had been obliged to warn Tefnakht who, naturally, had allowed Nemrod to leave so that he would believe his mission had been successful. Then, when the Nubians laid siege to Henen-nesut with their catapults and their raised platforms, Tefnakht's chariots would pierce the flank of Piankhy's troops and try to destroy the war machines. So Lemersekny believed.

Abilah had refused to remain in Khmun and Piankhy had not tried to persuade her otherwise.

267

Once again, his wife had confirmed her determination to stay at his side throughout this dangerous journey northwards. And the Black Pharaoh had known for a long time that the Great Royal Wife's magic was one of the most effective of weapons.

Cool-Head's stay in Khmun had allowed him time to bring his campaign journal and reports up to date. A state whose archives were not kept correctly stood no chance of lasting. Alas, it was already time to leave for Henen-nesut and check the thousand and one administrative details to which soldiers mistakenly paid no attention. And Cool-Head was longing for his family, who had remained in Napata. How many more days would it be before he could embrace his wife and children again?

Piankhy mounted Valiant, who was eager to gallop out across the wide open spaces. His neigh and his sparkling eyes expressed an infectious exuberance. Everyone who saw the shining tawny mane pass by was filled with a new energy.

*　　　*　　　*

Henen-nesut was in sight. The city walls looked just as solid as those of Khmun, but they did not impress Piankhy's soldiers. The methods they'd used in the last siege would produce the same results, wouldn't they? The pharaoh took good care of his men's lives, and that reassured each and every one of them. Confidence was at its height in the Southern ranks.

'Best go no further for now, Majesty,' advised Lemersekny. 'We must first secure the canal and the plain, and then bar the way to Tefnakht's chariots, which can only attack from the west. Then, and only then, we can put in place our catapults and mobile archery platforms.'

Piankhy gazed appreciatively at Henen-nesut. 'The City of the Royal Child' was built at the heart of a prosperous region made up of not only vast agricultural areas but also thousands of gardens of various sizes, which had flourished for generations in the hands of small landowners. The king delighted in the gentleness of this landscape— which he was going to transform into a battlefield.

'My men are ready,' declared Puarma.

'So are mine,' added Lemersekny.

'Pitch the tents and set up camp,' said Piankhy.

Lemersekny deplored this waste of time. An immediate clearing of the hilly areas where Tefnakht's chariots must have gone to ground would have been an excellent prelude to the capture of Henen-nesut. But the king set great store by his men's well-being.

'Majesty,' exclaimed Puarma in amazement, 'the great gate of the city has just opened!'

Queen Abilah smiled. She had been convinced her plan would succeed and that Henen-nesut would surrender to Piankhy without a drop of blood being spilt.

Prince Peftau, whose name meant 'Windy', had well and truly decided on a change of air. He was first to walk out of the city, at the head of a procession of nobles and unarmed soldiers, laden down with gold, silver and precious stones. There were also ten magnificent young horses, all in perfect health.

'It could be a trick,' suggested Lemersekny

suspiciously.

Valiant stepped out with a rare nobility, moving steadily along the road to the city. He stopped two yards from Peftau, who instantly knelt down and bowed his forehead to the ground.

'Hail, powerful sovereign!' he said, as loudly as his muffled, trembling voice permitted. 'The shadows had taken hold of my heart, darkness had invaded me, but I have realized the error of my ways. May the brilliance of your face give me the light I so greatly need. Henceforth, I shall be your faithful servant, for you are the far-off god whose head is formed from imperishable stars.'

Ignoring the gifts, the Black Pharaoh entered the reconquered city of Henen-nesut, whose inhabitants had strewn his way with iris flowers.

CHAPTER FIFTY-FOUR

The garrison of Henen-nesut had been fraternizing with the Nubians. Peftau had not stopped singing Piankhy's praises all through a banquet at which the guests included all the city worthies, dressed in wide-sleeved tunics, and their delightful wives, who had decorated their hair with lotus-flowers. After eating its fill, the pharaoh's mongoose had settled down to sleep—though with one eye open.

The most luxurious bedchamber in the palace had been permanently set aside for the royal couple. When Abilah and Piankhy were at last alone, the pharaoh stretched out on a gilded wooden bed whose feet were shaped like a lion's paws. It was said that two lions, Yesterday and

Tomorrow, protected the slumberer as he slept, so that he might die to yesterday and be reborn to tomorrow.

Abilah sat down beside her husband and gently caressed his chest. With every passing year, he seemed more and more the incarnation of a peaceful power against which misfortune must surely fail.

'Why are you so concerned?' she asked. 'We have just reconquered Khmun and Henen-nesut. From now on, thanks to the measures you have taken, these two cities will remain loyal to you, and Middle Egypt will once again be a bulwark against invasion from the North.'

'Not *all* of Middle Egypt, Abilah.'

'Do you mean you're thinking of marching further north?' When Piankhy did not reply, Abilah became angry. 'We have reconquered our lost cities, and Tefnakht is no longer threatening Thebes. Why must you continue this war?'

'Because I have been selfish and cowardly. My father Amon wanted me to be Pharaoh of Upper and Lower Egypt, but in my peaceful happiness I forgot half of my country. That is why a demon has risen up out of the shadows; Tefnakht is a brutal reminder of our duties, Abilah.'

The queen's beautiful face grew sad. 'I was hoping that we would take up residence in Thebes, close to our daughter, the Wife of Amon, and that we would spend the rest of our lives worshipping the gods.'

'We must destroy Tefnakht's power. Otherwise, like the serpent Apophis, who tries to hinder the ship of the sun as it crosses the heavens, he will regain his strength and once again sow discord

271

throughout the land, even in Nubia. This is not just a matter of a simple rebellion, as I had thought, but a real war. Tefnakht's army is intact, and it has regrouped further north.'

'Do you mean you want to capture Memphis?'

'Yes, Memphis, the capital of the golden age, the whitewalled city founded by Djoser, the shining city from the time of the pyramids. The city they call "the Balance of the Two Lands", built at the point that joins and balances the Delta and the Nile valley.'

Abilah was choked with emotion. 'The Northern forces still hold several strongholds between us and Memphis. And everyone knows that the fortress of Memphis is impregnable! Our royal line long ago abandoned all thoughts of governing it.'

'It's time to think of it again.'

'Piankhy . . .'

'You aren't afraid are you, Queen of Egypt?'

She nestled against him. 'Yes, I am. Afraid of losing you in battle, afraid of the suffering that will be inflicted on our army and our people, afraid of the terrifying consequences if we fail.'

'I'm afraid too—afraid of a task which goes beyond our human and material capabilities, but I refuse to heed those fears.'

'Why, my love?'

'Because we would be betraying Ma'at if we did not follow the path she has set out to its very end. And that end is the annihilation of Tefnakht and the return of Lower Egypt and the Northern provinces to the harmony of a reunified country.'

Her cheek against Piankhy's, her arm laid across his chest, the beautiful Nubian gave up the struggle. 'Even I shall never persuade you to change your mind.'

'No, because you agree with my decision. You are the guardian of the magic of Isis. You know that when people lack strong beliefs it leads to failure and misfortune. We shall throw all our strength into this fight, Abilah. If we are to die, we shall die together, giving thanks to the gods for allowing us so much happiness.'

*   *   *

The rat-faced man had not had time to finish his inquiries about Akanosh's wife, for there was a much more pressing need: to leave Henen-nesut as quickly as possible, rejoin Yegeb and tell him the truth about the dreadful events that had just occurred. The undertaking was difficult and risky, but he managed to get past the Southern army's guards under the pretext of visiting his family, who lived in a village a little way north of the city, and which might be supposed to have returned to Piankhy's control. The officer who let the traveller through commented cynically that this was the best way of verifying the situation: if he was killed, they would be justified in besieging the village.

Having overcome this first hurdle, the rat-faced man crossed the fields, stole some onions and figs, and reached the Nile bank in an area the Southern armies did not control. Alarming stories were circulating among the boatmen. People, they said, were talking about Nubian plunderers who would burn down villages, rape the women and slaughter the inhabitants. The fugitive managed to persuade a boatman to take him as fast as possible to Memphis. He must warn Tefnakht and ask him to

273

act at once.

The boat was continually stopped by river patrols, who made the rat-faced man explain where he was going and why—sometimes it took hours. This lost him precious time, which the Black Pharaoh would undoubtedly put to good use as he pushed deeper into Middle Egypt. The interminable journey did not end even at the gates of Memphis, for there he was questioned closely, and then given a two-week prison sentence.

But eventually the informer was received by an officer who took his story seriously and escorted him to Yegeb, who had set himself up in a scribe's office close to the Temple of Ptah.

'Why didn't you wait until I returned to Henennesut?' asked Yegeb. 'This is good news, I hope.'

'No, my lord, it isn't. Peftau has opened the gates of the city to Piankhy. And before that, the Black Pharaoh took Khmun.'

'What are you talking about? Prince Nemrod—'

'Nemrod lied! He has sworn allegiance to Piankhy again, just like Peftau.'

Yegeb felt his ankles swell, and he had a sudden urge to vomit. But matters were so serious that he had no time to tend his own ailments. He collected Nartreb, who was getting drunk in a tavern, and the two men took the informer to Tefnakht's headquarters.

The general listened attentively to the rat-faced man. Then he ordered, 'Pay him, and find him lodgings in the town.'

'We have taken many risks,' declared Yegeb as soon as his henchman had left, 'but we have succeeded in getting you accurate information.'

'Are you sure about that?'

'General, I am convinced the man is telling the truth.'

'So am I, but what are Piankhy's plans?'

'He has recaptured the two cities he considered his own, and he has re-established his former frontier, with the certainty that you will no longer be able to cross it.'

'If he is shrewd enough to know what my aims are, he knows that I will never accept a return to the old order, and that I will attack again.'

'But will he really continue further north?' asked Yegeb. 'That would be madness.'

'That Nubian considers himself Lord of the Two Lands, both Lower and Upper Egypt.'

'He'll burn a few villages,' predicted Nartreb, 'and then he'll go and pray to the gods in his beloved Thebes. When he thinks the situation has settled down, we'll give him a big surprise.'

Tefnakht imagined Piankhy seizing control of Middle Egypt, then turning his eyes towards Memphis—that's what Tefnakht would have done in his place. But then Tefnakht was a true war-leader, while Piankhy was a man of the South, devoted to peace, the past, and religion.

CHAPTER FIFTY-FIVE

Piankhy's fleet sailed down the Nile as far as the city of Illahun, at the gateway to the rich province of Faiyum. On board, there was an atmosphere of great joy. Although he regretted the unfortunate surrender of Henen-nesut, which had prevented his soldiers from showing their prowess, Lemersekny put on a brave face and challenged Puarma to ferocious games of dogs and jackals, which Lemersekny invariably won.

Piankhy's prestige continued to grow apace. Not only did he carry off incredible victories, but he was also careful of his soldiers' lives. Lemersekny had renewed his men's enthusiasm by promising them hard fighting. The now-penitent traitors Nemrod of Khmun and Peftau of Henen-nesut might have offered scant resistance, but things would be different with the other princes of Middle Egypt. They had always been loyal to the Libyans, and had everything to fear from the Southern army. They would therefore defend their cities fiercely.

Piankhy took a similar line. Far from reassuring his troops, he told them that the most difficult phase was about to begin. They were venturing into an unknown region, where no Nubian had set foot for decades. But this severe warning had only strengthened the Southern troops' resolve: they would fight to the death for the freedom and happiness of the Two Lands. To serve under the Black Pharaoh was an honour which future generations would envy.

Nevertheless, as Illahun came into view a heavy silence fell over the warships. Everyone knew that the fortified city was full of Northern footsoldiers who would also fight to the death. Since the battlements were higher than those of Khmun, no one was certain that the catapults would be as effective here. They could only hope that the Black Pharaoh would find a way of winning the victory.

When camp had been pitched, Piankhy summoned his two military advisers to his tent.

'What do you suggest, Lemersekny?' the king

276

asked.

'We can try the machines. But we can't expect a miracle.'

'I agree. What else?'

'Puarma's archers will find it hard to see their targets.' He pointed through the open entrance of the tent. 'Look how much cover there is on the walkway round the battlements.'

'That's observant of you,' said the king approvingly.

'The only option is a siege, and it may well be a long one. And that means Tefnakht will have all the time he needs to send reinforcements.'

Puarma spoke up. 'We could get the engineers to raise mounds of earth against the ramparts,' he suggested. 'That would solve some of our problems.'

'The labourers would be slaughtered by the Libyan archers,' objected Lemersekny. 'You're forgetting that this time they'd be unprotected.'

'Leave me alone,' said Piankhy. 'I want to think.'

Illahun . . . Very near here, Amenemhat III had built his famous palace, an immense complex of buildings—there were said to be over a thousand rooms. Under his influence, Faiyum had been transformed into a vast garden, whose fertility had become legendary. Set aside for hunting and fishing, it was placed under the protection of the crocodile-god Sobek, who caused a regenerated sun to rise out of the primordial lake and placed it at the highest point in the heavens. All things considered, it richly deserved its nickname of 'Beautiful Face'.

The Black Pharaoh did not remain deep in thought for long. He was about to leave his tent, when Abilah came in.

'What are you going to do?' she asked.

'You will not approve.'

'Piankhy, you are the king, the leader of this army, and you do not have the right to risk your life.'

'May your magic protect me, Abilah.'

Piankhy mounted his bay horse, swift as a red-eared jackal and formidable as the roar of a thunderstorm. His soldiers watched, astonished, as he galloped off alone in the direction of Illahun. Elated by the sensation of speed, Valiant stretched out his long, muscular legs and raced on with fiery passion. Yet Piankhy had only to tap the horse gently on his neck to bring him to a halt, close to the great entrance gate of the fortress.

The archers posted on the ramparts of Illahun had identified the Black Pharaoh from his noble bearing, his virile body, his gilded armour and the brightness of his robe of royal linen; but they dared not shoot their arrows.

When Piankhy raised his powerful voice, every defender of Illahun could hear him.

'You who are the living dead without knowing it, you lost and unhappy men, listen to me, listen to your king! If one more minute goes by without you opening this gate and swearing allegiance to me, you shall be slaughtered to the last man. Do not close the gates of your existence by refusing to obey me, do not place your heads on the headsman's block! If you respect the law of Ma'at and surrender your town to the Pharaoh of Upper and Lower Egypt, no one will be killed, no one will be plundered, and peace will reign. I await your answer, though my patience is already exhausted.'

On the battlements, people began running about in all directions. Officers and nobles rushed into the audience chamber and reported Piankhy's words to Osorkon, Prince of Illahun, a man of ancient Libyan stock.

'So, he has come—and he has come alone,' said the prince.

'We can easily kill him,' offered the fortress commander. 'Once he's dead, the Nubian forces will disintegrate and run away.'

'Fool! Have you never heard of the supernatural power that dwells within a pharaoh, granting him victory even when he is one against many? It was by that power that Ramses the Great defeated the Hittites at Kadesh, and it is because Piankhy possesses it that he is challenging us like this. No arrow will strike him, no spear will pierce his breastplate, because he is like an all-consuming fire that no human can extinguish.'

'Then what are your orders, Prince?' asked the commander.

Prince Osorkon left his palace, ordered the great gate of the fortress to be opened, and prostrated himself before Piankhy.

'May the shadow of God protect you, Pharaoh,' he said. 'It is Heaven which gives you your power: whatever your heart conceives comes to pass instantly. If we are capable of seeing reality as it is, it is only at your command. This fortress, this city, with all its treasures and all its inhabitants, belongs to you. Enter in peace, Majesty.'

Valiant galloped up to the citadel of Illahun. From its summit, Piankhy looked down on a town whose principal roads had been drawn with geometric care, crossing at right angles to each

279

other. Large, seventy-roomed villas mingled with modest dwellings only a hundred paces long and a hundred wide. Emerging from their numbness and their fear, the citizens cheered their liberator, while the soldiers of the garrison, who had exchanged their weapons for palm fronds, embraced the Nubians.

In less than an hour, the whole town was celebrating. Hundreds of jars of wine and beer were brought out of the palace cellars, low tables were set out with sliced meats and dried fish, and figs, dates and grapes were laid out on the ground. Everyone declared how happy they were to live in the reign of Piankhy.

'What's wrong with you?' Puarma asked Lemersekny. 'Anybody'd think you were drunk, but you haven't had a drop yet.'

'You really are the last word in idiots, archer. Nothing ever astonishes you. But me . . . I've never seen a man like that.'

'You're the idiot,' retorted Puarma. 'How many years will it take you to realize that he is Pharaoh?'

CHAPTER FIFTY-SIX

'Illahun has fallen,' Tefnakht told Daybreak.

'That is very bad news, yet you don't seem worried by it.'

'Prince Osorkon is a worn-out man who is afraid of the future. Piankhy will have had no difficulty at all in persuading him to open the gates of the city.'

'That damned Nubian now controls Faiyum!'

'Only part of it. If he tries to go further south,

280

the fortress of Meidum will block his way. I have appointed one of my most battle-hardened officers to take charge of it. He oversees his men's training exercises every day and has already killed several recruits he considered too weak. Meidum may not halt Piankhy's progress, but it will bring him to a standstill for many long weeks and he'll lose a lot of men.'

'Why not send reinforcements there?' asked Daybreak.

'I believe the Nubian is obsessed by a crazy dream: he wants to conquer Memphis.'

'Piankhy isn't a madman,' she objected. 'He knows perfectly well that that's impossible.'

'His petty victories have gone to his head. I prefer him to wear himself out on minor objectives and to go on believing that he's invincible. Then, at Memphis, he will come up against insurmountable walls and an army which is better rested and equipped than his own. And Memphis will be his tomb.'

*   *   *

Red had commanded the Meidum garrison for five years. It mattered little to him that the ancient city was 'the Dwelling-Place of Atum', the Creator. His one and only centre of interest was the barracks, where he trained soldiers in hand-to-hand fighting. Losses as high as one-fifth of his men did not bother him, since he was training true fighters, as vicious as he could wish. Since his appointment, he had not even thought of going to the site where a magnificent pyramid had been erected, the very first smooth-sided one, from which Khufu's

281

architect had taken his inspiration. Red dreamed only of bloody combat, and this time the opportunity was a wonderful one.

Since the moment when his watchmen announced the imminent arrival of Piankhy's army, Red had not paused for breath. He ran from one part of the battlements to another, checking his men's equipment and shouting orders, urging each man to be more alert than his neighbour.

At first, he thought he was mistaken. But then he saw that almost all the city's defenders were affected by the same phenomenon: they were trembling. Red would willingly have slaughtered them to cure them of their fear, but he needed all his troops. He yelled that the fortress had nothing to fear from the Nubian catapults and arrows, but he could tell that nobody was listening.

When Piankhy rode up alone to the great gate on his bay horse, one of the Libyan archers went down on his knees. Watched with horror by his comrades, Red slit the man's throat.

'You have two choices,' proclaimed the Black Pharaoh. 'Either you open the gates of Meidum, and you live; or you keep them closed, and you die. As King of Upper and Lower Egypt, I will not permit any city to deny me free entry.'

Red picked up the bow of the man he had killed, drew it, and aimed at Piankhy. But the arrow never left the bow, for three archers threw themselves on the Libyan, bludgeoned him to death, and threw his corpse over the battlements.

Immediately, the footsoldiers opened the great gate of the fortress, and Piankhy entered, his horse whinnying with joy.

*　　　*　　　*

'Meidum fell without a fight,' Yegeb admitted glumly. Nartreb followed him about like a shadow, looking more and more nervous.

Tefnakht was furious. 'What happened? he demanded.

'Red was betrayed by his own soldiers. Piankhy terrifies them—the wildest stories have sprung up about him. People say Amon wields the sword in Piankhy's hand, that he can read into his enemies' thoughts, that—'

'Enough of this childish prattle! Before Piankhy takes the road to Memphis, there is only one more obstacle: Lisht.'

'Let us not deceive ourselves, General,' said Yegeb even more glumly.

Sickened, Daybreak cut in. 'That is defeatist talk!'

'No, simply realistic. Lisht is smaller than Meidum and—'

'Perhaps its garrison will prove braver,' said Daybreak acidly.

'Let us hope so, Daybreak, let us hope—'

'Do not address me by my first name, Yegeb. You are not one of my friends. I have a title: use it.'

Yegeb swallowed. 'Indeed, Highness. But I maintain that Lisht won't hold out for long against the Black Pharaoh.'

'Such a lack of optimism could harm the morale of our troops, don't you think? I sometimes wonder if you and Nartreb aren't playing into our enemy's hands.'

'Highness, those words—'

'That's enough,' interrupted Tefnakht. 'Let us

283

not tear each other apart at the very moment when we must work together. My counsellors will see to the prosperity of the country. I shall attend to military matters.'

Yegeb and Nartreb withdrew, hand in hand.

Tefnakht seized Daybreak by the shoulders. 'Never do that again! It is not for you to criticize my counsellors.'

'Those two will betray you!'

'They are as attached to me as dogs are to their master. Without me, they would not exist.'

She pulled away from him. 'One day, you will have to choose between them and me. I love you, Tefnakht. All they do is use you.'

'Do you think I don't know that? But you can't exercise power without allies, and those two are highly effective.'

*   *   *

Lisht, 'She who Conquers the Two Lands', had been the capital of Amenemhat I, over a thousand years earlier. He had had his pyramid built close to the city, as had his son and successor, Senusret I, who had set his seal upon that wondrous time; among the great works of literature written then was the famous *Tale of Sinuhe*. Once stripped of its royal status, Lisht had become a simple staging-post between Faiyum and Memphis, a small town living more and more on its memories.

And yet its stronghold was not without its attractions. Lemersekny even cast covetous glances at it.

'Will you leave this one to me, Majesty?' he asked. 'A few shots from the catapult, and then I'll

284

take care of the rest.'

'No, Lemersekny. Why change tactics that have served us so well?'

'With respect, you shouldn't stretch your luck too far. Without you, we would be lost.'

'Why should the commander of this fortress be any more insane than those of Illahun and Meidum?'

Before the Black Pharaoh had even mounted his horse, the gates of Lisht swung open and its commanding officer, followed by his soldiers and a good portion of the population, submitted to Piankhy.

'The Two Lands belong to you,' declared the commander. 'The South and the North are yours, the riches they contain are your property. All the earth prostrates itself before you.'

As soon as he had passed through the gates of the city, the Black Pharaoh offered a sacrifice to the gods who had protected him, and paid homage to Amon. The whole of Middle Egypt had been brought to heel. Now the road to Memphis lay wide open.

CHAPTER FIFTY-SEVEN

The scout hurtled into the courtyard of the Lisht barracks, drew his chariot to a halt outside the headquarters and leapt down.

'I have a message for Captain Lemersekny,' he announced to the guard.

'He is resting. But Captain Puarma is here.'

'Perfect.'

In fact, Puarma was cursing Lemersekny, who, instead of doing his share of administration, was enjoying himself with the regular customers at an ale-house near the barracks. And he, Puarma, no longer had sufficient free time even to pay court to the headman's daughter in a neighbouring small town; she swooned every time she set eyes on him.

'This is recent, detailed information,' said the scout, handing Puarma a thick, sealed papyrus.

'At last! We've been waiting for this for weeks.' Carrying the precious document, Puarma hurried to the palace.

*   *   *

Abilah was swimming naked, with the incomparable, effortless grace of a woman of the Great South who had learned in infancy how to toy with the river's currents. When the heat became overpowering, the queen forgot her cares in the lake at the palace. And Piankhy tried to forget his by gazing wonderingly at his sublime wife, whose soul and body were the expression of an immutable beauty.

It was almost a year since the war between the South and the North had begun. After conquering Middle Egypt, the Black Pharaoh had appointed administrators from old local families; men who were determined not to allow princes like Peftau and his kind to stray from the way of Ma'at. Piankhy had put an end to these many years of corruption, unlimited personal power and the exploitation of humble folk. His stay in Middle Egypt had shown the nobles that from now on the pharaoh would rule with strictness and authority, paying no heed to clans who cared only for their own interests.

During this period of reform, the Nubian army had benefited from a comfortable existence, although they still had daily training exercises. The sick and wounded had had time to recover their health, while their comrades, although still on active service, had been sampling the region's relaxed way of life.

If Piankhy had not attacked Memphis immediately after capturing the fortresses of Middle Egypt, it was only because he had to be certain that the region was stable. That was now an accepted fact, and the king could turn his thoughts to the most perilous stage of his quest: the battle for Memphis.

He still needed reliable information on the fortifications and defences of the largest city in the land. The scouts contradicted each other, the reports were insufficiently precise, and the king was not going to embark upon this formidable venture before knowing the exact extent of the difficulties involved.

'Majesty,' said Cool-Head, 'Puarma is asking to see you urgently.'

'Show him in.'

The scribe was in an excellent mood, for Piankhy had recently given him permission to go to Napata, where he had spent a few all-too-brief days with his wife and children. Welcomed home like a hero, Cool-Head needed no prompting to tell everyone about the Black Pharaoh's exploits. However, he had not concealed the fact that the most difficult part was yet to come; or that recent events meant that, to Piankhy, Napata was now no more than a remote provincial capital. Struggling against gloom, Otoku had put on a little weight at a lavish banquet, and he was continuing to govern the city with a competence that delighted old Kapa.

Puarma was in a state of high excitement. 'Majesty, here at last is the report we have been waiting for.'

'Sit down and have a cup of cool beer.'

The dwarf reappeared. 'Majesty, Lemersekny also wishes to see you.'

His face crumpled and unshaven, his old leather kilt askew, the man with the acacia-wood arm walked in rather unsteadily. 'I had a dream, Puarma,' he said. 'You went to the king without me and showed him a plan of the fortress at Memphis, even though it was my scouts who obtained this vital information, at the risk of their lives and on my instructions.'

'Hurry up and sit down,' urged Piankhy, 'before you fall over.'

'As you command, Majesty,' said Lemersekny, slumping into a round-backed wicker chair.

'Shouldn't you bathe?' suggested the queen, emerging from the pool and covering herself with a veil of transparent linen.

'Bathing is bad for my aching joints, Majesty. On the eve of a campaign, the commander of the king's footsoldiers cannot afford to run the slightest risk.'

'I suppose you have already drunk your fill.'

'Not at all, Majesty. With this heat becoming more and more intense, we must struggle ceaselessly against water-loss, that cunning affliction which lies constantly in wait for us.

'Let me see this document,' demanded Piankhy.

Puarma broke the seal of dried mud and

288

unrolled the papyrus.

'The plans of Memphis,' said Lemersekny with relish.

'The city is vast,' observed the queen, almost alarmed by the size of the pharaohs' first capital, which had remained the centre of economic life in the Two Lands.

Equally impressed, Puarma read the inscriptions written in cursive hieroglyphics on the papyrus.

'To the south, there is a line of fortifications preventing access by land to the docks of the port of Peru-Nefer, "Good Journey". To the west, a canal runs between the outskirts of the city and the desert.'

'A weak point,' suggested Lemersekny.

'It only looks weak,' said the king. 'There's a garrison nearby which maintains a constant watch on it. And the point where it joins with the small canal that runs along the southern quarter is blocked by cargo vessels where archers are always stationed. An attack there would be impossible.'

Lemersekny pulled a face. 'If I understand this properly, all we have left is the Nile, to the east.'

'Three canals flow from it. The first leads to the docks, the second to the palace, the third to the old white-walled citadel in the northern quarter. But the inhabitants of Memphis have built huge ramparts, which prevent any invasion from the river.'

'Well,' said Lemersekny, 'we could skirt round the town using the eastern desert, follow the line of the burial-ground at Saqqara and swoop down on the north side of Memphis, where no one will be expecting us.'

'No, that wouldn't work,' said Piankhy. 'First, we

289

would have to cross the canal under enemy fire; besides, although the northern fortifications are older than those to the south, they are no less solid.'

Lemersekny drained his cup of beer impatiently. 'But there's no other way!'

'Looking at these plans, it would seem that that is so.'

Lemersekny would have liked to find an argument that proved Memphis was only a fortress like any other, but he kept silent. This time, the evidence had to be faced: the Southern army was not going to get beyond that frontier.

'We shall await your orders, Majesty,' said Puarma, disappointed, and the two officers went out.

Piankhy remained for a long time bent over the plans of Memphis.

'Puarma and Lemersekny wouldn't hesitate to give their lives if we had one single chance of succeeding,' said Abilah.

'So long as Memphis is in Tefnakht's hands, peace and justice will not rule over Egypt. Thanks to the wealth of this city, he can equip and feed his army.'

'So you refuse to give up. But what way will you take?'

'If it doesn't exist, Abilah, I shall create it.'

CHAPTER FIFTY-EIGHT

As evening fell, Yegeb and Nartreb were totting up the day's acquisitions. It brought smiles to their lips to see how steadily their wealth had grown since they had been living in Memphis. They had devised a new tax, the 'general contribution to the war effort', which could be levied at any rate they chose, had no upper limit and allowed them to hold both rich and poor to ransom, perfectly legally. As the Memphis dignitaries and merchants were anxious to retain the respect and trust of Tefnakht, their only protector against Nubian invasion, they must satisfy the demands of his two counsellors, whose conscientiousness and skill were so highly praised by everyone.

'How much longer are we going to put up with Daybreak?' askd Nartreb anxiously, as he rubbed his swollen toes with an expensive ointment given to him by the perfumer at the Temple of Ptah.

'That female is tougher than I thought,' admitted Yegeb, 'but the general has her under control.'

'Tomorrow she will become queen!'

'You are right to be worried, but baiting the trap with another suitor would be pointless—she'd be suspicious.'

'We cannot accept this state of affairs!' raged Nartreb, his moon-face puffing up with anger. 'That girl hates us, and she'll try to destroy us.'

'You can be sure I do not underestimate the danger.'

There was a knock at the door, and the two counsellors hurriedly rolled up the papyrus that listed all the details of their wealth.

Nartreb opened the door and saw the rat-faced man standing there.

'Oh, it's you. What do you want?'

A sort of rictus grin revealed small, pointed

teeth. 'If you pay me well, I can tell you some very interesting things.'

Nartreb grabbed him by the collar of his tunic and flung him into the room like a cheap parcel. The man got to his feet, blood dripping down his forehead.

'You will talk,' said Nartreb, 'and you will talk now. Afterwards, Yegeb and I will decide exactly how much you are to be paid. Remember this: no one who tries to blackmail us lives long enough to boast about it.'

Badly frightened, the informer cowered in a corner of the room. 'All right, my lord, all right! A man who hires out donkeys heard that I was looking for information about the past life of Akanosh's wife, and contacted me. I had to lay out a certain amount of money, and—'

'Get on with it!'

'Yes, my lord. This donkey-man knew her parents, who died when she was in her teens. They were a very devoted couple—'

'Is that the best you can do?' Nartreb raised his fist.

'Oh no, my lord! Akanosh's wife has suntanned skin, like you and me, but her father came originally from Nubia.'

'Her father was a *Nubian*?' Yegeb was astonished. 'Are you sure about that?'

'Well, that was only one witness, but there could be others.'

'Pay him,' Yegeb told Nartreb. 'I think we now have the solution to all our problems.'

*   *   *

Tefnakht and Daybreak were in bed in their huge bedchamber in the palace of the Tuthmosids, with its window overlooking the Nile. Tefnakht stroked the hollow of Daybreak's back. He slid his hand slowly back up her spine, then seized her by the hair and forced her to turn over.

'You're a savage!' she exclaimed in amusement, delightedly embracing her ardent lover.

The general's passion for Daybreak was never satisfied. With her, every duel of love was different. He had continually to reconquer her, and that war of conquest was rejuvenating him.

'What is Piankhy doing?' she asked him, when they were again lying quietly side by side.

'He is sinking deeper and deeper into the mire. He has realized that his army cannot take Memphis, but he is so vain that it will no doubt take him a long time to admit defeat.'

'What if he settles for his conquest of Middle Egypt?'

'It's only a temporary conquest. Piankhy won't stay in this region; he'll fall back to Thebes. Then I shall counter-attack and the traitors will commit treason again, this time in my favour. But I shan't make the same mistake as he did—he's a bad strategist. I shall have them all executed and then impose the methods of government devised by my counsellors.'

He kissed her breasts, which were as firm as sun-ripened apples. 'You don't know Sais, the city where I was born, which I shall turn into the capital of all Egypt. Tomorrow, I shall take you there.'

Daybreak was surprised. 'But aren't you needed here?'

'This journey was planned a long time ago, and

293

there is a strategic aspect to it.'

'What if Piankhy attacks?'

'Don't worry. Either he has given up, or he has gone mad—in which case his attack will end in disaster.'

'A chance to see the Delta and Sais. I would never have imagined . . .'

'It's a magnificent land, a hundred times more beautiful than the Nile valley. And our visit will enable me to introduce my subjects to their queen.'

'You mean . . .?'

'Yes, Daybreak. We shall be married in Sais.'

*   *   *

Piankhy spent hours galloping across the desert wastes, conversing with his horse, who chose the direction they would take. Valiant made light work of the dunes, avoiding the patches of soft sand. He seemed to leap as high as the sun and conquer the endless expanses where, in the crystal-clear air, the gods spoke with the voice of eternity.

Ten times, twenty times, Piankhy had spread out the map of Memphis and consulted with Lemersekny and Puarma. Despite their eagerness to capture the city, the two officers were unable to put forward any workable plan of attack.

Abilah remained silent. Despite her magic, she too was unable to detect a weak point which might give them hope of victory. In the Nubian camp, the atmosphere was becoming more and more gloomy. Would their tents still be pitched in these same positions in months to come, or even years? Everyone was waiting for the Black Pharaoh to make an announcement; they all knew that withdrawal would be tantamount to defeat. The brilliant Middle Egyptian campaign now seemed no more than a mirage, while the Northern army, under the command of the unwavering Tefnakht, remained intact.

As time passed, the scales had almost tipped against the king. Yes, Thebes was free; yes, Middle Egypt had been reconquered. But was that only an illusion, which a Northern invasion would rapidly dispel? By holding Memphis, Tefnakht possessed the key to the Two Lands, the centre of wealth and balance, which must be controlled in order to govern the country.

Today, without telling anyone, Piankhy rode further north, towards Memphis. Valiant automatically settled into a moderate pace which he could keep up all day without tiring.

Memphis, queen of the ancient empire! How beautiful and haughty she was. A screen of palm trees softened the harsh contours of her battlements, which lay there beyond the range of catapults and archers. The 'white wall' built by Djoser the Magnificent protected the city's renowned temples. Piankhy would dearly have loved to worship the ancestral gods there, but the wall rose up before him like an impenetrable barrier.

The Black Pharaoh rode as far as the first guard post. Alarmed, and afraid the two golden cobras curving up from the king's brow would strike them down, the sentries alerted their superior officer. He immediately requested help from the fortress commander, an ambitious scribe who had chosen to forge a career in military administration. He came out of his official residence and climbed up

295

on to the battlements. In Tefnakht's absence, it was up to him to take decisions.

The sight of the Black Pharaoh transfixed the scribe.

'I am your king,' declared Piankhy, 'and you owe allegiance to me! Hear me, Memphis! Do not close your gates, do not fight, O dwelling-place of the Light at the dawn of time. Let him who wishes to enter, enter; let him who wishes to leave, leave; let no man hinder those who wish to come and go. I have only one aim: to offer a sacrifice to Ptah, the lord of Memphis, and to the other gods who dwell in his city. In the Southern provinces, no citizen has been killed except those who rebelled against Ma'at. Let the gates be opened!'

The scribe emerged from his trance. On his orders, the gates of the guard post were opened, but only to allow a squad of cavalry to ride out, bent on capturing the Black Pharaoh.

CHAPTER FIFTY-NINE

There were at least fifty horsemen, all resolved to carry out the great deed, all determined to strike down the Nubian warrior who gazed defiantly back at them, apparently unmoved.

Piankhy drew his short sword from its scabbard and, with a swift, precise slash, slit his first attacker's throat. The tip of the second horseman's spear almost touched the Black Pharaoh, but at the last moment the king dodged to one side, and struck the man a fatal blow; then he skewered a third Libyan on his blade.

296

Although he and his horse were swift and agile, Piankhy knew he would be defeated by sheer weight of numbers unless his father Amon came to his aid. And sure enough, the god did manifest himself—in two strange forms. One was Lemersekny at the head of his elite footsoldiers, whose slingshots decimated the enemy; the other was Puarma, whose best archers wiped out the remainder of the Memphis cavalry.

When a volley of arrows rained down from the ramparts, the Nubians drew back to put themselves out of range.

'As we had received no orders, Majesty,' explained Lemersekny, 'we felt we ought to follow you. I'm sure you would have killed all those cowards without our help, but why tire yourself unnecessarily?'

Piankhy smiled. Yet his heart was sad, because Memphis had rejected peace.

*   *   *

The whole Delta was buzzing with excitement. Tefnakht had been acclaimed as the future master of Egypt, and he had announced his marriage to Daybreak, whose noble bearing enchanted the chiefs.

With a conqueror's fervour, the general extolled the virtues of total war against Piankhy, who was incapable of taking Memphis. All they had to do, to discourage him once and for all, was increase the number of soldiers quartered there. The force of conviction swept away all indecision, and he had no difficulty in raising another army. Meanwhile, Daybreak was delightedly exploring Sais, where the goddess Neith had created the world with seven words. A flurry of devoted servants were quick to satisfy the future queen's smallest whim.

Tefnakht joined her in the palace's audience hall, which she was having redecorated. In place of the usual friezes of papyrus reeds and migratory birds, Daybreak wanted pictures of her husband standing in his chariot and crushing the routed Nubian army.

'You don't think these scenes are too . . . warlike?' he inquired ironically.

'Confidence will inspire the sword-arms of all our soldiers. And it is here, in our palace, that such confidence must take root.'

'As you wish. Tomorrow, I am leaving for Memphis.'

'You're leaving me here alone?'

'You're the future queen, aren't you? In my absence, you shall govern my capital.'

Daybreak looked deep into her lover's eyes. 'Give me your instructions. I shall ensure they are followed.'

*   *   *

The scribe commanding the Memphis garrison tried to display resolute optimism. 'General Tefnakht, we drove back the Black Pharaoh's first assault without difficulty.'

'How many men did he send?'

The scribe cleared his throat. 'To tell the truth . . . not many.'

'Be more precise.'

'Well . . . at first he was alone, but then—'

'Piankhy dared to come in person to the gates of

298

Memphis?' said Tefnakht.

'A crazy gesture of defiance, my lord.'

'What did you do?'

'When he ordered me to open the gates, I did so, but only to send out our cavalry. If the Nubians hadn't rushed to help Piankhy, we would have captured him. When they saw how swiftly and resolutely we attacked they fled, and they won't return.'

'Nevertheless,' said Tefnakht, 'we shall take suitable precautions. I am sending you reinforcements of eight thousand men. A force of that size based in Memphis will deter Piankhy from trying to attack. He'll know he would be bound to fail.'

'Am I to understand that we are to . . . tell him?'

'Of course. Have the heralds proclaim to the people how many troops we have, and then allow two or three caravans to leave for the south. The Nubians are sure to intercept them and question the merchants—and from the answers they'll learn a truth that will terrify them.'

*   *   *

Daybreak was enchanted by the countryside around Sais, with its great stretches of cultivated land, its immense palm groves and its countless canals. She spent long hours walking with her serving-women through the pleasant landscape, which offered many places to shelter from the heat of the sun. And she often made a tour of all the rooms in the palace, to speed up the decorating work. Plasterers and painters were restoring the old residences, while masterbuilders and stonemasons were enlarging the Temple of Neith.

In the evening, Daybreak savoured the pleasure of a lukewarm shower running over her amber-skinned body. At dinner, she entertained Sais's leading citizens at her table, charming them and singing the praises of Tefnakht's policies.

One afternoon, as she was preparing to choose the dishes for dinner, she was outraged to find Yegeb in her antechamber, an ambiguous smile on his lips.

'Get out of my room at once!' she said angrily.

'Highness, you should hear me out.'

'Go back to your friend Nartreb. He must be getting bored.'

'This matter concerns you directly, Highness.'

'Does it? How?'

'I confess that Nartreb advised me not to do this,' Yegeb went on, 'but as I don't wish you any harm, I thought I ought to warn you of the grave dangers lying in wait for you. It would be better to stop dreaming before disaster strikes.'

'What dangers do you mean?'

'You were not born to reign. Leave Tefnakht and disappear.'

'You have gone mad!' said Daybreak with conviction.

'Follow my advice. If you don't, you will regret it.'

Daybreak snatched up a heavy silver vase, and Yegeb fled. He knew that she would ignore his threats and that she could no longer prevent him carrying out his plan. He was going to allow himself the inestimable pleasure of torturing her before triumphing.

As the end of the day approached, the heat had grown still fiercer. The Nile was at its lowest level, and the high ground was dried out and cracking.

Although he had increased his beer consumption, Lemersekny was still thirsty. And the arrest and questioning of a merchant travelling from Memphis had not improved his mood.

'Majesty,' he said to Piankhy, 'the Memphis garrison has just been reinforced by eight thousand men, well-trained Libyans from the Delta provinces.'

'Is that absolutely certain?'

'I'm afraid so. And that's not all. The city's granaries are crammed with wheat, barley and emmer-grain, the stables are well-stocked with beef cattle and the armouries are full of weapons.'

'So Memphis can easily withstand a siege, even a long one.'

'We wouldn't be able to starve the city into submission, or to deprive it of its means of defence.'

The Black Pharaoh gazed at the Nile. 'If a pharaoh cannot find a solution to his difficulties,' he said thoughtfully, 'perhaps he should make heaven come down to earth.'

CHAPTER SIXTY

As he rode through the gates of Sais, Tefnakht was thinking about his wedding to Daybreak. It would be spectacular, with thousands of guests, and the memory of the celebrations would endure for centuries. Despite his passion for Daybreak, the general never let himself be guided by desire alone. He knew that she was as ambitious as he was, and that she would both win the hearts of the Egyptians and provide him with an heir.

As soon as the period of celebrations was over, Tefnakht decided, he would return to Memphis and deliver a stirring address to the garrison, promising them a victory which in their minds they had already won. Piankhy would not try anything, because the fortress of Memphis was impregnable. The morale of the Black Pharaoh's troops was already being eroded by doubt and weariness. When they had to retreat, their ability to fight back would be rapidly diminished.

In spite of his desire to fight, Tefnakht had had the wisdom to be patient and use the time to his own advantage. Soon, his clear thinking would be rewarded.

*   *   *

Since the siege of Memphis would last for as long as Piankhy persisted in believing he had even a remote chance of capturing the city, Akanosh had decided to spend a few days with his wife in their province of Sebennytos. For them, the spectre of war was moving further and further away. When the Black Pharaoh, in his disappointment, turned round and headed back to the South, Akanosh would not join the Northern army of conquest but would remain in the Delta. The old warrior had permanently lost his taste for battle and longed only for tranquillity, far from all conflict.

As the prince's servants were finishing his packing, Nartreb burst in, followed by twenty guards armed with cudgels.

'Have you lost your mind?' demanded Akanosh. 'Get out of here immediately!'

'We are at war, Prince, and absolute loyalty to Tefnakht is the law.'

'Are you daring to accuse me of breaking that law?'

'Not you, no. But your wife—'

Akanosh slapped him hard. 'Get out of here, you vermin!'

The counsellor's thick lips swelled with anger. 'I have proof that your wife is a Nubian, and therefore an ally of Piankhy. The general demands that she appear before him immediately.'

'I refuse to allow it.'

Nartreb's smile was ferocious. 'If you persist in doing so, I shall use force.'

'By what right?'

'Those are Tefnakht's orders.'

*   *   *

Although cruel dreams still haunted her sleep, Daybreak was happy. Tomorrow, she would become Tefnakht's wife, and then she would share in the reconquest of her country. The war would undoubtedly cause much suffering, but there was no other way of getting rid of the Black Pharaoh. Even though he was doomed to defeat, Piankhy would fight to the bitter end, with the insane pride of a deposed leader. At the moment when Tefnakht struck the fatal blow, Daybreak would be useful to him, ensuring that his arm did not weaken.

Her maid placed on Daybreak's head a magnificent braided wig. It was a priceless creation made of almost blonde human hair, which softened the young woman's face and gave her the bearing of a great lady.

The weaver-women of Sais, the best in Egypt, had created a wedding-robe of royal linen which would mould Daybreak's curves to perfection and make her beauty dazzle everyone who saw her.

'Highness, are you ready for the fitting?' asked the maid.

'The fitting must wait,' decreed Yegeb's unctuous voice.

Daybreak swung round, as though stung by a scorpion. 'I told you to stop bothering me!'

'General Tefnakht wishes to see you immediately.'

'I haven't finished dressing.'

'He stressed the word "immediately".'

'Has something serious happened?'

'I don't know, Highness.'

Daybreak was alarmed. Had Piankhy launched a suicidal attack against Memphis? Anxiously, still dressed only in her under-bodice and a short skirt, she hurried to the audience chamber, followed with difficulty by Yegeb, who had to trot to keep up with her.

As soon as she entered the dimly lit room, which was shaded by thick curtains drawn across the windows, Daybreak felt great tension in the atmosphere. Tefnakht was pacing up and down. Nartreb was seated in the position of a scribe, staring at Prince Akanosh, who stood apart, his arms folded.

304

'Here you are, at last,' said Tefnakht.

'I was busy,' said Daybreak. 'What is happening?'

Tefnakht pointed at Akanosh. 'Do you know this man?'

'Yes, of course.'

'Are you sure about that, my dear Daybreak?'

'I don't understand.'

'I, too, thought I knew him. I even thought he was a loyal ally who would never betray me.'

The young woman was thunderstruck. 'Not Prince Akanosh!'

'No, not him,' snapped Tefnakht. 'Not him, his wife—his *Nubian* wife! Nubian—do you understand what that means? An ally of Piankhy, here in my own palace!'

'It is for me, and me alone,' said Akanosh furiously, 'to defend my wife against these disgraceful accusations. The fact that she is of Nubian parentage does not make her a traitor. Isn't her word—and mine—worth more than the word of two contemptible counsellors who think of nothing but lining their own pockets?'

'Unfortunately for your wife,' lamented Yegeb, 'we have proof of her guilt.'

Akanosh clenched his fists. 'You're lying!'

'Our men intercepted a letter which formally accuses your wife. The letter contains prooof that she was acting as a go-between, evidently without your knowledge.'

'A spy? Who was she working for?' asked Daybreak.

Tefnakht's eyes bored into hers. 'It's high time to stop this play-acting.'

'Play-acting? What do you mean?'

He seized her by the wrists, gripping them so hard she thought they would break. 'It was you who wrote that letter, you devil! You betrayed me because you hate me. You once wanted to kill me, remember? You used this treachery to get your revenge.'

'You're wrong. I swear that you're wrong!'

'I have identified the writing myself. It is yours.'

Tefnakht took a pace back from her and pulled out his dagger. A bead of blood stood out on her skin as the tip of the blade pierced her throat.

'I ought to kill you, you little bitch, but a slow death in a dungeon will be a much better punishment. Hour after hour, you will lose more of your youth and beauty.'

For a moment, Daybreak wanted to throw herself at Tefnakht's feet and beg him for mercy. But she chose instead to stand up to him: 'If you loved me, you would see the truth.'

'Take her away,' Tefnakht ordered his counsellors, who were only too pleased to seize the deposed princess and hand her over to the guards.

Alone with Prince Akanosh, overwhelmed by what had happened, the general took a more conciliatory line. 'Like me, you were deceived. Get rid of your wife, and do it quickly.'

'I trust her,' said Akanosh. 'I know she has committed no treason.'

'Look at the evidence, Akanosh, even if it is painful. The letter we intercepted proves that Daybreak, with the help of your Nubian woman, urged the fortress commanders to open their gates to Piankhy. Act at once; otherwise you will pay for it with your life.'

CHAPTER SIXTY-ONE

Cool-Head couldn't keep still. Ten times a day, he asked his assistants if the messenger from the South had arrived yet. Piankhy gazed endlessly at the river, so lost in thought that he quite forgot Memphis, whose white fortress sparkled in the sunshine.

At last the messenger arrived, bearing a wooden tablet drawn up by the specialists in Swenet.

Piankhy examined the tablet, which was covered in figures.

'What do you think, Majesty?' asked Cool-Head.

'It's perfect. Amon has answered my prayer.'

'How much longer must we be patient?'

'A few days.'

This short delay would be enough. Piankhy summoned Lemersekny, Puarma and the artificers and gave them their orders. They were to build platforms, erect climbing-poles and requisition every single boat, from the smallest to the largest, drawing up a list of owners so that they could be compensated.

The Black Pharaoh watched in wonder as the river swelled and leapt up to attack the river banks, with all the vigour of the new year. After careful checks carried out at the river-gauge in Swenet, the specialists had predicted a magnificent flood which would transform Egypt into an immense lake as the Nile deposited its fertile silt upon the land. It would reach the exceptional height of twenty-two cubits.

The earth was drinking thirstily. The water filled

the canals; whirlpools formed close to the river-banks. The purifying tide drowned vermin, and the scorpions and snakes fled into the desert. Soon nothing would remain but the islets and mounds on which the villages were built. Hapy, the god of the flood, was carrying out his work with enthusiasm, because the dog-star Sothis had appeared at the zenith of the sky, signifying that Isis had brought Osiris back to life.

Piankhy asked Abilah to conduct the ritual of making offerings to the Nile, without which the river would not look favourably upon him.

'One last time,' he told her, 'I am going to try to prevent thousands of deaths.'

'I and your officers are against this course of action,' she said anxiously.

Piankhy put his arms around her. 'Sometimes men give up their madness. I must try—you know that.'

*   *   *

The Black Pharaoh was as impressively tall as his horse was noble. The eyes of both man and animal were fixed on the ramparts, where the scribe who commanded the fortress had just made an appearance.

'This town is mine,' proclaimed the king. 'Open the gates immediately, and the inhabitants of Memphis shall be spared. As for the soldiers, they shall swear allegiance to me and I will forget their disobedience.'

'Go back, Nubian! My men outnumber yours, and you cannot so much as scratch our walls.'

An arrow whistled through the air, narrowly

308

missing Piankhy's head. Suddenly as enraged as a panther, he gave vent to an anger which paralysed the Memphis garrison.

'By my father Amon's command,' he roared, 'I shall descend upon this town like a thunderstorm!'

The Black Pharaoh wheeled his horse and galloped away. By the time the Northern archers came to their senses and let fly their arrows, he was out of range.

*   *   *

When the earth grew light in the dawn of the new day, immense movable bridges, made of boats of all sizes lashed together, had been carried by the current up to the walls of Memphis. The Nile had risen so much that the ramparts were now no more than a minor obstacle a few cubits above the Nubian warriors. The artificers leant ladders and climbing-poles and frames against what of the fortress walls remained above the waterline, and the archers began their battle.

Puarma's men proved swifter and more accurate than the Northerners. No sooner had they let fly an arrow and felled an enemy than they were ready to shoot again. Assistants constantly refilled their quivers.

'Forward into Memphis!' ordered Piankhy, whose rage had communicated itself to the whole Southern army. 'The Nile has defeated these walls. Let us cross them—no enemy shall stop us!'

Lemersekny's infantry launched their attack in continuous waves, like the thunderstorm Piankhy had predicted. They captured the ramparts while the Nubian fleet, commanded by the Black

309

Pharaoh himself, attacked the port.

Overwhelmed, the defenders tried in vain to beat back the Southerners, who were already mooring their boats to the houses built near the river; their doorsteps were only just above the water.

Lemersekny had fought with such energy that he did not even feel the pain from a leg-wound. Nevertheless, while he was getting his breath back, a doctor applied a honey dressing to the wound.

'This is the most glorious day of my life,' said the captain. 'Who would have believed that one day we would succeed in conquering Memphis?'

'Keep still, Captain, or the bandages won't hold.'

'Hurry up. I want to be first through the "white wall"—I'm certainly not leaving that honour to Puarma.'

The tireless Nubian archers continued to fire until all response ceased. Deep down, Lemersekny had to admit that Puarma had commanded his men with great authority.

The two captains waved to each other and, standing on the corpse-strewn battlements, looked down on Memphis. They saw Piankhy disembark and enter the city through the great double gate that opened on to the tree-lined road to the Temple of Ptah. The city's terrified inhabitants ran about in all directions and got in the way of their own soldiers, who no longer knew whose orders to obey.

Lemersekny decided that his men were sufficiently rested, and led them into the fray to clear the way for the Black Pharaoh. From bastions, circular walkways, the tops of the massive gates and the watchtowers, a band of Nubian warriors came rushing down, yelling with the joy of conquest. They poured into the barracks, into the scribes' offices, the papyrus stores and the commandant's house. Those who tried to hold back their advance were massacred, cut down by axes, clubs and swords.

Lemersekny saw an archer aiming at him, but it was too late to get out of the way. The arrow buried itself in his left thigh, forcing him to stop. Immediately, his men surrounded him.

'Get me some myrrh,' he ordered.

Lemersekny ripped open his own flesh with his dagger, pulled out the arrow, and washed the wound with tepid water given to him by one of his soldiers. Then the doctor gave him a root of bitter chicory to place on the wound, followed by a coating of myrrh. The pain eased, and the wound would soon dry out.

The captain went on his way, with a satisfied glance at the body of the archer, whom Puarma had killed.

'You're getting old,' Puarma told him. 'Next time—'

'Next time it will be victory, just like today! What could we possibly have to fear, when we are serving under a king who knows how to make the river his ally?'

The citizens, terrified that they would all be massacred, forced the remaining Northern soldiers to surrender. The last pocket of resistance was the ancient white-walled citadel. When Piankhy arrived there, flanked by his two captains, the scribe who had commanded the defenders was brought before him.

'Do you finally agree to submit?' asked the king.

311

'Yes, Majesty. Permit me to bow before you.'

The scribe walked right up to the king. As he bowed low, he slipped a double-bladed dagger out of his sleeve and tried to bury it in Piankhy's chest. But the blade sank into Lemersekny's acacia-wood arm, which he had swung forward to save the pharaoh. The scribe was so terrified that he made no attempt to defend himself when the captain smashed his skull with one mighty blow of that very arm.

'Getting old, am I?' Lemersekny asked Puarma. 'Well, I'm not too old to save Pharaoh's life!'

A clamour rose up from the streets and the alleyways; a clamour which quickly changed into cheers hailing the glory of Piankhy, the new master of Memphis.

CHAPTER SIXTY-TWO

Prince Akanosh had summoned Yegeb to his private apartments at the palace of Sais. The counsellor wondered delightedly what means the Libyan had used to rid himself of his beloved wife. Yegeb had written the vital letter himself, in a perfect imitation of Daybreak's hand, and he was more than a little proud to have struck down several other enemies at the same time.

'You wished to see me, Prince Akanosh?' he asked.

'I wanted to thank you for opening my eyes. I knew my wife's origins, but I had decided— wrongly—to forget about them. This war is a test of truth, and you are right to bring this out into the open.'

Yegeb bowed. 'I was only doing my duty.'

'I sincerely loved my wife, Yegeb. Now I don't know what I ought to do. Will you help me?'

'How?'

'I cannot bring myself to kill her myself, as Tefnakht asked me to. Would you take care of the matter, in return for a suitable reward?'

'What do you think would be suitable, Prince?'

'A bag of gold and a house in my province, Sebennytos.'

Yegeb thought for a moment. 'Let's say two bags of gold, the house and a proportion of the harvest tax.'

'You ask a great deal.'

'Is it not a "suitable reward"?'

'Come with me,' said Akanosh.

'You want me to take care of it immediately?'

'Let us lose no more time.'

Akanosh took Yegeb by the arm and opened the door of the bedchamber, where his wife was sitting in quiet resignation.

Yegeb decided to strangle her. That would be a slow, painful death. He took a step towards his victim, but was suddenly dragged brutally backwards by a narrow strip of leather which cut deep into the soft flesh of his throat.

'How happy I am to kill you,' murmured Akanosh. 'Thanks to the Nile floods, all the vermin are disappearing. Thanks to me, Tefnakht will be relieved of a louse.'

Yegeb died with a gurgle, his throat crushed and his swollen tongue protruding from his mouth.

*   *   *

313

'My lord, it is horrible, appalling!' Nartreb's voice shook as he spoke.

'What's the matter?' asked Tefnakht.

'It's Yegeb.'

'Well? Tell me what this is all about.'

'He's dead, my lord! His body has just been found in an alleyway near the palace. Someone strangled him.'

'He did dangerous work,' commented the general, 'and he had many enemies.'

'The guilty person must be arrested as quickly as possible!'

'Whom do you suspect?'

'Prince Akanosh. He left this morning for Sebennytos, together with his wife.'

'Did he?' said Tefnakht. 'An excellent idea. Locked away in her palace, the Nubian woman can do us no further harm. The Libyan leaders have a great deal of respect for Akanosh, and I have no intention of sentencing him to death. In fact, I shall offer him a high position in my government. Honest men aren't easy to find.'

'But . . . but he's a criminal!'

'Take care of your own fate, Nartreb, and leave me to decide that of my subjects.'

*   *   *

Tefnakht decided not to burden himself with a Great Royal Wife. In defiance of tradition, he would reign alone and be content with concubines to satisfy his desires. Daybreak's treason had opened his eyes for good. He must not trust anyone: real power should not be shared.

The general was not unhappy about Yegeb's death. He and Nartreb had been a formidable duo, who, sooner or later, would have begun plotting treason. Manipulating Nartreb, a perverted, violent creature, would present no difficulty: he could be used for all manner of underhand work. When the moment came, Tefnakht would replace him with someone even greedier.

'My lord.'

'What is it now, Nartreb? I told you, Akanosh is a valuable ally. Don't waste your time trying to compromise him.'

'My lord . . . Memphis has fallen. Piankhy is now master of the city.'

Despite the sweltering summer heat, a cold feeling crept over Tefnakht. 'How?' he asked. 'Did Piankhy attack?'

'Yes, but it wasn't an ordinary attack.'

'What happened to the garrison, the fortifications, the reinforcements I sent?'

'The Black Pharaoh used the flood to overcome the city's defences. Thousands of Northern soldiers have been killed, and the survivors have surrendered and have been taken into the Nubian army.'

'But Memphis was impregnable!' said Tefnakht, still unable to take in the news.

'Except at the height of the flood, when the river became Piankhy's ally.'

'His losses must have been enormous.'

'No, my lord. It was an easy siege, a rapid victory.'

'The population will rebel against him.'

'They would be massacred. But we are not yet defeated. The Libyan army contains many battle-

315

ready soldiers. The Delta will never surrender.'

'You're right, Nartreb. We must continue the struggle.'

*　　　*　　　*

The pharaoh appointed by Amon at last ruled over Memphis, the 'Balance of the Two Lands', which thus regained their centre of equilibrium. However, many of the citizens feared the Black Pharaoh's vengeance: by twice refusing to open their gates to him, they had put themselves at risk of terrible reprisals. Some of the most prominent citizens had already begged Queen Abilah for mercy, but she had made no promises.

As dawn drew near, Piankhy was in his new apartments in the palace of Tuthmosis I, close to the white-walled citadel, taking the measure of the great city. He had not yet decided upon a course of action, so his troops, still on full alert, had taken control of the city.

Lemersekny's wounds were almost healed, and he had questioned every single one of the Libyans who had chosen to fight under the Black Pharaoh's banner. Those who seemed suspect had been disarmed and put to work repairing the riverside embankments. As for the victorious footsoldiers, they were enjoying the comforts of the great barracks and the delicious food donated by the inhabitants in hopes of winning them over.

Dawn marked the triumph of light over darkness. The land grew brighter, and it really was a new day.

Piankhy announced his decision. 'Memphis must be cleansed.'

316

Abilah, Lemersekny, Puarma and Cool-Head were shaken. Why such cruelty, when the population had not shown the slightest inclination to rebel?

'Majesty, is that really necessary?' asked Puarma.

'It is essential,' said Piankhy. 'This war has soiled Ptah's city. Therefore I shall go and purify myself in the "House of Morning", in his temple. I shall make offerings of oxen, hornless cattle and poultry, I shall offer libations to all the gods, and lastly I shall purify the temple and the entire city with natron and incense. Then, and only then, we shall start dealing with material problems.'

*   *   *

Piankhy's coronation rites were completed in the Temple of Ptah, making him King of Upper and Lower Egypt in the eyes of all the inhabitants of the Two Lands. The pharaoh and his wife showed themseves at the palace's 'window of appearances' next to the temple, and were hailed by the principal dignitaries. Convinced that a new era of prosperity was opening up before them, the inhabitants of Memphis were jubilant.

Soon afterwards, Cool-Head received a message whose contents he passed on immediately to the king.

'Majesty, all the garrisons in the province of Memphis have abandoned their strongholds and taken flight.'

Piankhy seemed less than delighted by the news.

'You're thinking about conquering the Delta, aren't you?' Abilah asked him.

317

'The fortress of Kher-Akha bars the way to the western Delta,' he said. 'A hard fight awaits us.'

CHAPTER SIXTY-THREE

In the Libyan ranks, the men were gradually getting over the fall of Memphis. The defeat was a significant one, certainly, but Tefnakht had succeeded in keeping hope alive by bringing together the chieftains from the Delta province who had remained faithful to him. From Piankhy, they could hope for nothing but the punishment reserved for rebels; from Tefnakht, they could count on an enduring will to win and reconquer the lost territory. It had been proved that Memphis was not impregnable, so why not follow the example given by the Black Pharaoh? When the moment came, the great city would once again fall into the hands of the Egyptians.

'Despite the setbacks,' declared Tefnakht with a confidence that heartened his allies, 'our forces are large and quite capable of preventing Piankhy from invading the Delta. What I propose is this: we shall block the Nubian advance in two stages, first pinning them down at a specific point and then surprising them with a counter-attack. We shall pin them down at the fortress of Kher-Akha, one of the strongest and most ancient in the land. As it is built on a mound, the flood will be no help to the attacker.'

The first to speak in reply was Prince Petisis, lord of the town of Athribis. He was rich, a little overweight and had just turned sixty.

'This man Piankhy has become Pharaoh,' he said, 'and no one doubts any longer that he is under Amon's protection. Won't he take Kher-Akha, just like all the others?'

'To be honest,' replied Tefnakht, 'I think he may well do so. But his victory will weaken him, for the siege will be long and difficult.'

'That's certainly true,' said Petisis. 'And the second stage?'

'An even more difficult siege.'

'Where, General?'

'Once he has conquered Kher-Akha, Piankhy will wish to take the great city nearby, Athribis. Your role will be decisive, Petisis.'

'I shall hold out as long as possible, but . . .'

'And I shall swoop down with my entire force, all my archers, footsoldiers and sailors, whom from now on I shall be regrouping at Mostai, three days' march south-east of Sais. We shall attack Piankhy's camp with the speed of a falcon and while his army is rooted to the spot, besieging your fortress, we shall cut it to pieces.'

'This plan is a clever one and it should succeed,' conceded Petisis, and the other provincial leaders agreed.

*   *   *

Piankhy fed Valiant some salt. During the periods of fierce heat which caused heavy sweating, the horse needed more than usual. To stave off digestive problems, Valiant drank several buckets of water a day, and ate properly dried barley, plus a variety of fruit and vegetables. When evening came, Piankhy rubbed him down with a tuft of

319

fresh grass which absorbed the moisture and sweat, and he talked with him to draw up a status report. Up till now, there had always been brightness in the animal's eyes. This evening, he looked almost grim.

'Is he upset?' asked Abilah.

'No,' said Piankhy, 'but he fears the Delta, as we all do. It's a region none of our soldiers knows, and it is bound to be fraught with pitfalls and dangers.'

'Are you having doubts about whether to conquer it?'

'I must delay no longer. Lower Egypt is part of the kingdom Amon entrusted to me, and it must not remain in rebel hands. But the test is bound to be a severe one. We are going to fight Tefnakht in his own lands, and we shall have lost many men besieging Kher-Akha.'

'Wherever you lead them, Majesty, the men will follow you. They know that you are the Son of the Light, the brother of the river and the servant of Ma' at.'

Piankhy stroked Abilah's face gently. 'Without you, none of my deeds could be crowned with success.'

*   *   *

Nartreb was recovering quickly from Yegeb's death, and he had given up trying to find the killer. After all, he would get by very well without his accomplice, who had often regarded him with a certain contempt because he was less learned. Yegeb's knowledge of mathematics had enabled him to keep detailed accounts of his wealth, but today it was Nartreb who was reaping the benefits.

And since, Nartreb felt, he had the soul of a treasurer, he would not lose a single crumb of his wealth.

At Sais, the largest and richest town in the Delta, Nartreb was taking no risks. The Black Pharaoh would never venture this far, particularly after the hammer-blows Tefnakht would inflict on the Nubian army while it was encamped before Athribis. The general's plan was truly excellent, and the Libyan troops gathered at Mostai were thirsty for revenge.

The more Nartreb thought about it, the more he realized that Yegeb had been getting old and lacked ambition. He would have been content to contemplate his possessions, while Nartreb felt he himself had a political destiny. The war would last a long time, for after the victory at Athribis Tefnakht would try to reconquer his lost territory. He would need a government led by a minister who would stay well behind the battle-front and devote himself entirely to administrative matters. Nartreb's programme for government was ready: the post was his by right.

The head jailer of Sais prison was annnounced.

'The female prisoner wishes to see you, my lord,' he said.

'Daybreak does? But that prison is dirty and smelly.'

'That is why, if you agree to see her, I shall have the prisoner transferred to a place worthy of you.'

'Hmm. Have her washed and perfumed too.'

'As you command, my lord.' And the jailer went out.

This was an unexpected entertainment. When he had tried to rape her, the bitch had fought back.

This time she would be at his mercy. But what information could she have for him?

*　　　*　　　*

Daybreak was still beautiful, although her face bore traces of weariness. Barefoot and dressed in a short, pale-yellow dress which left her shoulders bare, she looked like a young girl scarcely in her teens.

Nartreb felt violent desire well up inside him. His fat lips swelled, his neck thickened and his pudgy fingers wriggled like serpents.

'What did you want to say to me, little one?'

Daybreak avoided Nartreb's greedy gaze. 'You and Yegeb, you were right. I wanted to avenge my father, as I had promised him I would.'

'Good, good. But your repentance is rather too late, don't you think?'

'My punishment is horrible. I can't bear that prison, that filth, that damp! Please pardon me, Nartreb.'

'That's impossible, little one. The sentence was pronounced by Tefnakht himself, and there is absolutely no scope for me to change it.'

'I beg you, have me locked up in a different cell, a clean one, without rats.'

'What have you to offer me, in exchange for such a privilege?'

Daybreak let her dress glide down her youthful body.

Nartreb's mouth watered at the sight. 'You will have to let me do anything I want.'

'Very well.'

'And you must do more than just lie there—I

322

hate apathetic women.'

'I'll do my best.'

Nartreb had no intention of transferring Daybreak to another prison. If Tefnakht found out, he would be furious. Since lying was one of his talents, Nartreb had some fine hours of pleasure ahead of him.

'Come and kiss me, little one,' he ordered.

Daybreak moved with the speed of a cobra. She sank her teeth deep into Nartreb's throat, making blood spurt out. Maddened with pain, he beat her off with his fists and knees. Knocked unconscious, she did not see death coming as he trampled her into the ground with a rage that was close to madness.

*   *   *

'How is Nartreb?' asked Tefnakht.

'Infection has set in, and it will be difficult to fight it,' said the doctor. 'I shall need large quantities of rare and expensive ointments.'

'Don't waste them. My army will need them.'

'Do you mean . . .?'

'Let him die, and don't ease his suffering. When a man reaches such depths of dishonour and barbarism, it is a sign that he lost his soul a long time ago.'

Tefnakht had seen Daybreak's body. In the name of the love that they had once shared, he owed her this final act of vengeance.

CHAPTER SIXTY-FOUR

As he rode towards Kher-Akha, Piankhy stroked his horse's neck and turned his thoughts to the sacred city of Iunu, whose approaches were guarded by the fortress.

Iunu, the city of Ra, the Divine Light; Iunu, the the birthplace of Egyptian spiritual life. Iunu, where the pyramid texts had been conceived and written, texts devoted to the incessant transmutations of the royal soul in the hereafter. It was here that the voice of God had made itself heard for the first time, sounding out over the land of Egypt.

The Black Pharaoh felt a surge of emotion, as if he were approaching the high point of his life. How could he, a son of far-off Nubia, ever have imagined that he would one day be so close to the source of this civilization, his very model and his reason for living? Yet he was also almost overwhelmed by sadness: how many soldiers must die in order for him to reach Iunu?

Abilah took Piankhy's hand gently in her own. 'You must have faith,' she whispered.

*   *   *

'There they are!' announced a watchman to the officer in charge of Kher-Akha's sentries.

The officer immediately left the ramparts and went to report to the fortress commander, a Libyan in his forties, with very delicate skin and the look of an aristocrat. The son of a rich Delta family, and

324

father of three children, he had enjoyed an easy, problem-free career.

'How many are there?' asked the commander.

'In my opinion, the entire Nubian army.'

'And the Black Pharaoh?'

'He's riding in the vanguard.'

'Are our men ready?'

'They will fight to the last man, Commander. And they will kill many Nubians, right up to the moment when the reinforcements arrive from Sais to finish breaking up the attacking force.'

'There will be no reinforcements.'

'No reinforcements? But. . .'

'We have received orders to hold out for as long as possible and cause the enemy as many losses as we can. But we can count on no one but ourselves.

'Understood, Commander. We have enough food and water for several months.'

'What do you think of the Nubians' catapults? Are they effective?'

'They're formidable.'

'And their weaponry?'

'First-rate.'

'How is the garrison's morale?'

The officer hesitated.

'I demand to know the truth.'

'It is not very high. Our men know that the Nubian warriors are courageous and the Black Pharaoh is stubborn. People say that Amon protects him and that his wife's magic enables him always to find the path to victory.'

'Every man is to hold his position resolutely. And may the gods look favourably upon us.'

*   *   *

325

'What a fine beast!' exclaimed Lemersekny when he saw Kher-Akha for the first time. 'Memphis, now that was too easy. This time, we're really going to have a fight on our hands.'

Puarma pulled a disapproving face. 'To raise one single scaling-ladder, we shall have to sacrifice fifty men. The Kher-Akhaian archers are ideally positioned, and there's a strong risk that mine will be ineffective.'

'When will you stop being so pessimistic? You're forgetting that it's Piankhy who's in command.'

Raising his gaze to the ramparts of Kher-Akha, Puarma was unable to subdue his fears. 'The artificers will have problems piling up banks of earth against the walls—perhaps insurmountable problems. There's a strong chance our losses will be very heavy indeed. And even if we do take this place, what army will we use to attack the Delta?'

'Piankhy will find the answer.'

Puarma was irritated. 'What's happened to your famous scepticism, Lemersekny?'

'If you were my commanding officer, I'd certainly despair. But there is a pharaoh in charge, and tomorrow, the sun will rise.'

*   *   *

It was a fine morning, with a light breeze to temper the fierce heat of the sun. Thousands of Nubians were preparing to give their lives to open up the approach to the Delta and the rich provinces of Libyan-occupied Lower Egypt.

Puarma's archers would try to provide cover for the artificers and footsoldiers, but Piankhy knew

326

that many of his comrades in arms would fall before the walls of Kher-Akha.

A profound silence fell over the Nubian ranks as they waited for the pharaoh to give the signal to attack.

Valiant whinnied, reared up, then grew calm and fixed his eyes on the great gate of the fortress, which slowly opened, as though in a dream. The Libyan commander stepped out on to the paved ground, threw down his sword and his bow, walked towards Piankhy and prostrated himself.

'Pharaoh was crowned at Memphis,' declared the Libyan. 'God has commanded him to rule Egypt and bring happiness to the nation. Why should I sow death and misery, when all I need do to prevent a disaster is obey? Majesty, accept Kher-Akha's submission.'

The silence lasted a few seconds more, as though the whole Nubian army had had its breath taken away. Then fear evaporated, and a powerful joy filled every heart. In indescribable jubilation, Piankhy's soldiers and the defenders of Kher-Akha rushed forward to congratulate each other.

*   *   *

The Black Pharaoh crossed the fortified hill of Kher-Akha and purified himself in the lake of Kebeh, where the Divine Light washed his face with water which had sprung forth from the primordial energy-source. Regenerated by this act, Piankhy headed towards the sandy mound of Iunu, where life had appeared for the first time. Standing before the rising sun, he offered up white bulls, milk, myrrh, incense and perfumes to the Creator.

Then the priests hailed him as he entered the Temple of Atum. They recognized him as Pharaoh, brother to the nine divinities who ceaselessly re-created the world.

The king spoke the ritual words designed to drive away visible and invisible enemies, put on robes purified in the temple's House of Morning, and tied on the headband which enabled him to see into the world of the gods. Then he climbed the staircase which led to the upper floor of the temple, from where he had his first sight of the granite obelisk. Granite was the primordial stone, in which the very first light had taken solid form.

Only one task remained: to go, alone, into the secret innermost shrine of Atum, whose name meant both 'Being' and 'Non-Being'. Piankhy broke the seal on the shrine's golden doors, opened them, and saw the mystery of creation, an eternal movement which was embodied in the never-ending voyage of the eternal ship of morning and the ship of evening.

Then the pharaoh knew why he had undertaken this long and perilous journey, why he had risked his life and the lives of those dear to him, why it was so vital that the Two Lands should be united and ruled by love.

CHAPTER SIXTY-FIVE

Under the spell of Iunu the secret city, sheltered by acacias and tamarisk trees, the royal couple had celebrated the holy rites in the temples of Ramses II and Ramses III. They had decked with flowers the Houses of Eternity of the ancient empire and paid homage to the bull Mnevis, the earthly incarnation of the power of the Light.

Piankhy particularly loved the temple of 'Atum of the Sycamore', and the shrine of the sacred tree, on whose leaves a priest, wearing the mask of Thoth, had written the Black Pharaoh's coronation names. Groves, orchards, olive groves and man-made lakes made Iunu a good place to live, one where with every step you took you could sense the presence of the gods.

Only Lemersekny was in a foul mood.

'We're wasting time,' he complained to Puarma. 'Look at our soldiers! They're wearing wide-sleeved shirts, pleated kilts decorated with little bell-shaped motifs and embroideries of gazelles gambolling in the savannah, and they even spend all day being perfumed by lovesick damsels! And then there are all these dignitaries, from the chief scribe to the crown-bearer, who never stop singing Piankhy's praises. We're enjoying our past successes and we're losing our taste for battle. This isn't the way to take Athribis.'

Puarma smiled. 'Have a little faith, Captain. Pharaoh will find the answer, won't he?'

*   *   *

Athribis, whose symbol was a black bull, was a rich, powerful city ruled with pride by Prince Petisis, whose name meant 'the Gift of Isis'. Despite the economic chaos that had accompanied Libyan occupation, he could boast of having fed all the inhabitants of his capital, and that its garrison was loyal to him.

Each day, after enjoying a lukewarm shower, Petisis sat down at the well-laden breakfast table which Egyptians called the 'cleansing of the mouth', for before eating it was customary to purify it with natron. He had an excessive fondness for goat's cheese and dried fish.

But the news his head scribe had just brought had robbed Petisis of his appetite.

'Kher-Akha has surrendered without a fight? That's impossible!'

'The commander recognized the sovereignty of the Black Pharaoh. So he had no further reason to sacrifice his garrison.'

'Tefnakht ordered him to resist and he knew the price of that courage! Where is Piankhy?'

'He has taken up residence in Iunu,' said the scribe.

'He will lose no time in attacking us. Summon all the officers of the garrison.'

'Prince Akanosh has just arrived from Sebennytos and he wishes to speak with you.'

'Show him in.'

The two men greeted each other warmly. They had liked each other for a long time.

'Did you travel all night, my friend?' asked Petisis.

'I set out as soon as I heard that Kher-Akha had fallen. Has the news been confirmed?'

'The fortress commander opened his gates to the Black Pharaoh. Piankhy did not even have to attack, and he did not lose a single soldier.'

'So the first part of Tefnakht's plan has been a total failure.'

'And Piankhy's intact army is about to arrive at the gates of Athribis,' said Petisis worriedly.

'We must put an end to this war,' decreed Akanosh.

'Are you suggesting I should . . .?'

'Yes, you, too, should open the gates of your town and submit to the true pharaoh.'

'Do you fully understand the implications of that advice?'

'This is not treason, Petisis. Under Tefnakht's command, we tried to defeat Piankhy and we failed. He is the pharaoh and we owe him obedience. Why make our provinces suffer for nothing?'

Akanosh had risked everything. Petisis could order his arrest and send him to Sais, where he would be executed.

'I have a secret to tell you,' said Petisis. 'I am not Libyan, but Egyptian. To see Athribis return to the bosom of a true pharaoh would be the joy of my old age.'

*   *   *

'You look wonderful,' Puarma told Lemersekny. 'That shirt with the short, wide sleeves suits you to perfection.'

'That's enough, archer! I loathe these boring social events.'

'This one is hardly boring. Watching the Prince of Athribis hand his town back to Piankhy isn't something you do every day.'

'We're soldiers, not courtiers. I'd have preferred to conquer this fortress at the point of my sword.'

'Keep your strength for Sais,' said Puarma. 'Tefnakht won't surrender, you can be sure of that.'

The two men headed for the riverside, to watch

331

the ceremony.

Piankhy and Abilah landed at the port of Athribis from the royal ship. Prince Petisis had had a canopy of gilded wood erected to welcome the royal couple and shelter them from the sun's rays.

'Enter into your dwelling, Majesty,' said the prince, kneeling before them. 'All its treasures are yours—my gold ingots, a heap of turquoises, necklaces, amulets, golden dishes, robes of royal linen, beds spread with fine linen, oil of frankincense, pots of unguent and many horses from my stables.'

'Are you offering me the finest of them?'

'If anyone is hiding his finest horses from you, Majesty, may he die on the spot!'

'Rise, Petisis.'

'I am the son of an Egyptian, Majesty, and I am grateful to you for giving Athribis back its freedom. As for those Libyans who are the sons of Libyans, today they submit to your authority.'

The first to step forward was Prince Akanosh, accompanied by his wife. Piankhy appreciated their nobility, which showed no signs of weakness.

'We are vanquished,' said Akanosh. 'Henceforth, the province of Sebennytos belongs to the Pharaoh of Egypt. I pray that he may show mercy to my subjects and to my wife, who is of Nubian origin but faithful to her clan.'

'You are to be praised for your wisdom,' replied Piankhy. 'Serve this country and her king faithfully, and remain as ruler of Sebennytos.'

'You are placing your trust in me, a Libyan?'

'I place my trust in a man whose preoccupation is safeguarding his province and its inhabitants. Since you place their lives above your own, you will know how to make them happy.'

Mayors, administrators, counsellors, judges and officers—some of Egyptian origin, others Libyan—came one by one to swear an oath of allegiance to the Black Pharaoh. The prince of the rich city of Khem did likewise. To each, Piankhy set out the role he must play in respecting the law of Ma'at and preserving the unity of the Two Lands, whose inflexible guarantor he would be. The celebrations did not begin until late in the evening, after the government of most of the Delta had been put in place.

As he chewed on a roast duck thigh, washed down with sweet white wine, Lemersekny could not resist musing loudly, 'There's still Sais. The last battle and the finest of all.'

Piankhy's mongoose leapt on to his acacia-wood arm. 'Ah, there you are! You'll protect us to the very end, won't you?'

The little carnivore scurried up to the soldier's shoulder and licked his cheek.

'The pharaoh is right,' Lemersekny went on. 'We must carry the task through to its end. It would be a pity to die at the last hurdle.'

CHAPTER SIXTY-SIX

The last warriors faithful to Tefnakht had gathered around the general in his palace at Sais. The intransigents were advocating total war against the Nubians.

'Athribis has betrayed us,' revealed Tefnakht, 'and the majority of the Libyan chieftains have

333

submitted to Piankhy.'

'What does that matter?' shouted an old officer. 'We won't miss cowards like that. At least we know who we can rely on. Come to Mostai where our troops are gathered, General, and you'll see that we're ready to fight.'

'You should know that I shall never surrender. Our army is still sufficiently strong to prevent Piankhy from taking Sais, which he dreams of putting to fire and the sword.'

A young officer said heatedly, 'You're wrong, General! Piankhy has not killed a single civilian, and those who have recognized his sovereignty have nothing to complain about.'

'You're the one who is wrong. The Nubian has only one objective: to destroy me and every Libyan along with me. Up to now, he has slyly pretended to be merciful. Tomorrow, he will reveal his true nature, which is pitiless cruelty.'

'Your argument is unconvincing, General. Facts are facts.'

'Do you wish to leave my army?'

'Let us accept defeat, General. Piankhy will grant us his pardon.'

The old officer stabbed his dagger into the young man's chest, and he sank to the ground, his eyes filled with amazement.

'We shall fight and we shall win,' declared the murderer.

*   *   *

On the map of the Delta, there remained only one province which had not been subdued: Sais, where Tefnakht reigned.

'The last hurdle,' said Lemersekny.

'Tefnakht has kept his best men around him,' commented Puarma. 'Up to now, Majesty, you have saved many lives. But this battle will be murderous.'

The mongoose perched on his shoulder, Piankhy was deep in thought. 'If you were in Tefnakht's position, what would you do?'

Lemersekny scratched his wooden arm. 'Not one single fortress has resisted us. Sais won't be an exception to the rule. Staying locked up inside it will give him no chance of survival.'

'So,' went on Puarma, 'he has massed his troops elsewhere—it must be on one of the routes to Sais.'

'I can tell you exactly where he's waiting for us,' said Piankhy. 'At Mostai.'

'Majesty, how . . .?'

'I received the information from the Libyan princes. But I wanted to test your powers of reasoning.'

Lemersekny protested, 'If Tefnakht knows his allies have abandoned him, he'll also know they have told you about Mostai. He'll have changed the place of his ambush.'

'We can't be sure of that,' said the king. 'He needs favourable terrain on which to manoeuvre his chariots, and moving footsoldiers and boats at the same time is not so easy.'

'Let me check this,' said Lemersekny.

*   *   *

Cool-Head was torn between joy and pain. Joy at seeing the Black Pharaoh's triumph, pain at being separated for ever from Napata and Nubia.

Piankhy had warned him that he would be in charge of an important ministry, so the scribe was thinking of bringing his family to Egypt. But where would the royal couple live, at Thebes or at Memphis? No doubt in the North during the summer and in the South during the winter, in order to show that Pharaoh neglected neither Lower nor Upper Egypt.

It still remained, though, to lance the abscess that was Sais, the last one afflicting the great body of the gods' beloved land. Despite the joyous, relaxed atmosphere which reigned at Athribis, Cool-Head sensed that Piankhy was uneasy. Although Tefnakht was greatly weakened, the king feared he would do something violent and unexpected, a gesture of madness which would steep the North in blood. And Piankhy was also worried about Lemersekny, whose mission was taking longer than expected.

As for Puarma, he was champing at the bit. If he had not been a disciplined soldier, he would willingly have disobeyed Piankhy's orders and gone to look for his colleague, who was no doubt in difficulties. By chancing his luck, Lemersekny had perhaps lost the game.

*   *   *

He was dusty, tired, thirsty and fractious, but he was alive. Lemersekny refused to talk before he had drunk a jar of cool beer and washed his acacia-wood arm, which positively bristled with thorns.

'I had to travel through the groves,' he explained, 'and fight off snakes and scorpions. Then I got stuck in a swamp near Mostai. But I saw

336

them. Boats on a canal and an encampment of footsoldiers.'

'Many of them?' asked Piankhy.

'Not as many as we have. I propose that we attack the canal and the camp simultaneously. Our boats will easily force a way through, our archers will take out the two guard posts, and our chariots will use the Northern route to decimate the footsoldiers.'

Puarma voiced no objections.

'I would have liked a day or two to rest,' added Lemersekny, 'but it's better to act quickly.'

Piankhy could have demanded help from the Libyan princes, but he decided that this final battle should be fought only by his own army, the troops who had served him with total loyalty ever since their departure from Napata.

Puarma dared to say what it was that was troubling him. 'Majesty, if this battle were to end in failure, all your work would be reduced to nothing, and chaos would reign again.'

Lemersekny blazed at him, 'It was I who observed the enemy's strength and positions, not one of your archers. There are no traps awaiting us.'

'But what if a Libyan reserve army with chariots and—'

'It doesn't exist, Puarma! These are Tefnakht's last forces, and we shall destroy them.'

*   *   *

Piankhy and Abilah were out on the boating-lake at the palace of Athribis, the king himself wielding the oars. The queen was dressed in a net gown which

337

covered less than it revealed, and was protecting herself from the sun with a sunshade.

'This is the final hurdle, isn't it?' she asked.

'Yes, I think Lemersekny is right.'

'And yet your officers are anxious.'

'That's true,' he said. 'One would swear that the spectre of defeat was gnawing away at their souls.'

'The evil eye. It's trying to slip into our ranks. We must ward it off before we launch the attack.'

'What do you suggest?'

'We shall celebrate the most ancient of our rites, the breaking of the red vases.'

*   *   *

The night before the Nubian army was to leave for Mostai, Queen Abilah, acting in the name of Sekhmet, took several red vases covered with Tefnakht's name and shattered them on the paved floor of the temple. In this way, she was depriving the Libyan of the god Set's energy and violence, which were expressed by the colour red.

Shortly after the end of the rite, Puarma felt himself freed from the oppression which had been constricting his breathing for several days, and a number of soldiers experienced the same relief.

Queen Abilah's magic was more effective than Tefnakht's. So the Nubian army set off, singing, to conquer the last Northern bastion.

CHAPTER SIXTY-SEVEN

Tefnakht could no longer bear the inaction, and he had decided to attack Piankhy's troops stationed at Athribis. With the advantage of surprise, he would inflict heavy losses on them before withdrawing and preparing other surprise attacks.

The Libyan soldiers were almost ready. Straps criss-crossed their chests, their hair was braided and their slender beards shaped into a point, and there were warlike tattoos on their arms, chests and abdomens. All that remained was for them to stick two feathers into their headdresses. Neither the sick nor the old had been willing to remain in the rear, and even old Pisap, a seventy-year-old chariot officer, had come out of retirement to take part in the fight that would give Tefnakht's troops back their confidence.

The general had been unable to go to sleep. It was a restless night, filled with painful visions of the Nubians pouring down on him like the waves of an enraged Nile. He walked through the sleeping camp, which was bathed in the light of the full moon, and for the first time he felt doubt.

He doubted himself, the validity of what he had done, and the usefulness of fighting. Heaven and the gods had sent many signs to open his eyes. Sent by Amon, recognized as Pharaoh, Piankhy had set out along the path of the just and had spread joy and peace, while he, the rebel and causer of strife, found himself on the verge of the abyss.

The dawn was coming up, but the birds were not singing. A distant rumble had frightened them. A rumble that was getting louder with every second that passed—Piankhy's chariots!

The general gave the order for the trumpeters to sound the alarm. Jolted awake, the footsoldiers leapt up and hastily gathered up their weapons while the chariot crews harnessed their teams. Puarma's archers had already killed the sentries, and Piankhy's flotilla was now attacking Tefnakht's boats, whose terrified crews could muster only a feeble response.

Tefnakht swiftly realized that his only chance of destroying the Nubian attack was to defeat the opposing chariots. At the head of his best troops, the general had no choice but to meet them head-on.

'Forward!' he yelled, and he leapt into his chariot.

He found Pisap there, firmly attached to the shell of the chariot by a leather strap and gripping the reins tightly.

'Where is my charioteer?'

'Vomiting,' said the old man. 'It's the fear of death. Don't worry, General, I know how to handle your horses. Just kill as many Nubians as possible!'

The Libyans lacked neither courage nor skill, but the bumpy terrain quickly proved unfavourable to them. Several chariot wheels broke, while those of Piankhy's army stood up to the speed and irregularities of the track, just as the carpenter had promised him in Napata.

Thrown off balance, the Libyan archers and javelin-throwers missed most of their targets, while the Nubians struck home with almost every shot. And then came a miracle. There, less than fifty paces from Tefnakht, was Piankhy astride his bay horse! Piankhy, within range, oblivious of the danger he was running. Tefnakht drew his bow, aimed and fired.

Valiant made a mighty leap to avoid a Libyan chariot which had just overturned, and the arrow brushed past the nape of the Black Pharaoh's neck.

'General,' said Pisap in despair, 'we must make a run for it.'

Tefnakht turned round. His chariots had all been disabled.

'Push on towards the canal,' he ordered.

Thinking the general had thought of a plan to counter-attack, Pisap forced a way through.

Tefnakht jumped down on to the ground, ran to the nearest moored boat, seized a flaming torch and set fire to the sail. The morning wind fanned the flames, the stern caught fire, and the conflagration spread quickly to the next boat.

Pisap was aghast. 'General, why . . .?'

'Piankhy is not going to get his hands on my fleet. Now we are going to die. We shall return to the fray.'

'No, we must escape.'

'That's impossible.'

'We can take the path which runs along the canal, and go north across the wheatfield. In the Delta marshes we will find shelter. I know hiding-places Piankhy's soldiers will never discover.'

'The chariot is too wide.'

'Go on there, my children!' roared Pisap. 'Go on!'

The horses galloped away.

*　　　*　　　*

341

Of the whole Libyan army only a few survivors remained, and most of them were mortally wounded. Tefnakht's forces had been wiped out. Piankhy ordered the doctors to take care of the injured, then rode out before his soldiers, who greeted him with cheers.

'You did not fight for the glory of a man,' he told them. 'You fought for Egypt and her pharaoh, the earthly representative of the celestial law of Ma'at. This war is over, and today you have become the builders of peace. Harm no one, protect the weak, guarantee the safety of the people. By doing these things, you will achieve your greatest victory of all.'

With Lemersekny and Puarma, Piankhy scoured the battlefield, searching for Tefnakht's body. The Nubians cut off the right hands of the dead; this enabled them to calculate the number killed, which the scribes noted down on their palettes.

Twice Puarma thought he had identified the general, according to the description given to him by a Libyan charioteer who had been wounded in the shoulder. But each time, when the charioteer was shown the body, he told Puarma he was mistaken.

After comparing several witnesses' accounts, Lemersekny arrived at the conclusion that Tefnakht had fled the battlefield in a chariot, heading north. With the aid of several scouts, he found the canal path which still bore the imprint of the chariot's wheels.

Piankhy did not hide his annoyance. 'So Tefnakht is still alive.'

'I shall send a number of detachments out to look for him,' Puarma promised.

*   *   *

Curled up in a ball, the mongoose slept on Piankhy's lap. The king was sitting on a throne of gilded sycamore wood, in the darkened audience chamber at Sais where formerly Tefnakht had imposed his law.

Now that it had submitted to the Black Pharaoh, the city of the goddess Neith had sunk into a sleepy daze of perfect tranquillity, certain that Piankhy would spare its inhabitants. As for the Black Pharaoh, he had not been able to sleep, and he had come to gather his thoughts here where his adversary had dreamt up his insane plans.

In the silence of the deserted palace, Piankhy thought of his vanquished enemy, deprived of all support. Tefnakht had pursued his dream to the very limit of his strength, with a conviction that successive defeats had scarcely dented, but he had been mistaken about his own destiny and that of Egypt.

Barefoot, Queen Abilah walked forward into the darkness, sat down at the foot of the throne and laid her head against her husband's knee. 'What have the searches revealed?'

'Nothing,' replied Piankhy. 'Tefnakht knows the marshes and islands of the Delta very well. He will travel from one hiding-place to another.'

'Why not abandon him to his solitude?'

'Because he himself will not be satisfied with that. He will gather together a band of boatmen and fishermen, loot the villages and spread insecurity all round the edges of the country. And that is something I cannot permit.'

343

CHAPTER SIXTY-EIGHT

Tefnakht was not as alone as Piankhy thought. As he journeyed further into the strange, dangerous world of the Delta swamps, he thought of the little communities of fisherfolk whom he might band together to struggle against the Nubians. Old Pisap had family among the boatmen who roamed the canals north of Sais, and they would certainly come to his aid.

The two Libyans had abandoned their chariot, which had become useless, and were now travelling about with the aid of a papyrus boat, sailing along between tall banks of reeds. No Nubian would manage to follow them in this maze; it took detailed knowledge to reach the islets on which the fishermen built their huts.

It was to one of these islets that Tefnakht and Pisap were heading. A good size, and hidden behind thickets of papyrus where dozens of birds nested, it had been levelled off to receive a stone shrine dedicated to the snake-goddess Wadjyt, she who had the power to revive and restore energy. The treasurer of the Libyan army had hidden gold and precious stones there when he came to hunt in the region. Thanks to this small fortune, Tefnakht would be able to pay mercenaries and wage incessant raids against Piankhy.

There was a hut on the islet. After dining on fish cooked over a small fire, the two men went into the hut to sleep.

In the middle of the night, Tefnakht heard a suspicious noise, like the beating of wings. Sword in

344

hand, he went outside.

Despite the lack of a moon, which was veiled by clouds, it was as clear as day. Perched on top of a papyrus stalk twelve cubits high sat a swallow with a human head, staring accusingly at him.

So, the myth was true. When the ancestors returned from the hereafter, the Light did indeed cause them to take on the form of birds with human faces. The swallow's features changed. Tefnakht thought he saw the faces of the Tuthmosids, the Amenhoteps, Ramses the Great . . . And all these pharaohs were reproaching him.

A strong wind blew up, darkness swallowed up the brightness, and the swallow flew away, leaving behind it a turquoise trail.

*   *   *

'I have an important mission for you, Pisap,' said Tefnakht. 'Take this message to Piankhy.'

The old man scratched his ear. 'I must have misheard you, General.'

'You heard me perfectly.'

'You, Tefnakht, you want to surrender?'

'No, I want to negotiate. As envoy of the province of Sais, you have nothing to fear.'

'Do you mean you're giving up the fight?'

'Yes, I am. Tonight, my ancestors appeared to me and they convinced me that I had taken the wrong road. Today there is a true pharaoh, crowned at Iunu, Memphis and Thebes, and it is him we must all obey. The Black Pharaoh has achieved the unity I dreamt of. My eyes were closed; they have just been opened. Since Egypt at last knows peace, I must no longer be a destroyer.'

345

'You know what awaits you, whether you negotiate or not?'

'As a rebel, I shall be condemned to death. Pharaoh is obliged to take that decision—in his place, I would do exactly the same. But I want to die standing up and looking my judges in the face, not like a fugitive, struck down with an arrow in the back. Also, I hope that my submission will pacify the last rebels, and that war will leave their hearts. Lastly, I want Pharaoh to grant me his pardon, so that I may defend my cause before the court of the Otherworld.'

*　　　*　　　*

'Hurry up, Lemersekny,' urged Puarma. 'We're going to be late. You should be washed, shaved and dressed.'

'I'm sleepy. Go on your own.'

With the utmost care, Puarma took hold of the young lady with the delightful breasts and slender hips who was the cause of Lemersekny's tiredness, and evicted her from the bed. She gave him a wonderful smile, but unfortunately he had no time to pay homage to her charms.

As Lemersekny was turning on to his side to dive back into his blissful dreams, Puarma overturned the bed.

The shock of falling on to the paved floor half woke Lemersekny. 'I hate these military ceremonies,' he grumbled, holding his back.

'Will a bit of iced water make up your mind for you?'

'Oh no, not that!'

'Then hurry.'

346

'Can't you just imagine the reprimand we're going to get because we haven't yet caught that damned Tefnakht?'

'Nevertheless, we have to obey Pharaoh's orders and go to this ceremony. I'm going to throw a reasonably clean tunic on your back and then you're coming with me—without arguing.'

Still somewhat befuddled, Lemersekny left his bedchamber.

Standing amid the crowd of courtiers, he was asleep on his feet when Piankhy began handing out the golden flies that were given as a reward to distinguished soldiers for acts of bravery and determined attacks on the enemy.

Then the pharaoh announced, 'The moment has come to honour our senior officers. I am thinking first of a man who without hesitation risked his life again and again to contain the enemy before striking him down. Because of his valour and that of his archers, Captain Puarma deserves to be raised to the rank of general.'

Lemersekny's eyes opened wide in amazement. He saw Puarma leave the throng and present himself before the king. Puarma a general! An archer who had no sense of strategy and would never have the slightest idea of how to plan an attack properly. But then again, why not? The archer was young, he didn't lack courage. He'd make a bad general, of course, but no worse than anyone else.

'The same praise and the same rank must be granted to Lemersekny,' Piankhy continued.

The man with the acacia-wood arm thought he had misheard. He stood rooted to the spot, unable to step forward. Puarma came and fetched him,

347

and led him to the king, who decorated him with the golden fly.

'I am proud of you, my generals. You will jointly command the Egyptian army, in which Nubians, Libyans and Egyptians now serve together. It is up to you to ensure the cohesion of our troops.'

*   *   *

'General Lemersekny,' said Cool-Head, visibly agitated, 'an ambassador from Tefnakht is asking to see His Majesty.'

'I'm in the middle of an official reception,' muttered Lemersekny thickly.

'General, this is serious.'

To celebrate his promotion, Lemersekny had invited his men to a party. They drank strong oasis wine, undiluted with water and, as was only right, the new general had set an unstinting example.

'The man's name is Pisap,' Cool-Head went on, 'and he carries a document bearing Tefnakht's seal.'

A second miracle in one day! Lemersekny threw the contents of a water-pot over his head, but the mirage did not disappear: the scribe was indeed real.

Trying to behave with the dignity befitting a general, Lemersekny listened to Pisap's explanations and agreed to take him to the king, who was rubbing down his horse.

The sheer size of the Black Pharaoh terrified the old Libyan, who suddenly found himself unable to utter a word.

'Does this envoy really have a request to present to me?' asked Piankhy.

Lemersekny took the papyrus from Pisap's hands, broke the mud seal, unrolled the document and read out the text.

* * *

From General Tefnakht to the Pharaoh of Upper and Lower Egypt: may he live, may he prosper and enjoy good health. Peace be with you, Piankhy, since no one may look you in the face, since no one can withstand the fire that gives you life and shines in your eyes. You are the bull, with a powerful, victorious arm. Must your heart not grow calm after the defeat which you have inflicted on me? I, Tefnakht, am a lost, ruined man. Judge me with mercy: cut the dead branches from the tree, but do not tear up its roots. Yes, I am afraid of you, and that fear tears at my belly and racks my bones with agony. Since the day you vanquished me, I have eaten nothing but the bread of hunger, I have drunk only the water of thirst; my clothes are torn, my body is nothing but suffering. Will the goddess Neith herself, patroness of my town, forgive my errors? You continue to hunt me down, you impose an interminable flight upon me, and I am at the end of my strength. That is why I beg you to cleanse me of my misdeeds. Take my possessions, take my horses, and add them to your own treasure, but grant a favourable answer to my request, so that anguish may leave my heart.

Piankhy had been watching the mongoose, which, after sniffing Pisap for a long time, had fallen asleep. So Pisap presented no danger.

'Have you any other message for me?' the king asked the old man, who was still trembling.

349

'Yes, Majesty. Tefnakht wishes to meet, you and he alone, in the Temple of Neith.'

CHAPTER SIXTY-NINE

Fat Otoku and crusty old Kapa were sitting side by side on the trunk of a fallen palm tree, Kapa's gnarled hands resting on the pommel of his walking stick. Together they gazed out at the Nubian desert.

'The news is excellent,' said Otoku. 'From now on, the North, South, West and East will all be obedient to Piankhy. Not a single province remains unsubdued, and every town pays homage to the Lord of the Two Lands.'

'Good, good. But all the same,' mused Kapa, 'I would willingly have slit the throats of Peftau and Nemrod, those princes who were so quick to commit treason.'

'Peftau is sick and will soon withdraw from public life. As for Nemrod, he has become Piankhy's most ardent supporter—and he has absolutely no freedom of action.'

'Where is the pharaoh going to reside?'

'At Memphis, to keep a permanent watch on the Delta.'

'A wise decision,' said Kapa.

'But Memphis is so far away . . .'

'Resign yourself to it, Otoku. You will continue to be a good governor, and we shall grow old peacefully together, in our good old city of Napata. Piankhy has left us so many fond memories that we shall spend our time reliving them. His present task is as vast as Egypt itself.'

'It is a triumph indeed, but it deprives us for ever of the king and queen's presence,' said Otoku sadly.

'Their destiny cannot be compared with ours, for their lives do not belong to them. In the face of the happiness and prosperity of the country and its people, their personal wishes count for nothing.'

With a heavy heart, Otoku chewed on a few warm flatcakes piled up on top of each other. Why did this old man always have to have the last word?

*　　*　　*

As they waited with the king outside the Temple of Neith, General Lemersekny, with the full agreement of his colleague General Puarma, voiced his disapproval. 'It's much too dangerous, Majesty. I don't believe for one moment that Tefnakht has repented. He has lied to soften your heart and he is setting one last trap for you. If he wants to meet you alone, it is only to kill you.'

'I am quite capable of defending myself.'

'Yes, but why take useless risks, at a time when the country needs you so much?'

'At least let me search him,' said Puarma.

'There he is!' announced a watchman.

Piankhy turned and went into the temple.

Driven by Pisap, the defeated general's chariot was in a terrible state. The shaft was splitting, the body was coming apart, and the wheels were in imminent danger of breaking. Piankhy would have seen only the terrible state of the exhausted horses. Knowing the king's views on the subject, the stable-men immediately led them away to the palace

351

stables to take care of them.

Lemersekny took Pisap by the shoulders.

'The Black Pharaoh's going to kill Tefnakht, isn't he?' asked the old man.

'You're an old soldier; you know the law of war. Come and have a drink. It will take your mind off what's about to happen.'

Tefnakht's hair and beard had grown long, and he was dressed in rags. His time in the marshes had transformed him into a pauper, but there was still pride in his eyes. He walked between two rows of astonished soldiers and up to the threshold of the temple, where Puarma was waiting for him.

The Nubian searched him, and found no hidden weapons. Besides, the mongoose, which was perched on the head of a lion statue whose task was to drive away non-believers, showed no hostility.

'The pharaoh is waiting for you inside the temple,' said Puarma.

Tefnakht walked through the massive gateway, crossed the great open courtyard and entered the first Hall of Pillars, whose door had been left ajar.

The Black Pharoah was wearing the double crown, symbolizing Upper and Lower Egypt, a broad golden collar, a white kilt and white sandals. He stood stock still, caught in a ray of light.

Seeing him at such close quarters, Tefnakht understood why he would never have succeeded in defeating him. His athletic build was matched by an indomitable spirit, capable of venturing along unknown paths and confronting the impossible without ever weakening. Piankhy did not even dream of triumph; he simply advanced, whatever the obstacles, and victory had been offered to him as a bonus.

'I am in your hands,' declared Tefnakht.

From a gilded silver scabbard decorated with an image of Amon with a ram's head, Piankhy withdrew a dagger.

Tefnakht trembled, but he did not recoil. As he had wished, he was staring his death in the face.

'I demand an oath of allegiance from you,' said the king.

Driven by a force greater than himself, Tefnakht prostrated himself for the first time in his life.

'I will not transgress the law of Ma'at,' he promised. 'I will obey Pharaoh's orders, I will put his decrees into practice, I will not attack his allies and I will act in accordance with his wishes.'

When he stood up again, the dagger was back in its sheath.

'Prince Tefnakht,' said Pharaoh, 'I entrust you with the government of the town of Sais, which you know better than anyone else. Take care to make the inhabitants of your province happy by rigorously applying the directives I shall give you. Each day, you shall go to the temple to be purified. Each month, you shall reside there for three days, far from the cares and affairs of this world, to hear the word of the gods and to silence any desire within you to rebel against Ma'at. Do you promise, on your life and that of Pharaoh, to respect these duties?'

'I promise, Majesty.'

*   *   *

As the Nubian fleet approached Napata, Otoku thought of the exhausting administrative work that awaited him. Piankhy had kept his word and sent gold, silver, copper, precious fabrics and rare essences for use in the Temple of Amon. An inventory of these treasures would have to be drawn up, under Kapa's watchful eye, and Otoku knew that the old man would not permit even the smallest mistake. If only Cool-Head could have taken care of these formalities. Otoku had no confidence in any other scribe, and he preferred to take care of this chore himself.

The entire population of Napata had gathered on the quayside to welcome the soldiers who were lucky enough to return to Nubia. Their comrades had remained in Egypt, either at Memphis or at Thebes, under the command of General Puarma and General Lemersekny.

People sang, kissed each other, shouted Piankhy's name, and heaped praise upon the sailors who, before disembarking, had offered up a sacrifice to the gentle north wind.

'Kapa!'

'What is it, Otoku?' said the old man through clenched teeth. These noisy demonstrations annoyed him.

'It's—it's Cool-Head!'

'My sight isn't as good as it was. Are you sure?'

'He's running down the gangplank.'

The crowd parted before the dwarf, whose reputation as a great dignitary was no longer in question.

Otoku should have rejoiced, but he was so astounded that he could hardly breathe. 'Look, Kapa, look carefully!'

'I've just told you I have bad eyesight.'

'There, in the bows of the flagship, that's

354

Piankhy—Piankhy and Queen Abilah!'

'You're talking nonsense, Otoku.'

'The pharaoh has come back!'

The fat man's huge body wobbled as he ran. With all the agility of an elephant, and not without crushing a few feet, he rushed towards the gangplank to be the first to bow before the royal couple.

'Majesty, is it you? Is it really you?' he cried.

'Have I changed that much?' asked Piankhy, smiling.

'I thought you'd stay in Memphis.'

'My mission is done, Otoku. Egypt is one again, the Two Lands are at peace, each province has its leader, and all are obedient to the pharoah. My place is here at Napata, close to my father Amon. It is he who guided me, he who protected me, and it is to him that I had to return. The law of Ma'at now reigns over the Delta, as it does over the valley of the Nile, and happy days are measured by the rhythm of festivals and rites. If, tomorrow, the people of Egypt need my arm to prevent the tyranny of misfortune and injustice, I shall leave again.'

While the celebrations were being organized, Piankhy and his wife set off for the sacred mountain. The sun turned the desert sand to gold and illuminated the gates of the great temple.

'You alone know my secret,' the king told Abilah. 'You alone know that power is not the goal of my life, and that the only journey I wish to make is the one mapped out in this temple by the gods and the ancestors. Neither the clash of weapons nor the courtiers' hymns of praise could ever become the harmony of my life.'

'You have accomplished a masterpiece of magic by opening hearts so that they may discover their true duties and by putting each man back into his proper station. You have not changed our world, but you have given it a meaning. Each day we shall make offerings to the gods and pray that they will enable us to withstand the enemies who await us on the path to old age.'

'We shall win that battle, too,' promised the king.

'Yes, Piankhy, because the goddess of love is making the stars dance with joy in heaven, our true country.'

Together, Pharaoh and the Great Royal Wife stepped through the massive gate of the temple, 'Heaven on Earth', where darkness was transformed into light.

AUTHOR'S NOTE

Piankhy was one of the pharaohs of the XXVth dynasty, and he reigned for a little over thirty years (747–715 BC). It is difficult to give an exact date for his reconquest of Egypt: was it around 730, or at the end of his reign?

His wonderful adventure is told by a huge stele (1.80m tall and 1.84m wide), which is preserved in the museum at Cairo (Journal of accessions 48862, completed by fragments JA47086–47089). It was discovered in 1862 on the site of Gebel Barkal, 'the Pure Mountain', and exhibited by Auguste Mariette in his museum at Bulaq before being transferred to the present Museum of Antiquities.

This stele has been the object of several translations and numerous general or specific studies, of which the following are among the most significant:

E. de Rougé, 'Inscription historique du roi Pianchi-Meriamoun', *Revue archéologique*, vol. 8, 1863, p. 94f.; *Chrestomathie égyptienne*, no. 4, 1876.

F. J. Lauth, 'Die Pianchi-Stele', *Abhandlung der königlichen Akademie der Wissenschaften*, vol. 12, 1871, pp. 241–314.

H. Schäfer, *Urkunden der älteren Aethiopenkönige*, vol. I (Urkunden, vol. 3), 1905, pp. 1–56.

J. H. Breasted, *Ancient Records of Egypt*, vol. 4, 1906, pp. 406–44.

N. C. Grimal. *La Stèle triomphale de Pi(ankh)y au musée du Caire*, Cairo, 1981.

M. Lichtheim, *Ancient Egyptian Literature*, vol 3, 1980, pp. 66–84.

C. Lalouette, *Textes sacreés et textes profanes de l'ancienne Égypte*, vol. 1, 1984, p. 124f.

A number of Egyptologists believe that the name of this pharaoh should be read as Piy or Piyi (not Piankhy), according to Nubian dialect, but the meaning remains the same: 'the Living One'.